D0419459

# DEPOSED

# DAVID BARBAREE
# DEPOSED

twenty7

First published in Great Britain in 2017 by

Twenty7 Books
80-81 Wimpole St, London W1G 9RE
www.twenty7books.co.uk

Copyright © David Barbaree, 2017
Maps © Rachel Lawston, 2017

A CIP catalogue record for this book is
available from the British Library.

Hardback ISBN: 978-1-78576-267-3
Ebook ISBN: 978-1-78576-268-0

1 3 5 7 9 10 8 6 4 2

Typeset by IDSUK (Data Connection) Ltd

Printed and bound by Clays Ltd, St Ives Plc

*For Anna*

# THE ROMAN EMPIRE

**Main map labels:**

GERMANY

LOWER GERMANY

UPPER GERMANY

BRITAINNIA

RAETIA   NORICUM

CISALPINE GAUL

GALLIA NARBONENSIS

AQUITANIA

GALLIA LUGDUNENSIS

TARRACONENSIAN SPAIN

LUSITANIA

FURTHER SPAIN

CORSICA

SARDINIA

Balearic Islands

ITALIA

•Rome  •Naples

SICILIA

NUMIDIA

MAURENTANIA

AFRICA

•Sabrata

CYRENACIA

•Cyrene

MEDITERRANEAN SEA

EGYPT

ARABIA

SCYTHIA

DACIA

MOESIA

PANNONIA

ILLYRICUM

ADRIATIC SEA

CRIMEA

BLACK SEA

•Constantinople

PONTUS A...

BITHYNI...

THRACE

MACEDONIA

ACHAIA

•Athens

•Sparta

•Troy

ASIA

GALA...

LYCIA

CILICIA

CYPRUS

CRETE

RHODES

SYRIA

JUDAEA

PARTHIA

RE...

## Inset map (top)

PANNONIA

ILLYRICUM

ADRIATIC SEA

•Ravenna

•Ariminium

•Bononia

•Luca

•Perusia

•Mevania

•Trebiae

•Nursia

PICENUM

•Corfinium

•Cosa

•Rome

LATIUM

•Ostia

ELBA

•Canusium

•Brundisium

•Thurii

•Nerulum

•Naples

▲Mt Vesuvius

Baiae

Misenum

Herculaneum

Pompeii

CAPRI

TYRRHENIAN SEA

Naulochus

Messana

Mylae

•Locri

•Rhegium

▲Mt Aetna

SICILIA

▲Mt Eryx

... SEA

Compass: N E S W

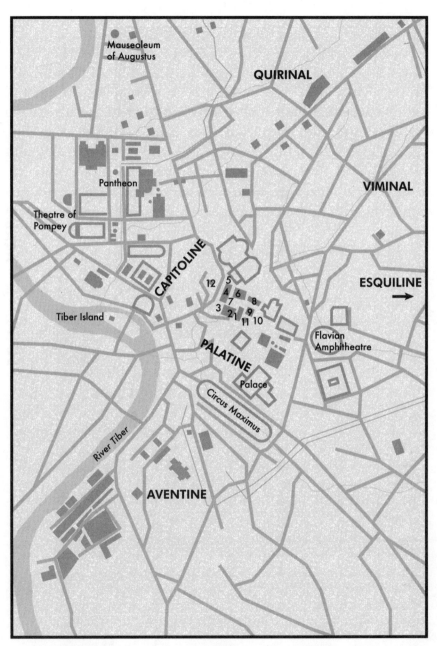

Mauseoleum
of Augustus

QUIRINAL

VIMINAL

Pantheon

Theatre of
Pompey

ESQUILINE
→

CAPITOLINE

Tiber Island

12  5
    4 6
    7   8
3  21  9
   11 10

Flavian
Amphitheatre

PALATINE

Palace

Circus Maximus

River Tiber

AVENTINE

1.  Temple of Castor and Pollux
2.  Basilica Julia
3.  Temple of Saturn
4.  Temple of Concord

5.  Carcer
6.  Senate House
7.  Rostra
8.  Basilica Aemilia

9.  Temple of Divus Julius
10. Regia
11. Temple of Vesta
12. Temple of Jupiter
    Optimus Maximus

# Author's Note

Romans divided their days into twenty-four hours, twelve hours of sunlight and twelve of darkness. Noon was the sixth hour of the day and midnight the sixth hour of the night. Romans also referred to their days as one of eleven successive periods: after-midnight, cockcrow, still-time (when cocks have finished crowing but the world is still asleep), dawn, morning, afternoon, sunset, vesper (for the evening star), first torch, bedtime, and depth of night. I have used both systems throughout this work.

I come to bury Caesar, not to praise him.
The evil that men do lives after them,
The good is oft interred with their bones;
So let it be with Caesar.

William Shakespeare, *Julius Caesar*

# I

## An Introduction
### A.D. 68

# NERO

## *8 June, depth of night*
## *The Praetorian camp, Rome*

My interrogation resumes with a splash of water. It's poured onto the top of my head with slow, malicious ease, and a cascade of icy murk soaks my hair and slides over my face and the back of my neck; a quiver runs down my spine. My head snaps back and I suck in one long, panicked gasp. I try to move, but rope still holds me to the chair, concentric circles wrapped from my chest down to my belly.

I open my eyes. Standing in front of me is a soldier, one of my Praetorians, holding an empty bucket.

'Up now!' he says. 'Up, up, up.'

Grudgingly, my wits return. Cuts and swollen bruises pepper my body, and with each breath a sharp pain shoots through my ribs like an arrow.

The soldier tosses the bucket aside. His silver cuirass catches the fire-light and shines the colour of Spanish gold.

He steps forward, places his hands on the arms of my chair, and leans in, until our noses are only inches apart. I unwillingly breathe in the stink of cheap, sour wine. He lingers, staring into my eyes . . . Fear. That's what he's after, any trace he can scavenge. But I won't let him have it. I refuse to be afraid of a mere soldier. It's undignified: as far beneath me as it should be beyond him.

This one, though – this one has it in for me.

Earlier, before I lost consciousness, still tied to the chair, he asked if I remembered him. He genuinely believed that I should know him personally from the hundreds of thousands of soldiers at my beck and call. He described a night – years ago – when I made him serve a dinner party dressed as Venus. On my orders, he was forced to wear a silk stola, wig, and make-up, and sent marching amongst tables of guests. He's only known as Venus now – or so he says. The rank and file, the officers, even the prefects – no one remembers his real name. He was red in the face when he told me, a girlish quiver to every word. Who knew that a Roman soldier could be so sensitive? What's a bit of eye-shadow compared to a German horde?

I, of course, remembered none of it. After I told him as much, that I didn't recall him or that night, but it sounded like quite the party; he beat me viciously. I'm not sure he would have stopped if the centurion hadn't told him to. The last thing I remember before losing consciousness is the soldier, my erstwhile Venus, panting like a dog after his outburst.

Thankfully, before he can lay his calloused hands on me again, the centurion calls out to him. He gives me a knowing wink before joining his superior by the fire.

We are in a dark, cavernous room the gods above know where. The only light is from a fire burning to my left. The bricks beyond – interlocking stones of black volcanic rock – seem to move with the flicker of the flames.

I count three soldiers, the same three who dragged me from my bed hours before. I watch them pass around a skin of wine. Each man takes a long, deep swig. I could use a drink myself. When I tell them as much, one soldier laughs while the other two, Venus and the centurion, ignore me.

The centurion's helmet is off revealing a sweaty mat of ginger. I doubt he's of Italian stock. Likely he's from Gaul, near the Rhine, where such a look is common. I find this comforting somehow, his treachery easier to understand. You can never trust a non-Italian. Their hearts are never truly in it.

The soldiers continue to talk. I watch the flames of the fire to pass the time.

Their voices are getting louder the more they drink. They're sharing their theories on me, debating how best to capitalise on my value. One of them refers to treasure buried in the shores of Carthage. 'He knows where it is,' he says. 'He knows.' (Why do the rabble always think Caesar buries his treasure rather than spend it?) Another thinks there's gold in my veins, flakes of it floating in my blood, like leaves on a pond. He wants to cut and drain me like a pig, and boil down what he collects, leaving only the ore. 'The Greeks did it to Priam,' he says, 'and he's richer than Priam.'

I take a deep breath. Wait. Their time will come. Many remain loyal: soldiers, courtiers, senators, the poor in the streets. Despite the recent unrest in the provinces, despite one or two legions acting out like petulant children, the majority love me still. Someone will come. Someone will stop this. And when they do . . . These three will have to be punished. There's no avoiding that now. Their execution will have to be public – public and somewhat gruesome. I'm not a monster, but precedent will need to be set. This can never happen again. Granted, I will promise one of them – just the one – a quick death in exchange for the names of the men who betrayed me. But that is a minor cost well worth the return. When it's all over – after they're crucified, bled and their grey, stiff bodies are left for the crows – balance will be restored. Then I'll drink, fuck and go to the races. The Greens are due for a win after all – the Greens and me both.

The soldiers finally finish their discussion. Whatever deal they've struck, it's commemorated with a handshake and more wine. The skin is passed around one final time. Venus guzzles his fill and then wipes his mouth dry. He watches me as he does it, as he slides his hand across his face.

I breathe deeply, willing my heartbeat to slow.

Venus goes to the fire and removes from the flames a long, thin dagger. The blade glows a translucent yellow-orange in the gloom. Steam whispers off the steel. He holds the weapon above his head and turns it from side to side, inspecting the blade. All of my effort to remain resilient vanishes. Fear overwhelms me. I feel it in the pit of my stomach, an empty expanse that grows and presses on my bladder until warm piss trickles down my leg.

Venus walks towards me. He's smiling again, his rotting teeth illuminated by the glowing blade. I grow frantic, writhing uselessly against my bonds. I call out to the redheaded centurion. I offer him coin, titles, even a distant niece's hand in marriage. I offer him Cyprus and mean it. The centurion just stands there, watching. His only response is a shrug.

# MARCUS

*10 June, afternoon*
*City jail IV, Rome*

I climb the stairs without stopping once. The sound of feet sliding on dusty brick – *scrip-scrape, scrip-scrape, scrip-scrape* – fills the whole stairwell. When this happened before, I'd worry someone was following me. Every few steps I'd stop and look behind me, but the sound would stop as well and there wouldn't be anyone there. It took me ages to get to the top. Last winter I told Elsie. She said it was a ghost, but there were ways to make sure it wouldn't bother me. She boiled bits of python in wine – its guts and skin and even its *eyes*! – for one day and two nights. Then, when it was a sticky, black paste, she rubbed it on my chest each morning until it was finished. It itched and the smell made my nose tingle. But it worked. I can still hear the ghost when I climb the stairs, but it never bothers me. So now I can go all the way without stopping.

When I reach the top of the steps, I lean against the big, heavy door until it slowly swings open with an old *creeeak*. Inside his cell, the prisoner is curled up in a ball, snoring. I move quietly, hoping the freedman won't wake up until after I'm gone. But when I shut the door and the latch *clicks,* he wakes up.

'Morning, pup,' he says. His voice is fuzzy with sleep. He stretches, then props himself up on an elbow. 'What've you brought me today?'

I walk to his cell, kneel, and pull out from my basket a loaf of bread.

'Bread,' he says. 'Surprise, surprise.' He sits up. Sticks of hay slither and crunch. 'You're trying to poison me, aren't you? Feeding me that stale shit.'

He points his chin at the roof and scratches his neck. He didn't have a beard before but now he does. There's a scar on his cheek where the hair doesn't grow. It looks like a chubby, pink leech.

I push the loaf through the bars and hold it there.

He gets on his knees, then his feet. He's short – nearly as short as me. But he's as wide as an ox, so he moves like one, with big swishing steps. He lumbers over.

'Did you do as I asked?'

I'm not supposed to talk to prisoners. I've never once spoken to him, but every day he talks and talks and talks, asking me to carry messages for him. It makes me nervous. Elsie says to ignore him and finish my chores, so that's what I do.

'Well?' He stares at me with little green eyes. I aim mine at the bricks. When he sees I won't look him in the eye, he says, 'Whelp.' He says it quietly, but angry all the same. He takes the bread. Then, with his free hand, he points at my bare arm, which is purple with bruises. 'Loyalty,' he says, 'to a master who does that is misplaced, boy.'

Outside, a cow's bell clatters. *Clack clack clack.*

He walks back to his bed of hay, sits, and leans against the wall. He says, 'Come on, boy. Show some backbone, some initiative.' He rips off a piece of bread with his teeth and starts chewing. Little white pieces fall out of his mouth as he talks. 'You're a young pup, I know, scared of your master. Your little balls shrink at the thought of him. But you'll never change your lot in life following the rules. I was a slave once too, you know. I've told you who I am, haven't I? Galba's freedman. Icelus.' He points his chin at the roof and a bulge slides down his throat. He rips off another mouthful. '*The* Icelus. The city must be talking about me by now.'

Every day he says this; every day he tells me his name expecting me to know who he is. I've heard of Galba – the whole city is talking about the Hunchback raising an army in Spain – but I've never heard of an 'Icelus'. Anyway, even if I *had* heard of him, there's nothing I could do.

He says, 'I'm no thief or murderer, you know – at least, that's not why I'm here. I'm a political prisoner. A partisan. Do you know what that means?'

I fill a cup with water from the bucket against the far wall and carry it back to his cell.

'It means I made a bet. I bet on a man, that things would turn out in a certain way. If I lose . . .'

He stands up with a grunt and walks to the edge of his cell.

'If I lose, I'm dead. Or it's off to the mines. But if I'm *right*? Well, cunts and coin is what I used to call it, my ambition in life –' he winks '– until Master Galba taught me to speak with more class . . .'

He grabs the cup and pulls it through the bars.

'I've been here for, I think, twenty-two days. You see me locked up, destitute, and alone. You probably think I'm buggered. But the mere fact that I'm alive means something. My party cannot be doing all that badly. Now, say the man I've backed loses and I'm left to rot or, the gods forbid, killed. Do you know what will happen to you if you send one tiny, insignificant message for me? Nothing. No one will ever know. On the other hand, say I'm released . . . if I'm released, who knows what I can do for you. You can come and work for me if you'd like. And maybe, after a few years of faithful service, I set you free. I mean, look at me . . .'

He points at himself with the hand holding the cup; water sloshes out over the rim.

'I was a slave once. But I'm a freedman now. To a Sulpicii no less. And believe me: I didn't get here by being loyal. Do you think Galba was my first patron? Uh, uh. I moved on when the opportunity presented itself.' He finishes the cup off in one swift glug. 'You need to think about this, boy. Your life could change with only a little cunning.'

He stares at me, waiting. What does he want me to say?

I wait a moment and then point at his pisspot. Icelus turns to see what I'm pointing at. Then he sighs and his shoulders slouch. 'Empty,' he says. 'Nothing to be done there. But –'

He's cut off by the sound of horses outside.

'Expecting anyone?' he asks.

I shake my head. No.

I go to the window and grab two rusty bars and, standing on my tiptoes, look out over the ledge. Across the valley, I can see the city, hills of white stone, red-tiled roofs and shinning white marble. From here it looks quiet, but I know it's never quiet.

'What do you see, boy?' Icelus says.

I look down below and see two black horses tied to a post. I can't see who rode them.

And then we hear the door downstairs open with a heavy *bang*, followed by the jangle of metal and the stomping of feet. The noise gets closer and closer, and louder and louder, but then it stops, and all we hear is their breathing, long wheezes back and forth on the other side of the door.

Icelus backs away from the bars. He whispers, 'Do me a favour, pup. Forget I told you my name. OK?'

The door shakes as somebody wallops it three times from the other side. *WHACK WHACK WHACK*. I want to hide but there's nowhere to go. So I just stand there, shaking like the door.

Why don't they knock, whoever it is? Why not holler 'open up' instead of breaking down the door?

The fourth *WHACK* is the hardest. Wood cracks and the door flies open. Two soldiers rush in – shiny breastplates, wobbly helmets, swords bouncing at their hip – dragging a man by the arms. They pull him into one of the empty cells and then drop him. They don't say anything, they just drop him to the hard, brick floor.

'Boy –'

A third soldier walks in. He has to dip his head so the top of his helmet – the hairy bit that looks like a peacock's bum – doesn't catch on the door's arch.

'Boy –' he says again.

I don't move. My legs feel heavy and I'm shaking.

The soldier by the door takes off his helmet and holds it against his hip. His hair is orange and sticky with sweat, and his eyes are small and black. He looks like a fox.

To me, he asks, 'Do you work here?'

I nod.

'Where's the key? Fetch me the key. Now.'

I move quickly, happy to get away. I walk past the other two soldiers, who are still standing in the cell over the man they dragged in. One of them hiccups. They have the same look in their eyes that Master Creon gets when he drinks too much: lazy eyes; eyes that can't see you even when you're standing right in front of him.

I grab the ring of keys hanging from a hook on the wall. I bring it to the Fox. He takes the keys and tells the soldiers to get out of the cell.

He shuts the door behind them. The new prisoner is face down on the bricks. He hasn't moved. His tunic – purple and hemmed in gold – is filthy and torn. The Fox starts trying the keys in the lock and picks the right one on his second try.

To me, he asks, 'What are your duties here?'

I try to answer but inside my chest bunches up into tight little knots and my voice dies in the back of my throat. I'm ashamed of this, which makes it even harder to answer. I can only spit out one word at a time. 'Bread,' I say. 'Water.'

'Anything else?'

I point at Icelus's pisspot. 'Toilet.'

'And your master? Does he come here?'

I shake my head. No.

'Good. Very good,' the Fox says. 'All right, boy, listen to me very carefully. Do you see this man?' He points at the prisoner. 'This man is an enemy of the state, an enemy of Rome. He is dangerous. While he is a prisoner here, you must be wary of him. He will try to fill your head with stories. He will tell you that he is rich and powerful, and that he can reward those that help. He may even tell you that he is Caesar. This is a *lie*. He is nothing more than a common criminal. While he remains here, he receives no special treatment. Nothing. Understand?'

I don't know what to say. This day is very strange and I just want it to be over.

'Understand?' the Fox asks again.

I try to say something, but the words don't come. I clam up like I always do. I take too long and the Fox becomes angry. He takes a step toward me. I try to step back, but trip on my own feet and fall to the floor. My bum hits the bricks and a lightning bolt of pain shoots up my back.

The soldiers laugh. One of them hiccups again.

'This one is brave, isn't he?' the Fox says to the soldiers. 'A young Achilles.'

I sit up.

The Fox is serious again. 'Do you understand me, boy? The prisoner receives the same treatment as any other. I don't need to tell you what will happen if you disobey me, do I?'

I shake my head. No.

'Good,' the Fox says. Then, for the first time, he turns to look at the other cell. Inside, Icelus is cowering against the back wall, with his head buried into his arms and knees.

The Fox says, 'You are the Hunchback's freedman?'

Icelus peeks his head out. He looks at the Fox, then at the other two soldiers. 'I . . . am.'

'Your master is no longer a usurper. I have a message I wish for you to deliver to him.'

'And if I refuse?'

'Then I cut your throat.'

Icelus looks up at the roof, like he's thinking. Then he stands up and pats the dust off his thighs. He smiles. 'Well, I suppose I should accept then.'

The Fox waves his hand and one of the soldiers unlocks Icelus's cell. The rusty hinges *screech* as the door swings open. Icelus steps out and says to the Fox, 'Where to?'

The Fox ignores him. To one soldier, he says, 'Stay on the door by the road until I have you relieved. Save for the boy –' he points at me '– no one enters without my say-so.' Then to Icelus, he says, 'We will send you to your patron. But first the prefect desires a word.'

They walk to the door. Icelus is smiling. He winks as he walks past me.

The Fox is the last to leave. He pauses at the door, turns back, and says, 'Nero, I will see you again soon enough. May the gods take pity on you for all of your crimes.'

With that, the Fox walks out, leaving me alone with the new prisoner.

I stare at him for ages. He's in the same spot where the soldiers dropped him, face down, his arms spread wide. I don't think he's moved. Is he dead?

I didn't ask the question out loud but he answers it anyway: he moans. Then he starts to move, wiggling slowly, like a worm. He raises his head, showing me his face. A rag – sopping wet and stained a purply-brown – covers his eyes and a thick line of dark red stains each cheek. It looks like he's been crying tears of blood.

I bend over and start spitting out my breakfast. A puddle of retch collects on the bricks.

'Water,' the prisoner says. He rolls over on to his back. 'Water.'

I feel better after retching. I'm still scared, but I begin to feel sorry for him. I've never seen anyone this bad before. Prisoners always come with cuts and bruises, but never anything like this. Can I bring him water? The Fox said not to give any special treatment, but water isn't special. Everyone gets water.

I go to the cell door and stick two fingers into the keyhole. I feel the latch I'm looking for and flip it up. *Click*. Then, with a tug, the door swings open. The rusty hinges *screeeech*. Once the door is open, I fill a cup with water and bring it back to the cell. I kneel beside the prisoner and I'm about to speak when I suddenly realise that I don't know what to call him. The Fox said he's a liar and a criminal. But then he called him . . . he called him the most famous name in the world. But it can't be him. It can't be the man Master and Mistress pray to every night and worship like a god. He wouldn't be here. He wouldn't look like this. Would he?

'I . . . I have water.'

The prisoner's head darts around, trying to see who is talking. I put my hand on his shoulder, letting him know it will be OK. With one hand, I hold the back of his head. With the other, I bring the cup to his lips. Propping himself up on his elbow, he puts his free hand on the cup. Together we tip the cup and water pours into his mouth. He drinks all of it, every last drop. He's out of breath when he's done.

'Thank you,' he says.

I help drag him to his bed, which is just a pile of hay in the corner. He sits, pressing his back against the wall. He gestures for more water. I fill the cup and sit down beside him. He puts his hands on the cup and we raise it to his lips. He takes a sip.

I stare at his face. Under the bloody rag, he has bruises, big and dark and purple, and his beard is sticky with syrupy blood, so red it's almost black. I think again of the name the Fox gave him. Is this really him? On the other side of the circus, there's a lake. Caesar's lake. Beside it, there's a statue as tall as a giant. It's supposed to be the Sun God, but everyone says it looks like the Emperor. Like Nero. I look closely at the prisoner's beat-up face and coppery beard. I try to match his face to the statue. But I can't. There's too much blood, too many bruises.

He asks, 'What's your name?'

'Marcus.'

'You are a slave?'

'Yes.'

He nods.

'You are . . . Caesar?'

'Yes.'

The prisoner tries to lie down but he can't do it himself, so I grab his shoulders and help him down on to the hay.

He says, 'Thank you, Marcus. You are a kind boy.'

He doesn't say another word. He just curls up on his new bed of hay and falls asleep.

# II

## A Hand in the Forum
### A.D. 79

**Eleven years later . . .**

# TITUS

*9 January, cockcrow*
*The Imperial palace, Rome*

Ptolemy whispers in my ear, 'Titus,' and I open my eyes.

It's too early yet for the sun, so a lamp is in the boy's hand. Amber light dithers along marble columns; drapes of Tyrian purple look an empty, bottomless black. I always forget how winter does this: paralyse the night until it bleeds into the day.

Once I pull back my sheet and sit up, the room comes alive. Slaves materialise out of thin air, drawing back curtains, beating dust from a rug of hide; braziers are lit. One stands ready with my belt. Another clutches the wool cloak I wear most mornings at my desk, as I read and attend to state business.

On campaign, I had two slaves, maybe three, attending to my needs. I grew used to such conservatism. I've tried to apply these values to my life here in the capital, amid the extravagance. It hasn't worked. I often find myself sending slaves away to other parts of the palace, to my sisters or brother, to my father, or even my daughter who the gods know has more than enough hands waiting on her. Yet they always return – they or others like them. The one holding my belt is new, I think. She's young, with chestnut hair, and thick eyebrows that meet above her nose.

I take breakfast in my study, as I review the letters and official dispatches that arrived during the night. The governor of Mauretania calls the province a backwater. He would like to return to Rome before his term is up. Would I put in a good word with the Emperor? (No, likely not.) In Asia, measures were taken to supress a cult, one of the newer superstitions from the east. The proconsul believes the followers of Christus are particularly seditious. (Aren't they all?) Cerialis writes from Thrace. The letter is more than two weeks old, which means the winds were poor or our Imperial service continues its decline. Tomorrow, Cerialis will finally move against the latest False Nero and his army. (Father will be pleased. We've let that wound fester far too long.) The eunuch Halotus writes again to request a meeting. He claims I summoned him to Rome and he would like to know why. I don't recall making such a request, but I have neither the time nor the inclination to explain. I have better ways to spend my days than with Nero's chief poisoner. I write on the letter itself 'no' and instruct Ptolemy to personally deliver it to the eunuch. The astrologer Balbilus writes to say that a comet was possibly observed the night before last. This is Balbilus's third inauspicious report in a month. He and I will have to talk.

'Is that all?' I ask Ptolemy.

'One more, sire,' the boy says. He walks towards me, unrolling the letter. 'It only just arrived.'

'Who from?'

He reads: 'Lucius Plautius. He is in Italy.'

Strange. I didn't know Plautius was in Italy. Father had granted him a respectable post in Syria, a favour to his demanding aunt. Has his term ended already? I put out my hand. I've time yet before the ceremony begins.

*5 January (from Baiae)*
*Dear Titus Flavius Vespasianus (prefect of the Praetorian Guard):*

*I should start with the good news: I am in Italy. I'd meant to keep this a secret. After all my years away, toiling in the east, sweating under the desert sun, rubbing elbows with barbarians – tamed barbarians, but barbarians nonetheless – I'd yearned to sneak back to the capital unannounced and surprise those I hold dear. I'd hoped to see the look of joy form spontaneously as I walked into so-and-so's atrium one evening. But I have bad news as well – information that concerns the Emperor – so I have spoiled the surprise. I will explain all of this in a moment. First, however, I hope you will permit me a few cathartic words on the state of the Empire.*

*I had expected to feel a shift once I'd returned to Italy; a sense of morality, something tangible I could feel growing in the soil or floating in the air.*

I'd looked forward to this more than Italian wine, or its temperate sun, or its tart, mouth-watering lemons. Civilisation was what I was truly homesick for. However, since touching my foot to Miscenum's cement pier, I've bore witness to such debauchery and vice that I feel as though I've entered a Greek port, brimming with unruly sailors and pirates and whores, rather than the jewel of the Empire, a mere day's ride from the capital.

How did we Romans let the Bay of Naples descend into an endless brothel and bottomless cup of wine? What would our noble ancestors say if they could visit Baiae today? What would noble Brutus, the man who banished kings and established a republic – what would he say at the sight of a senator in the arms of an Alexandrian courtesan, with her black eyes and artificial charms, while his wife and the mother of his children is miles away in Rome? What would dear Cincinnatus, the man who declined the ultimate power of the dictatorship because he preferred the country life, working his plough and tilling the dark Italian earth that he loved so much – what would he say at the sight of his descendants betting their ancestral homes on the roll of a single die, and then shrugging at an ill-fated toss because there is always more credit to be had?

And yet I know the extreme does not mark the whole. I look forward to my return to Rome. I know there are good, moral men in the capital; men who will help guide our Empire back towards the noble, wholesome values that made Rome mistress of the world. You, my dear Titus, are one of whom I speak. I often hear of the good you do every day in Caesar's name. If you occasionally apply a strong hand, I know circumstances require it. Rome cannot fall back into another civil war. The months that followed Nero's suicide were dark and destructive. Eighteen months of civil war, one man after the next grasping for power, taking the principate by force, until your father finally emerged victorious and brought peace to our borders. We must remain vigilant in order to ensure such evil does not happen again . . .

But I digress.

You are, no doubt, wondering why I've come to the Bay first, rather than Rome. The answer is simple: I am on the hunt for a summer home – an obvious necessity if I am to be resident of Rome once again. I'd sent my freedman Jecundus weeks ahead of me to secure a suitable residence.

*But his choice was terrible. It was too small, coldly designed and terribly outdated: frescoes in the old style, two-tone mosaics, et cetera, et cetera. It was, simply put, a calamity. In the end, however, there was no harm done. Just yesterday I sold the outdated abomination and purchased a home more to my liking. It is, in a word, perfect. It has all of the modern amenities, including a pond of lampreys and spectacular mosaics. The location is also exquisite: the breeze from the sea is pleasant, the temperature warm-to-moderate, and the view of the blue Tyrrhenian is stunning. It is a good distance from the orgies of Baiae and the barracks of Miscenum. The perfect retreat and only a day's ride south of Rome. I look forward to having you visit.*

*But enough of myself: enough of the trivial concerns of a private citizen. I will now relate a story that – if correct – could concern the safety and security of the Emperor.*

*There is a woman here, introduced to me by my freedman Jecundus – a whore if you must know, whom Jecundus met after several weeks at sea – who claims to have information concerning some sort of plot against your father. Two weeks ago she told her story to Jecundus (I shall not pollute my letter with the 'why' and the 'how'). Before I could track her down and have her explain the tale in more detail, she went missing. For days, Jecundus and I searched for her. But then, in the end, we happened upon her by chance – in the market, of all places. The woman was frightened when we confronted her, but in the end she proved quite forthcoming.*

*She calls herself 'Red'. You are, no doubt, picturing an inferno of red hair on the top of her head; however, I assure you, the name is a misnomer. (Her hair is a common, muddy brown.) She has given herself the title on account of the passion to which every man who beds her will – so she says – inevitably succumb. It seems an effective method of trade. Many will hear her name and think, I'll have to see what all the fuss is about. (As Jecundus can attest.) In fact, despite her low birth and occupation, she is not altogether uninteresting. In addition to her idiosyncratic adopted cognomen, she carries herself with considerable dignity during the day, as though she were patrician born, not a prostitute, without the slightest hint of irony. You should have seen her in the market when we confronted her, Titus. It was as though a slave had disturbed a king.*

*We had a long talk, she and I. It is difficult to sift fact from fiction, given her state of agitation. She is scared and recalls the incident with a growing sense of irrationality. In any event, this is what she says.*

*Seven days ago, she attended the home of a Pompeian knight by the name of Vettius. It was late when she arrived, well after sunset. He took her to the atrium. After drinking some unmixed wine, he had her disrobe. He was, I presume, about to begin, when there was a knock on the door. Concerned that it could be his wife – or so he said, what wife would knock on her own door? – he told the woman to hide behind a curtain. The material was such that with her eyes close to the fabric, she could see through it, while those in the dimly lit atrium could not see her. So, hiding behind the drapes, stark naked and shivering, she watched as four men burst into the room. Her knight tried to run, but two of the intruders caught him and held him to a chair; a blade was brandished and pressed to the knight's neck.*

*The story becomes harder to follow at this point. I gather that the knight was asked a series of questions. He shook his head again and again, until he began to cry. One of the four, apparently not appreciating the responses, gave some signal to the others, and the knight was gagged and then rolled up in a carpet. Two of the men heaved the carpet onto their shoulders, and then off they went.*

*There is, of course, more. I would not waste the prefect's time with the disappearance of a mere Pompeian knight. The whore swears on her life that amongst the questions put to the man, she heard the words 'poison' and 'Caesar'. This is what she told Jecundus several days ago; and this is what she repeated to me. I pressed her for specifics, but she had none to give.*

*It is frustrating we do not have all the answers, but we are moving in the right direction. After some quibbling over price, she agreed to go with Jecundus and me tomorrow to the victim's home. She is quite scared of what she knows, or what she thinks she knows, but she could not resist the promise of compensation. She is a whore, after all.*

*In all likelihood, it is merely a false alarm. I cannot imagine anyone foolish enough to cross the Emperor, especially after the hard line you took here less than a month ago. In any event, I will investigate and determine exactly what is going on. I aim to return to Rome in three days time, before the Agonalia. I shall tell you in person all that I have learned. Leave it to me. I owe you and your father much. I will not let you down.*

    *Yours,*
    *Lucius Plautius*

I read the letter twice before yelling for Ptolemy. He arrives out of breath.

'This letter is dated the fifth of January. Why am I only getting it now? Campania is a day's journey away.'

Ptolemy shrugs. 'It arrived last night.'

'Has Plautius come to see me?'

Ptolemy shakes his head.

'Have there been any more letters from him?' I ask.

'No,' Ptolemy says.

'Are you certain?'

'Yes. That –' he points at the letter in my hand '– is the only letter we have received from Plautius in months. Why? What's wrong?'

The procession snakes its way through the forum in rows of two. Oxblood red togas mark the occasion. I alone stand out in my cuirass, polished steel embossed with golden hawks, wings spread wide. Buildings of cream-coloured brick and gleaming marble loom on either side. Somewhere the sun is rising, but it's hidden by January's cold, grey haze.

We haven't moved for some time. Each man wages his own private battle to stay warm: shifting his weight back and forth, rubbing his hands together, or tucking his chin down into the folds of his toga. Some commit a small sacrilege by inviting an attendant slave to enter the procession to rub or hug their patron until the line starts to move again.

In front of me, at the head of the procession, one priest is pulling on a ram's leash, trying to drag it up the temple steps. His colleague pushes on the animal's haunches. They push and pull but the ram won't budge. The animal's victory is complete when both men have to pause to catch their breath, each bending at the waist like two runners after crossing the finish line. I'm reminded of a joke, one my men tell after too much wine: how many priests does it take? But I can't recall the punch line.

'Cousin,' I say, 'don't you have a better way to get the animal to the altar?'

'Of course, Titus, of course,' Sabinus says without offering an alternative. He, like the other priests, wears the long folds of his burgundy toga over his head like a hood, the requisite reverence for the gods above. Despite the cold, his forehead and round, pink cheeks are spotted with a nervous sheen.

It was a mistake to name him pontiff. For years I'd warned against giving him any appointment, let alone one of the city's most prestigious. But after Baiae Father insisted. 'We need to close ranks,' he said. 'Only use men we can trust.' This year he filled the colleges and Imperial posts with only those with proven loyalty to the party, particularly our relations, with no regard to capability. He chose loyalty over competence, which is fine in theory; in practice, however, the logic isn't sound. What good is loyalty if the regime is a laughing stock?

The two priests start again, pushing and pulling, groaning as though they're relieving themselves on the temple steps.

The ram doesn't move.

I can feel the vigour with which I began the day slowly start to seep from my bones. Seneca teaches that anger is the most dangerous of all the passions, that it robs a man of reason and harms the man who wields it as much as the target. Lately, after these last few years confined to the capital, I've wondered whether he was wrong, whether it is frustration – not anger – that is the most damaging. At least, as Aristotle says, anger can help focus the mind in order to work towards a result. Frustration, on the other hand, sucks the life from you, one day at a time.

The priests pause again to catch their breath. The ram nibbles on one of their togas. Behind me, someone suppresses a laugh. I take a deep breath.

'Allow me, cousin,' I say to Sabinus.

I walk towards the ram, drawing the sword at my hip. With a nod of my head, I signal for the second priest, the one overseeing the ram's arse, to move. I draw the sword back and swing. Using the broad side of the blade, I hit the animal firmly on its backside. Startled, it trots up the temple steps. Roles reversed: the ram drags the priest with the leash up the steps and onto the portico.

I retake my place beside cousin Sabinus and the procession starts again.

We climb the temple steps, thirty or so, and pass between two grooved marble columns – two of twelve that ring the Temple of Concord's massive rectangular porch. It's darker here, in the pediment's shadow, a dusk-like grey, broken only by the hearth's fiery glow. Dozens of temple slaves mill about, naked from the waist up. Smoky tendrils of incense waft through the air: rosemary, frankincense and others I can't place. The temple's doors sit slightly ajar.

The portico continues to fill. Conversations – none higher than a whisper – overtake the quiet.

Cousin Sabinus takes his leave and heads to the altar.

Flames crackle and spit. Behind me, a senator lets out a sacrilegious chuckle.

I turn and scan the crowd looking for Plautius. His letter was dated four days ago, plenty of time for him to make his way from Baiae to Rome. Plautius has always had a flair for the dramatic, but his letter has piqued my interest. I would like to hear what he stumbled upon in the south. But behind me, amongst a sea of burgundy-hooded priests and bareheaded attendants scattered across the portico, the temple steps, and spilling out into the forum itself, I see many of the city's elite, but no Plautius.

'Good morning, my prince,' a voice over my shoulder says. I turn to see Senator Eprius Marcellus. In the morning's grey light, old Marcellus is all divots and curves: bent back, gaunt cheeks, protruding brow. With his weathered, scaly skin and narrow eyes, he looks more snake than man.

'Marcellus,' I say.

A young temple slave slips by on padded feet.

'Do you think it will be long before we resume?' Marcellus nods his head towards the hearth. Cousin Sabinus and another priest are arguing in whispers. The former is pointing at the ram, the latter at the hearth. I can't hear what they're saying, but it's obvious they're arguing about what step to take next. The pause between procession and sacrifice is slowly shifting from acceptable to mildly embarrassing.

'Resume would mean the ceremony has stopped,' I say. 'It hasn't.'

I can feel the eyes of the other men on the portico. It's a familiar sensation in Rome: a room full of eyes, watching and weighing, noting every gesture, recording every little tic. If only I could have held my soldiers' attention like this on campaign. Jerusalem would have fallen in a day.

'It seems ironic, doesn't it?' Marcellus asks.

'What does?'

'To make the god of beginnings wait for his rites to be performed.'

Most men in this room are terrified of me. Rightly or wrongly, they see me as the Emperor's attack dog. Very few would dare talk to me the way Marcellus does, or make a joke at the regime's expense. Marcellus, however, is very rich and very patrician. He simply doesn't have it in him to bow and scrape to a provincial like myself, someone who can't trace his origins to one of Rome's founding, patrician families, no matter what office my father currently holds. He was once a great friend to our family. Father relied on him, especially during the regime's early years, after Nero's suicide and the civil wars that followed. But the relationship has become strained. His cousin Iulus was implicated in Baiae, but the rot began before that. It's hard to pinpoint when or why.

I say, 'I doubt that Janus will care when the ram is cut.'

'Well,' Marcellus says, 'I suppose I should take the word of a prince on issues of theology over a mere senator.' The comment is meant to annoy, so I ignore it. Marcellus presses on. 'Your father is not in attendance this year? I recall him attending last year. And the year before that.'

'He is feeling under the weather.'

'Well, I hope your father hasn't found that he has grown too great for the Agonalia. It has a long history in Rome. His decision not to attend could be viewed by some as . . . distasteful.'

'Some?' A bolt of frustration travels up my spine. 'I trust you do not share such sentiment. My presence – the emperor's oldest son and prefect of the Praetorian Guard – should be honour enough for the Agonalia. Wouldn't you agree?'

I'd meant my reply to sound witty, a snappy retort, but I've missed the mark. It sounded petty, like spouses arguing in public.

'Of course, Titus,' Marcellus says. His expression is cold and impossible to read. 'If you will excuse me.'

He gives a slight nod before pushing his way through the crowd.

That was a mistake – a mistake but not a fatal one. Marcellus will get over it. It's too early to talk with that viper.

I turn my attention back to the altar. Thankfully, temple slaves have taken over from the inexperienced priests, my hopeless cousin included. One slave is tending the hearth; another two are collaring the ram.

'Good morning, Titus.'

Another voice over my shoulder. I turn to see Cocceius Nerva. The senator is short, nearly a full foot shorter than me, and with a large alp of a nose, which today is sticking out from under his priestly hood.

'Nerva,' I say.

'Was Marcellus giving you a hard time?' Nerva's voice – as always – is calm, controlled and a touch too quiet. It's an ingenious way to counter his height disadvantage: it requires his interlocutors to, as I am doing now, lean forward or even crouch to hear what he has to say.

'Isn't he always?'

'I have to hand it to him,' he says. 'The confidence he must possess to annoy you, the great general.'

'Politics is a different animal. In Rome, he's the seasoned veteran.'

'Still,' Nerva says. 'After Baiae, I'd have thought he'd proceed with a little more caution.'

I don't respond. What happened in Baiae is not something I wish to discuss. But Nerva – who has survived the rise and fall of six emperors – is expert in ensuring he does not lose favour with whatever regime is in power. Sensing my discomfort, he changes the subject seamlessly. 'Any news from Thrace?'

'Nothing of substance.'

'Shouldn't Cerialis have the False Nero in chains by now?'

I smile. 'I'm always surprised at the impatience of senators. Wars take time, even small ones. Cerialis is a force of nature. I don't doubt that we will hear of his victory any day now.'

Nerva bows in an exaggerated way to show defeat.

I ask, 'Do you know Lucius Plautius?'

'Not well,' Nerva says. 'We've only met a handful of times. Where is he posted? Syria?'

'He was,' I say. 'His term ended a few months ago.'

'You must know him well from the war.'

'I do,' I say. 'I received a letter from him this morning. He was in Baiae, but the letter was dated several days ago.'

'The post is unreliable these days, isn't it?'

I study Nerva, weighing his tone. Is he asking for another appointment? Father has already been quite generous – though like Marcellus, he is not as close to Father as he once was. This is what Rome has done to me. I worry that evil lurks behind every comment. If a man says, tomorrow it will rain, I think he's plotting murder. If he says it will be sunny and temperate, I think the murder is already done and the blade wiped clean.

A bell finally rings and cousin Sabinus begins a low, steady chant. Two priests attend to the ram, the same two who had tried but failed to bring it inside. One dribbles wine onto the ram's head. The second follows with a cake of spelt, crumbling it in his hands. White crumbs fall like flakes of snow before embedding in the ram's wine-soaked fur. The priests step back and the slaves step forward. One grabs the animal's chest, the other its back legs. An older slave with a white beard and protruding ribs stands directly behind the animal. He grabs the ram's chin and pulls it up, exposing the neck. He brandishes a knife with his free hand and, in one swift movement, he slits the animal's throat. Thick, dark-purple blood pours out of the animal's neck and splashes onto the temple floor. A puddle collects at the ram's feet. Cousin Sabinus flinches and momentarily suspends his chanting.

Gods, please tell me no one saw our new pontiff swoon at the sight of blood.

The ram's body relaxes as the last whispers of life run from its limbs. The old slave with the knife runs the blade along the animal's chest and belly. The skin silently parts, revealing the animal's pink insides; ribbons of steam twist up into the cold air. The slave cuts off a piece of flesh and hands it to one of the priests, who then tosses the meat onto the bright, burning coals in the hearth.

Cousin Sabinus resumes his chanting but in a softer voice than before – so soft that it's difficult to make out the words. At least now no one will hear if he makes a mistake.

The old slave with the knife begins to pull the animal's insides out of the cadaver and onto a silver plate. The wet, slapping sound overtakes cousin Sabinus's chanting. A haruspex walks to the altar and begins inspecting the entrails. His colleague takes notes, pressing his stylus into a wax tablet. The temple slaves begin carving up the ram's carcass, which will be handed out to the poor in the forum later today.

When the haruspice are finished, a bell chimes again marking the end of the ceremony. The crowd takes its time in exiting the temple. Many forgo a quick exit and casually resume discussions amongst themselves. Nerva takes his leave. I stay where I am, hoping to avoid conversing with another senator. I've had my fill for the day.

Suddenly there is a commotion somewhere in the crowd, and an excited hum travels from one man to the next. I watch as the throng – first in the forum, then on the temple steps – slowly parts, making way for an invisible traveller. Eyes are aimed down. A few look indignant, others amused. Finally, materialising from a break in the crowd, I see a mutt – bulging ribs, brown hide with spots of black – casually trotting up the temple steps and onto the portico. The animal arrives unmolested at the altar and stops.

She's holding something in her mouth. Saliva drips from her bared teeth.

The throng mutters.

'A stray,' someone says.

I signal to a slave to remove the dog. But before he can reach it, the animal turns, faces the crowd and opens its mouth. Whatever it was carrying drops to the temple floor. The slave bends down to pick it up. He stops. His eyes widen, filled with terror. I walk towards the dog. Before I reach it, I realise what it dropped; so too does the crowd. The men talk excitedly. One man cries out; others laugh. I hear the word 'omen'.

Once I reach the dog, I squat to take a closer look.

Lying strewn on the portico is the hand of a grown man, severed at the wrist, palm up, with its fingers curved towards the gods. My eyes fix on the signet ring – the thick, gold ring of a senator or knight – glistening with the sheen of the dog's saliva.

The ring spins on my desk: a gold, mesmerising blur. The revolutions slow and it begins to wobble, like a drunk at the end of the night, before finally toppling over. I pick the ring up and hold it to the lamp's flame. The ring's inscription has been scratched away with a series of frenzied scores, making it impossible to read; any clue of its former owner now buried and lost. This, of course, I already knew. But frustration and a lack of a better idea compel me to check again. Once I'm finished, I place the ring back on the desk and spin.

The mutt interrupts my train of thought with a whimper. I look down at the bear hide spread out on the floor. She is curled up on top, sound asleep. Her leg muscles twitch as she dreams. She is somewhere else, chasing game. A hare, maybe. Lucky girl. She has no idea the trouble she's caused. Soon the whole city will be talking about her – if they aren't already.

Maybe I made a mistake taking the ring, but I had to think quickly. When I realised it was a senator or knight's ring on the hand, lying there on the temple floor, I removed it before anyone noticed. I thought I would be able to determine the owner. I didn't want the ring starting talk of a murdered senator – if that's actually what happened. As for the mutt, I'm not sure why I brought her back to the palace. But she's relevant somehow. Who knows, maybe she'll shit out something useful.

'Master.'

Ptolemy is standing across the room holding a lamp. His face palpitates in a yellow shade.

'Yes.'

'I'm sorry to disturb you. Regulus is here. He says you are expecting him.'

'Send him in.'

Moments later Ptolemy returns with Regulus. The young man looks immaculate, even at this hour: a fresh shave, stainless red cape, polished cuirass, the hint of lavender – every inch the patrician blue-blood I have resented my whole life. He has never seen a battlefield and yet, because of his connections, here he is, a military tribune in the Praetorian guard.

'Titus,' Regulus says. He stands at attention when addressing me, as he should, but he lacks the rigor one can only learn under the conditions of war. That pretentious purse of his would never last in the barracks.

'What do you have for me?'

'Exactly what you asked for,' he says. 'A list of every senator and a list of every appointment abroad.'

'Good,' I say. 'Tomorrow, be here bright and early. We're going door-to-door.'

Regulus looks incredulous. 'Isn't that . . . beneath us?'

I ignore the question. I hold out my hand and Regulus hands me the two rolls of papyrus.

'May I?' he says, pointing at the seat across from me, on the other side of the desk.

I stare at the young tribune, waiting to see if he has the gall to sit without my leave. He doesn't sit, but he continues to speak, still brimming with confidence.

'Can I speak freely, sir?'

He takes my silence as leave.

'It seems to me the party is at a bit of a crisis point. There are people out there disparaging your father. Disparaging *Caesar*. I don't know what you have planned tomorrow by going door-to-door, but I'm not sure if it will be as effective as other avenues. I've been told that there are those who would talk. Well-meaning citizens who could provide us with information about our enemies.'

'I think, Regulus, the word you are looking for is *informer*. You have informers waiting to provide us with information. You're not suggesting that we use informers, are you? Or do I need to provide you with a history lesson?'

Regulus thinks my questions are rhetorical. He just stands there with his mouth slightly pursed.

'How old are you?' I ask.

'Twenty-two.'

'Twenty-two. So that would make you how old during Nero's last great purge, after Piso and his accomplices were discovered? Eight?'

'Thereabouts,' he says. 'Maybe seven.'

'And did you lose anyone during that purge?'

'My uncle.'

'Your uncle. On which side? Was he of the Regulii?'

'No. He was my mother's brother. A Sulpicii,' Regulus says. 'I'm not sure what you're getting at. My uncle was a traitor. He was in league with Piso, Scaevinus and all the rest. He provided them with money, information and who knows what else. Nero was perfectly within his rights to have him killed.' Regulus' voice is rising. He hadn't planned on this becoming personal. 'I'm surprised you're acting so naive. Emperors occasionally have to take drastic measures. Otherwise, they're done. It's that simple. Nero did it with Piso and he held on to power; and it was his failure to do it again with Galba that guaranteed his downfall. If he'd done what was necessary, if he had found each and every one of Galba's supporters and killed them, as was his Imperial right, then he'd still be alive and in power today.'

The nerve of this spoilt shit. He speaks as though this is my first week on the job, as though I haven't been fighting to keep Father in power for nearly a decade, sniffing out plots, stamping them out before they can bloom. He speaks as though it would be *his* throat slit in a coup – rather than Father's and mine.

I get up from my desk and walk to the wine. It's airing out in a bowl on a side table. I have to step over the dog to get there. She's still sound asleep, but her whimpering has stopped. Maybe she caught that hare. I dip two glasses into the bowl, and then pour seawater from a terracotta pitcher into the cups, diluting the blend. I only add a splash. Tonight we both need something strong. I hand one to Regulus and then motion for him to sit. I take a seat facing the young tribune.

Now that I've calmed down, I can proceed with more precision. I start again.

'I wonder,' I say, 'did you see any of your uncle's transgressions? Did you see him hand gold pieces to Piso or Scaevinus? Did you see him at any of the conspirators' clandestine meetings? Did you see him put up his hand, volunteering information?'

'I was seven. Obviously not.'

'But you're certain he did such things. You're just not sure how you know what you know.' I pause to take a sip of wine. It burns the back of my throat as it goes down. It's the sour variety, the type that only the legions drink: a thick, acidic blend that is as impervious to time and temperature as any soldier. After all my years on campaign, it's all I can drink. The higher-end vintages from Spain or Italy taste like water now. 'May I ask what happened to his estate?'

'Nero confiscated most of it. My other uncle, his younger brother, was allowed to retain his real estate holdings in Italy,' Regulus says. He raises the cup, takes one whiff and his face contorts like a child asked to eat his vegetables. He lowers the cup without taking a sip. 'But that's common practice,' he adds.

'There,' I say, 'you've hit the nail on the head.' I take another sip of wine. It burns less this time. 'Informers often stand to benefit from their informing. It's implicit in the act. Why else inform?'

'For the good of the Empire,' Regulus says. 'For the good of Rome.'

'I thought you frowned on naiveté.'

'You think my uncle was betrayed by his own brother?' Regulus asks, incredulous.

'That I do not know. What I *do* know is that informers, like everyone in this city, are only looking out for themselves. You can often trace the source of a man's ruin to where the spoils land. Maybe others stood to benefit from your uncle's demise. Maybe *they* are the reason for his ruin. I don't know. But I would be surprised if he – the uncle accused of conspiring – was actually involved. I've never heard of your uncle. I can't imagine he was an integral part of a plot to overthrow Nero.'

Regulus is quiet for a moment. When he speaks again his voice has a new bitterness to it. 'Speculate all you like,' he says. 'But culling disloyal citizens ensures stability. It guarantees power remains intact. Tiberius ruled for eighteen years using informers to locate and purge his enemies. And Nero's failure to do this was his downfall.'

'Tiberius was Augustus' heir,' I say. 'He could have ruled for another eighteen if he'd done away with the practice.' The rumour – never proven but to which I subscribe – was that Tiberius was suffocated with a pillow by his unhappy staff. 'Informers and purges didn't prevent his downfall. They caused it. And no purge would have stopped what happened to Nero. Legions in Gaul and Spain revolted and the Praetorians turned on him. Then, with the help of his freedman, he took his own life. No purge of the senatorial ranks could have stopped that.'

I take another sip of wine before continuing. I'm going slowly now. I'm enjoying watching the look of contrition form on this pretty, patrician boy's face.

'It's unfortunate that you haven't had more time on campaign,' I say. 'All you've ever known is Rome so it's hard for you to see it for what it really is.'

Regulus bristles. 'I've been throughout Italy, and to Greece and Egypt.'

'Those are recreations of Rome but on a smaller scale,' I say. 'Miniature Romes but with different weather and systems of roads that make sense. The provinces are merely copies of the capital. The system of government, laws and regulations – everything is the same. The people are the same as well, though again on a smaller scale. Less rich, less ambitious – but Roman nonetheless.' I lean back into my chair, hoping to show how at ease I am. 'No. There's nothing you can learn about Rome by visiting miniature Romes. But on campaign, after only a few days living as a soldier, you would know more about Rome than from another ten years living here.'

Regulus looks unimpressed. He may have rolled his eyes, but I can't say for certain in the lamp's dim light.

'It's true,' I continue. 'The selfishness of this city, the unchecked greed, and the obsession with status – all of this is obvious to the soldier. It's obvious because the life of a soldier is different. By necessity it is the very opposite. Selfishness in an individual will get the group killed. The army must work as one unit not only to conquer, but to survive. In Rome, a selfish man is rewarded with his dead brother's farm and widow. In the field, however, a selfish man is rewarded with death. If you lived as a soldier, even for a short while, you'd see that. You'd view these *helpful* citizens wishing to inform on their fellow Romans with scepticism. Their motivation would be obvious.' I tilt my head back and drain the last drops from my cup. 'Informers, like everyone in this city, are only looking out for themselves. You would do well to remember that.'

'And how was Baiae any different?' Regulus asks. 'You cut down two men without so much as a trial.'

The boy catches me off guard. I let my pettiness distract me.

'In Baiae there were no informers. There was no purge,' I say, without much conviction. It's now my turn to let emotion seep into my voice. 'Those men plotted openly against the Emperor. I saw their treachery with my own eyes. There was no opportunity for a trial, nor was there any need for one.'

Regulus is at a loss. The purse to his lips is back. He didn't like my answer any more than I did.

'It's late,' I say. 'Go home to that pretty wife of yours. Be here tomorrow before sunrise.'

Regulus gets up to go. He places the glass of wine on the desk. The cup is full.

'Bad luck, that,' I say, pointing at the wine.

Regulus reluctantly picks up the cup. He looks at it like Julia looks at her vegetables. But I will say this for the boy: he has manners. In one fell swoop, he tilts his head back and drains the cup. He coughs violently – so much so that he has to place his hands on my desk to brace himself. The mutt wakes up and raises her head from the rug to watch the commotion.

'I don't know how you drink that swill,' he says.

'I'm a soldier,' I say. 'Remember: bright and early tomorrow morning.'

DAVID BARBAREE | 35

Regulus salutes me before turning to go.

Absently, I turn back to my correspondence, unrolling a letter from the governor of Gaul. But before I've read more than two words, I hear someone clear his throat. I look up to see Virgilius standing at attention. I nod my head and the centurion relaxes. I gesture at the chair opposite my desk.

'General,' he says before taking a seat.

My old friend's presence immediately puts me at ease. He has a lean frame, a mop of white hair and a thick, salty beard. Old and battle-hardened, he is everything Regulus is not.

'How much of that did you hear?'

'Just the last bit,' he says. 'His uncle did it, if you ask me.'

I give the smile he was looking for.

'Did you find Plautius?' I ask.

'No. But his wife is here.'

'Did you speak with her?'

He shakes his head. 'Just the staff. They said Plautius was expected in Rome two weeks ago. But letters have been coming in from the Bay saying he's got further business to attend to.' Virgilius looks over at the mutt. 'You think that was his hand?'

I lean back in my chair. Plautius' letter is on my desk. *She heard the words 'poison' and 'Caesar'*, he wrote. *I will investigate. Leave it to me.*

'I'm not sure,' I say, 'If it's not, I'd like to speak with him.'

'Should I go find him?' Virgilius asks. 'Or at least try to.'

'No. Not yet. I need you with me tomorrow. Domitian is there now.'

'Your brother is in Baiae?'

I nod. 'He's been there nearly a week, doing whatever it is young men do in Baiae. I will write to him. I will ask him to find Plautius. It will be good to put him to use.'

Virgilius nods, then asks: 'If that wasn't Plautius's hand, what do you make of it?'

'Accident or not, it will give us trouble. You know how this city loves omens.'

I don't need to say anything more. Virgilius knows me well enough to see I'm done talking. He stands and says, 'I will see you tomorrow then.'

He leaves.

I look again at the letters spread out on my desk. The dog – awake now – trots over and places her head onto my lap. Her large, dark eyes stare up at me lovingly.

'If only you could talk,' I say to her.

I pick the gold signet ring up and hold it to the light of the lamp's flame. After I inspect those familiar scratches, I place the ring onto the desk and spin, losing myself in the gold, mesmerising blur.

# III

## Working Together
### A.D. 68

# NERO

*14 June, cockcrow*
*City jail IV, Rome*

I decide to kill myself the second time I'm lucid. For days, I've been consumed by crushing pain and feverish dreams – dreams more vivid than this world will ever be again; nightmares of white-hot blades piercing my eyes and purple-black blood gushing down my cheeks, pulsing out in a constant, endless churn. Until now, only once has the fever broken and the pain subsided enough that I could think clearly. I squandered those hours, as I cried out in anger, cursing the men who did this to me and the gods who let them do it. I'm lucid a second time and I don't want to waste it. I refuse to be a bargaining chip, or the consideration paid for titles or coin, or whatever it is they plan to do with me. I want a good, clean Roman death; a death deserving of Caesar.

The question is: how?

Everything is black. The world has been reduced to touch, smell and sound. There is little left of my Imperial self, nothing but broken ribs and chewed-up flesh, bruises on top of bruises; my beard is caked with my own blood, a coagulated paste that stinks of the butcher's block; and every one of my bones aches. But all of this pales in comparison to the pain emanating from whatever is left of my eyes, which may occasionally wane, but is always too much to bear.

I'm lying on my back in what I presume is a prison cell. A thousand pricks of hay irritate my back and neck. It's quiet, save for the clatter of a cow's bell, a dwindling staccato off in the distance. They must have taken me outside the city walls. I hope they will return my remains to the city proper, to our family's crypt. I hope they will grant me that.

I test my surroundings, sliding my hands out in every direction over the dusty brick, searching for anything to use. My right hand brushes the wall and I happen upon a loose brick. I get onto my knees, slowly, with extreme effort, and then wiggle the brick with a ferocious shake until it dislodges from the wall. I hold the brick above my head and swing it down against the floor, again and again. It smashes on the sixth try. I slide my hand over each piece, until I find one that's shaped like a spearhead, a jagged shard, which tapers to a point. It will serve.

Still on my knees, I raise the terracotta shard to my neck and press it against where I think the vein is. I apply enough pressure to break the skin; a trickle of blood slides down my neck . . .

I hesitate.

My mind wanders. I imagine my subjects – not mourning their lost emperor or even rejoicing at his fall – but indifferent, going about their day as they would any other. I think of my mother. I picture the look of satisfaction she'd have if she could see her son at this very moment, dethroned and on his knees like a beggar, about to open his veins. I think of the men who did this to me, alive and well. Not just the soldiers who took my eyes, but the men in positions of favour who must have been involved: senators, generals, my ungrateful Imperial staff – the men who truly stood to gain from my fall. At this very moment, they're probably enjoying a cup and a laugh that the whole affair has come off without a hitch, that the man they'd worshiped as a god now sits in a cell, blind and helpless.

I scream, a frothy, wordless torrent of anger; my body quakes with rage. I scream a second time, then a third.

Exhausted, I crumple to the bricks.

Time passes. I breathe. Long. Deep. Breaths.

Something has changed.

I put the shard of brick aside. I will use it, but not yet.

# MARCUS

*15 June, afternoon*
*The fullery of Proculus Creon, Rome*

'How many times do I have to say it?' Master says. 'The slower you go, the less money I make. Is that so hard to understand? So why in Jupiter's good name do you children take so long? You're not composing poetry; you're collecting piss. Yellow, white, green, or red – I don't give two figs. Just bring it here, to the fullery, so I can turn it into *money*. Does this look hard?'

Master holds up a pisspot and a fat terracotta urn, the kind we carry from building to building. He pretends to pour the pisspot into the urn. Both are empty, but the sound of the women behind him, sloshing away in the vats cleaning and rubbing clothes, makes it sound like they're full.

'Do you see that? How long did that take? I've had sneezes take longer.'

Master tosses the urn and pot to Socrates; he fumbles but doesn't drop them.

'Do you want a hard life? I can whore you out to the degenerates of this city, if you'd prefer? Then, instead of dawdling from apartment to apartment with the sun on your back, you can feel the hot stinking breath of some lonely knight in your ear.'

Me and the other children start shaking our heads, protesting.

Master rests his hands on his fat belly. 'No? Then *hurry*. Collect the piss and move on. Bring it to the fullery so the women can clean.'

Master stops; the women keep splashing around in the vats.

'Well? What are you waiting for?' Master says. 'Go!'

The children scatter but Master calls me over before I leave. He talks as he's inspecting cloths. 'I had a soldier visit me.'

My heart starts racing at the word 'soldier'.

'He said the freedman is gone, but they've already brought in a new prisoner. Is that right?'

I nod my head, too scared to say anything about the new prisoner.

'Well, you do the same for this one as you did for the other. Yes? It's a lucrative contract to run that prison, and I won't lose it because of you. Water and bread, collect the piss, then move on. Understand?'

Master snaps his fingers. 'Understand?'

I nod my head.

'Good.' Master goes back to inspecting the clothes. 'Go. Get moving.'

I use the gate called Pig. I forget its real name, but it's beside a canteen with a pig painted on the wall, long and fat with its tail in a twist – so I call it Pig. After I'm through the gate, I follow the road north.

The road is empty except for a cart pulled by an ox and an old man slowly flicking the reins. The sun is straight up in the air and hot as an oven. My tunic sticks to my sweaty back. I walk along the road until I reach a dirt path and then I take it east. Soon I can see the jail, red-orange brick all by itself in a green field.

I used to like the walk. It was quiet, away from Master and Mistress and Giton and everyone else. I'd walk beside the dirt path, through the tall grass. Sometimes the grass would be slippery and cool, and I could feel it crunch under my feet. Some days I'd spot a hare, or a cow, and in the spring there are lots of red poppies along the way.

Now I don't like the walk, not since the soldiers came. Now each day my heart starts pounding faster and faster the closer I get, and I can't get a proper breath because it keeps slipping out of me. But I have to go, like Elsie says.

She's the only one I told about what happened. That night, after the soldiers brought the new prisoner to the jail, I snuck back to Master's late. I came in through the kitchen from the alleyway and Elsie was there, kneading dough for the next day's bread. She saw me and right away knew something was wrong. She wiped her hands on her apron and then bent down so our eyes could see each other. She said: 'Tell me, child. Tell Elsie.' That's all she said.

I told her everything. I started going and couldn't stop. I cried and she pressed my head against her bony chest. Her grey hair was up, but a few itchy strands hung down and tickled my neck. She wasn't angry with me, and she didn't tell me I did anything wrong – which made me feel better, but for some reason I cried even harder.

She said, 'Everything is fine, child. Yes? Listen to Elsie. Everything is fine.'

The next morning, before anyone else in the house was awake, Elsie hurried me down to the Subura. It was so early its narrow streets were nearly empty. She pulled me into a dark alleyway. At the end of it, there was a man sitting cross-legged on the bricks. He was naked, I think, except for the red paint that covered half of his body. He was so fat that his big round belly covered his thighs and crotch. Elsie kneeled in front of him and motioned for me to do the same. Then she told the magi everything. When she was done, he waved his hand and said the remedy was simple. 'Lion fat with rose oil rubbed between the eyebrows. It grants popularity with kings,' he said. 'It will work with emperors. Even their ghosts.' Elsie paid him and then he rubbed lard on my forehead.

Elsie said it was best not to tell anyone about the prisoner, at least until the magic ran its course. 'Keep doing what's expected of you,' she said. So every day I keep going to the jail, doing what I'm supposed to. And I haven't told anyone but Elsie about the prisoner.

The whole city is talking about Nero. Some people say he's dead; others say he's gone north to raise an army – or east, or west. Even Master and Mistress can't agree. Last night, I heard Mistress tell Master she thinks Nero is on his way to Parthia to buy an army from their king. Master said, 'Don't be stupid, my dear. Nero is gone. He's as dead as our dinner.' And he held up a half-eaten drumstick.

There's a new emperor now. His name is Galba, but people call him the Hunchback. Elsie says he's old – older than she is – with a crooked back and a bald head. He was governor of Spain before being named emperor, so he isn't in Rome yet. Master says he'll likely be here by the end of the summer. Some people aren't happy that he's the emperor. Yesterday there was even fighting in the streets. I heard Master tell Mistress it started in the senate. Senators made speeches against Nero. (One name sounds like Nero. Nera or Nevi or Nerva.) Later, in the forum, Nero's friends laid flowers on the rostrum and made speeches about him. Other people started to boo and hiss. Both sides started yelling at each other and throwing rocks. Then the fighting started. I heard Master tell Mistress a few people were killed. 'Torn apart,' he said, 'like the legs off a cooked chicken.'

'Is Rome safe?' Mistress asked.

Everyone in the room – me, Elsie, and all the other slaves waiting on them – we all looked at Master waiting to hear what he said. He shrugged. 'Rome hasn't had a civil war in eighty years. Not since the republic came to an end. Rome is safe. Don't you worry.'

Everyone had been holding their breath waiting to hear what Master said, and when he said we'd be OK, everyone started breathing easy again – everyone but me and Elsie. We knew he was wrong. He didn't know if Rome was safe, just like he didn't know Nero was still alive.

Outside the jail there's a soldier. He's sitting in the dirt with his back against the wall. When I get closer, I can see he's asleep. Or drunk. His mouth is open and he is holding a jug, which is tilted sideways. I can see dark circles in the dirt where the wine dripped out. It's usually this one out front, or his friend; the same two that were with the Fox that first day. The soldier doesn't wake up when I walk past.

I go inside, climb the steps, push open the broken door and, there in his cell, I find the prisoner lying down on his bed of hay. I see right away he's not shivering. Since the first day, he's had a fever. Sometimes his body was burning hot and wet with sweat. Other times, he'd be freezing cold. And nearly every day he'd mumble or even yell in his sleep. Once he yelled, 'My Thebians, my Thebians.'

I told Elsie all about the prisoner's fever. She said to leave him alone, like the Fox told me to. But I said, 'What if he dies and they blame me?' Elsie agreed that wouldn't be good either. So she told me how to clean his cuts with a rag, and how to make sure he drinks lots of water. I also took two blankets from Mistress's cupboard to keep him warm.

Today, I start in the way I've done each day so far. I go inside his cell, kneel beside him, and whisper, 'Sire, I have water.' I have to go in his cell because he's too weak to come and take the water through the bars. He's never once said anything besides his strange, feverish mumbles. But today – after he murmurs and wiggles around on the hay – he actually says something.

'What news from the city?'

I don't say anything. Elsie said I shouldn't have spoken to him that first day and I shouldn't again. So I keep my mouth shut. I help the prisoner sit up, and then I sit down beside him. I can't tell if he looks any better. He still has the rag wrapped around his head covering his eyes, or where his eyes used to be, and he still has his cuts and bruises.

'Please,' he says.

It's funny to hear him say 'please'. I told him I was a slave, but he must have forgotten. I shake my head to let him know I can't say anything, but then I realise he can't see. So I say, 'I can't. I'm not allowed.'

I start tearing the bread up into little pieces on my lap and then place one into his hands. He lifts it up and puts it in his mouth. He chews gingerly.

He gulps the bread down, then says, 'Who said? Who said you're not allowed?'

I realise it was a mistake to talk at all because now I'm talking to him. I figure it's best to say just enough to answer his questions, and maybe then I can stop altogether.

'The soldier,' I say. 'The one who brought you here.'

'Ah, I see. Well, do you know who that soldier was?'

'No,' I say.

'Nor do I. Which tells us something. He's not important. The men he's working for may be. But he is nothing.'

I don't know what to say. He didn't seem like nothing to me. He locked the Emperor in jail. I don't say anything else and neither does the prisoner. I put another piece of bread into his hands. He chews and chews. He's quiet for a while. Then he says, 'You speak Latin well enough. For a slave, I mean. Are you from Italy?'

I shrug. 'Not sure.'

'Well, I suppose it doesn't matter where you are from, does it? You are a Roman now.'

I figure that's a funny thing to say, because slaves aren't Romans. Not citizens at least. We're just slaves.

He asks, 'Your master. Who is he?'

'Master Creon.'

'And who is Master Creon?'

'My master.'

'We're going in circles, boy.'

I'm not sure what he means, so I don't say anything. I stand up and get water. I come back with a full cup and sit beside him. Then I help him take the cup in his hands. Water spills out over the side when we make the switch.

'I've never heard of your master,' the prisoner says. 'Senator?'

'Freedman.'

'Ah,' the prisoner says. He takes a sip of water. 'And how does Master Creon make a living?'

'He owns a fullery. And buildings.'

'So he collects Caesars and piss, does he? Well, he must like me. Freedmen have done well under me.'

Master used to talk well of Caesar. But yesterday Master said something about knowing the direction the wind is blowing, and told Socrates to get rid of the figurines he had of Nero. 'Pulverise them,' he said. 'Don't leave a trace.'

I tell the prisoner the first part, but I leave out the last bit. He nods his head, like he expected as much. He says: 'You said there was fighting in the city?'

'Yes. I –'

I realise I didn't say anything about fighting in the city. He tricked me. He got me talking and then asked me again about the city. I don't know how he guessed about the fighting, but he did. I tell the prisoner about it because I figure it's too late now: he's already tricked me.

# NERO

◆

*15 June, afternoon*
*City jail IV, Rome*


The boy tells me some story about speeches in the senate and how it inspired treachery in the forum. It's amazing what the dregs will drink up like honeyed wine. I press the boy for more. His understanding of events is a muddied mess, but sifting through the dirt, I find the nuggets I need to piece the story together. The senate has named the Hunchback emperor. What folly! Galba has a temper worse than Hera, and the intelligence of a mule. Worst of all: half the world thinks I'm dead. I've been gone a handful of days yet men are already clamouring to piss on my grave.

If the boy's story is true, Nerva's duplicitousness is staggering. I raised him up from nothing. He comes from obscure plebeian stock. How many consulships did the Cocceii have before me? One? Without my favour, little Nerva and that mountainous nose of his wouldn't have advanced past aedile. But now that I'm gone, he's disparaging Caesar! This won't do. I can't have it. Apollo, grant me patience . . .

And then doubt creeps in. What if Nerva – a man I relied on a great deal – what if he was involved in the coup? Doubt is like poison: a drop can spread and infect the whole. I've been reluctant to point a finger at those closest to me, to think seriously about who it was who betrayed me, but someone in my inner circle must have been involved. Four men were entrusted with a key to my chamber: Spiculus, the ex-gladiator and my personal bodyguard; my chamberlains, Epaphroditus and Phaon; and Tigellinus, one of two Praetorian prefects. And whoever it was, they wouldn't have acted alone. None could have hoped to seize the throne themselves. At least one senator orchestrated the whole affair, a man who knew, if I was out of the way, he could be accepted as Caesar. The question is: who? Who thought themselves equal to Caesar? Galba is the obvious answer, given his quick rise to the principate. But he was in Spain – a difficult spot from which to plot a coup. Who else thought themselves up to the task? Who was ambitious and grasping enough to dare to bring me down?

I will not put it off any longer. Steps must be taken to right what has been done. I order the boy to fetch me a ram for the appropriate sacrifice to Apollo. He gives me excuses as to why this isn't possible. I tell him this is unacceptable, but when he offers me some cockroach walking across the prison floor, I surprise myself and accept. This is new to me. Compromise.

He hands me the insect, placing it upside down in my palm. Its tiny legs furiously maim the air. I don't see this, of course; but I feel a tiny breeze along my palm and experience fills the void that blindness leaves.

I say the appropriate rights in Etruscan, invoking Apollo's name, asking he guide me in the days to come and in what I must do. Then I snap the cockroach in two.

# MARCUS

*15 June, afternoon*
*City jail IV, Rome*

The *crunch* is the loudest sound I've ever heard. Nero says he was making a sacrifice to the gods so they can help in the long road ahead, but the strange language he used makes me think it was a spell.

Nero hands me the dead bug and says, 'Dispose of this in the appropriate manner.' I don't know what the 'the appropriate manner' means, but I don't want to ask. He's already frustrated with me because I didn't know how to secure a ram. So I stand up and throw the bug out the window, first the head, then the tail. I watch each piece pass between the rusty bars and fall out of sight.

He keeps talking. He's happier now, after saying his spell. He tells me to stay clear of the fighting in the city as best I can. 'The masses often need to work this kind of thing out physically,' he says, 'with violence.'

He doesn't ask me any more questions. I figured he'd ask me to carry messages to the city like Icelus had done, but he doesn't. He finishes his bread without saying anything else. When he's done, I leave him with his back against the wall and a cup of water in his hands. I shut the cell door.

I'm on my way out the door when he says, 'Marcus, bring me wine next time. Yes? And fish sauce. I can't eat this stale bread without fish sauce.'

I start to tell him I can't bring him wine and he waves his hand in frustration. 'If we are to work together . . . I cannot keep hearing excuses. Leave me.'

I nod before turning to leave. When I'm outside and walking along the dirt path, I wonder what he meant by working together.

# IV

## The False Neros
### A.D. 79

# CALENUS

*10 January, cockcrow*
*Across-the-river, Rome*

Flat on my back, arms crossed, staring up into empty black, I listen
to them whisper; no choice, really. Back and forth they go, faster and
faster, until they're laughing – giggling like there aren't eight of us
crammed into one room six storeys up. What hour is it anyway? I
figure it's still early because the wine in my belly hasn't turned to
poison (not yet at least), and the hole the landlord calls a window has
a nice silver glow.

It's a useless habit here in the teat, waking before the sun rises. In the
barracks, as a raw recruit, they drum it in to you. 'Up, you rogues! Up!'
the centurion screams each morning, and up you get. One moment
you're dreaming of the pretty girl that you left a hundred miles south,
and the next you're jumping out of your blanket in the dark, and it's
cold as a Thracian's tit. And then it dawns on you that the voice you
just heard was an ugly monster of a man, with more hair on his back
than a pony, and the girl you were dreaming of is far away, and your
heart aches.

But then, over time, experience breaks you in; habit takes over. One
day, when the centurion yells 'Up!', you're already awake, lying on
your back, arms crossed, and you're hoping the moments you've got
before all the drills and marching and digging frozen dirt stretches
out just a wee bit longer. And you don't jump when you hear the
centurion's voice, which is now more familiar than that pretty girl's.
Instead, you give a mighty sigh and slowly stand up like the good
soldier you are.

There was a man in my cohort by the name of Publius. He said waking early isn't learned by habit. Sleeping late is what young men do, he
said. If you're awake before the centurion comes in, it means you're

getting old. He'd say, 'Calenus, you're old. You're damned near ancient. Make your peace with it.' Then I'd tell him where he could go.

I miss those days, from time to time. Not the centurion yelling – nobody misses that. But I miss Publius and the rest of my cohort. Good boys, the majority.

More giggles in the dark. It's the Syrian, I'd wager. He never has trouble keeping his bed warm. The others always get after him for bringing back girls and boys. I can't begrudge him, though. This is our lot: if you're born in an attic, you can't sleep in a palace.

I roll over on to my side and try to get a few more hours. I think of my wife, to calm my nerves. I think of her curls, a bird's nest of black, and the way she'd touch my arm, right above the elbow, when she'd whisper something sweet in my ear. A good thought on a cold, dark morning.

I hear the forum before I see it: laughter, bartering, bargains, cursing, catcalling, a cock crowing, and two angry pigs crying out like a couple of newborns. As I slow down, my knee begins to throb. It's bad on mornings like this. It's cold – too damned cold for the teat. Everyone has been complaining, not just cripples like me. Rome's coldest winter in two hundred years, they're saying – not many Romans have woken up beside the Rhine, with snowdrifts up to their waist, and the only heat you'll feel for months is the smoky-steam twisting up from your piss – and I know I've been living in Rome too long because I'm starting to agree. I'm softening into the southerner I've despised my whole life. But the body forgets; the blood thins out, like watered-down wine.

I turn the corner out of the alleyway and I'm met by an army of citizens flanked by towering walls of white marble and stone. I cut through the middle of the square, from one corner to the next, dragging my bad leg as I go.

I push my way through faded tunics. Rooster red, olive green and icicle blue. To my right is a senator, in his spotless white toga, with a legion of slaves trailing behind. To my left, on the steps of the courts, a few kids are playing pirates and soldiers; I walk close enough to

hear the marbley-crunch of their pieces banging together. A woman –
heavyset, with cheeks pinker than a sunset – looks me up and down as
we pass each other, like she's pricing a cut of meat. Hidden somewhere
in the crowd, a snake hisses. In front of the Temple of Saturn, two
soldiers are giving a freedman a hard time. One is holding the man's
basket upside down. The other is patting the man's sides, searching
for a coin or two.

I reach the other end of the square and stop at a fountain. Water
gushes out of a fish's mouth into a pool. I stick my head into the
stream, hoping cold water will soothe what's turning into a hangover.
The water is nice enough, but the fiery spear of pain between my
temples stays put.

'Calenus!'

The hands of a giant pull me in for a hug. When the giant's hands
finally let me go, I wipe water away from my eyes.

'Morning, Fabius,' I say. 'Long time.'

Fabius looks up at the sun. 'Morning? Barely, I'd say. You know you're
a long way from the barracks if you consider hour three the morning.'

I look up at the same sun. 'No, we can't be free of the second hour.
Anyway, we're both a long way from the barracks.'

Fabius looks older than I remember, fatter and greyer, especially his
beard. But he's still built like a gravestone. He asks, 'Do you have time
for a dip?'

'Not today,' I say. 'I'm expected somewhere.'

'Well, at least grab a cup with me.'

Fabius sees me thinking it over. He grins and says, 'Whoever it is,
they'll wait to speak with the great Julius Calenus.'

'One cup,' I say.


'I'm making good coin, working for Montanus,' Fabius says. 'You should
think about joining up.'

The vendor pours us both a double cup. Red, the cheapest he has,
sour as a lemon. Fabius and I are standing, leaning over the bar,
looking into the canteen, our backs facing the bustling street. Inside,
two women are descaling fish. Behind them, oil sizzles.

'Don't think so,' I say. 'I never liked Montanus. The man couldn't take orders before. I can't imagine what he's like now that he's the one giving them.'

Fabius and I both served in I Germanica, a legion of 6,000 good men stationed near the Rhine, which had the bad fortune of fighting against Vespasian in the civil war. After he won, Vespasian, in all his wisdom, sent each and every man in the first packing, as though it'd been our decision to oppose him, rather than the whims of a few greedy legates. But I'd had enough before that. I deserted after Cremona fell – after I'd watched a four-day-long sack of a city, and I'd seen enough murder and rape and all the rest of it, and I said, 'Fuck the legions and fuck the Empire,' and I ran. It was a cowardly act, one that will haunt me the rest of my days. What makes it worse, though, is that if I'd stayed on like Fabius, just a few months longer, I'd have been dismissed anyway, and I'd be in the same spot as I am now. Ten years after the war and Fabius and I are both here in the capital, doing our best to earn a living.

Fabius works for Montanus now, another soldier we served with. A giant of a man, twice as tall as any I ever knew, and three times as mean. I've only got an idea of how he's making money in Rome, and I don't want any part of it.

'It's not the best way to earn a living,' Fabius says. 'But it beats holding the line if you ask me. Montanus has us doing heavy work, sure. But there's no killing. I don't carry a sword or a spear. Now all I have is a stick.'

'A stick?'

Fabius nods. 'The size of my arm. Everyone in this city acts tough, but shake a stick in their face and most of them will crumple up like papyrus.' He makes a fist, crushing paper he doesn't have. He laughs at his own joke.

Half a dozen slaves walk by carrying a litter above their heads; drapes of blue silk sway in the breeze. The parting crowd stands on their tiptoes, trying to catch a glimpse of whoever's inside. Nearby, a mule squeals bloody murder.

Beside us, two freedmen are talking about a wolf in the Forum. Fabius sees me staring.

'You didn't hear what happened yesterday?'

I shake my head.

'Diana's blue tit! How did you manage that? You must have been deep in the drink.'

'Well?' I say. 'Out with it. What happened?'

'A wolf crashed the Agonalia. Walked right in, mid-ceremony. If you can fucking believe it.'

'A wolf?'

'Mm-hm. As big as a horse. But that's not the best part. Do you know what the animal was carrying?'

'What?'

'Some poor bugger's hand.' Fabius shakes his head. 'Virgil couldn't make this stuff up.'

I sip my wine.

'I would've paid money to see it,' Fabius says. 'Bunch of senators standing around, patting each other on the back, thanking the gods for all their land and coin, when in walks a wolf. This city is going to the dogs.'

'Or the wolves,' I say.

Fabius laughs. 'Right back to where it started.'

I finish off my wine and reach for my purse, but Fabius grabs my arm. 'I've got this one, old friend. You can get the next.'

As I'm walking away, Fabius says, 'If you change your mind, you can find us near the Capena Gate. The Painted Pig. You know it?'

'No,' I say. 'But I won't change my mind.'

The portico is filled with dozens of men and women down on their luck, waiting to beg for coin or an invitation to dinner. I see it and shake my head. I tell myself what I'm doing is different. I'm working for it.

I trudge up the walkway and through the front door, bypassing the line. A few of them glare at me, but no one says a word. I'm not a big man by any stretch, but people always seem to know I'm a veteran. I don't think it's the limp or the scars. My wife thought it was my shoulders. I always kept them square, she said, to whatever lay ahead, even when turning a corner. I know she was only teasing, but there may have been something to it.

Inside, in the middle of another crowd, I see the man I'm looking for. 'Morning, Appius,' I say.

Appius is Senator Nerva's chief slave. He's short, with a solid frame, and hair as black as squid ink, flecked with grey. In the crook of his arm, he's holding a wax tablet. He'd been talking with an old man in a faded blue tunic. The old man looks upset at the interruption, but then quickly bows his head to wait.

'Is it morning? Barely, I'd say,' Appius says. 'You know, if everyone came at the hour you do, Calenus, he'd never be able to leave his home.'

Damned house slaves. Every morning this one acts like the king of the atrium, even with freeborn men like me. Nothing to be done, though – nothing except to leave the bounds of his kingdom as soon as possible.

'Let him know that I'm here, will you,' I say.

'No need,' Appius says, reluctantly. 'He is expecting you. Follow me.'

I follow Appius down the hall. The old man in the faded blue tunic keeps his head bowed as we walk away.

We find Nerva in the colonnade. I spot his little frame and big nose from a mile out. Behind him, in the garden, there is a slew of green, trees mainly – olive and fig, I think. Between the trees are paths of polished stones, white ones, worming their way across the yard. Nerva is sitting in a chair, his legs barely touching the ground, presiding over the woman in front of him, who's on her knees, kissing his gold ring. Behind Nerva, one slave is holding a jug of something; another's standing guard over a wooden chest; a third is holding rolls of papyrus.

'Thank you, Nerva,' the girl says. She looks young except for the lines around her blue eyes.

'Of course, child.' Nerva says. His voice is always just above a whisper, which makes me always have to lean forward to hear him. 'But if you will excuse me, I must attend to my next guest.'

As the girl walks away, Nerva says, 'Two children, a dead husband, and barely eighteen. Sad, isn't it?'

'Life is hard,' Appius says with a shrug. 'Don't spend too much time with this one,' he says pointing at me. 'We still have a lot to get through and the day's already half done.'

'Fine, fine,' Nerva says, waving Appius away with his hand.

When Appius is gone, Nerva says: 'Well?'

'Caecina hasn't left his house after dark all week.'

'No? Not once? I find that very surprising. I'd heard differently. Is it possible he's sneaking out? In disguise?'

I shake my head. 'No. After sunset, no one's gone in or out.'

'Well, keep watching the Turncoat. He's planning something. I want to know what.'

Nerva has had me following Senator Caecina for weeks. He's never said exactly what he's looking for. He hints that Caecina is up to something, but I think he just *hopes* he's up to something. Senators are like children, waiting for the moment when they can rat each other out; it's a proven way to rise. And Nerva has proved quite able. If the Turncoat gives him an inch, Nerva will turn it into mile – especially with Caecina's reputation.

'OK,' I say.

Nerva doesn't get out his purse, so I change the subject. 'Is it true what they're saying? About what happened yesterday, at the Agonalia?'

Nerva smiles. 'Is the city talking about that already? What exactly are they saying?'

I tell Nerva what Fabius told me. I ask: 'You were there?'

'Of course.'

'Is it true?'

'It wasn't a wolf,' Nerva says. 'It was only a stray dog.'

'What about the hand?'

'Yes, that part is true.'

'Bad omen, that.'

'Bad? It's an embarrassment, is what it is.' Nerva says. 'Nine years ago, after the civil wars, Vespasian arrived in Rome with an army and a story – well, he had a few stories, but the one the people liked, the one that stuck, was the story of the hand. He claimed a dog came to him at dinner one evening, carrying a man's hand. A divine omen from the gods, he said, a sign that power would change hands. Complete nonsense, but the people liked it. After more than a year of civil war they'd like any story. But now, nine years later, it actually happens, and while he's emperor?' Nerva shakes his head. 'An unmitigated embarrassment.'

'Something like that,' I say. 'It can't be an accident. Can it?'

'Who's to say?' Nerva says. 'But I will say this: our fair city never ceases to surprise me.'

Strange to hear Nerva talk badly of Vespasian Caesar. He was close to him once – I'd thought, anyway. Nerva was named consul a few years back – and that's the highest honour for a senator. It's hopeless for an old pleb like me to follow politics. It's like watching the races from outside the stadium, and all you have is the roar of the crowd to judge who's in the lead.

Nerva snaps his fingers and a slave runs in with a purse of coin. 'Here,' he says. 'This should cover your services to date.' Nerva tosses me the purse. I catch it above my shoulder. It has a good weight to it. 'Before you go,' Nerva says. 'There is one more thing. There are two provincials coming in from Spain tomorrow. They will arrive in Ostia. I need you to meet them there and bring them to the city.'

'Who are they?'

'A man named Ulpius and his nephew.'

'A senator?'

Nerva sneers. 'With this Emperor, anyone can buy a seat.'

'Ah, they're rich,' I say. 'You're planning on squeezing a bit of juice from the lemon?'

Nerva smiles. He thinks I've paid him a compliment. This won't be the first time he's taken advantage of a provincial; I've seen him do it before. Wealthy families will come to Rome, hoping to make a name for themselves, and Nerva will offer his assistance. He'll make the right introductions, organise a meeting or two with an influential senator or an Imperial secretary. And soon enough they'll be indebted to him, and they'll be willing to lend Nerva coin, favours, votes – whatever he needs. Nerva must have spies in the provinces letting him know when a big fish makes his way to Rome.

'Make them feel welcome,' Nerva says. 'They're my honoured guests, et cetera, et cetera. Get them to Rome safely and let me know immediately when they have arrived. I am told the older one is a cripple. At least you will have something in common. Keep your eyes and ears open. I want useful information.'

On my way out, I push my way through the crowd of men and women come to beg Nerva for coin. I tell myself what I'm doing is different. I may no longer be a soldier, but at least I'm working, at least I'm earning my coin, rather than begging for it.

# TITUS

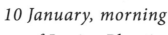

*10 January, morning*
*The home of Lucius Plautius, Rome*

We are in the tablinum. There's a breeze coming in from the garden. It's another cold January day. Antonia is wearing a blue stola, hemmed in gold, with fur draped over her shoulders. She's sitting on the edge of her chair, leaning on the arm. Her big eyes are staring straight into mine.

I remind myself why I'm here: Plautius. I am looking for Plautius.

'You must have something to eat,' she says. 'It's really no trouble.'

'Thank you, Antonia,' I say. 'But I really can't stay long.'

She looks slightly older than I remember. Her thick brown hair is less thick, less lustrous, and her eyes ... she still has the eyes of an ox, but they're calmer now, more distinguished. She's still beautiful, though. She was always very beautiful.

A slave pours wine into my cup. Another pours warmed seawater. Steam slithers out; cinnamon and cloves perfume the air.

'I cannot believe you are here,' she says. 'How long has it been? Five years?'

'I'm not sure.'

'Well, it's been too long.'

She looks down at her wine.

Finally, I ask: 'Have you heard from Plautius?'

Her husband's name breaks the spell. She sits back in her chair. 'Not for a few days,' she says. 'Maybe a week.'

'When do you expect him back to Rome?'

'I thought you'd know better than I would. He said he was staying on to finish up something for you?'

Antonia's fur slides off her shoulder exposing a smooth white collarbone.

Memories – nothing more than fragments – occur to me for the first time in years. A lamp-lit room, frankincense burning, an arched back. She had a particular smell, if memory serves; a sour, slightly bitter willingness.

She pulls the fur back onto her shoulder.

I try to focus on the task at hand. 'Did he tell you anything else?'

'No. Other than that he called it his "mission", whatever that means. I assumed he was buying you some expensive vintages. He never understood that you prefer the cheaper blends.' She gives me a subtle look that says she's always understood this. 'Why? Don't you know what he's doing?'

Plautius said in his letter he'd be in Rome by now. It doesn't auger well if his own wife hasn't heard from him.

'I'm afraid not,' I say, trying as best I can to hide my unease. 'I've received only one letter from Plautius. He said he'd be back to Rome by now, but apparently his plans changed.'

'I see,' Antonia says. She sips her wine. 'You know I've been back in Rome for several weeks now. You haven't visited.'

'An oversight,' I say. The word is wrong, too formal. 'My duties keep me very busy.'

She looks down at her wine.

I feel compelled to add, 'I've wanted to.'

'Well,' she says. 'I'm sure you have more business to attend to today. I don't want to keep you.'

'Yes,' I say and hand my wine to one of the slaves hovering at my side. 'I should be going.'

'You promise to come again?' she asks.

'I will,' I say before standing to go.

On the street outside, six Praetorians are waiting for me. The four rank and file are standing, their backs straight as arrows. Virgilius, meanwhile, is leaning against the building, with his thumbs tucked behind his cuirass. The mutt is on a leash, sitting quietly beside him. She's staring at the house and, when she sees me, her tail starts to wag and her whole body sways from side to side as though there is an earthquake.

That morning Regulus and I had split the list of senators in two. We've gone door-to-door trying to confirm the whereabouts of each and every senator who is supposed to be in Rome. The aim was to determine by deduction the owner of the hand in the forum and its golden ring – if it indeed belonged to a senator. Regulus may be insufferable, but he was right: the task is monumental. I thought taking a break to call on Antonia might prove more fruitful.

The mutt jumps up when I get close. I pat her head and say (in a sweet tone I rarely use), 'Yes, yes. I see you.'

Virgilius smiles. He has never seen me like this, with animal or man. 'Any luck?' he asks.

'No, she thinks Plautius is safe and sound on the Bay.'

'Is he officially missing then?'

'Let's wait to hear what Domitian says. Are you ready to go?'

Virgilius shakes his head. 'There's been a change of plans.'

'Oh?'

'We had a message from the palace. Your father requests your council.'

The morning is nearly done and we have nothing to show for it. And now useful hours will evaporate at the palace. But Caesar calls. 'Fine, fine,' I say. 'Lead the way.'


Long, wide, sun-stealing swaths of dark purple shrink the room. It's midday, yet the weak pulse of a lamp is the only source of light. The air is stale. Father is sitting at a desk inlaid with a sheet of green marble. Phoebus, the Imperial secretary, stands behind Father's left shoulder, a letter in his child-sized hands. Epaphroditus, the exchequer, is sitting opposite Father. Both are freedmen – men who began as palace slaves, but who have risen far since earning their freedom. Epaphroditus especially. He was a chamberlain once, charged with wiping Nero's arse. Now he runs the Imperial treasury.

Senator Secundus is here as well, sitting across from Father, resting both hands on his deluge of stomach. He's breathing heavily, as he always does, sending eruptions of hot air through his tangle of milky-white beard. Secundus currently has command of the fleet in Miscenum, but Father relies on his counsel so much he is in Rome more often than with his fleet. And finally there is cousin Sabinus, our useless newly appointed pontiff, who is leaning against the wall.

'General Titus,' Phoebus says, smirking. 'We'd given up hope.'

For a freedman, Phoebus is too impertinent by half. He calls me 'general' feigning respect, but he means it to sting. From undefeated general to prefect of the Praetorian guard, from hard-earned glory to a post traditionally held by drunkards, philanderers and the odd farmer's son. It's not a move to be envied. But Father asked, so I obeyed, for the good of the family, for the good of the party.

To Father, I say, 'I need to speak with you.'

'Fine, fine,' he says. He's bent over the desk as though his chest is cemented to the marble. In this light, his skin has an unhealthy purple pallor. 'We will talk,' he says. 'Later.'

He motions for me to sit. I cross my arms, letting him know I will stand.

'As I was saying,' secretary Phoebus continues, 'word came this morning from Thrace. Cerialis has finally attacked the False Nero and sacked the city of Maronea, which was harbouring known sympathisers.'

'Good,' Father says.

'But,' Phoebus continues, 'it seems the imposter and a handful of his followers escaped.'

Silence follows Phoebus's announcement.

This is not good news. Father wanted this handled quickly and quietly. A Nero in Thrace, genuine or not, undermines our position. The damage grows with each day that passes.

Cerialis had been sending his updates directly to me. Did he write to Phoebus this time? Or does Phoebus have a man in Cerialis's camp? A problem for another day perhaps.

'So the imposter has run off?' Father asks, shaking his head.

'Madness,' cousin Sabinus says, hoping to contribute.

I ask, 'How do they know he's missing? A sacked city is chaotic to say the least.'

'It's not a large city,' Phoebus says. 'They would know if the false tyrant remained inside its walls. Cerialis is putting some of the survivors to torture to learn more.'

Father sighs. It is the sigh of an old man. He asks, 'The tyrant has been dead how long? More than ten years, no? Yet we are still haunted by his ghost.'

'It *is* interesting, isn't it?' Secundus asks rhetorically. 'Nero was a monster. The rabble remembers, certainly. Yet there persists a fascination. I have often wondered whether it was the way he died, running the way he did, into the night, never to be seen again.'

Eyes in the room look to Epaphroditus, Nero's former favourite, who was supposedly with the tyrant in his last hours, before he took his own life. But Epaphroditus's expression – beneath his black goatee and black eyes – is impassive. It's as though we are discussing the races, not the end of a dynasty he witnessed first hand. No wonder he has survived the rise and fall of so many emperors. The man is as readable as a rock.

Father, always the pragmatist, mutters: 'Opinion is never universal. I'm sure some miss the tyrant. The extravagance, the pageantry, et cetera, et cetera. We should tell the rabble of the debts he left. That was his worst crime, if you ask me, the Imperial deficit.'

Secundus continues as though no one had spoken. 'I would think a second factor is the chaos that followed: three civil wars, one after the next. Who wouldn't believe Nero simply ran east to form an army?'

'What's past is past,' I say. 'Let's focus on what to do now. Yes?'

Father nods. 'Please.'

'It's important that we not let the trail run cold,' Phoebus says. 'We must inform Cerialis to pursue this False Nero to the ends of the earth.'

Father, then the entire room, look to me.

'This is not two boys chasing each other in the yard,' I say. 'Cerialis just sacked a city.'

Phoebus grimaces. He squeezes the letter from Thrace in his little hands.

'We must move quickly,' Phoebus says.

'Obviously,' I say, 'but not rashly. Cerialis must secure the city and root out all of the False Nero's remaining supporters. He should send riders out in every direction to see if the imposter can be spotted. But Cerialis is an experienced general. I am sure he's already taken these steps. I suspect the problem is you're getting your information from someone other than the general himself. Maybe it would be prudent to wait and get our information straight from the horse's mouth, yes?'

Phoebus's grimace hardens and I know I've hit the mark. There was a time my victories came over armies, not palace freedmen. Even so, I will enjoy the win, however slight. In a city full of vipers, you're either using your fangs or feeling the bite of another's.

'Madness,' cousin Sabinus says again, to no one in particular. 'Madness.'

When it's just the two of us, father and son, I draw back one of the curtains, letting natural light brighten the room. It's not direct sunshine, only a grey radiance, but it's welcome all the same. Father's purple pallor morphs to a more traditional antique white. I take a seat in front of his desk.

'Before you start, I want to talk about your sister,' he says. He's fiddling with a dagger the size of his hand, pressing the dull point into his left index finger and twisting it like a screw. His eyes are on the blade. He's not looking me in the eye, which has me worried. 'We're slowly losing numbers, people we can count as friends. You see that? Senators who were once friend are now, possibly, foe?'

I give a slight nod in response.

'And you know some have more influence than others. Some are shepherds rather than sheep?'

'Yes.'

'And you would agree that Marcellus is one of those shepherds?'

Old, scaly Marcellus who is more snake than man. I don't like where this is going.

'I agree with the premise, but not necessarily its application.'

Caesar exhales. His eyes remain on the blade.

'I want you to hint to Marcellus that I would be open to marrying Domitilla . . . to him.'

'Is that so?' My jaw clenches. 'Do you intend on actually following through this time? Or is your daughter to be the carrot once again – the carrot while your oldest son plays the constant stick?'

'Which would you prefer, Titus?'

He's looking at me now, defiant. He puts the dagger back on to the desk. I can see the handle, which is fashioned from the tusk of a boar. It's the knife he was given by the governor of Britannia after he halted the sack of Calidunum. A gift of thanks. I remember the firelight in the camp that evening, as the governor handed Father the knife to a round of cheers. I was only seventeen. I remember hearing those hurrahs and thinking that my father was a god. Where has that man gone? I wonder. Is it the weight of office? Or is it the gout that afflicts his legs? Does constant pain make the task of leading an empire too heavy to bear?

Caesar asks again: 'Which would you prefer? Would you rather I renege or marry her off?'

'Neither. I would prefer neither because both are folly. You have done this before, used the prospect of marrying Domitilla to woo dissatisfied senators. But they're on to the plan. Marcellus is not stupid. He will see it for what it is. A ruse. You've refused to marry Domitilla for ten years. You know what they call her, don't you?'

'I know.'

'The Widow,' I say, carrying on regardless. 'They say she is cursed.' My poor sister's husband died on their wedding night. She was only fifteen. Father had married her off to a man three times her age, and he died hours into their marriage. 'You won't marry her because you don't want to give up the asset. But people say that no one wants her. They say she's cursed and marrying her means death.'

'I know, I know.' Father waves his hands at me. He leans back in his chair but his back stays bent and his shoulders slumped.

'Ambitious men are growing restless, Titus. I can feel it.'

Now it's my turn to say, *I know*. I stay silent, though. He knows I know.

'We need to do something,' Father says. 'What you did in Baiae was good. It rid us of a few enemies and it sent a message. But now? This business with the hand – it's the smell of blood in the air. Aspiring minds are salivating.'

Silence eats at us for a moment. Our anxiety breathes.

'What do you make of the hand?' I ask. 'We haven't spoken of it yet.'

Father gives a sarcastic *harrumph*. 'Oh, it was planned. I've no doubt. Some senator who doesn't have the figs to do anything but fake an omen. Find a senator with a cock this big' – Father shows me a short distance between his thumb and index finger – 'and we'll have our man.'

'But how would someone plan it?'

Father shrugs. 'How should I know? Our enemies are industrious.' He sighs, collects himself, then says, 'What was it you wanted to speak with me about?'

I fish out what I need from between the leather and steel of my cuirass. I reach my hand out, open it, and the gold ring falls onto the desk. Father squints, scrutinising the circle of gold with his opaque eyes. His top lip curls slightly.

'What . . . is that?'

'A ring. A gold ring. It was on the hand.'

'And?'

'It means the hand likely belonged to a senator or knight. Not some drunk pleb in a back alley. And there's more.'

I fish out Plautius's letter and drop it on Father's desk. He picks it up and reads. He rolls his eyes three times before his expression changes. 'Ah. And you think this hand belonged to this missing knight, Vettius? Or Plautius himself?'

'I'm not sure. At first, I didn't think very much of the letter. You know what Plautius is like. But he said he'd be in Rome by now. I called on Antonia today and she's not seen him in weeks.'

Father shakes his head. 'No one would be fool enough to kill a Plautii. They're too close to our family. We've had an alliance for more than forty years. They're almost our kin. But I agree: none of this is good.'

'I have Domitian looking for Plautius.'

'Domitian?' He shakes his head, letting me know what he thinks of Domitian's chances. 'You couldn't have found someone more capable?' He reads the letter again. 'None of this is good, Titus. None of it.'

We reach the forum as the sun is starting to set. Vendors are closing up shop; a lawyer exits the courts with an entourage of slaves carrying rolls of papyrus; and half a dozen vestal virgins tiptoe towards home, all in white, a cloud of incense trailing behind.

We enter along the Clivus Capitolinus, which snakes its way down the Capitoline Hill's steep slope, between the tabularium and the Temple of Saturn. As we're making the descent, I see a boy with his back to us, writing on the wall of the senate house. At our vantage, I can't see what he's writing. Graffiti on a public building should not be the prefect's concern, but often I find it's indicative of the people's mood, a weathervane of public sentiment. I signal for my escort to stop and make my way toward the boy alone.

He is dressed as a common pleb: worn tunic, bare feet, and a mange of strawberry-blond hair. He pauses and cautiously looks to his left then his right, but he doesn't see me coming from behind.

When I'm directly behind the boy, I can see what he's scrawling on the wall:

## Nero Lives

Questions run through my mind, the sort a confident general would never ask, but which occur often to Caesar's son. Does he know about the False Nero in Thrace? Has he been hired to write this? Is this part of a larger campaign to undermine my father . . .? Underneath the insecurities of Roman politics, I know, odds are, this boy is just that: a boy; one who probably couldn't think of anything more clever to write. Nearby there is a girl, hidden, watching after she was asked to, deciding whether this boy's bold act impresses her or not.

I hear a dog panting behind me. I turn to see Virgilius and the mutt. Virgilius looks at the boy, then at me. He sardonically arches his left eyebrow. *Orders?*

I give him a wink and then silently walk the remaining five yards to the boy. When I'm directly behind him, I say, 'It would help if you could give us more details. Such as *where*.'

The boy freezes. He turns around slowly. When he sees my armour, he starts to shake. (Does he know I am Caesar's son?) He drops the brush and runs.

Virgilius watches as the boy disappears into an alley. 'You'll make him pine for Nero even more now.'

'Fear is good. It makes everyone more compliant.'

Virgilius gives me a mock bow to feign defeat. When he bends down, one of his gloves, which was tucked into his belt, falls to the ground. He kneels to pick it up. But before he can, the mutt snatches it in her mouth. She tries to run away but the leash stops her. Virgilius has to use both hands to stop her from running away.

'Strange,' Virgilius says. 'She's behaved all day.'

The dog is aiming her snout at the Temple of Concord. The leash is taut. She wants to run.

'Let her go,' I say.

Virgilius, good soldier that he is, drops the leash without a word. The mutt – still carrying Virgilius's glove – trots toward the Temple of Concord. We follow.

We follow her across the forum, up the steps of the temple and onto its portico. The dog is near the temple doors. She slowly turns to face us. She opens her jaws and drops the glove.

When the glove hits the portico, Virgilius and I stop in our tracks. For a moment, we stand there, in front of the dog and glove, dumb-founded.

'How did she do that?' Virgilius asks. 'Again.'

The dog is panting, her tongue lolling out to the side of her mouth. She's content now that her job is complete.

'She was trained,' I say.

'Why?'

'The question is *who*, Virgilius,' I say. 'The question is who.'

# V

## Magnificence of Mind, Part I
### A.D. 68

# MARCUS

◆

*21 July, afternoon*
*The home of Proculus Creon, Rome*

'You don't know who Hector is? Or Achilles?' Giton is laughing. 'What *do* you know?'

We're outside, under the colonnade. Master and Mistress are somewhere inside taking their siesta. Their son, Giton, is sitting on the steps that lead to the garden. He tosses a piece of fish to the puppy that's spinning in circles at his feet. Somewhere in the city people are fighting – like they have nearly every day since Galba was named emperor. We can hear it, but it's so far away it only sounds like giants whispering.

'I know some things,' I say. I'm holding a palm fan but I stopped swishing it when Giton started making fun.

He says, 'I know some things, *sir*.' Giton wants me to call him 'sir' even though he's younger than me and smaller. He says I should show the proper respect, because he's my master, just like his mother and father. 'Well,' he says, 'what is it? Tell me something? You don't know anything, *do* you? I'll be twice as smart as you when I'm your age.'

'I know . . . I know how to get the favour of kings.'

Giton crooks his eyebrow. 'What?'

'I know how to get the favour of a king. Or an emperor.' I shouldn't say anything: Elsie took me to the magi in secret. But I hate when Giton teases me. When he starts, he doesn't stop. 'I know a potion. It works.'

Giton frowns. 'Well? Tell me.'

'Lard of a lion, mixed with rose water,' I say. I point at the spot between my eyes where the magi rubbed the lard. 'You've got to rub it right here.'

'How do you know it works?'

I open my mouth but don't say anything; Giton starts to laugh.

'See, you don't know anything. You're so stupid. I should tell Father to whip you for talking like that, for making things up.'

Giton tosses the plate onto the ground and it smashes into a hundred pieces.

'Tell mother you did it,' he says. He does this sometimes, breaks things for no reason and tells me to say I did it. He stands up. 'I'm Achilles. You're Hector. I always win. That's all you need to know about Homer.'

He walks way along the colonnade, the little puppy nipping at his heels.

Elsie is in the kitchen. She's busy chopping white-green leeks. I ask her who Hector is. Without looking up, she says, 'Stories? I don't have time for stories.'

I say, 'Giton says I don't know anything.'

Elsie looks up and her face changes. She comes over to me and bends down and looks into my eyes. She says, 'I have a better story for you. Yes? The story of how I found you. Should I tell you this story?'

Elsie takes me out into the alleyway. It's hot and dusty and the sun is just peeking in over the neighbours' roof. We sit on an amphorae lying on its side like a log. Elsie's hair is grey and thirsty. She keeps it tied into a big knot, but a few loose strands are hanging down to her shoulders. She swipes at them and sticks them behind her ear. Then she takes out a handful of pistachios and drops them in her apron. I pop one into my mouth and it's so salty I'm thirsty right away. She tells me a story – one I've heard before, but I like hearing again.

'Let's see. Maybe I start at the beginning. Yes?'

I nod.

'I was born free – a point of pride for your Elsie, yes? – on the other side of the Middle Sea. Our village was small – too small for a name – surrounded by trees as tall as the Palatine.' She looks up at trees that aren't there. 'One day, when I was still just a girl, I was playing with my sisters in the forest. We were laughing and singing and hiding, carrying on like we always did, when suddenly raiders appeared, a dozen of them, covered in furs and boils, with beards as long as your little arm.'

Inside, Mistress is hollering for boiled water.

A big blob of sweat trickles down my back.

'The raiders took me and sold me to soldiers, and the soldiers brought me to Rome and a knight named Quintus Proculus purchased me. It was in Master Proculus's home that I met my Silva. Silva was much older than me. His hair was grey, like mine is now, and his skin was droopy –' she pulls at the loose skin on her neck '– like mine is now. But he was kind to me, in his way.'

She plops a pistachio into her mouth. She rummages around with her fingers and pulls out the shell.

'Master Proculus had Silva teach me Latin and some Greek. We spent hours and hours together. Silva declared his love very early.' Elsie smiles. 'Too early. He began the first lesson with, 'This is the letter "A", and ended with, "I love you with all of my heart." I wasn't interested. He was old, like I said. But my Silva was persistent. He wore me down. Months later, when he said, "This is the letter 'Z,'" I said, "I love you with all of my heart."' Elsie squints, thinking. 'The heart is strange. Yes? I'm not sure what changed. Maybe, after so much hardship, Silva's kindness was all I wanted. We weren't allowed to marry, but Master Proculus let us share a room. We lived like that for many years until, finally, I was with child. But then – suddenly – Master Proculus died. Silva and I had hoped Master Proculus would have freed us in his will, but others were given that privilege. Instead, he – what's the word? Bequeathed? Yes, he *bequeathed* us to his former slave, a freedman named Creon.' She makes a face like she smelt spoilt milk. 'You know who I mean.'

A cart pulled by a mule slowly crosses the entrance to the road; its wheels squawk like birds.

'As my belly started to bulge, Mistress told me I would be able to raise the baby in their home. But, because I was their property, my child was theirs, according to law. The law, the law, the law.' She sighs a big, heavy sigh. 'Our baby was born in March. A little girl. Silva and I raised her for five years. You should have seen her, Marcus. She was as pretty as an empress and as smart as a banker. She was my pride and joy. But then one day Master decided she wasn't welcome. He said she didn't have *value*. So Master sold my little girl. I don't know to who. The day the traders came to take her away, Silva – seeing my tears – fought to keep her, throwing his old arms around like he was a boy of twenty. But the traders were young and strong. One of them hit my poor Silva on the head so hard it slowed his wits for good. He slurred his words like a drunk for a year and then he was gone.'

For a moment, I think Elsie is going to cry, but she doesn't.

'For two years, I cried and prayed to Diana for relief. I wanted to die.' She flicks another pistachio into her mouth. 'In the mornings, before

Master and Mistress would wake, I would walk by the Tiber, looking at the deep-green swirling water and I would think of my little girl. Each morning I would think about jumping in. Each morning, I would think: tomorrow I will jump. Tomorrow. But then, one morning, as I was walking along the shore I heard a mighty howling. I thought I was dreaming again – dreaming of my little girl crying as the slavers dragged her away – but the sound didn't stop. So I trudged into the water, up to my waist, and found in the reeds a baby boy, pink and screaming.'

'Was it me?' I ask, even though I know it was.

'It was you, howling like a wolf.'

'Why was I in the reeds?' I ask this every time. 'Did my mother not want me?'

'Oh no,' Elsie says. 'Diana left you for me. I prayed for months and months and this was how she answered.' She nods. 'I took you to a Chaldean priest – the best in the Subura. He said the heavens foretold greatness for you, and I thought: this boy could be anything! Maybe one day he will own a bakery or learn a craft, like painting. Maybe he could own slaves himself! Imagine that!'

Elsie is smiling again.

'I knew Master Creon wouldn't sell you. How could he after what the Chaldean said? So I brought you home. Master and Mistress agreed that I could look after you, though by law you would be their slave. I named you Silva. But as you grew older, Master Creon could never remember your name. He'd see you in the atrium, or under the colonnade, or at the fullery, and he'd ask, "And who is he?" And I'd say "Silva", and he'd say, "But Silva is dead." Then, one day, he told Mistress you needed a new name, so he wouldn't be confused any more. Master said, "Let's name him after a consul. We'll never forget a consul's name." It was September and the consuls were Marcus Arruntius Aquila and Marcus Vettius Bolanus. So they named you Marcus, and you've been Marcus ever since.'

Elsie's story makes me feel better. (She always makes me feel better.) But I still don't know who Hector is. It used to be she was the only person I could ask questions; she was the only person I knew who wouldn't laugh or yell at me. And if she didn't know the answer, then I'd never know it. But now . . . now there is someone else.

# NERO

◆

*22 July, afternoon*
*City jail IV, Rome*

The boy and I have a routine now. He visits in the afternoon and, as I take my bread and water, we talk. We discuss – or, more precisely, I lecture and he listens – about any manner of things. I tell him stories about my grandfather, great-great grandfather, or the Divine Julius. Or I explain which wine to pair with wild boar, or duck, or venison. I talk and talk and talk, sometime with purpose, but usually to fill the hours. He listens quietly, occasionally asking questions. We rarely talk politics and I don't press him for information. He remains nervous about engaging with me and I don't want to scare him away. I enjoy his company; at the moment, he's all I have.

Besides, when it comes to politics, the boy only understands half of what he hears. When he does provide me with information of his own volition, it often requires considerable parsing. From what I understand, the current state of affairs is this: the Hunchback, the newly appointed emperor, is now making his way from Spain to Rome. The city waits in suspense. Violence has occurred on occasion, but hasn't yet taken root. The city is teetering on a precipice. Yet Galba is dawdling in Gaul, securing cities and dolling out punishment to those who took their time flocking to his cause. He is not due in Rome for some time. I wonder whether the Empire will last in the meantime.

I don't know why I'm still alive. There could be any number of reasons. I am in the dark, literally and figuratively. Thankfully, the pain is lessening. I will never be self-sufficient; my eyes will never miraculously unpluck. But as the fog of pain lifts, I am regaining my wits. And with my mind intact, I will have agency – and with agency I can find the men who did this to me.

As I see it, I have two immediate problems. Escaping this cell is one; coin the other. By now the Hunchback, or possibly the senate, will have appropriated the Imperial treasury. There is a chance I have another fortune at my disposal. But Africa feels a world away. And I won't know for certain until I lay my hands on it. I have time, though. I am content to rest and recover my strength. I am content to plan and think of the days and months ahead. Apollo willing, I will be away before Galba reaches Rome.

The boy lingers this afternoon, more than usual. He asks me who Hector is. *Hector.* His chronic ignorance is galling, even when one takes into account his station. Since he knows next to nothing of Homer, I have to start from the beginning. Son of Priam, husband to Andromache, brother to Paris, saviour of Troy until he wasn't, until he fell victim to the Greeks, to the terrible Achilles. I tell him how after a valiant fight, Achilles killed Hector and dragged his body around the walls of Troy, tied to his chariot, while carrions circled overhead and Hector's wife, up on the walls of Troy, wailed. This upsets the boy; I can hear it in his voice. I tell him there is no reason to be upset. Hector fought with dignity and his name lives on. It didn't matter how long he lived. I make the argument from memory, without conviction, while rubbing my shard of terracotta brick.

# MARCUS

*27 July, sunset*
*The home of Proculus Creon, Rome*

The guests arrive before sundown. There are seven of them, each with their own slaves. One guest named Otho shows up with ten slaves. Ten! I heard Master talking with Mistress about him this morning. He said Otho is a senator, 'very important, very important.' He's a close friend of the Hunchback. Master invited him but couldn't believe he said yes.

I know it's an important dinner because Master spent money on oysters, good ones from somewhere called Lucrean. They're the first course. We spent all morning cleaning and opening them and laying them on ice from the Alps. Next will be peacock, roasted with its feathers on. (Elsie says the feathers have to stay on or the taste isn't right.) There's also a boar that's bigger than me. Elsie and Socrates had to lift it onto the counter together. They skinned it, stabbed it with a long spit, and roasted it all day.

Otho is the last to arrive. His ten slaves walk in first. The one at the front announces his master by name and then Otho walks in. His hair looks like a rug, blond and tufty and thick, with little twists that fall in front of his eyes, and his smile is as wide as the front door. He sees me in the front hall, as he walks inside, and says, 'And who is this?' He bends down and, with his hand, tilts my chin up until our eyes meet. He does it gently. I don't like it. He says to Master, 'Is he yours, Creon? What's his name?'

Master's smile is from ear to ear. 'Marcus. His name is Marcus.'

'Marvellous.' That's all Otho says before introducing himself to Mistress.

Dinner is served in the triclinium. Lamps are lit as the sun goes down. Guests are given their very own couch. Master's made sure he's right beside Otho. Master tells me to wait on Otho personally, so I've got to stand directly behind him, holding a jug of wine ready to fill his cup when asked. All the other guests want to tell Otho how great he is and how great Galba is. (No one calls Galba the Hunchback in front of Otho.) They say Galba is going to adopt Otho, so he'll be next in line for the throne. Otho looks in to his cup, a big smile on his face, and says, 'It's impertinent to speak of such things'. Even *I* know he doesn't mean it.

The boar is brought in and everyone claps.

Otho says, 'As grand as any meal in the palace,' and Master looks like he's going to faint.

Master and Otho start talking between themselves.

'I suppose you're wondering why I accepted your invitation?'

'I was honoured, senator. Properly honoured.'

'I don't make it a habit visiting the homes of freedmen, Creon. It can hinder the reputation of a man of my standing. But it can be done strategically, on certain occasions.'

'Yes. Of course. Of course.'

Master Creon talks differently with Otho. He nods his head, instead of shaking it, and he hasn't yelled, not once.

'My presence here tonight means that you are remarkable, and I will tell you why. You're rich, Creon, but in Rome, there are many rich freedman. I've been told that something sets you apart from your *nouveau riche* contemporaries, that you're a man with vision. Are you such a man?'

'You've heard right,' Master says. 'I built my little empire up from nothing. I owned one apartment when I started. Now I've got six, a jail, and a fullery that's just humming along.'

'Yes. I've heard. You have done well in business. However, business is not the arena in which a Roman, a true Roman, defines himself. Wouldn't you agree?'

'No . . . I mean, yes, I'd agree.'

'Politics, Creon, that is how a man truly makes his name live on. Not those massive graves your fellow freedman erect. Pouring all of their money into four walls of stone, engraving "here lies so-and-so, who made a fortune doing such-and-such," as though the world will remember a baker once his ashes are cold. I hope you have grander plans than that.'

Otho looks into his glass and sniffs. Master snaps his fingers, which means, come fill the man's cup. Otho smiles at me as I'm pouring. My skin feels itchy.

Master says, 'But I'm a freedman. I'm not likely to get into the senate.'

Otho's eyebrows shoot up into his forehead; he laughs. Everyone in the room smiles, even though they couldn't hear what made him laugh. 'Oh, Creon! You misunderstand me. You've no place in politics yourself. Come now. But you can align yourself with a politician. That's how you can move into the political realm. It is, after all, your civic duty.'

Master looks into his cup. 'You need money.'

'Yes, obviously,' Otho says. 'But I want *your* money. Fortune is giving you a chance, Creon. A chance to become a friend –' his voice goes to a whisper '– of the next emperor. Are you surprised? Don't let my feigned modesty fool you. The Hunchback is old and childless. But the senate and the people want certainty. They want stability. Galba knows this. He should be in Rome before the year is out. By that time, I have no doubt I will be named his heir. I have corresponded with his representatives, and the auguries have been propitious. It is inevitable. But I will need money, Creon. Power does not come cheap. I want your money. Call it a loan – one which the Imperial treasury will easily pay back – with interest – when I am emperor.'

Master nods his head. 'I'm honoured, senator. Honoured.'

After dinner, Otho points at me and asks Master, 'Is the boy for sale?'

Master says yes, he'd gladly sell Otho anything he needs. He starts to name a price, but Otho waves his hand. 'I am not going to bargain with a freedman. I'll send someone to come haggle another time.'

When the party is over and I'm cleaning with Elsie, I tell her what Otho said, about how he wants to buy me. She shakes her head. 'Poor child,' she says, 'though you've been lucky up until now.'

I ask her what she means, but she doesn't say.

# NERO

## *28 July, afternoon*
## *City jail IV, Rome*

Today the boy gives me an account of his dinner last night, as though it was a feast to end all feasts, not a little meal given by an inconsequential freedman. He alludes to some story about being sold. I feel compelled to ask questions as though I care.

'A knight, you said?'

'Senator.'

'Well, given your age and the way the man talked . . .' I shake my head. 'The man's cupbearer will likely be asked to do more than hold his cup – if you understand my meaning. A bad outcome for you, certainly, but it is better than the mines or the hold of a ship.'

The boy starts to cry; a reasonable reaction, though I doubt he only has a vague sense of what fortune holds for him.

'Don't cry,' I tell the boy. 'It's undignified, even for a child your age.'

'How do I stop it? How do I stop the man from buying me?'

'You don't. You're a slave. You go. You endure.'

'You don't know how then?'

The boy's impertinence is galling. Without my eyes, locked up like a criminal, the proper hierarchy is torn to smithereens, and a slave feels comfortable chastising me. Bile fizzles on my tongue . . . and yet I ask questions despite myself.

'Who?' I ask. 'Which senator wants to purchase you?'

'His name is Otho.'

I laugh for the first time in ages. I might have cried if I still had my eyes. That bald lecher is back in Rome, is he? I made it quite clear that if I ever saw him or his wandering hands again, I would have him thrown from the Tarpeian Rock. Now that I'm gone, I suppose the coward thought it safe to slink back to the capital.

'You're in luck, boy. I will take great pleasure in setting Otho back. Tell me everything you can about Otho and what he said to your Master.'

# VI

## The Provincials
### A.D. 79

# CALENUS

◆

*11 January, morning*
*Pier XIV, Ostia*

'I'm looking for someone,' I say. 'A man by the name of Ulpius.'

The clerk is sitting behind a desk covered in papyrus, rolls of it, like he's a librarian or something equally as dull. There's a green awning overhead blocking the sun. To my left, there are ships – hundreds of them across the bay – bobbing up and down in the Tyrrhenian's swell. Some are fixed to the pier, sails furled, oars quiet; the rest are cutting through the blue. The air has a chill to it, so my bad knee aches; but the sun is out for the first time in days.

The clerk looks up from his rolls.

'Ulpius?' he asks. 'A strange name, that. A debtor?'

'No,' I say. 'He's coming in from Spain.'

'You look like a creditor is all. A man come to collect.'

'He's not a debtor.'

'From Spain, you say?'

The clerk looks down at his papers. His skin is a knobbly mess of callouses, sunburn and wrinkles. He looks old, but with freedmen, after a life of servitude, it's always hard to tell. Likely, he's tied to one of the port barons, with nothing better to do with his hard-earned freedom than to work for his former master, doing the same job he was forced to do before he was set free, but this time for a small fee and less pride.

'Dangerous journey at this time of year, isn't it?' he says with his nose buried in the papyrus. 'Spain to Ostia.'

I travelled most of the night to Ostia, Rome's port on the sea. I've been here all morning looking for Nerva's rich cripple, walking up and down the pier, and my patience is running thin.

'Be careful, friend,' I say before turning to go. 'You might end up wasting the wrong man's time.'

I've walked only a pace or two before I feel a hand gently pulling on the crook of my elbow. I let him turn me around.

'Didn't mean any offence,' he says. Now that he's standing, I can see that his back is crooked, and he has to cock his head back to look me in the eyes. 'You look like a creditor, is all. I see a lot of creditors here, trying to find debtors before they take to sea. Interesting lot, creditors, don't you think? They come here with coin in hand, ready to spend a few denarii to loosen tongues or hire extra muscle. Sometimes they'll spend more coin than the debt is actually worth.'

There it is. I've lived in Italy for close to ten years now, but I always forget how damned corrupt it is. Even some lowly freedman working the pier expects silver for his trouble.

I reach into my purse and pull out one coin, silver and embossed with Vespasian's fat cheeks. 'Well?'

The freedman's face lights up with a toothless smile.

'You creditors are a fickle bunch. Just before you ran off, I was about to say –' he takes the coin from my hand '– we had a Spanish ship come this morning. I don't have all the names presently. But if your man's from Spain, he'll be on it.'

He points in the direction of the eastern pier. As he's turning to go, I grab him by the arm.

'You can hold onto that coin if you like. But it's mine until we find Ulpius. Understand?'

His eyes look unnerved but his toothless smile never leaves his lips. 'Of course, of course. No problem, friend.'

We find the Spanish ship on the southern pier, port gunwale parallel to the shore. Men are carrying crates over the gangplank and stacking them onto two carts. They're all sailors, near as I can tell: exposed chests the colour of old leather, and hair to their shoulders, tied back or braided.

Then I spot two men by the carts who aren't sailors. One is short, stocky, and dressed like a Parthian: trousers and a crimson jacket embroidered with gold, with matching gold chains, and make-up, black lines traced around his eyes like a woman. The other one is bent over a chest. His skin is dark, his tunic green, and his head as hairless as a newborn's. I take one look at him and I know he's a killer. I don't know for certain – and I've been wrong before – but there's something in the way he moves; everything is economic and smooth. I'm not sure if he was a legionary, though. I don't think he would have fit into the standard-issue cuirass. He has the chest of a young buck, all bluster in the spring.

The Big Buck is testing the lock of a chest, giving it a ferocious wiggle. When he looks up, I spot his eye patch, which covers his left eye, and a thick scar that runs across his cheek.

He notices me and we have a moment. We stare at each other, eye to eye. He jumps down from the cart. He's a bit long in the tooth, but he swings his legs down to the pier smooth enough. A killer for certain.

'Can I help you, friend?' he says as he's walking over.

'Maybe,' I say.

He's in front of me now, closer than I'd like.

'I'm looking for someone,' I say. 'A man named Ulpius.'

'Lucky you,' he says.

His tone is casual. It's hard to tell if he's angling for a fight or whether I've actually found Ulpius.

The clerk takes this opportunity to slink off, my coin in hand.

'I think what my friend here is trying to say –' a voice to my right says '– is that you don't need to look any further. You've found your man.'

I look to see a man stepping onto the pier. His hair and beard are the colour of copper with patches of white, and wrapped around his head, covering his eyes, is a rag. His left hand is on the shoulder of a kid who's guiding the way; in his other hand, he's holding a stick, which he taps as he walks. *Tap tap tap.*

So, Nerva's cripple is blind as a rock.

'You know my name,' the cripple says, 'may I have yours?'

'Calenus,' I say. 'Julius Calenus.'

The cripple doesn't have an accent. I've never met a Spaniard before. I was expecting an accent. I thought he'd be rich too. You'd have to be for Nerva to take an interest in you. But this one isn't dressed the part. His light-brown cloak is almost as plain as my tunic.

I don't like the look of the kid. A spoilt, patrician shit by the looks of him. Hair trimmed short, expensive silk tunic, clean-shaven despite being on a ship for days. I bet there's not one callous on those milky-white hands of his.

'Cocceius Nerva sent me,' I say. 'Asked me to help escort you to Rome.'

'Ah,' the cripple says. 'He didn't want the blind man groping his way along the Tiber.'

I shrug. I don't care if his feelings are hurt. It's probably best he thinks I'm here because he's blind, not because Nerva's planning on fleecing him for some of his gold. (If he's got any.)

'Well,' the cripple says. 'I wonder if you're required. One only needs to follow the Tiber east, and a touch north, isn't that right? Are you able to offer anything other than directions?'

'You've been before?'

'Rome is everywhere, my friend,' the cripple says. 'One would be hard pressed not to have been there.'

I've never spoken to a blind man before. I wonder whether all of them talk like this, staring off at the moon?

'I meant the city itself,' I say.

Suddenly two sailors drop a chest and one end slams against the pier. Wood cracks and the top of the chest swings open. I nearly shit myself at what I see: coins, gold and silver, and jewels, green, red, and turquoise, more than I've ever seen in one place. A few coin spill out onto the pier. I look at all those chests lined up on the carts and wonder how many of them are also filled with coin.

The two sailors who dropped the chest look like they *actually* shit themselves. Their mouths are wide open.

It isn't the Big Buck who's the first to react; it's the kid – which is a bit of a surprise, really. He walks to the chest and kicks it closed. After he looks to make sure none of the other sailors on the boat saw the mint hidden in the chest, he bends down, picks up the spilled coin, and presses them into the hands of the two sailors.

'Our secret,' he says quietly. It's probably two years' worth of wages. Then the kid says louder: 'We'd like to make Rome before sunset.'

The two sailors exchange a quick look before pocketing their money. They start loading the carts again like nothing happened.

Pretty deft move, I have to admit, for a patrician shit and all.

'Marcus,' the cripple says to the kid. 'Come introduce yourself to Calenus here. We should be getting on the road as soon as we can.'

We're on the road out of Ostia by mid-afternoon. I should have them inside the city gates before nightfall.

The kid and the cripple are in the first cart, the Big Buck and the Parthian slave in the second. I'm on horseback, between the Tiber and the road. They're a quiet group, for the most part, except for the Parthian. He keeps asking me question after question. What do I make of the Emperor? Is Nerva my patron? Does he ever consult with the Emperor? Questions where the answer is no one's business but my own. Or maybe Nerva's. He asks me, 'What is Rome's mood?' like the teat is my wife and we're in a spat, not a city bursting with a million plus.

He doesn't stop, so I give my horse a little kick and I speed away. When I'm beside the cripple, I slow down to a walk. I decide to see if I can gather information from Ulpius that I can sell to Nerva.

But before I can start, he says, 'What legion did you serve with?' His head is aimed straight ahead when he asks, like he's watching the road. The question gives me the jitters. I never said a word about being a soldier.

'How'd you know?' I ask.

'Know?' He keeps staring straight ahead. 'Know what?'

'That I used to be a soldier?'

He considers the question. He's rubbing something in his hand, a piece of brick I think, that's rounded and smooth.

'I didn't – I wasn't certain, at least,' he says. 'I merely presumed and asked the second question, who did you serve with? I tried to save us both time. Unsuccessfully, it seems, but I tried.'

'But what tipped you off?' I ask.

'Oh, a number of items. Your walk being one. *Right-left-right-left.* It conjures up a triumphal procession. Hmm. What else? You didn't back away from Theseus. That was another clue. Pride overruled common sense, which is often a product of training. And your patron. Men like that always have extra muscle on hand.' The cripple shrugs a satisfied shrug. 'More than anything, it was your smell. You stink of sour wine; it's dripping from your pores. And no one drinks that swill but the rank and file or generals looking to slum.'

Whatever information I could sell to Nerva isn't worth talking to this prick. I pull on my reins and my horse slows, letting the cripple pull ahead.

We're on the road for less than an hour when we spot four men on horseback coming the other way. One of them is a legionary. The other three aren't soldiers; hired thugs by the look of them. One is tall and the other two are stocky. Trailing behind them is a woman. Her hands are bound, and the soldier on the horse has another rope tied to her hands, like he's taking a dog for a walk. The woman has seen better days: her stola is torn, her top lip is swollen and bleeding, and her hair, which may have been up before, but is messy now, falling every which way. The whole thing doesn't look right, but one of them is a soldier so it's none of my business.

As they draw closer, no one says a word. But the kid turns back on his seat and exchanges a look with the Big Buck.

When our group meets theirs, the kid reins in his horse and stops the cart. The soldier reins in as well.

'Good afternoon,' the kid says.

The soldier nods at this.

I can see now that the woman's gagged. She's staring at us with wide eyes.

'Looks like a dangerous prisoner you have there,' the kid says, nodding his head to the woman. 'Parthian or German.'

The legionary is oozing confidence. It's hard not to when you're wearing armour, with the strength of the legions behind you. I remember how good that armour felt, and the confidence that came with it.

'Clear the road,' the soldier says. They're on horseback and could easily go around the carts. Ignoring the kid's question and giving an order is his way of putting the boy in his place. I expect the boy's balls to shrink after the soldier speaks to him like that but they don't. Instead, the kid asks again: 'Parthian or German?'

The plume of the soldier's helmet, which is parallel with shoulders, marks him as an officer. When it dawns on him that some little shit is talking to him like this, things are going to turn quickly. I look at the Big Buck to see what he's doing, whether he's as unnerved as I am, but he's barely paying attention. He's looking up into the trees at some bird. Worst of all, the cripple is humming like he's the happiest man in the Empire.

The kid keeps going. 'Or maybe she's a Celt.' He's got the look of someone who doesn't like heights but climbs up a rock face all the same. I'm not sure whether he's brave, crazy, or just acting the part. 'Is she for sale? I've always wanted to own a Celt. Let me buy her from you.'

Then the kid takes out a coin and flings it at the legionary. It flies end over end a good fifteen feet and hits the soldier straight in the cuirass. *DIIIINNNNGGGGG.* The kid forces a smile to his lips, a crazy fucking smile.

The legionary has had enough. To his companions, he says, 'Ten lashings for the boy.'

Two of them dismount and start walking toward us. They pull out wooden cudgels from somewhere inside their tunics. They're walking towards the kid but he isn't content to wait. He jumps off the cart and sprints straight at them. This catches them off guard just enough that the kid can land a quick punch right on the stocky one's chin. With the one dazed, the kid grabs him by the tunic and runs him right at the tall one. Then all three of them fall to the grass.

'Marcus, don't dally,' the cripple says. 'We want to get to the city before dark.'

This group is madder than a Thracian priest.

The centurion looks at the third thug and says, 'Teach the boy a lesson. Twenty lashes.' Then the officer points at me and the Big Buck. 'You two stay where you are.'

The third thug gets off his horse and makes his way to the three bodies rolling around on the grass.

I look at the Big Buck. He still hasn't moved. Not even an inch. He either trusts the kid can handle three grown men all on his own, or he's hoping the boy breathes his last in the not so distant future.

Nerva will be livid if I let his rich provincial die on the trip from Ostia. He'd never use me for anything again. But if I get involved it likely means laying a hand on a legionary. Usually, that's a very, *very* bad idea. The best way out of this is to let the boy take the twenty lashes and hope that's the end of it.

Once the third thug reaches the mess of bodies on the ground, the Big Buck finally moves. Like I said: he's a bit long in the tooth but damned if he doesn't move well. He's down from the cart in a blink of his one good eye, and he covers the distance to the scrum just as quick. He's not armed, but he catches the third thug by surprise, landing a punch square on the chin. The poor bastard crumples; I wonder if he'll ever get up again.

After the thug collapses, the Big Buck shoves his hands into the threesome rolling around on the grass, trying to help the kid.

The officer has seen enough. He draws his sword and spurs his horse forward. He drops the rope and the girl takes off. She heads to the tree line, taking strides as long as her ankle length tunic will let her.

The situation has escalated like I feared. If the officer cuts down the Big Buck and the kid, his day will be that much easier if he just kills me and the cripple. My difficult decision isn't a decision any longer. I'm now tied to this group until this is all sorted. Despite reservations to the contrary – despite having no armour or sword, and just a little dagger shoved in my boot – I spur my horse at the officer. I yell one of my old battle cries, wondering if it will be my last.

# TITUS

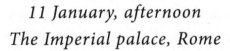

*11 January, afternoon*
*The Imperial palace, Rome*


Domitian finally sends word from Campania, in not one but two letters.

Ptolemy finds me after the baths, in my robe, making my way to my study. He waves two letters in the air, explaining that Domitian sent both, a day apart, but somehow they arrived at the same time, with the same carrier. Which means the Imperial service has more problems than I'd thought, or Domitian – despite my explicit order that he move with haste – failed to do so.

In the hall, still dripping from the baths, I say, 'Give them to me in order.'

Ptolemy hands me the first letter.

*10 January (from Baiae)*
*Brother:*

*What gruelling tasks you assign. Sniff out the whereabouts of a Plautii, you say, like some mastiff let off the leash. Is this how you think to keep me feeling involved in the matters of state? Really, I'd rather spend my days here relaxing, which, I will remind you, is the reason I came to the Bay. Also, I will have you know, it is not all the debauchery the moralists allege. I have been reading and attending elegant parties where the conversation is good enough; and by that I mean there is substance to it, but it is not too Greek one feels effeminate.*

*In any event, I cannot find Plautius or any other Plautii. The Bay is bereft of squashed noses and green eyes. (Thank the gods. I never understood Father's affection for that family.)*

*As for your inquiry about Vespasia, I'm not sure I will pay her a visit. Capri feels an empire away (though it is only a short boat ride).*

*Anyway, I doubt I am welcome. I look too much like the brother she currently despises, though with more hair and smaller jowls. (I am only poking fun, brother. Lower your back, please.)*

*I will return when the weather in the capital is better or, I suppose, if a social event trumps my need for iceless blood and warm toes. Must I keep searching for Plautius in the meantime? Please say no.*

*Your Brother,*

*T. Flavius Domitianus*

'And the other,' I say to Ptolemy, and he hands me the second letter in exchange for the first.

*11 January (from Baiae)*
*Titus:*

*I may have spoken too soon. Last night, after I'd written to you of my lack of success, I attended a dinner party in the foggy hills above Baiae. Secundus's nephew, the know-it-all Gaius Caecilius, was also in attendance. After he'd trapped me in conversation, he casually referred to a discussion he'd had with Plautius the week before. Once I'd picked my jaw off the floor, I asked him where, when exactly, and in what circumstance. As it turns out, he shares a mutual friend with Plautius, a merchant named Cinnius, whom Plautius was staying with while here on the Bay. According to the know-it-all, about a week ago, Plautius – somehow, without explanation – disappeared. I called on Cinnius later that evening to confirm the tale; or, at the very least, to hear the more accurate, less interesting version. But Cinnius not only confirmed the story, he showed me Plautius's trunks of linens, amphorae of wine, and half a dozen slaves cluttering up his portico. According to Cinnius, Plautius arrived by ship in late December. He was with Cinnius for nearly two weeks before he went missing. Apparently, the night before, Plautius had been bragging about performing some important, clandestine task for the Emperor. The next day, Plautius and one of his freedman left early, before the sun rose, never to return.*

*After my meeting with Cinnius, I ran home, dictated this letter and ordered the carrier not to stop until he handed this letter to you personally.*

*Has your paranoia finally led to something of substance? Send instructions to your brother – his interest is sufficiently peaked.*

*Yours, Domitian*

'Find my father,' I say to Ptolemy. 'I need to see him right away.'

# VESPASIAN CAESAR

◆

*11 January, afternoon*
*The Servilian gardens, Rome*

I'm the new man. This is how I will always be known. I'm a retired general, with distinguished service in Britannia and Judea. I have earned the regalia of an ovation and a triumph, and I have held the consulship eleven times. I am Caesar, the Emperor of Rome. Still: I am and will always be the new man. The *provençal*. Italian, yes, but not from Rome. No matter how just or cruel, how wise or stupid, no matter how many years of peace I foster, or the state of the Empire's coffers, I am simply the emperor whose father and grandfather did not hail from Rome; who began their careers as centurions before, respectively, lending money or collecting debts. At one time, there was even a rumour that my grandfather, Petro, was not even Italian, but a Gaul. The rumour began (and ruined) my first attempt at aedile more than forty years ago.

After the votes were counted and the aedileship lost, and once the sting of failure had lessened, I returned to our family estate near Reate, in the Sabine hills, to confront my father. It was late January, crisp and green. I found him in the fields, watching slaves repair a harness. The beast of burden, a shit-brown ox, was chewing leisurely beside the gaggle of men hard at work. My father had an injury from his days in the legions, which left one of his arms useless. He kept it in a sling, tucked into his belly. It was half the size of his good arm from lack of use; it was the arm of a boy, but withered and wrinkled. Father was old then, bald with a crooked back. He was chewing a reed, as he always did.

'Ho! The politician!' he said as I approached, walking my horse through the long grass. 'How did you do? Another win?'

I wasted no words. 'I lost. Was grandfather a Gaul?'

He shrugged. 'Officially? No. Definitely not.'

My face reddened. 'And unofficially?'

The slaves slinked off to the barn, preferring not to learn more family secrets than they had to.

Father shrugged a second time. 'Who's to say? The gods, maybe. Not I, certainly.'

I spat venom. 'You don't know?'

'Like you, I'd heard the rumours. But you remember your grand-father. He was a republican – the old, angry Cato-type. He was a veteran, the dominus. He expected a warm meal every evening and an obedient son. He rarely spoke. I never asked and he never told me. It's as simple as that.'

'You don't care whether our blood's polluted?' I demanded.

My father – always patient – considered the question. He held the elbow of his crippled arm. 'Not particularly, no.' He chewed his reed. 'It's my opinion that anything in concentrate is bad. Wine, invest-ments, blood. It's better to dilute, to diversify. You wouldn't put all of your money in one apartment block in Rome, would you? Why, in one night your fortune could go up in a puff of smoke. You'd be destitute. And look at Tiberius, your Emperor. Does any man have a better pedi-gree? Claudian blood adopted into the Julian line. One can't improve on that lineage. But where is he at the moment? On Capri, raping and drinking, while the public coffers foot the bill.' He spat. For the first time, I thought he spat like a Gaul.

'What about my career? It's over before it started.'

'I thought you wanted to be a politician. You'd let a rumour keep you down?' He threw his good arm around me. He shook me with warmth. 'Listen: Petro may have been a Gaul; he may not have been. I don't know and neither do you. No one does, except maybe your grand-mother. But she'll not utter a peep if it's bad for us. If there are family secrets, she'll take them to the grave. But it doesn't matter. The past is lost. People want a story, give them one. Truth is for philosophers and engineers, not politicians. Someone used a rumour to beat you. Use a better rumour to win. Better yet, forge documents.'

The next year, I did as my father suggested. Letters of my great-great grandfather, a man of Italian decent, were 'found' and copies circu-lated. Money made its way to the right people. I won the aedileship handily.

That was forty years ago. At the time, the issue was life and death. But the world is changing. Today, if a man's grandfather were a Gaul, his advancement would not be blocked, not necessarily. Now, every day, we have provincials coming to Rome and making a name for themselves. One day there may even be an emperor who hails from Gaul. Maybe. There may even be a time when such an emperor is not known as a *new* man, and is simply just a man. Then again, without these distinctions, how would a Roman know who is below and who is above? Hierarchy is the stuff of life. I'm Roman enough to know that.

Graecina, matriarch of the Plautii, visits during the eighth hour, as she does every week. We have wine; a weak blend, from the north, diluted with water, boiled with a handful of cloves and sage, and then honey is ladled in. It is the drink of the old, for those with weak teeth, weaker bellies, and dwindling energy.

We meet in the Servilian gardens, under a fig tree. We sit; bones creak. We manoeuvre, slowly twisting in our seats like a screw, searching for relative comfort.

'A cold week,' I say, 'thus far.'

'There have been colder,' Graecina says.

'For Rome, I mean.'

She considers the distinction. She has seen winters beyond Italy, in the north. 'Yes, this is true. A cold week for Rome.'

A bowl of pistachios sits between us. Graecina uses her mouth to open the shell, like a squirrel feasting on an acorn.

'You've heard about this business with the hand?' I ask.

'I do not live under a rock.'

'What do you make of it?'

Graecina takes a shell out of her mouth and flicks it to the ground.

'I think it is embarrassing for the principate, for the Empire . . . for you. Who is responsible?'

'We are investigating.'

Grey eyebrows furrow. 'You mean Titus is investigating.'

I nod, then say, 'There is something more. One of your kinsmen may be missing.'

'Who?' Traces of concern crease her already wrinkled skin, and there is a sudden sheen to her milky eyes. 'Tiberius?'

'No,' I say. 'Lucius Plautius.'

'Oh,' Graecina says, relieved. 'Plautius is worthless. Do not waste resources tracking that one down.'

'The Flavii and the Plautii have a long history together,' I say. 'Our family owes yours a great deal. I would not be emperor if not for the Plautii.'

'You owe my deceased husband – gods rest his bones – a great deal, not the Plautii. And you have done more than enough to pay him back. Now you and I are friends – friends who are old and complain together for sport.'

I served under Graecina's husband. He was the best general I'd ever seen. I fear he will be one of the great generals rarely remembered. He conquered Britain, but Claudius Caesar (who had not lifted one of his stubby fingers) received the triumph, while Aulus Plautius was given a mere ovation.

'There is more,' I say. 'Plautius wrote to Titus from Baiae, weeks ago. Before he went missing.'

I hand her the letter. She reads. Occasional derisive snorts escape her dry, cracked lips.

She looks up halfway through. 'He protests too ardently, no? He sounds like a man complaining of dwindling morality while he can. The man has always been a hypocrite. Look for him in a brothel.'

'The important part follows the moralising,' I say.

She finishes reading the letter.

'Titus has Domitian making inquiries across the Bay,' I say, 'but so far there has been no sign of Plautius. I take it he never wrote to you, explaining what he was doing on the Bay?'

'No. He did not.'

Graecina sips her sweetened wine.

I explain everything to Graecina. I explain the hand, the gold ring, Titus's latest discovery, how the dog was likely trained to drag the hand into the forum. There is no need to hold anything back – not with Graecina.

'The ring was solid gold,' I say. 'By law it belonged to a senator; or, at the very least, a knight.'

'And you think this hand in the forum belonged to my kinsman, do you?'

'I don't know. But I'm not sure it matters. If your nephew is missing, I will consider the matter quite serious. A close friend of our family – a Plautii no less – learns of a plot to poison Caesar and then disappears?'

I shake my head in frustration. In the early days, when many still pined for Nero, stories like this, rumours of plots on my life – it infuriated me. I'd spit fire and demand blood. But, after a decade in power, they became familiar, a chore to attend to, like chewing my nails or taking my morning shit. And now, rather than fire me to action, they suck my energy, like a leech I can't quite pull off. But these latest developments have the feel of something different, like ambitious men are converging on the principate, as though they're coming at me from all sides. No one has ever dared move against one of the Plautii, a family so intertwined with ours that we are practically kin.

To Graecina, I say, 'What do you make of all this?'

She gives the letter one last look before dropping it beside the pistachio bowl. 'I think it is the weak mind that looks for coincidence. I think you are probably right, there is a murdered senator or knight, and you should find out who. But I am not sure it has anything to do with my worthless kinsman, who is lost in a brothel somewhere in the south.'

Graecina does not stay long. We both appreciate a short, efficient discussion. After she's finished her wine, she snaps her fingers and two slaves are at her side, helping her stand.

'Caesar,' she says with a nod.

Graecina, with a slave on each hip, makes her way through the gardens. She passes Titus who is headed in the opposite direction. His expression is grim; a roll of paper is crushed by an iron grip.

One should never be filled with dread when their son visits, unannounced. But such is the life of a new man in Rome, I suppose – at least one who holds the title Caesar.

# VII

## Magnificence of Mind, Part II
## A.D. 68

# MARCUS

*28 July, first torch*
*South of the Imperial palace, Rome*

The entrance to the palace doesn't look like an entrance at all. It's only a dark crack in the brick, tucked behind a huge tree and covered in ivy. Nero told me how to find it. 'Follow the aqueduct to the palace, heading south-east. When you get close, maybe a dozen paces or so, you'll see a wolf painted on the wall. The passageway is right below it, behind an ancient oak.'

Nero was right: I could see it in the moonlight, but only just.

'Don't concern yourself with guards,' Nero said. 'Only emperors know of this passageway. Augustus built it, years ago. Squeeze through the crack and there will be a stairwell on the other side. It leads to the upper levels of the palace, into my personal quarters . . . the Emperor's personal quarters. At the top of the steps is my bedchamber. The door will take you through to my study. What you need is in there.'

The passageway is narrow, barely wider than my hand, and pitch black. I don't want to go in – even if Nero said the palace would be empty. But then I think of Otho, how he held my chin, the way he stared at me. My skin starts to itch and I think I could go anywhere if it meant Otho wasn't my master. I take a deep breath and squeeze through the crack.

Inside, like Nero said, there's a flight of winding stairs. I follow them up in the pitch black, holding onto the wall to make sure I don't fall. Soon there's moonlight and, when I climb higher, I can see a skylight overhead.

At the top of the steps, there's a hole cut into the stone the size of a wagon wheel. On the other side of the hole, there's cloth. Nero told me to expect this. 'From your perspective, it will look like a circle of fabric. On the other side, it's a beautiful tapestry.' I push on the material, easing the tapestry away from the wall, and then I jump down into the room.

The room is as big as Master Creon's atrium, bigger even. Overhead, there's another skylight, with the moonlight streaming in, silver and bright. The bed is big enough to hold a Cyclops. The whole room is a mess: chairs are overturned; the sheets are torn half off the bed.

I cross the room and open the door. Luckily, there's another skylight. At one end of the room there's a desk covered in rolls of papyrus and a bronze scale, with a big wooden chair pushed up against it. In front of the desk are three couches. Behind the desk, there's a picture on the wall, made from little tiny stones, of a younger man carrying an older man. Behind them, a city is burning. The stones are purple and black and white in the moonlight.

Nero said there'd only be one letter in the drawer. But when I open the drawer, there's more than one. I can't read, so I don't know which one to take. I don't know what to do. My heart starts pounding and I can't get a hold of my breath. I shouldn't take all of the letters because that'd be stealing. Then again, when I told Nero I didn't want to take anything from the palace, he said, 'They're my letters, boy. Don't forget that. Everything in that palace is mine by right. Think of this as an errand you're running for Caesar.'

I'm still trying to decide what to do when I hear voices. My heart starts pounding even harder – so loud I can hardly think. The voices aren't coming from the bedroom, but from down the hall that leads to the rest of the palace. I stuff all of the letters in my tunic and run for the bedroom. The voices get louder and louder, and then the hallway is lit up with lamplight.

They are about to walk in . . .

I drop to the ground. Luckily – somehow – I'm behind one of the couches. I can see their boots when they come in, but they can't see me. Quietly, I slide myself along the marble until I'm under the couch. I have to move very slowly so the papyrus doesn't crunch between my chest and the floor. I lift my legs up so my sweaty skin doesn't stick to the tiles and squeak.

'Did you leave that door open?'

'Which?'

'The bedroom . . . Check it.'

There are four feet. Two walk into the bedroom. They come back a moment later.

'Empty.'

The other feet disappear behind the desk.

'What is it, Terentius?' the man behind the desk asks. 'You think you're above checking a bedroom?'

'I didn't say that.'

'You didn't need to. It's your demeanour, that hangdog expression of yours. Has cutting out Caesar's eyes gone to your head? Don't forget you are merely a centurion and you did it on my orders.'

'Yes, and you did it on the orders of another.'

'I wasn't ordered to do anything. I'm prefect of the Praetorian Guard. I was asked to participate. I was asked by my colleagues, not my superiors.'

'Of course, they are your *colleagues*. And where are your colleagues now that the plan has gone to shit?'

I can hear the man at the desk lean back in his chair. He says, 'There has been a snag or two. I will admit that. But we've hedged our bets.'

'So you say.'

'Nero is alive. That's worth something. The Hunchback will pay for Nero, and reward us for our trouble.'

'And you're not concerned about crossing your colleagues?'

'We will deal with that when it arises. In the meantime, I'll send another letter to Galba.'

'Another? Is there any point? Either your letters are not getting through or he is content to wait until he arrives in Rome. You put too much faith in that freedman of his, Icelus. He's blocking your letters, seeing how he can profit from what he knows.'

'I'm going to send an envoy this time. Someone I can trust to deliver the message . . . What is that you're fiddling with? Not that figurine again?'

'What of it? This is my small reward for doing your dirty work. Caesar's lucky charm . . . Shit!'

Something clatters against the floor. I can see it skitter along the marble, something small, made from dark stone. A little statue, I think.

The man standing bends down to pick it up. I keep dead still. Luckily, he's turned facing the desk, away from me, so he doesn't see me under the couch. I keep so still I don't even breathe. As he kneels down and reaches his hand out for the figurine, his head comes low enough to the floor that I can see the side of his face. It's the Fox. Somehow – even though I didn't think it could – my heart starts beating faster, a throbbing drumbeat – so hard I think it's going to pop out of my chest and gush out of my ears.

'For gods' sake, Terentius. Put it away.'

The Fox stands up without seeing me. My heart doesn't stop pounding.

I hear the desk drawer open.

'Where are my letters? They're gone.'

'They can't be,' the Fox says.

'You thought I was being paranoid about the door,' the man behind the desk says. 'Jupiter's *piss*!' The drawer slams shut. 'The thief couldn't have gotten far.'

Chair legs *screeeech* along the floor.

'Those letters . . . we have to find them.'

The man at the desk runs out of the room. I watch the other legs, the Fox's legs, follow. When they're gone, I get up and run.

# NERO

◆

*29 July, dawn*
*City jail IV, Rome*

It must be morning when the boy comes back. I'd wondered whether a bit of adventure might make him less woe-is-me, but he quickly dashes any such hope. He arrives shaking uncontrollably and muttering about foxes, as though he went for a walk in the woods.

When we examine the letters, an odd problem presents itself: he has three rolls of papyrus instead of the one I'd sent him for. I left one letter in that particular drawer. I am certain of this. From what I gleaned from the boy's confused retelling of the conversation he overheard, it sounds as though the soldiers that did this to me are using my office for their own personal use. It's unnerving, but no more unnerving than soldiers cutting out Caesar's eyes. Anyway, at the moment, this isn't our chief concern. The problem is that neither of us can read the letters to determine which is the one we need. I'm blind and the boy is as ignorant as a mule.

I pine for the days when presented with a problem I could merely wave my hand and tell my minions to fix it. Self-reliance is tedious and dull.

The boy and I discuss the problem. He adds little, but we eventually come to the following conclusion: if he can see and I can read, we must combine these abilities. We develop a system. The boy traces my index finger over each letter, as though we were painting over the words. He does it slowly at first, with a good pause in between each particular letter, so that I can determine what it is. First we establish the letter, then the word, then the sentence. We improve as we go, and, luckily, the task is straightforward. It takes only a sentence or two to determine that the first two letters are of interest, but clearly not what we were looking for. The third is the one we need.

Despite our success, the boy is reluctant to leave. He is afraid to continue. I've concluded he requires a particular type of guidance, a healthy mix of encouragement, inspiration, and a gentle shove in the right direction. Fear, however, affects him – so much so that it could sink us. It is the elephant in the room that must be addressed.

'You're young yet,' I say, 'so I will not go so far as to name you a coward, but fear clearly has hold of you. If we're to have success in our scheme, you must – at the very least – control your fear.'

The boy, as always, is struck dumb. I press on.

'I am not one for advice, so I offer the following anecdote. There was once a soldier by the name of Corbulo who, for a time, was Rome's greatest general. On the topic of courage, Corbulo once made a distinction that I think correct. When it comes to fear, when faced with danger, whether mortal, social or whatever else, he said there are two types of men: those who can think and make decisions without hindrance, as though fear did not affect them; and those who cannot. The former have been blessed by the gods, according to Corbulo, and we should envy them. The Greeks call it "magnificence of mind". My grandfather, the great Germanicus, is a recent example.'

A story could inspire the boy; and I know which I should tell. But am I able to tell it – my mother's favourite – without conjuring up that damned woman's ghost?

I press on.

'No doubt you know of my grandfather by his Germanic victories, how he avenged the disaster of the Teutoburg Pass, Rome's worst defeat in nearly a thousand years. But even as a boy he acted with daring. When he was eleven, not much older than you are now, he was sent to meet his father, my great-grandfather, who was on campaign in the east. He was sent by ship to Dalmatia, where he was then to proceed through the hinterland by horse. Four soldiers accompanied him. While stopped for the night, Dalmatian bandits raided their camp. All four soldiers were killed. The bandits took everything of value, including the legionary standard, the golden eagle that we Romans value so highly. The bandits debated taking my grandfather to ransom later but ultimately decided against it.

(They were evidently unaware of his identity and the Imperial windfall they'd happened upon.) One bandit knew the Latin word for sea. He pointed in the opposite direction that they would eventually take and said, "Sea." And then off they went.

'My grandfather was completely alone. He could have easily turned back and made his way to the coast, and the mere fact that he survived would have been considered a victory, a commendable start for a boy his age. However, he refused to allow the loss of a legionary standard. Clearly, the Claudian streak of stubbornness was embedded in his bones, even at such a young age. He decided to follow those bandits through the wild mountains of Dalmatia – and follow them he did.

'He was an experienced hunter, so he followed the plodding barbarians easily enough. The bandits stopped for the night as the sun started to set. They roasted rabbit over an open fire and ate before retiring for the evening. My grandfather watched them, hidden in the surrounding forest. When he was certain the bandits were asleep – they were too stupid or arrogant to place a guard – he went into the camp to retrieve the standard. The smell of the cooked rabbit stopped him. He'd travelled all day without anything to eat or drink. The sizzling flesh dripping with fat made his mouth water.'

At this point in the story, my mother would ask, *And do you know what he did next?* and she would always pause for effect, daring her audience (usually her young son) to interject. I try to think of a way around it, but nothing comes to mind.

'And do you know what he did next?'

One. Two. Three.

'He stopped for dinner. He sat down by the fire, crossed his legs and ate: roasted rabbit and bread. And, when he was done, he washed it down with a draught of wine. Then he stood up, wiped his mouth, stepped over the sleeping bandits, removed the standard and made his way back to the coast. He'd marked his path as he'd followed the bandits through the forest, etching an "X" into trees with his knife. So he followed this path back to the sea and reached the coast the next evening. The following day, my eleven-year-old grandfather had a new caravan assembled and he was on his way to meet my great-grandfather, legionary standard in hand.

'Now Corbulo,' I continue, 'Corbulo did not count himself among the Germanici of the world. Fear affected him. It might even have crippled him. But in the end, this didn't matter. He'd found that foresight and training could overcome this handicap. He trained harder than any other soldier when he was rising through the legionary ranks. He studied harder and longer than any other man. Before he would go to battle, he would set out a detailed plan, anticipating any contingency, so that he did not have to think when danger was before him. The lesson lacks the mystique of tales told by other generals, but I think it honest. At dinner parties, Corbulo would be asked, "And how, great general, did you bring the Parthians to heel? Bravery? Unmatched physical strength?" To which he would reply, "Diligence and long nights," and the party would give a collective groan. He was a particular type of Roman, now rarely seen: an honest man who outworked his rivals.

'I doubt you are a Germanicus, Marcus. You are young – nothing is impossible – but I think it unlikely. In the end, though, it doesn't matter. You can make yourself a Corbulo. I will rehearse with you what must be accomplished. We will rehearse until you have it perfect. You will outwork fear.'

# MARCUS

### *29 July, vesper*
### *The Happy Cock, Rome*


The canteen has four long, wooden tables, with large men sitting around them laughing and yelling and swigging wine. Shadows rise and fall in the lamplight. No one notices me when I slip in. I walk to the bar, stand on it and say, as loud as I can: 'If Doryphorus is here and would like to make some coin, he only needs to ask.'

I say it all like Nero said, just like we practised again and again. He wouldn't let me leave until I had it perfect. I was worried they'd laugh at me or yell and tell me to leave. But Nero told me they wouldn't. 'Every man in this city desires two things,' he said. 'The first is coin – mention silver and you are credible, immediately. The second is what you are trying to avoid giving to Otho, so there is no point in offering it up.'

Nero is right: no one laughs or tells me to go away. They all went quiet to hear what I said and now that I'm done, they've gone back to doing whatever they were doing before.

I sit down at the table and a man takes a seat beside me. He's short and pudgy, with eyes the colour of ice, and a beard, mud-brown and bushy. 'And who might you be?'

Nero had told me about Doryphorus. 'The man is an actor by trade. You cannot do your sad, quiet routine with him. He takes directions for a living. So tell him what you need from him, not the other way around.'

'You'll need to shave,' I say, just like Nero told me to.

The man laughs. 'Is that so?'

'How's your patrician accent?' I ask. 'And your Greek?'

'Come now, boy. You've got me salivating. What's the plan? Who sent you?'

The next morning, I meet Doryphorus in the forum. His beard is shaved and he's wearing a toga, white and clean.

'Good morning, slave-with-a-consul's-name.' This is what he calls me. It takes him a long time to say but I think that's part of the joke. He laughs every time he says it.

'Morning,' I say.

He asks, 'And how do I look?'

'Fine,' I say.

'Better than fine, I'd wager.' He looks himself over. 'Well, best get on with it, haven't we? Lead the way.'

The magistrate is bent over his desk, squinting at a ledger. His eyes are swirls of milky white, like his hair. 'You said your name was what?'

We're sitting on the other side of his desk. The room is all marble, emerald green with black, swirling lines. Outside, the forum grumbles and hums.

'The deceased's nephew.' Doryphorus's voice is different with the magistrate. He pronounces each word exactly, and he uses long words, like a proper patrician.

'And him?' The magistrate points his wrinkly finger at me.

'My slave.'

'And you've arrived from Alexandria today?'

Doryphorus answers in a different language. He leans back in his chair, satisfied with himself.

'Fortune is smiling on you, sir,' the magistrate says. 'The estate – your unclaimed portion at least – was to escheat to the Emperor at the end of the week.'

'Was it?' Doryphorus says, as though he's surprised, even though I told him as much, after Nero told me. 'I left Alexandria as soon as I received your letter. But the seas were terrible. We spent several weeks in Sicily, waiting for clear passage.'

'Yes, well, it is of no consequence now. Here you are. Once you provide some information to confirm that you are who you say you are, I will be able to sign over your inheritance.'

'Please.' Doryphorus opens his arms wide, like he's looking for a hug. 'Ask me whatever you like.'

Nero has been right about everything so far. He knew senator Florus had recently died and his estate hadn't been distributed yet. 'Because I kept the letters to his beneficiaries,' Nero told me. 'Leading the Empire isn't all campaigns and banquets. It's also about fulfilling the state's needs, including its coffers. If a beneficiary doesn't come to collect, then it escheats to the Emperor. Now, I suppose, Florus's money is to go to the Hunchback. But not if we get there first. Find Doryphorus,' Nero said. 'Tell him to impersonate the deceased's nephew. But do not give him all the information. He is trustworthy, but only up to a point, like any man.'

The magistrate asks Doryphorus all sorts of questions, about him, about his dead uncle, and Doryphorus knows each answer. Then he asks: 'And could you please produce the letter I sent to you?'

Doryphorus looks to me. From my tunic, I pull out the letter I'd taken from the palace and hand it to the magistrate. He reads it closely. Then he says, 'Excellent. I will get everything in order.'

'Sir,' Doryphorus says. He wiggles to the edge of his chair. This is the trickiest part. 'If I could trouble you . . . your assistance would make my affairs here in the capital much easier than they need be. You see I have two debts that require payment immediately. Rather than making out one letter of credit to me, if you were able to make out *two* letters of credit, one to a man named Doryphorus, the other to a freedman named Creon.'

The magistrate looks up at us with his milky eyes.

My heart drums. *Thump thump thump.*

'As you'd like,' he says. He starts to write. 'I commend you, sir, for your sense of responsibility. These days, most would run back to Alexandria, silver in hand, leaving his creditors out in the cold.'

Later that night, I'm called into the atrium before dinner. I find Master sitting with Doryphorus.

'This is the one?' Master asks.

Doryphorus says, 'He is, indeed,' and then hands Master a little roll of paper. Master gapes. Without looking up, he tells me that I'd been selected to assist at the Imperial palace. I am to attend each day and only return at night, when they were done with me. 'You're on loan, boy. So don't embarrass me.'

This was Nero's plan. He didn't want to purchase me outright because he didn't know where I'd live or how I'd eat. He also didn't want anyone new being sent to the prison. 'I've grown used to your company,' he said.

'Are you forgetting something?' Doryphorus asks.

'Hmm,' Master looks up from the letter of credit. 'Oh yes, of course.' To me he says, 'You're to bring two amphorae to the palace each week, one of wine and one of fish sauce. Why the palace needs my fish sauce, I've no idea. But there you have it.'

'Now Creon,' Doryphorus says, 'there will be no hitting or touching of an Imperial slave. Do you understand?'

Master makes a face: *who me?*

'I see the bruises, and I've also asked around. This boy is now Imperial property. Keep your hands off or *your* hands will come off. Understood?'

Master – still looking at the letter of credit – waves his hand. 'Yes, yes.'

'I've heard that Senator Otho was interested in purchasing the boy,' Doryphorus says. 'I don't need to tell you that he is now Galba's property, the Emperor's property.'

'Otho was going to buy the boy. But you beat him on terms, fair and square. I'll find him a different boy, there are thousands in this city. It's easily done. See our guest out, Marcus.'

I follow Doryphorus to the front door. In a loud voice he says, 'Tomorrow, boy. Be at the palace bright and early.' Then, pretending to adjust his sandal, he bends down and whispers, 'A pleasure, Marcus. Whoever cooked up your little plan, I don't give a fig. Just give him my thanks. And let him know Doryphorus is a man of his word. I didn't have to do this last bit, fooling your master. I could have taken both letters of credit and ran. But I did as I promised.'

Doryphorus turns and leaves.

# NERO

◆

*30 July, afternoon*
*City jail IV, Rome*


The boy recounts the story like a conquering hero. The canteen, the magistrate's office, his master's ignorance – it is the greatest day of his life. He relishes the ruse played on his master the most; I can hear it in his voice. Yesterday, he was sick with dread at the thought of providing false information to this Creon character, as though his master were something more than a freed slave, but now he is content with his victory.

He did well, all things considered. I'd thought he'd wither at one point, collapse under the weight of his own cowardice. But he didn't. There's even a tinge of confidence to his demeanour this morning, a slight hint of swagger.

He's how old? Nine? Ten? It's hard to say without laying eyes on him. But he lacks the croaking voice and stinking torso of a teenager ... I was his age, or thereabouts, when I rode in the games of Troy. I was tiny then, so small that my helmet didn't fit. Before the manoeuvres, mounted in the yard, it kept sliding forward, covering my eyes. I'd push it up, but it would only stay a moment before sliding down again, with each rollicking step of the horse. Uncle Claudius told me to dismount. 'You're too young,' he said. 'You'll be hurt.' Mother wouldn't have it. She kissed me on the cheek and gave me one of those talks only she could give. 'You carry the blood of two great families,' she said. 'From the Julians, you have inherited fortitude, from the Claudians pride. You and I share the same blood and thus the same qualities. If you fail today, if you embarrass me, it will wound me deeply because I am a Claudian. But I will be able to bear it because I am a Julian.'

The other boys were older than me, teenagers all. We cantered out into the arena to a beating drum. When the crowd saw me, they thought my presence precocious. There were cheers and whistles at each turn

I made. My helmet fell, but I kept my position and finished without it. 'Little Germanicus,' they yelled, 'like his grandfather.' Mother, however, was apathetic. 'You did nothing to set yourself apart.' I waited until she had left the yard before starting to cry.

I make a point – maybe out of spite, I'm not sure – of telling the boy he did well. He is struck dumb – again. It may be the first compliment he's ever received.

Later, he asks me about Hector. He hasn't forgotten what I told him; he only wants to hear it again, like going back to a good bottle of wine: you remember the taste, but you want to feel it on your tongue. I take my bread with fish sauce and a cup of white, my spoils from our little plot. As I eat, I tell him the tale.

I'm in the midst of my story when we hear the *creak* of the door.

The boy goes quiet, as do I.

I hear feet shuffling across the dusty brick.

Then silence . . .

To Marcus, I whisper, 'Who is it?'

'The actor,' Marcus says.

More silence, then, quietly at first, no more than a whisper: 'Caesar.' The voice grows louder, more passionate. 'Caesar, is that you?'

It's good to hear that title again, to hear it spoken with reverence.

'I knew it! I knew you were alive.' The voice – Doryphorus's voice – morphs, from reverence to incredulity. 'Three-fucking-figs, Caesar! You look awful.'

# VIII

## An Invitation to Dinner
### A.D. 79

# CALENUS

*12 January, dawn*
*The slave market, Rome*


'What did you do with the bodies?'

I hold my hand to my nose to block the stink. Slave markets have a particular smell – like shit mainly, but also the maggoty stink of rot, the battlefield two days after the fight. Nerva's doused himself in perfume and a cloud of prissy I'm-not-sure-what follows him everywhere he goes. He smells better than the market, but only just. I'm surprised he isn't retching with that big beak of his.

'We left them there,' I say. 'Away from the road, in the forest aways, but right where it happened.'

Nerva says, 'And the other two ran off?'

'Mmhm. The centurion and the other one.'

We're walking side-by-side between rows of slaves tied to posts. All of them are men, down to a loincloth and dusted with chalk.

'Him?' Nerva points at a muscly Ethiopian.

I squat down and tell the slave to open his mouth. He does, showing me brown and yellow teeth. I spread open his right eye and peer in. He has a sad, glazed look to him, like he's drunk. But this lad – I'd wager – hasn't had a drink in a long time. No one would waste drink on a man not long for this world.

I look up at Nerva and shake my head. We keep walking, kicking up sand as we go.

'Could you identify the centurion?'

'Yes,' I say. 'I gave him a nice cut, right below the eye.'

Nerva nods. 'You come to me first if you ever see the man. Yes? I will pay you for the information. As I always do.'

'If you want,' I say.

I point to a man who's all skin and bones, struggling against his chain. Nerva looks dubious.

'I was looking for help to guard my person, Calenus. Someone intimidating.'

The slave is bald, thin, with skin the colour of boiled leather. But he's wily, I think.

'I like his fight,' I say.

Nerva frowns, but he trusts my opinion, so he doesn't say 'no'. He doesn't say anything, which means *start your due diligence, please.*

I take two steps forward and the slave lunges at me. The chain stops him just short of getting his hands around my throat. He claws the air like a wild dog. It's possible he's only crazy, not wily. I raise a fist above my head. I'm planning on giving him a good smack to see how he handles it, but the dog collapses to the sand and curls up into a ball.

I shake my head at Nerva. We keep walking.

'You travelled back to Rome together.' Nerva asks, 'How did you leave them?'

'We didn't talk much on the ride back. I brought them to their house on the Aventine, as planned.'

'What were they like afterwards?'

'Nothing fazed the cripple. I'm not sure he's all there. As for the others? Their blood was up. You could see that. But otherwise fine, all things considered.'

Nerva considers that for a moment. 'You think there is more there than meets the eye?'

I shrug. 'I'm not from Delphi, am I? All I'm saying is they seemed OK during and after the whole mess.'

We walk past an old, hairless man coughing up his insides. Nerva pulls up his toga as he steps over the man's legs.

'And why didn't they call on me? They understood I'd sent you, and that I was expecting them after they arrived?'

'They knew. But –' I step over the legs of a man who's asleep or dead '– if I had that much coin, I'd expect people to come to me.'

Nerva strokes his chin, thinking.

'What about him?' He says, pointing at a man sitting in the dirt, leaning against the stake he's chained to, hugging his knees. He looks tall – tall and strong.

'Perhaps,' I say. As we get closer, I see a tattoo on his arm, blue ink with a scar running right through the middle of it. If I hadn't seen one before, I wouldn't be able to make out what it was. But I'm certain the tattoo – before a blade sliced it in half – was a German battle shield being lapped by blue waves.

'I think you're in luck.'

'Oh,' Nerva says.

I keep my voice quiet so the traders don't hear. 'He's a Batavian.'

Nerva's face doesn't change. He'd be a good dice player.

'Here?'

Slaves that will fetch a good price are normally shown at auction or taken to the home of rich patricians known to spend. It's odd to find a prize like this in the market.

'I don't think they know what they've got. Tattoo's mangled from the scar. You wanted intimidating. You won't find better than a Batavian.'

'Will he take orders?' Nerva whispers. 'I've heard they can be difficult.'

I shrug to let him know I haven't the faintest idea.

Nerva says to the slave, 'Do you speak Latin?'

The slave looks up at Nerva. His eyes are bluer than the Tyrrhenian.

'No,' the slave says. He says it in Latin. He goes back to staring straight ahead.

'Stand up,' Nerva says.

The Batavian's eyes slowly circle up to take Nerva in, before circling back, unperturbed. He doesn't move.

Nerva takes me aside. 'He's wild. He could prove difficult.'

I shrug. 'Resale value alone . . .'

'Can you help?'

'I'm no slave driver, am I? I wouldn't know where to start.' I look over my shoulder at the Batavian. Nerva does the same. 'Unlikely you'd break him. Not in this lifetime. But you're smart, aren't you? Can't you outsmart him?'

Nerva – always a man of commerce – says: 'Fetch me a good price.'

The traders agree to a good number, considering the return. After Nerva pays, I squat so my face is level with the Batavian. My Aedui is different than his Chatti – night and day, really – but I know some Cananefates. Seeing as how they neighbour the Batavians, he should be able to understand. So I ask the Batavian if he'll come like a good boy or whether he's going to put up a fight.

He answers. His accent is a kick to the ears, but I get the gist. He says, 'How does your Roman master –' he nods at Nerva '– normally take you. The arse or the face?'

I shake my head at Nerva. He signals for help and four traders surround the Batavian. I figure he'll lash out, get beaten to a pulp, and then dragged off to Nerva's. But the boy's got *some* sense. He sees the traders and just lies down on the sand, with his legs and arms spread wide. After a moment scratching their perplexed arses, the traders unlock the chain tying him to the post, then each of them grabs an arm or a leg, and they hoist the Batavian into the air and carry him out.

*10 January (from Capri)*
*Dear Domitilla (in Rome):*

*Capri is beautiful, sister. I wish you had come. It has been the escape I had hoped for. Julia and young Vip have been a pleasure. (Thankfully, Julia did not inherit her father's dourness. She can enjoy a holiday.) We have spent our time reading and going for long walks in the sun. One of the palace slaves has shown us the island. He took us to where Augustus wrote his last will and testament, and where Tiberius Caesar performed those wicked acts that brought his mother endless shame. He may have given too much detail for the girls' young ears, but he is old and meant no harm by it. Anyway, I do not believe they understood half of what he said.*

*As you predicted, I have had time to reflect; indeed, I have had nothing but time these last three weeks. I have thought often of what Titus has done, examining it from every angle. When we parted, you were certain I would eventually forgive him. You said I would see his act as necessary, one made to protect our family. Give it time, you said.*

*I am sorry, sister, but I cannot forgive Titus. My husband was not guilty of anything other than telling a joke that was not funny. He had no intention of taking the title 'Caesar'. That was the joke. He was lazy, selfish and unintelligent. He did not desire the principate; nor did it suit him. Our brother murdered my husband for a punchline gone wrong.*

*I did not love Asinius. He was mean, a quality which makes one hard to love. And I do not think he cared for women. He took me the one time, on our wedding night, but it was mechanical. After that, he did not so much as look at me. He preferred the pretty young men he kept company with, and he was not jealous when I pursued love outside of our marriage. We were strangers, really.*

*I did not love Asinius, but I cannot forgive Titus. It was an embarrassment – one that I shall never truly recover from. My own brother murdered my husband. He didn't arrest him or put him on trial. He didn't investigate the claims against him or interrogate anyone allegedly involved. Why would he? Our brother's sole aim is power – or at least the artifice of it. Is it any wonder Domitian has turned out the way he has?*

*I have been thinking about our brothers. How they are so very different and how that came to be; why Father favours the one and shuns the other; why one will succeed Father as emperor and the other is already forgotten. I've concluded brothers, like everyone, must carve out their place in the world, but they must do so in a manner that will not intrude on their sibling. Titus came first. He took certain qualities as his own: confidence, boldness, strength. Domitian came nearly ten years later. He took what was available to him: cunning, cynicism, fecklessness.*

*It is the same with sisters. Is it not? You came first. You took decorum, intelligence, pluck. When my turn came, I took what was available: vitality, wit, desirability.*

*Proof of my theory is the rivalries we often see between siblings. You and I have disagreed over the years, though we love each other. Titus and Domitian have also fought – though, given the ten-year gap between them, it has always been less of a fight, and more a child lashing out at a man.*

*If it were Domitian who'd murdered my husband, I would be angry, but I would understand. The world has dictated its terms to Domitian; he grew into a mould. Titus, however, chose to be the man he is. He chose to be Father's attack dog. He wants the Empire to shiver as he passes by. He chose to be the man he is. I cannot forgive him.*

*I will remain in Campania until the weather turns. The girls may stay with me. As I said, they are a welcome distraction.*

*Please send word from Rome. I miss the city, its politics and – yes – the gossip.*

*With all my love,*

*Vespasia*

# DOMITILLA

◆

*12 January, afternoon*
*The Imperial palace, Rome*

'He wasn't perfect,' Lepida says. 'I'll be the first to admit it . . .'

She scrutinises a fig with narrowed eyes. Beside her, a slave stokes the coals of a tired brazier.

'And,' she continues, 'I'm sure Titus had his reasons. He is prefect of the Praetorians after all. I know it falls to him to keep Caesar alive and the Empire safe.' She looks up from her fig. 'May I ask, Domitilla: are these figs from the palace gardens?'

'Somewhere from the south,' I say. 'This recent cold streak has wreaked havoc on the palace gardens.'

Lepida smiles. 'Too bad. I'd heard such fantastic tales of the palace figs . . .'

Finally, she takes a bite – no, not a bite; it is a mouse-like nibble.

'. . . I only wish Titus to know – and you are his sister, so I know you will tell him – I only wish him to know I had nothing to do with whatever it was that happened in Baiae . . .'

Lepida drops her nibbled fig on a side table and adjusts her shawl. She is dressed in black – black stola, black shawl. She is in mourning. Even so, beneath her shawl, her blonde hair is quaffed and teased and pinned up into elaborate, fashionable curls; blue eye-shadow darkens her lids; and gold hangs from her neck and wrists. She may be in mourning, but that is no excuse to look drab.

'. . . maybe my husband was a traitor,' she says. 'Maybe he was in league with Asinius. A trial may not have been necessary. But please understand I had nothing to do with any of it.'

As I always do, I come to Titus's defence.

'There is more to the story than we realise,' I say. 'We don't know what information Titus had or what steps he took to ensure their guilt. Nor is it our place to question his tactics.'

'I agree,' Lepida says. 'I agree wholeheartedly. But, as I'm sure you can appreciate, a wife cannot control her husband, and she is not always privy to his affairs. Your sister was obviously not involved. How could she have been? She is Caesar's daughter after all. I hope your brother won't hold me to a different standard.'

Last month Titus put to death two men: Asinius, his brother-in-law, and Lepida's husband, Iulus. According to Titus, both were plotting against Father. Lepida is here to make sure Titus won't turn his scrutiny to her. Her plan – and it is not a bad one – is to link herself with Vespasia, my younger sister, Asinius' wife. But I think she has overestimated my influence with Titus.

Lepida asks, 'How long was Vespasia married to Asinius?'

'Ten years, I think.'

'Yes, that's right. Ten years.' She smiles. It is a joyless smile. 'Not much longer than I was married to young Iulus. And I think Vespasia held her husband in as much esteem as I held mine.'

'Yes, well, Asinius was an unhappy man.'

'As are all men who fail to find Caesar's favour,' Lepida says. 'He probably expected more as the Emperor's son-in-law. But there is only so much of it to go around.'

Her joyless smile, her light-hearted tone – Lepida is surprisingly at ease given the circumstances.

'Speaking of Vespasia,' Lepida asks, 'where is she? Is she still in Rome?'

'She's gone south, to our home on Capri.'

'Ah, to escape the gossip. A wise decision.'

'To relax,' I say. 'To relax and to reflect. It's a difficult event, losing one's husband. Something you can appreciate.'

'Well,' Lepida says, 'I would leave Rome as well, but I fear how it would look. With my past . . . your brother might think I was running away.'

Lepida speaks of her past so casually one would never know she was once accused of treason. Many years ago, her first husband, Caius Cassius, was caught plotting to kill Nero. She was implicated as well. I wasn't in Rome at the time – I was too young and Father made sure I spent most of Nero's reign away from Rome, on our family's home in Reate – so I've only heard the rumours. But it's said Lepida and her friends were performing 'ghastly religious practices', whatever that means. Lepida's husband was banished to Sardinia. Another man was put to death. Lepida miraculously escaped punishment other than one month's house arrest. She seduced Nero, people said, with her green eyes and feminine wiles. (She's a bit older now, but in her heyday Lepida was a great beauty.) Others said she cast a spell on Nero. But these are very familiar Roman refrains: women are matrons, pure as the driven snow, or witches poisoning their husband's dinner. As a girl, it would drive me mad studying history. It still does. If I am no more than a line in the record books, I will consider it a life well lived.

Lepida slides to the edge of her chair. Earnestly, she says, 'We're friends, Domitilla. Isn't that so?'

This is the first time I've spoken to Lepida in a year. She is only here because she's concerned for her safety. She is only here to ask Caesar's daughter for a favour. We are far from friends.

'The very best,' I say.

Lepida smiles her joyless smile. 'Good. Then I know you'll do what you can with your brother. You'll speak to him of my innocence.'

'Of course.'

Later, after Lepida has left, Titus pays me a visit. A dog – all sinew and bone – slinks in after him.

'I'm late.'

'Titus Flavianus is a busy man,' I say, teasing. 'His relations are merely happy that he calls at all. Something to eat?'

Braziers crackle with welcome warmth.

'I can't stay long.' Titus collapses into the chair beside me. His shoulders slump, as though a cord were suddenly cut. He rubs his hairline, which is retreating, like his enemies of old. He does this often now, as though he hopes to drag his hair back towards his face. What happened to my eldest brother? Where is the young man who would ride into Rome unannounced, with stories of foreign lands and epic battles that would leave his younger sister in awe? His hair was full then, the colour of sawdust, and his shoulders stout. He would talk of danger and war with a gleam in his eyes that made his family puff up with pride. Vespasia and I thought he was invincible. Now? Now he looks tired and hungry, with his bloodshot eyes and cheeks studded with bone. He looks lonely – though his sister who loves him is sitting beside him. Prefect of the Praetorians does not agree with Titus: the petty squabbling, the syco- phants, the violence. Father relies on him too much, expects too much.

'Jacasta,' I say. 'Bring my brother some water. Maybe something to eat as well.'

Jacasta is under the arch leading to the tablinum. She signals for two slaves to carry out my request. They will probably delegate the task a third time, and so on down the line until the slave on the lowest rung in the household fills a pitcher with water.

'Wine,' Titus says. 'Something sour.'

I stare at him disapprovingly.

'Please do not give me that look, Domitilla.'

'What look?'

'It's one cup.'

I wave my hand nonchalantly, like I'm indifferent to my brother's consumption of wine. The last thing he needs is more criticism.

'And what is that?' I ask, pointing at the dog, which is now curled up under a table.

'Her name is Cleopatra,' Titus says.

What he doesn't say – what he wants the city, including his dear sister – to be left guessing, is whether this dog is the same one that dragged a man's hand into the forum on the Agonalia. The act is very Titus-like, to usurp a bad omen and make it his pet.

A slave – a newer one that I don't know, young and pretty – brings a bowl of olives and almonds. I catch her flashing Titus a smile as she bends down to hand him the bowl. She brushes up against his knee and he returns the smile. I thought my brother was looking old, his days of womanising behind him, but clearly he hasn't lost all of his charm.

'How goes the search?' I ask.

Titus nibbles on an olive. 'What search?'

'For three days now you have been knocking on doors all over the city. Everyone is talking about it.'

'Who is everyone?'

'Titus, I am Caesar's eldest daughter. You forget how many call on me day in, day out.'

Titus frowns. 'What are they saying?'

I shrug. 'Different things. Rumours mainly. Some think you're seeking support against Caecina.'

'The Turncoat?' He looks surprised. 'The people love that rivalry, don't they?'

It's remarkable how the people will remember certain events, how a story will grow and take on a life of its own, compared with what they will forget in a flash. One year, when they were both quite young, at a festival (I cannot even recall which), Titus and Caecina fought with wooden swords, the kind gladiators train with. Neither backed down; both were young men looking to prove themselves. They went for near an hour and beat each other to a pulp. The people have never forgotten the story, or the rivalry. Caecina's conduct during the civil wars hasn't helped. He changed sides three times, betraying men he'd sworn oaths to on each occasion, before finally defecting to Father's cause. Ever since, the city has waited for him to do so again.

Titus smiles. 'I suppose you won't be taken in by such rumours.' His sharp edges are beginning to soften. It always takes time for him to let his guard down, to remember he can set aside the city's politics with his sister.

I return the smile, adding an air of mock-modesty. 'Never. Anyway, the idea doesn't make sense, frankly. The city always thinks you're on a mad hunt to bring a senator down, but I know better. And as far as Caecina goes . . . well, he's known as the Turncoat, but I think his days of switching sides are over. There's no side to switch to. Now he's just a playboy. His schemes and betrayals occur in the bedroom.'

'You sound like you speak from experience,' Titus says. His face is pained when he asks. The skin around his mouth and eyes tightens. The Turncoat is the one man he would not approve of.

'Not to worry, brother. His type doesn't appeal to me.'

He relaxes again, relieved.

'Speaking of men calling on me, you received my note about the eunuch Halotus?'

'I did.'

'He says you called him to Rome but now refuse to see him.'

'A half truth – though I suppose we can't expect more from a eunuch. I never called him to Rome. But it's true I refuse to see him. I have more pressing matters than to listen to a eunuch's complaints.'

'Well, I was forced to meet with him, given your refusal. He was impertinent as always.'

Titus raises an eyebrow.

Before he can start, I say, 'Nothing you need to worry about, brother. He is harmless, so long as he's not preparing our dinner.'

Halotus served two emperors before Father. Under Claudius Caesar, he was a chamberlain. Chief taster to be more exact, which meant he was charged with ensuring the Emperor's food was free of poison. So when Claudius Caesar suddenly died – healthy one day, gone the next – and Nero succeeded him and *promoted* Halotus, the city whispered that Halotus was behind it. They said that rather than ensuring the Emperor's meal was free of poison, he guaranteed it. But the allegations never rose above rumour, whispers behind his and Nero's back.

Titus nods and then nibbles an olive.

'So are you going to tell me who you're searching for?' I ask. 'Or will you make me guess?'

Titus considers the question, before eventually confiding in me. 'Lucius Plautius,' he says and then proceeds to tell me about a letter he received from Lucius just before he went missing.

'"Caesar" and "poison"?' I shake my head. 'That's all he wrote?'

'Essentially, yes. Enough information to pique my interest but not nearly enough to act on. And now he's missing.'

Poor Titus. These plots against Father are growing in frequency, I'm sure of it. Baiae was only last month and already there is another one. The pressure Titus must feel. If he doesn't catch whoever is involved, no one will.

'Lucius has always been dramatic,' I say, offering what little comfort I can. 'I'm sure he was exaggerating.'

'Let us hope.' Titus's eyes lock onto Jacasta who, at the mention of Plautius's name, has been watching us intently. 'Your maid,' Titus says, 'I recall Plautius was once quite fond of her. You'll let me know if she hears anything from him?'

'Ah, yes,' I say. 'I'd forgotten.' Years ago, when Father and what felt like half the Empire spent part of the winter on Capri, Plautius invited – and probably paid – Jacasta to visit him every night. He was quite taken with her. I think she was fond of him as well.

'Of course,' I say. 'If Jacasta hears anything, you will be the first to know.'

I decide to change the subject.

'Will Father name Domitian consul this year?' I ask.

'I don't know.'

'He should. Domitian needs experience in administration. He could end up ruling one day.'

'I know.'

The strained look is back on Titus's face. He takes Domitian's super-fluousness personally. Poor Domitian. More than ten years junior to Titus – the great, indefatigable Titus: Father forgot all about him. Titus does his best as an older brother, to provide the guidance and advice Domitian requires, but there's only so much he can do.

'Jacas—'

Before I can finish the thought, she's beside me, pouring wine into blue crystal. Jacasta has been with me so long, she knows my moods better than I. Titus's brow crinkles, subtly acknowledging his moral victory. *See*, he says without saying anything, *wine helps*.

'Have you heard from Vespasia?' he asks.

'Yes.' My eyes look to the cup in my lap. 'The weather has been good, warmer than Rome.' I force myself to look up. 'And she's enjoying her time with her niece.'

'Did she say anything else?'

Poor Titus. He's more sentimental then anyone realises.

'She's upset, Titus. She thinks her husband was innocent. She did not love the man, but you know Vespasia. She's very . . . proud. We both know that. She finds the whole affair hurtful and humiliating. She just needs time.'

Titus sizes me up, reading my expression. Is this the gaze that so many senators crack under? He should know sisters are made of sterner stuff.

'Give her time,' I say. 'There is nothing more to it.' I try to change the subject. 'Was there another reason you came?'

'Yes.' It's now Titus's turn to stare at his cup. 'I've come to warn you.'

'Oh,' I say, 'that sounds ominous.'

'Father intends to approach Marcellus. About marriage . . . to you.'

My heart sinks, but only a smidge. Father has started down this path before only to turn back. He prefers me a lonely widow. My value is higher that way.

'Is that so?'

Titus looks sympathetic, but what does he know? If Father follows through, it's not Titus who will have to share his bed with an old man.

'I have advised against it.'

'Well, let us hope Father listens to you.'

The strain is back: Titus's eyes are slits.

Jacasta is called away. When she returns, she says, 'Mistress, there is a man at the door that insists on delivering a message to you personally.'

'Was he searched?' my paranoid brother asks. His Praetorians patrol the Palace at all hours. Titus knows any caller, known or unknown, is checked three times before setting eyes on me.

'He was,' Jacasta says nodding. 'He said his name is Cyrus. A foreigner, I think.'

'What was he like?' I ask.

Jacasta says, 'He has many gold chains and bracelets, and black make-up painted around his dark eyes, like a woman. And he is wearing pants.' Jacasta raises her eyebrow on this last item to signal she considers it the strangest. 'He says he has a present for you, from beyond the Silk Road. I know how you favour good silk. He let me inspect it.'

'Oh?'

She smiles blissfully. 'It was very good.'

The man named Cyrus enters the room with enough pomp it borders on the comic. He walks in with his head held high and his chest puffed out, with long, jumping steps. He is short and plump, with a dark complexion and a thick waist. His coat and trousers (the one's Jacasta disapproved of) are a deep green embroidered with gold stitching. Gold chains are piled on his neck and they *clink* and *rattle* with each of his bombastic steps. Trailing behind him are two strapping young slaves, carrying a large chest over their heads. Cyrus bows to me first, then Titus, in the deep ingratiating way Romans aren't capable of, because republican blood still runs in our veins.

Cyrus waves his hand and his slaves lower the chest to the floor.

'In Parthia,' he says, gaze averted, 'men talk in court of the unrivalled beauty of the Emperor's daughter. The sort of beauty one feels in the knees.'

'You are Parthian then?' Titus asks, trying to assert control of the conversation. He is Caesar's eldest son after all.

'By birth, yes. But I am here in the employ of another; a Roman citizen.'

Cyrus claps his hands and the two slaves fling open the trunk. He pulls out a bolt of light blue silk and brings it over to me, displaying it on his arms. 'My patron sends you these gifts. He has heard you are a woman of impeccable tastes, with an eye for fine fabric.'

'Has he?' I ask. The man's hyperbole is somehow both grating and pleasurable. 'And are all those for me?' I nod at the trunk.

'Yes. He only asks that you accept an invitation to dinner at his home. Many of the city's notable families will be there, but without Caesar's eldest daughter, my patron fears the evening will be a failure.'

This man is too much – too many compliments, too much make-up around his eyes, too much of everything.

'Who is your patron, sir?' Titus asks. His annoyance at being ignored is becoming obvious to more than his sister.

'The illustrious Senator Lucius Ulpius Traianus of Spain.'

Titus and I exchange looks.

'Who?'

# TITUS

*12 January, first torch*
*The home of Eprius Marcellus, Rome*

Marcellus's slave answers the door. He's nearly as old as Marcellus, but where the latter is all bone and sinew, the slave is loose skin, long arms and glassy eyes. Following him through the atrium into Marcellus's study feels an eternity. Beside me Secundus rolls his eyes. For Secundus – always the academic – time spent travelling is a waste unless a slave is reading aloud from one of his books.

Marcellus is in his study, sitting at his desk. A weak blend of lemony incense tries but fails to supress the room's damp staleness. Two slaves – no more than boys – stand behind their master holding rolls of paper. On the desk, a lone lamp burns oily black smoke. Murals of vermillion look a dark, muddy brown; I make out a few trees, a nymph, and a satyr balancing his oversized member on a tree stump. The woodland scene is oddly playful for such a serious, unhappy man.

Marcellus is squinting at a roll of paper an inch or so from his face. His slave announces our presence. Marcellus, however, finishes reading – just a line or two – but enough to send the message: *you are in my home now*. I doubt he knows why we've come. But he knows Caesar's son is visiting him, which is a victory in itself. If I were here as prefect of the Praetorians, sword in hand, I would not wait for his slave to lead me into his study.

'Ah –' he finally looks up from the page '– Titus Flavianus and . . .' He squints. '. . . Secundus.' He feigns standing by raising his backside three inches from his chair. 'Please.' He points at the two chairs across from his desk.

We sit. Secundus's chair creaks under his massive bulk.

We hear a cough from the back corner of the room.

My skills have dulled here in the capital. The general who took Jerusalem would enter a room and note every detail: the number of people, their age, their weight; whether they were left handed or right;

whether they carried arms or were likely to carry arms; their disposition towards the Emperor; whether the man harboured republican
sympathies; whether his father did; his father's father. I turn around
and see the girl I'd missed, lost in the shadows. She is almost naked,
save for a blanket of wool wrapped haphazardly around her hips. Her
eyes are wastelands, listless and white, blankly staring at the wall.
Her back and bony shoulders are bent toward the floor. Her cheek is
bruised. She coughs again – a choleric, sickly cough. What any man
does in his home is his own business. Still . . . Why is she just sitting
there, bruised and half naked? At the very least, it lacks decorum. I
turn back to Marcellus. He pays no attention to my having noticed
the poor girl or the look of disgust I am not bothering to hide. Empty
regret shimmies up my belly and stabs my heart. Poor Domitilla.

'To what do I owe the honour?' Marcellus asks.

Secundus – sensing my disgust, my desire to leave without another
word – is the first to speak. 'We've come to make a proposal to you,
Marcellus. On behalf of Caesar.'

'Oh,' Marcellus says bitterly. 'Caesar remembers me, does he?'

'Caesar will never forget the good work you did for the party,'
Secundus says.

At one time, Marcellus was one of Father's closest advisers. He
was particularly instrumental in fighting the Stoic opposition. Those
years were eye-opening for me. Before I'd viewed power through the
lens of war. It was about might and logistics. You won a war if you
had strategy, better training, more advanced arms and more men.
If I answered honestly what ultimately won us the war in Judea, if
I had to boil it down to one advantage, I'd say it was armour. We
had it, the Jews didn't. Political power is different. In Rome, power
is about increments and measuring yourself against another; the
measure of one's political power is merely the inverse of another's.
The Stoic opposition sought to undermine Father – not to gain the
throne themselves – but merely for the sake of undermining him.
They thought: bring the principate down an inch and we'll go up that
same inch. And this is why we are here tonight. Father is conceding an inch to Marcellus, rather than sitting back and watching him
reach for it. We cannot have every man in the Empire looking to gain
an inch or we will bury ourselves.

'Never forget?' Marcellus repeats Secundus's words with sarcastic inflection. 'Never forget, you say. I've been shut out for years. No appointments, no honours, no nothing. Caesar either forgot me or he spurns me on purpose.'

I cannot remember why Marcellus fell out of favour. Allegiances also occur in increments. We push away an inch, he pushes away two, until we are on opposite sides of the senate floor.

Marcellus continues, 'Why his own son visits my home and doesn't say a word.'

Everything is a slight to the dignity of an entitled senator. Even silence. I decide to cut our visit short. Despite my dislike for Marcellus, we need his support.

'Father is willing to offer Domitilla,' I say abruptly. 'She will marry you, but in exchange you must not only cease your diatribes in the senate, you must fight whatever trouble we are facing now.'

Marcellus is silent. He was not expecting this. It is a reversal in fortune and it takes him a moment to digest it. Finally, he asks, 'Trouble? You mean this business with the hand?'

'For a start,' I say. 'And there is the False Nero. You know he is still on the run.'

Marcellus nods.

'A dissident senator could make much of such a story,' I continue. 'But the incident could be turned to our favour. Cerialis was victorious. We would like your support, rather than your dissent. On this and any other issue.'

As the offer begins to sink in, Marcellus's serpentine lips tighten into the echo of a smile. He says, 'I will consider your offer,' but I know he has already accepted.

I stand up. Secundus does the same.

'You have until this time tomorrow to decide.'

On our way out, I keep my eyes in front of me, avoiding even a glance at the bruised, choleric girl in the corner.

Secundus and I make our way through the dark streets of Rome, quickly marching down the slope of the Esquiline Hill, escorted by a dozen Praetorians and just as many slaves. Torches light up the deserted streets. As we near the bottom of the hill, we spot Virgilius and a group of Praetorians waiting for us where the road levels out.

'You're up late,' I say, 'well past your bedtime.'

Virgilius doesn't answer; his face is grave.

'What is it?' I ask.

'I will take you.'

We follow Virgilius south, toward the Capitoline Hill. At night, it looks like a mountain of black shadow rising up from the city's centre. At its peak, the Temple of Jupiter's domed roof of bronze looks a silver-green in the moonlight. We round the Temple of Caster, in to the forum, to the foot of the Capitoline.

The southern side of the hill is a sheer rock, straight up and down, like a palisade. Directly above is the Tarpeian Rock, a ledge ten storeys above the forum. During the republic, those guilty of treason would be thrown from it to their death. Under the principate, however, it has fallen out of fashion. Capital punishment, especially under the Julio-Claudians, was administered in more creative ways.

A cluster of Praetorians at the foot of the hill part as we get closer, revealing a mound of linen – no, not linen. A body.

Secundus and I look up in unison, imagining the man's fall. Then we look down. The man's arms are spread out, like he's been crucified; and his left leg is bent and twisted in the wrong direction. He seems deflated after his fall, like he's missing half of what made him substantial, a tent with the poles removed. His skull has spilt open in the back, and a mess of red gore has spilled out onto the road. His face is bloodied and swollen. Despite his disfigurement, the man is familiar. I know him, though I cannot quite place him.

'You'll note he has both his hands,' Virgilius says. 'Which could be good news or bad, depending on how you look at it.'

Virgilius means this man's death was not related to the hand Cleopatra dragged into the forum – not directly at least.

I notice half of the corpse's left index finger is missing. The wound is old though; the tissue well healed.

Secundus has his hand to his mouth. For a moment, I wonder whether he will retch. But he swallows back whatever was bothering him and asks, 'Who is he?'

'I had a hunch.' Virgilius kneels and starts to pull up the man's tunic. 'And I think this proves it correct.'

Virgilius points at the man's exposed crotch. 'One cock. Zero balls.'

'They could have been crushed in the fall,' Secundus says.

'You can see the scar,' Virgilius pushes the corpses' member to the side. 'It's an old scar. This man was cut, long ago.'

'Halotus,' I say.

'Ah, the eunuch,' Secundus says. 'I'd thought he had a procurator-ship somewhere. Asia, maybe.'

'He's been back in Rome for a week or so,' I say. 'He'd been trying to meet with me, but I hadn't had time. Or the desire.'

Secundus scratches his beard. His shock has faded and he is once again the academic. 'It's a serious thing,' he says, 'to kill a procurator. The eunuch was universally despised; even Caesar did not like him. But still, one cannot kill a man vested with Caesar's power. It's like an attack on the Emperor himself.'

Virgilius inspects the body, pressing and patting, looking for more evidence on how he died, when we hear an odd sound, like the crinkle of paper. Virgilius looks up at us, his eyebrow raised. He presses the man's torso until he pushes on the right hip and hears the sound again. He takes a small dagger and cuts a hole in Halotus's tunic and pulls out a roll of papyrus. He stands and unrolls it. The page is filled with strange writing, letters I've never seen before. Nearly half of the page is stained with the eunuch's blood.

'That's not Latin, is it?' Virgilius asks quizzically.

'No,' Secundus says. 'Nor is it Greek.' He points at the paper. 'May I?'

Virgilius nods and hands it to Secundus.

'If I had to hazard a guess,' Secundus says, 'I'd say it was German. Which particular dialect, I've no idea.'

'Can you translate it?' I ask.

'Possibly,' Secundus says.

I look around us, confirming none of the other Praetorians can hear our discussion.

'Secundus is right,' I say. 'An attack on the procurator is akin to an attack on the Emperor. And with Plautius still missing . . .'

I have been denying it for too long. It is time I admit the state of affairs.

'. . . we are at war. There is a concerted effort at work, aimed at undermining the Emperor. We must assume the ultimate aim is to seize the throne. Until we know who the traitors are, we must min-imise the damage.' I point at Halotus's corpse and, to Virgilius, say, 'Have this cleaned up. For now, the name of the man who died does not go beyond the three of us. Understand?'

Secundus and Virgilius nod in agreement.

'What will we do, Titus?' Secundus asks.

'We will find the men who did this,' I say, 'and we will bring them to justice.'

# IX

## The List
### A.D. 68

# MARCUS

◆

*2 September, afternoon*
*City jail IV, Rome*

'No. No, no, no, no.'

It's wrong. Everything I do is wrong.

'You've missed its other leg,' Doryphorus says. 'Otherwise, it's just a "P".'

Doryphorus is standing over my shoulder. His finger is pointing at my 'R' – the 'R' I've messed up. Again. I'm holding a wax tablet and a stick, whittled and smoothed. I've pressed lines into the wax to make my 'R' but I guess it's just a 'P' right now. My bum hurts from sitting so long. I've never had to sit so much before.

'Draw its other leg,' he says. He's puffing air like a bull again. I get scared when he does this. I can't think very well. All I do is clam up and wait till it's over.

'Come *on*,' he says again. 'Draw the other leg.'

He grabs my hand and forces me to draw a sideways line from the middle of the letter, down and away.

'There,' he says in between angry puffs. 'That's an "R".'

Nero is sitting cross-legged on the floor of his cell with his back against the wall. A clean bandage is wrapped around his eyes. His coppery beard is getting long.

'At this rate,' Doryphorus says turning to Nero, 'he'll be my age when he learns to read.'

Nero doesn't answer Doryphorus. To me, he says, 'Marcus, will you come sit with me a moment.'

I sit beside Nero, outside his cell, with only the prison bars between us. He's rubbing a scrap of red brick with his thumb. The one that's shaped like a spearhead and he carries around with him everywhere.

'Are you enjoying your lesson today?' he asks. He doesn't wait for me to answer. 'Don't let the actor fool you. Learning one's letters is difficult. The "P" and "R" are very similar, twins almost. The Castor and Pollux of letters. It will take time to learn all of this. But the effort will be worth it.'

Doryphorus is fiddling with the wax tablet. The sad afternoon sun is coming in the window and three rusty bars cast long shadows across the bricks.

'Do you want some advice?' Nero asks. 'A titbit of wisdom I had to learn the hard way. Maybe, if you hear it now, you can avoid future heartache. I have found that the pupil has the tendency to form an opinion of the master, to hold him in esteem, before understanding *who* the master really is – the parts that make up the whole. Take Doryphorus, for example . . .'

Doryphorus is watching us now. He's scowling.

'. . . yes, he knows his letters. But he remains just a man; he has faults and vices like any other. What vices, you ask? Well, he has a temper. That's obvious, isn't it? Don't grow up to have a temper, Marcus. Believe me. All it does in the end is make people uncomfortable. Can you imagine listening to a man yell at a boy as he's trying to learn his letters? Do you know how uncomfortable that would make an audience? Why it's as awkward as a first kiss. Worse even. At least with a first kiss there's the hope – the faint echo – of the orgasm to follow.'

'Are you done?' Doryphorus asks. He's still scowling.

Nero ignores Doryphorus. To me, he says, 'What I'm trying to say, Marcus, is this: make sure you understand the man before you take anything he says to heart. Doryphorus knows his letters. Listen to him. Learn from him. But don't take anything he says to heart. Not until you're ready. Do you understand?'

'Yes,' I say.

'Good,' Nero says. 'Now run along. You should be getting back to Creon's.'

These are my days now. Each day Nero and Doryphorus take turns giving me lessons. In the morning, I learn history and literature and sums; in the afternoon, I learn my letters. I have to learn my letters before I can learn to read. But so far, things aren't going very well. Doryphorus is probably right: I don't know if I'll ever remember them. Each one is a mystery. So when they are jumbled together on a page or carved into buildings – the mystery seems impossible. It's like when I stare at all those temples in the forum and wonder how they were built – how did people *do* that?

My lessons started the day after Doryphorus found us. That day, Nero told me to leave, so he could talk with Doryphorus alone. The next day, when I came back to the jail, Nero's blindfold was off and Doryphorus was sitting on a stool, with his arms through the bars, applying a strange green paste to Nero's cuts and the tender pink scars where his eyes used to be.

While Doryphorus and Nero talked, I prepared Nero's bread, tearing it up into little pieces, and I poured out the wine and fish sauce Nero had tricked Master Creon into giving him. They talked about people I didn't know. Nero would name a person and Doryphorus would tell him what he knew – where the man was, what he was doing.

When Nero was finished eating, he told Doryphorus that he was tired and needed to rest. They spoke in voices so low that I couldn't hear. And then when Doryphorus stood up to go, I heard Nero say: 'And see to the boy.'

Doryphorus glared at me. Then he grabbed me by the tunic and dragged me out of the room, all the way to the top of the steps. He knelt, so our eyes were level, shook me by the tunic and said, 'What of your education?'

I didn't know what he meant, so I didn't say anything.

He said, 'Don't clam up on me, boy. I don't have time for your silent act. I want to know what kind of work we have ahead of us. Your education: how far has it progressed? Can you read?'

I shook my head. No.

And he said, 'Do you know your letters?'

I shook my head. No.

'Gods. You'd no education before you were taken slave?'

I shrugged.

'Well, slave-with-a-consul's-name,' Doryphorus said. 'Our friend has decided that you are to be educated. It is your reward. Is it a fair price for a few sips of water and a loaf of bread? Who am I to say? It's only *my* time and energy. Your lessons start tomorrow. Be here bright and early.'

And my lessons started the very next day.

# NERO

◆

*2 September, afternoon*
*City jail IV, Rome*

I took Doryphorus to bed on his seventeenth birthday. He was a palace freedman at the time, so he had no choice in the matter. Nevertheless, given his artless attempts to seduce me for several months prior, one can assume he was a more than willing partner. Ever since, he has loved me unconditionally. Even after my decision to discard him, weeks later, once the inevitable sense of boredom set in.

In my sexual tastes, I generally inclined to females, blondes in the main, at least one foot shorter than me. (Caesar cannot feel *petite*.) On very rare occasions, something different would catch my eye. In contrast to my choice in women, I preferred young men with a dark complexion and whose body types mirrored my own: lean, muscled, effervescent. At the time, Doryphorus met the bill: slim, short but not too short, and thirty-three puddle-shaped moles from head to toe. (I vaguely recall counting them one morning, tracing my hand across his swarthy flesh.) Without my eyes, I'm no longer able to see whether he still meets my prior standard. Yesterday, however, he was sitting beside me and my elbow grazed his midriff. I was shocked at the blubbery give. Age, I suppose, catches up with us all, and with it loose skin and fat bellies.

I was generally fair to my discarded lovers. I would provide stipends and a place to live once I was bored with them, if I wanted them clear of the palace out of respect for whichever woman happened to be my wife at the time. My enemies would often try to exploit my kindness, to claim it evidences some sort of weakness on my part; stories would circulate from time to time. I vowed not to let this dictate how I behaved. Doryphorus, however, is a rare, unfortunate example of Caesar falling short.

I took Doryphorus not too long after Piso's conspiracy was unearthed. The senate felt anger and unease after so many of their own were sentenced to death. Doryphorus provided my enemies with an opportunity to manufacture weakness. Rumours began to circulate that

Doryphorus made love to *me*, not the other way around – a common refrain in Roman politics, but one which nevertheless causes harm. So when I grew bored of Doryphorus, with these rumours circulating, I did not provide him a stipend or a residence, as was my usual practice. Instead, I showed the manly virtue of indifference: I sent him packing from the palace without a coin to his name. I also had one of my staff start a rumour that I had Doryphorus killed for some trivial offence. Better they think Caesar unpredictable and cruel than sentimental.

One month later, I was plagued with guilt. It came on me suddenly and unexpectedly. I sent Spiculus to track him down. The gladiator returned the next day. He'd found Doryphorus acting with a troupe in a canteen near the circus. He was, according to Spiculus, alive and well. As I'd instructed, Spiculus presented a gold piece, holding it up so Doryphorus could see my face embossed in the shining ore, and told Doryphorus I was sorry and wished him well. Apparently, Doryphorus began to cry. ('Blubbered' was the word Spiculus used.) Doryphorus said he loved me and was happy to be wherever Caesar thought best. If it was away from the palace, acting in a troupe, then that is where he would be.

I met Doryphorus once more, years later, when attending a play in the Subura. On certain nights in Rome, under the cover of dark, with a small retinue of friends and disguised guards, with swords strapped under their togas, I would escape the palace and make my way amongst the commoners. We would attend plays, brothels, canteens – wherever the night took us. On the night in question, we attended the Happy Cock, a canteen which doubled as a theatre. That night, the long tables were removed and replaced with seats all aimed at the stage; firelight danced along the brick walls.

My companions and I entered just before the show was to begin. There was a hush followed by a buzzing sense of glee – the Emperor is here! *Here.* Space near the front was cleared; half-drunk plebs gave up their seats. One man cried like a little girl. The show began shortly afterwards. Poor Doryphorus: he didn't know I was in the audience until he was on stage. He nearly fell over when he saw me.

When the show was over, I sent word backstage that I wished to speak with him. Out he came, nervous, angry, bewildered, and still as lovesick as when we parted, though he tried to hide it. He said that he had been acting with the same troupe for two years. He was happy.

When we parted, I gave him a feathery kiss on the cheek. My guilt, if I had any left, eased. I wouldn't hear his voice again until my eyes were gone and my Empire lost.

The day he found us, Doryphorus bribed the guards out front to gain entry to the jail. After speaking with me and learning the centurion appeared to be the one in charge, he bribed the rank and file again to organise a meeting with the centurion, the man Marcus calls the Fox and we now know is named Terentius. He then bribed Terentius for the privilege of visiting me on an ongoing basis. Doryphorus thought he seemed completely at ease, even phlegmatic. 'Why?' I asked. 'Because,' Doryphorus said, 'the world thinks you're dead. Or off in the east somewhere raising an army. And no one would believe a washed-up actor anyway. Why not make the extra coin?'

According to Doryphorus, the jail is now guarded by four soldiers at all times. They rarely come into the jail, preferring to drink and dice outside. Other than those we know are involved, Doryphorus believes the rest have no idea who is being held inside. They are content because they have been given one of the more comfortable posts a Praetorian can have.

I don't know why Doryphorus followed Marcus here. He claims he had a hunch I was alive. I have my doubts. I wonder if he had a change of heart and intended to bludgeon the boy, once he figured out how to make a profit from it. But when he saw me, all of his old feelings came back (or so he says). He is devoted to me (I think). Whatever his motivation, I am not in a position to be turning away friends.

Doryphorus thinks I should take back the purple. He says the people would rally around me once they knew I was alive. I have my doubts. True: the people love me still – how could they not? But at the moment, from what Doryphorus tells me, and from what I have gleaned from Marcus's tales, Nymphidius, the remaining prefect of the Praetorians, has taken over the city in Galba's absence. He is holed up in the palace and executing those who question his authority. He has even killed a senator. If – and it is a big 'if' – we were able to overpower the gaggle of guards out front and escape, Nymphidius would have me cut down before I'd mounted the rostrum.

I also remain physically helpless, pathetically so. An Emperor must be able to lead his troops in the field; he must be able to watch the look of contrition form on a foreign king's face as he bends the knee. I, however, can't even manage my meals on my own. The boy effectively chews for me, when he rips up my bread and douses it in fish sauce, like a mother bird tending to its chick. In any event, there is something I desire more than the principate; more than the title Caesar; more than the godlike power I wielded. Retribution.

Doryphorus has procured us two wax tablets, the kind clerks use or schoolboys when learning their letters. The first we use exclusively for Marcus's lessons. On the other Doryphorus has written out a list of those who may have been involved in the coup. I cannot see it, but I can trace my fingers over the indents in the wax; I can run my hand across each name, line by line, and I can feel the names of the men who have, or *may* have, broken their oath.

Plots against Caesar spread like wildfire. Once a man gets wind of a chance to rise, he inevitably wants to be involved; and given the nature of Rome and its politics, and the measures I had in place protecting my person, any successful plot would require Imperial secretaries, soldiers, and senators, all working together to bring me down. We have a list of eleven names so far, four of which we know were involved.

| *Guilty* | *Guilt unknown* |
| --- | --- |
| *Terentius (centurion)* | *Epaphroditus (chamberlain)* |
| *Venus (soldiers)* | *Phaon (chamberlain)* |
| *Juno (soldiers)* | *Spiculus (bodyguard)* |
| *Nympidius (Praetorian prefect)* | *Tigellinus (Praetorian prefect)* |
| | *Galba (False Emperor)* |
| | *Otho (covets the throne)* |
| | *The Black Priest (?)* |

I drank heavily the night I was taken. I remember the soldiers bursting in and the godforsaken cave they dragged me to, but the night is otherwise a soggy blur. Every night, at a minimum, there would have been two members of my personal bodyguard (all ex-gladiators) and two Praetorians outside my door. That night Spiculus and Hercules were the gladiators on duty. I'm almost certain the two Praetorians were Venus and Juno. (I was never given the other rank and file's name, so I have named him after a goddess as well, as I did for his colleague.)

Only four men had keys to my bedchamber: Spiculus, Epaphroditus, Phaon and Tigellinus. One of them had to be involved, unless they were subdued somehow and their key taken. As for senators, I now no longer think Galba was involved, not directly – not with the letters Marcus found and the conversation he overheard in the palace. The letters show I wasn't the only person Nymphidius betrayed that day. Doryphorus has read them aloud so often I can recite each word for word.

*10 June (from Rome)*
*Nymphidius:*

*The tyrant is dead, yet somehow your task was a failure. How could this be?*

*After the deed was done, you were to bring our chosen man immediately to the Praetorian camp and have him proclaimed Emperor. But you waited too long – far too long – and then the senate – unmolested, free to pick whomever they pleased because your soldiers were not breathing down their necks – named another man emperor. The plan was simple – so simple that, given its failure, we are left with one conclusion to draw: you have betrayed us.*

*We had a pact, sworn before the dark god, sealed by the Black Priest and bound by blood. You know what we are capable of. The gods help you, because we shall not.*

*10 June (from Rome)*
*Servius Sulpicius Galba (in Spain):*

*The world is changing rapidly, but I believe there is a chance to profit should we work together. Tigellinus is gone. I am now the lone prefect of the Praetorians. I speak for the three cohorts stationed in Rome. On my orders my men blinded and imprisoned the tyrant. I have released your freedman Icelus and sent him to you with this letter. He will confirm my account. Only I and three of my associates know Nero is alive. The world thinks him dead. I leave it to you decide his fate.*

*The Praetorians require a bonus of 2,000 sesterces a man. I also require one million sesterces for my continued loyalty, and the loyalty of the guard. This is a small price to pay for the Principate. I await your word.*

*Nymphidius Sabinus,*
  *prefect of the Praetorian Guard*

The letters show Nymphidius only sought to seek the Hunchback's favour once the original plan had gone to shit. The soldiers who stole me from my bed – Nymphidius, the centurion Terentius (or the Fox, as Marcus calls him), and my two goddesses, Venus and Juno – they were working with another group, one that had chosen a different man to take the purple. Who exactly the Black Priest is, who he is working with, and who they wanted to put on the throne – these are all questions we do not have answers to.

This evening, like every evening, after Marcus leaves, Doryphorus and I go over the list. I can hear him pacing, as his voice travels from one side of the room to the other.

'We know for certain four soldiers were involved,' I say. 'Venus, Juno, Terentius, and Nymphidius. The question is whether the other prefect, Tigellinus, was involved.'

'You are certain Marcus is correct?' Doryphorus asks. 'You are certain he actually heard what he thinks he heard in the palace?'

'You don't credit the boy enough,' I say. 'I think what he reports is more or less correct. Terentius was receiving orders from someone. And the letters he stole are damning, in my opinion. Nymphidius was working with another group, one led by this Black Priest. Once that plan failed for whatever reason, they brought me here, to this particular jail, because only the Praetorians and I know it exists.'

Based on descriptions given by Doryphorus and Marcus, I have determined I am being kept in one of the jails, which is north of the city, near the Tiber. I know the one. It is usually used by the vigiles, to hold runaway slaves or some debtor who hasn't paid his bill. But emperors and the Praetorian Guard have often used it over the years, to torture and kill whomever they pleased, away from prying eyes. It's always been maintained by a freedman in return for the prisoners' urine and the prospect of having connections within the vigiles and the guard. (Marcus's master Creon must hold the contract.) What a wretched turn of fate that Caesar's secret prison now holds Caesar himself.

'If the letters are genuine,' Doryphorus says, 'it begs two questions: who is the Black Priest? And who was their "chosen man", the man they'd pick to be emperor?'

I shake my head in frustration. At the moment, these questions are impossible to answer.

I say, 'Have you heard anything further on the Imperial staff?'

'No,' Doryphorus says. 'Your freedmen have all gone into hiding. It's not safe for anyone who was one of your favourites.'

'When they begin to resurface, we will have a better idea of their complicity.'

Doryphorus sits beside me. I can hear his stocky frame flap against the ground and his sigh as he relaxes against the wall. He places his hand on my knee. An innocent act meant to imply less innocent out-comes. Am I still attractive in my current circumstance: eyeless, broken and imprisoned? I'd never have guessed. Or maybe Doryphorus's tastes have a deviant side. In any event, it doesn't matter. I pick up his hand and cast it aside. I do not explain myself; nor should I have to. I am no longer the man I was. I have only one purpose now, and reaching orgasm is not it.

Doryphorus leaves without a word, but I know he will be back tomorrow. As I wait for sleep to come, I hold the wax tablets with my left hand and run my right across the names. The list is a work in progress. But at the moment, I have nothing but time.

# X

## The Exchequer
### A.D. 79

# TITUS

◆

*13 January, sunset*
*The Imperial palace, Rome*

I find Father in the palace, sitting on a balcony, looking south. On the edge of the valley below, running south-east and away from the palace, is the aqueduct. Three storeys of arches, endlessly repeated, it looks like a giant caterpillar of brick easily stepping over whole apartment blocks, then green fields, before disappearing over the horizon. Directly below us, rising out of the valley floor, is Father's amphitheatre, a hill of stone and shadow, surrounded by scaffolds. Beside it, taller than any building in Rome, is a bronze statue of the sun god. The ghostly sound of hammers striking chisels drifts through the air: *chip chip chip.*

Father points at the unfinished project. 'I thought they would be farther along now.'

'Oh?'

Father is leaning back in his chair. A slave on her knees is massaging his swollen, gout-ridden feet. She is as old as Father: grey hair, withered shoulders. The balm she is applying is a sticky grey paste, a mix of wool-grease, woman's milk, and white lead. It burns my nostrils, even from a distance.

'Yes,' he says. 'I was hoping they'd be done. Was that too much to ask?'

'It was.'

Caesar snorts. 'What happened to my son the general? I used to say, "Titus Flavius gets the job done. Give him a day and he'll take the hour."'

Father considers himself a motivator of men. He takes different tacks, depending on the subject. With his eldest son, he provides equal parts pride and disappointment. Historically, it has been quite successful, especially when I was the young soldier trying to prove himself. On this occasion, however, it will miss the mark. The valley below was once home to Nero's golden palace, a sprawling marble complex surrounding a garden and man-made lake. After the civil wars, Father wished to remove all memory of Nero and the illustrious Julio-Claudians, so he had it torn down. In its place, he wanted the largest amphitheatre ever built. The message: Nero built for himself; Vespasian builds for the people. It was a monumental task and it is coming along at a reasonable pace. I tell Father as much. I also blame the engineers who continuously change their plans and budget.

Father winces as the slave continues massaging his aching feet. He asks, 'Will it be complete by the end of the year? You never know which will be my last.'

'Nonsense,' I say, 'you've years left.'

'Do I?' He frowns sardonically. 'If my procurators are being struck down in the capital, and members of the Plautii, our family's closest friends, have gone missing – how long until Caesar is struck down himself?'

Today, it seems, Father intends to rely more on disappointment, rather than pride, in his interminable quest to motivate his eldest son. I try to keep calm. 'Halotus was killed *yesterday*. You may want to allow more time than the morning to find his killer.' My voice remains low, but there is an edge to it. 'Don't worry, Father. You sit here on your balcony, enjoying the view, and I will find those responsible for the eunuch's death. And I will find Plautius.'

'You will? Oh good.' Father's tone is sarcastic. 'I was worried you wouldn't be able to find Plautius, seeing as how you've been completely unsuccessful up to now.'

This is how Father governs. He is with you, until – suddenly, out of the blue – he is against you, and then you're buried under a mountain of bitter complaints. 'You are exaggerating,' I say. 'It was only confirmed two days ago that Plautius was missing.'

Father swats at the air. 'Bah! Excuses, excuses. And what about that damned hand? Where is your answer for that? At the moment it's causing me more trouble than anything. The hand and this godsforsaken cold streak. The people think the gods are against me.'

'Since when do you care what the people say?'

The slave gently places Father's foot down onto the stool before starting with the other. Father sighs with relief.

'It matters, Titus. All of it matters.' His voice is calmer now that his pain has lessened. It's often this way: his frustration with governing rises and falls with the pain in his legs. 'Omens matter – real or fake, whether or not the gods are involved. If the people think power will change hands because a dog dragged some poor buggers hand to the forum, they will be indifferent to treason. Or they will expect it. And it emboldens the ambitious. It's the same with my procurator being killed or a Plautii missing on the Bay.'

I had planned on telling Father of the Germanic scroll found on Halotus, which Secundus is attempting to translate. But it's best to keep this to myself for now. I will wait until I have something more concrete to report. There is no point in aggravating Father's anxieties.

Father points at his left foot; the skin is bloated, with a marbled-purple hue. Half in jest, he says, 'I suppose my health doesn't help, does it? I don't inspire confidence. Not any more. I used to be something fearsome, but now I'm not much more than a cripple. I rely on you to protect our family and the party. We'd be lost without you.' He pats my hand. His tone is conciliatory now. 'Move quickly, Titus. Crack whatever heads you need to. Just find out who is working against us. Expose them and bring them to justice.'

'Yes, Father,' I say, as though this was not already patently clear.

Father adjusts his position; he winces. 'Speaking of cripples, I understand you've been invited to dine with Ulpius.'

'I have. Why?'

'Are you planning to attend?' he asks.

'I thought it would be prudent, to learn more of this rich provincial.'

'Prudent, yes,' Father mumbles, 'but behave civilly, please. Our family owes the Ulpii.'

'What? I've never heard of the man. You know his family? How?'

'There were several families who provided financial contribution to us during the civil wars. The Ulpii were one of them. And one of

Ulpius's kinsman served in Judea, during the rebellion. He's now posted in the provinces. You should try harder to remember the soldiers who bled for you.'

'I'd forgotten. Very well, I will be civil.'

Now that we've discussed Halotus, I'm waiting for Father to finally ask about Marcellus. He sent me, after all. He should have to ask.

To fill the quiet, I say, 'Cerialis has written again. He's confirmed the False Nero is missing. He believes he's run east.'

Caesar nods. 'I've heard. Another embarrassment.'

'Having Cerialis pursue the False Nero may make practical sense, but it will hurt us politically. It gives the man more credence.'

'And what would you suggest?'

'I thought we could bring Cerialis back with the rebels he *has* captured. Give him honours and a parade. A show of force to remind the people of Caesar's might.'

'Not a triumph, surely.'

'No, no,' I say. 'Something smaller. But the games will be sizeable, and that is what the people care for anyway.'

Loath as I am to admit it, when Father nods and says, 'Yes, that's a good idea,' bubbles of filial pride well up inside of me, an echo of my days as a boy, constantly seeking the general's approval.

The slave on her knees rises, packs up her balm and towel, bows and leaves.

Father circles back to Plautius – a topic we have already covered. He is avoiding speaking of Marcellus.

'What of Plautius then?'

'He remains missing,' I say.

'Yes, obviously. Have you had any more information? What is your plan?'

'I'm not sure.'

For a change, rather than simply complaining, Father offers advice. 'What about the knight Plautius mentioned in his letter? Do you know anything of him?'

'Vettius? No,' I say. 'Not yet. All we have is the name. It is difficult to make inquiries without more information.'

Father considers this, then says, 'Ask the exchequer. Get his people on this.'

I nod. 'Yes, good idea.'

'And go visit Plautius's wife again. Read whatever letters he's sent. There may be something more in those letters. And who do you have in the south now, making inquiries.'

'Domitian continues to search.'

Father makes a face, like he's bitten a rotten fig. 'I don't know why you gave such a task to him. It is beyond his capabilities.'

'You underestimate your youngest son,' I say. 'He is capable. He only requires the experience. That is why you should name him suffuct consul this year.'

Father laughs. He once again has a sarcastic tinge to his voice. 'What? You're not serious?'

'Yes. He needs the experience in administration. He needs to learn how to lead.'

'Why? What does it matter what experience the boy has? You will lead when I am gone. You will have a son.'

'You can't be certain of that.'

Our voices are rising again. We have had this argument before, but every time emotion gets the better of us.

Father says, 'I'm certain Domitian would be a disastrous emperor.'

'Not with the right training.'

'I will consider it,' Father says, ending the discussion.

We sit in silence for a moment. Finally, Father asks about Marcellus. 'And how did it go? The proposal.'

'Fine.'

'He accepted?'

'Yes, though he wouldn't admit it. He intends to make us wait. I gave him until this evening to give us his answer.'

Father nods. 'Good. You did well.' Father looks at me and sees something. Disgust, maybe. He pats my hand. 'He won't be such a bad husband,' he says. 'There have been worse.'

I think of the girl in Marcellus's study, naked, bruised and relegated to the corner. I think of his thin, serpentine lips.

'Perhaps.'

I call on Antonia, Lucius Plautius's wife, in the afternoon. At my request, she takes me to Plautius's library and shows me his letters.

Rather than leave me alone to read, Antonia sits on the arm of my chair, her soft, warm hip resting against my arm. Occasionally, she will lean in to read over my shoulder, twisting her torso so her breast touches my shoulder. Slaves slowly retreat from the room, sensing their presence is not desired. I find myself skipping words as I read.

It was Antonia who seduced me all those years ago. We both happened to be staying with the governor of Syria. I was there to raise more troops for the war. Plautius had gone south for some reason or another. On my third night, after days of what I considered harmless flirting, I returned to my room after dinner to find her lying on my bed, naked as the day she was born. She hadn't been touched in months, she told me afterwards, as we were enjoying a cup of wine in the lamplight. She was unhappy and lonely and nothing filled the void better than a general, fresh from war. We spent every night together for the next month. Then I went back to war and we never spoke of it again. Is she hoping to pick up where we left off? Stealing a man's wife is unethical, but especially so when that man is missing and possibly dead.

I stand up suddenly. I move so quickly, Antonia almost falls when she jumps to her feet.

I start packing up the letters. 'I will have my staff review these.'

Embarrassed, Antonia looks at the floor. 'Very well. I shall have someone see you out.'

A slave announces my presence.

'Master, prefect Titus is here to see you.'

The exchequer, Epaphroditus, looks up from his cluttered desk.

A ribbon of incense meanders through the murk.

The freedman stands. He is built like a spear: tall, skinny, no curves whatsoever. As always, he is immersed in black – black eyes, black hair, black robe; his dagger-like goatee is the outlier, which, though black, is dusted with white. He says, 'Prefect Titus. Sir.' He wipes his hands on his thighs and then waves his right at the chairs opposite his desk. 'Please.'

I move slowly, taking in the room. Taking in the rolls of papyrus, the ledgers, and the clerks against the far wall, who slide their chairs back and silently depart. Taking in the mosaic behind the exchequer's desk of Ulysses tied to his ship's mast, smiling.

Epaphroditus sees me staring over his shoulder. He turns to look. He says, 'I've spent nearly ten years in this room. I often forget he is there.'

'He looks happy,' I say.

'Does he?' Epaphroditus frowns. 'I thought him mad. Temporarily, at least. If he weren't tied to the mast, the call of the sirens would have him steer his ship into the rocks.'

'I suppose that's true,' I say. 'But isn't life more enjoyable when someone else is steering the ship?'

The freedman blushes slightly, embarrassed I have brought philosophy to his room of numbers.

I change the subject. 'You are the man who knows where the money is.'

It's not a question; nevertheless, he nods.

'There is a man I wish to learn more of,' I say. 'A Pompeian knight named Vettius.'

'Do you have any more information? Another name perhaps?'

'No.'

'Assuming we can find this man,' the exchequer says, 'what do you wish to know?'

'Whatever you can tell me. When he became a knight, what he does. Anything you can provide.'

Epaphroditus's lips move, as though he's whispering his way through sums. 'Well, obviously I do not know anything of this man, not off the top of my head.'

'That's fine. Report back to me after you have made the inquiries you need to.'

'Of course, Titus.'

There is a moment of silence and my mind wanders. I think of the man in Thrace claiming to be Nero and the followers he's gathered. As I find myself sitting before one of Nero's old favourites, questions suddenly occur to me. I ask: 'What do you make of the newest man claiming to be the tyrant?'

'I think him an imposter,' Epaphroditus says abruptly.

I weigh his words for a moment and then say, 'You've an odd biography. No man – none that I can think of – has ever cut the throat of their head of state and then continued working for the state – day in, day out – as though nothing happened.'

His eyes look uneasy. 'Am I being dismissed? Have I done anything to offend you or your father?'

I shake my head. 'No, I didn't say that. I am merely curious. Another Nero gallivanting around Thrace has my mind wandering.'

I see wine distilling on a side table. I go to it and pour us two cups, equal parts wine and seawater. He watches me with uneasy eyes. I hand him a cup and retake my seat. I am uncreative in putting people at ease. But wine works – why try anything different?

'I was in Judea after the civil wars,' I say, 'when my father returned to Rome and was named Caesar. By the time I was called back to the capital, those who received pardons were already back to work. Humour me. Explain to me how this happened.'

He sips his wine and relaxes slightly.

'It happened in June,' he says, 'Nero . . . I mean the tyrant's death. His suicide.' He takes another sip. The wine gives him confidence and his voice fills out. 'Not long afterward the senate declared Galba emperor. He was in Spain at the time.'

I nod. All of this is well documented, but foundations must be set.

'Galba took his time getting to Rome,' he says. 'He conquered cities as he went and –' he considers his words '– made examples of those slow to declare their support . . .'

What he means is that the Hunchback, on whatever pretence he could dream up, killed a good number of men whose loyalty was suspect. When power changes hands, there must be a certain amount of blood spilled. Galba, however, was indiscriminate.

'. . . Galba didn't arrive in Rome until October, after the Ides. The months before were dangerous. The prefect of the Praetorians, Nymphidius Sabinus, took control of the city. He besieged the palace and intimidated the populace. The senate sent emissaries to meet Galba in Narbonne, begging him to hurry back. The other prefect, Tigellinus, went into hiding. I did the same. I thought it only a matter of time before they had me executed. So I ran to my villa, south of the city. I stayed there for weeks. Nymphidius was mad . . . you remember what happened to him.'

'Yes,' I say. 'One doesn't forget a thing like that.'

'When Galba finally arrived in Rome, he put a price on my head, fifty thousand sesterces. But I was to be taken alive. Soldiers found me and dragged me to the palace.' The exchequer laughs a bitter, incredulous laugh. 'I thought that was it. But he wanted to congratulate me, for killing Nero – even if it was at the tyrant's request. He made me his guest of honour at dinner that night and for weeks afterwards. Every night I would have to tell the story, how it happened, what Nero said.'

Having Epaphroditus repeat, again and again, the story of Nero's suicide – how he needed his freedman's help after he lost the nerve – it was useful, politically. But those first weeks after Nero's fall were crucial. Galba clearly did not do as much as he could. If he had, maybe False Neros would not continue to plague the Empire.

'Galba's time as emperor was –' Epaphroditus again chooses his words carefully '– unfortunate. The decimation, the riots, his choice of heir. He did not last beyond January the next year. But by then he'd already installed me in the palace again, though he moved me from secretary of petitions to the exchequer, a promotion for killing the tyrant. The emperors who followed Galba left me where I was.'

'Fortune and the webs she weaves,' I say.

'I was fortunate,' he says. 'I won't deny it.'

I lean in, conspiratorially. 'What was it like? Cutting the throat of the emperor?'

Epaphroditus' back straightens; his eyes divert, nervously. 'Treasonous,' he says coolly.

His answer is rehearsed – one he has given for years. Now that I've heard it, I'm not sure there was any other he could have given. (He is talking with Caesar's son, after all.) I hate asking questions that have only one answer. I appear slow-witted.

I stand to go. 'Find out what you can on Vettius. Do it as soon as you can.'

Before turning to leave, I take in Ulysses's smile one last time. I think: I'm not smiling – that's obvious. Hopefully, I'm the one steering the ship. Then again, this ship – the Empire – it's so vast, so amorphous, it often steers itself.

# XI

## Rumour's Sparrows
### A.D. 68 to 69

# MARCUS

*24 September, sunset*
*The home of Proculus Creon, Rome*

Master and Mistress are eating dinner. Master says, 'I'm telling you –' he swigs his wine and then wipes his mouth '– it's getting to the point where it's affecting business.'

'Oh?' Mistress asks.

Master waves me over. I take three quick steps forward and pour wine into his empty cup. He puts his hand up and I stop. Socrates follows with water.

Master says, 'I don't know why they need to do it in the forum. Can you imagine? I'm there trying to negotiate a deal and then we hear murderous chanting.'

'How did they do it?' Mistress asks.

'There were dozens of them. They dragged the poor bastard, kicking and screaming from his litter. I don't know how they spotted him behind the curtains, but they did. They dragged him right into the middle of the square and then started scratching and tearing at him, until he was a bloody mess – I think, anyway. I ran. I didn't need to see that.'

Mistress shakes her head. 'Terrible. Though he was rotten from what I heard.'

Master shrugs. 'I never had any problem with Phaon. Out of all of Nero's freedman, there were worse. Believe you me.'

I try my best to remember what Master says. Nero will want to know. Phaon. The forum. Bloody mess.

# NERO

◆

*25 September, afternoon*
*City jail IV, Rome*

We cross Phaon off the list. It's possible that, despite his murder, he was nevertheless involved in the coup. Possible, but I don't think so. It likely happened as the boy's owner thinks: old scores were settled and Phaon's life was the only payment that could square the account. Either way, he's gone now, so we cross him off the list.

| <u>Guilty</u> | <u>Guilt unknown</u> |
|---|---|
| *Terentius (centurion)* | *Epaphroditus (chamberlain)* |
| *Venus (soldier)* | ~~*Phaon (chamberlain)*~~ |
| *Juno (soldier)* | *Spiculus (bodyguard)* |
| *Nymphidius (Praetorian prefect)* | *Tigellinus (Praetorian prefect)* |
| | *Galba (False Emperor)* |
| | *Otho (covets the throne)* |
| | *The Black Priest (?)* |

It's unfortunate I can't help those who were close to me and now find themselves in danger. But where were they when their emperor's eyes were being plucked out? Asleep in their beds, fat and rich on the spoils of empire – that's where. Phaon sealed his own fate. He took bribes, extorted, embezzled. I turned a blind eye because he did as I asked and he was capable. If men are seeking revenge now that I'm gone, it's no fault of mine.

These random murderous outbursts have Marcus spooked. Phaon isn't the only man to be killed since my fall; nor will he be the last.

So long as the Hunchback remains absent from the city, and with Nymphidius pursuing his own ambitious ends, chaos will replace the rule of law. It will be the same as when a city is sacked: no one is watching, so do as you'd like. But what can I tell the boy other than to keep his head down and avoid it as best he can.

The latest news is that the Hunchback is now in Gaul, killing whomever he pleases and solidifying his position. Meanwhile, my pain lessens and my strength grows. Hopefully, I will be ready by the time Galba comes to Rome.

# MARCUS

*3 October, first torch*
*The home of Proculus Creon, Rome*

Belly and Mole are visiting Master. They're sitting with him under the colonnade. Belly brought mead. They have been drinking for hours. Usually they'd be drunk by this time, but not today. Today they're quieter.

Belly and Mole aren't their real names. I don't know their real names. I call Belly 'Belly' because he's so fat his belly sinks between his knees. And I call Mole 'Mole' because he has a brown mole on his cheek the size of my thumb. It's round like a hill, with three thick hairs that stick straight out and wobble when he moves. Belly and Mole are merchant freedman, like Master Creon.

'Mad as a Thracian,' Mole says. 'I always knew it.'

'You didn't,' Belly says.

'I did!' Mole says. 'I told you more than a month ago: Nymphidius thinks he's Caesar.'

'You didn't!' Belly says again.

Master says, 'Hold on, hold on. You may have said that, but you didn't know *this* would happen. Did you?'

Mole says, 'I had an idea.'

'Like hell!' Belly says.

Master looks over to me and Socrates who are standing with the pitchers of mead. 'Marcus, get us some more olives. And tell Elsie to cook something, for fuck's sake.'

I go to the kitchen, tell Elsie what Master said, fill a bowl with olives, and go back outside.

'Do you think it was true?' Mole asks. 'Do you think Caligula was his father? His mother *was* a slave in the palace.'

Master says, 'Doesn't matter whether it's true or not. How many slaves do you think Tiberius or Claudius conferred children on? You could fill the circus with them. Even Augustus – a prude by all accounts – even *he* had little Octavians running around the city. But none of them could ever be emperor. They were born to a slave for the love of Jove.'

Mole shakes his head. 'Mad as a Thracian.'

'Still,' Belly, says, 'his men turned on him awful quick. Cut his throat in the blink of an eye.'

'Those Praetorians are cold-blooded,' Master says. 'I heard it was his centurion that gave him up. Stole Nymphidius's letters and told the whole camp what he'd planned. Man by the name of Terentius . . .'

My heart jumps up into my throat when I hear the Fox's name.

'. . . he's named himself prefect in Nymphidius's place. The other prefect, Tigellinus, is still missing.'

Mole says, 'I'm not sure I blame them. The Hunchback has been cutting disobedient throats in the provinces. What's he going to do when he gets to Rome and sees the head of the Praetorians saying he's Caligula's love child and *he* should be emperor? Galba would've killed Nymphidius and anyone he thought was with him. No, I can't say I blame them. I'd've done the same.'

Later in the evening, when they are eating dinner alone, Master says to Mistress, 'Otho will be adopted by Galba once he gets to Rome. And then Otho will be the next in line for the purple. Then the principate will owe me – *me!* – a cool million sesterces. We will be set for life, my dear. Any appointment, any business venture – anything we want, will be ours.'

Mistress is doubtful like she always is. 'And how do you know Galba will adopt Otho. How do you know? I've heard there are other candidates.'

Master snarls. 'Who? Who is being considered?'

'I heard it will be one of the Pisos.'

Master laughs. Crumbs fly from his mouth. 'One of the Pisos? Please, my dear!' He puts his hand up like he is being attacked. 'Please stop turning your mind to the world of men. You have no conception of politics, of Rome in its eight hundred and . . . in its current year. Those old families are just that: *old*. They are relics, ancient and dusty and dying. The senate will be rejuvenated with men like Otho, with families from Beneventum, Ferentum. Families from the Sabine hills. And while those men move up to the senate, who will fill the classes below?' He points at himself. 'Entrepreneurs. Men of Minerva, like your dear husband.'

I try to remember all these names. Otho, Piso, Galba the Hunchback. I keep saying the names, so I can remember tomorrow. Otho, Piso, Galba.

Otho, Piso, Galba.

Otho, Piso, Galba.

# NERO

◆

*4 October, afternoon*
*City jail IV, Rome*

Today Marcus brings more news. He's becoming quite the little spy. And his Master's precocious participation in politics has proven useful.

Nymphidius is dead. He was clearly involved in my downfall. But he is gone and therefore unable to atone for his crime. So I am crossing him off the list.

| *Guilty* | *Guilt unknown* |
|---|---|
| *Terentius (centurion)* | *Epaphroditus (chamberlain)* |
| *Venus (soldier)* | ~~*Phaon (chamberlain)*~~ |
| *Juno (soldier)* | *Spiculus (bodyguard)* |
| ~~*Nympidius (Praetorian prefect)*~~ | *Tigellinus (Praetorian prefect)* |
| | *Galba (False Emperor)* |
| | *Otho (covets the throne)* |
| | *The Black Priest (?)* |

This man Terentius – the one Marcus calls the Fox – is more treacherous than I'd imagined. We must be cautious. Clearly he believes there is value in keeping me alive. But once his opinion changes, he will act swiftly.

Doryphorus has news as well: he has learned where Tigellinus is holed up. He was once the most hated man in Rome; so the mere fact that he's alive points to complicity in the coup. But I cannot be certain. I must speak with him. I want to look him in the eye – so to speak.

Answers will come. In the meantime, we wait.

# MARCUS

♦

*7 October, afternoon*
*City jail IV, Rome*

We're in the middle of a lesson when *he* comes in. The Fox.

I haven't seen him since I snuck into the palace. He walks into the room slowly. He's holding his helmet at his hip and his armour makes a rattling *clink-clink-clink* with each step.

Doryphorus whispers under his breath, 'Terentius,' so Nero can hear.

The Fox is smiling, but it's a strange, unhappy smile. Another soldier – the one Nero calls Venus – waits by the door. The Fox comes to a stop outside the cell. The door is wide open. I'm sitting cross-legged on the floor. Nero and Doryphorus are on the bench.

The Fox sees me and sneers. 'You do have a passion for slumming it, don't you, Nero?' He clasps his hand on the cell door and moves it back and forth. The rusty hinges *screeeech*. He sees the amphorae of fish sauce and wine. 'Industrious, even without your eyes, I'll grant you that. But you've taken the freedom I've allowed a bit far, haven't you? What's next? Bludgeon the guards outside and retake the throne?'

'Oh, I wouldn't worry,' Nero says. 'My ambition left with my eyes. Maybe you inherited it?'

The Fox sneers. He looks at Doryphorus. 'You do keep yourself informed here, don't you? I suppose you've heard I'm prefect now. What of it? I didn't hasten Nymphidius's demise. He did that himself. I had nothing to do with his decision to claim he was Caligula's love child. I didn't make him lust after the purple.'

The Fox notices the wax tablet in my hands. 'Lessons?' he asks. '*What* on the gods' green earth could you wish to teach some frightened slave boy?'

Nero says, 'Slave? I see no slave.'

The Fox frowns. 'Your lack of eyesight notwithstanding: a slave is a slave. Teach him what you want. He will remain a slave or, at best, a freedman. Your efforts won't change that.'

'I disagree,' Nero says. 'I have a pupil named Marcus. He has an aptitude. He absorbs information like a sponge. I know of no slave.'

This isn't true. It takes me for ever to learn anything. And I'm a slave. That's obvious. I don't know why Nero said I'm not.

'He is chattel,' the Fox says. 'I can cut his throat to prove the point. I would be within the law, so long as I pay his master compensation for the loss.'

For a moment, no one speaks.

The Fox smiles. 'Yes, maybe I *will* do that. I will cut the boy's throat. Not today, but I will murder – no not murder, he is chattel after all – I will *ruin* a man's property. This will prove the point. Will it not?'

My heart is beating loudly now, faster and faster – so loud I think it might explode – and my legs feel flimsy.

Nero doesn't answer the Fox but instead speaks to me. 'Marcus, have we discussed an honourable death yet? Its constituent parts?' His voice is calm, like he's teaching a lesson. 'Every soldier will give you a slightly different definition, but the important distinction is this: wounds to the back show cowardice; wounds to the front, bravery. The reason is simple: a cut to the back shows whether you were running from your enemy or not. I raise this point now, Marcus, because, when the time comes, I hope your knife goes into this man's back and reveals the coward he is.'

No one speaks. My breath squinches up and stops. I think the Fox is going kill me right here and now.

But he laughs; he waves his hand. 'I see you lost your mind with your eyes. How far the mighty have fallen.' Then he turns to me. 'It appears, boy, a compact has been made, between you and I.' He's still smiling but his voice is hard. 'Good luck.'

I want to scream. I didn't say anything. I didn't threaten to stab him. I didn't call him a coward. But I clam up like I always do and the skin on my face starts to boil.

'We've paid you good money, Terentius,' Doryphorus says.

'Yes . . . yes, you have. And I've given you generous allowances – allowances I can take away at my leisure. Remember that,' the Fox says. 'But I didn't come here to scare a slave. I came for information.'

The Fox looks around the room and sees the stool. He fetches it and places it outside the cell. He sits.

'Your holdings, personal and the Imperial treasury, which I gather are one and the same, will soon be seized by the Hunchback, if they haven't already. The Praetorians expect Galba to provide a bonus for ousting you, the bonus Nymphidius promised. I am sceptical. From what I hear, the Hunchback is difficult, the what-have-you-done-for-me-lately type. I knew a man who served under him in Gaul. He said initiative was punished as come-uppity, while loyalty and hard work were not rewarded but considered the execution of duty. I have no interest in taking orders from such a man, and I doubt very much he will provide any bonus, let alone the figure promised by Nymphidius.'

The Fox keeps chewing on his lip.

'As I said, the Imperial holdings are to be seized by Galba. I cannot benefit. But there is talk . . . of Dido's treasure.'

'Those are only rumours,' Doryphorus says.

'More than rumours,' the Fox says. 'You sent an expedition to Carthage to find it. They acted on bad information, a mistake when unravelling the cypher. But you discovered the error. You cracked the cypher.'

'Quite the tale,' Nero says.

'There's no point denying it,' the Fox says. 'The night we questioned you, you were reluctant to divulge what you knew, even after we took your eyes. Ever since, I have been hunting down your former courtiers, torturing or bribing them, and slowly learning the truth. The world thought your quest for Dido's fortune was pure vanity and a failure. But I know you cracked the cypher.'

Nero shakes his head. 'I'm sorry to disappoint.'

'I'm making you an offer, Nero,' the Fox says. 'I cut your eyes out. So what? You're alive, aren't you? That's a better spot than most would have left you in. We were paid to kill you, but we hedged our bets. We kept you alive, and I intend to profit from it. There's no point in fighting it. Let's make a deal. We scrounge up enough coin to leave Rome and go find that treasure of yours. We split it, down the middle. You can spend your remaining days in Greece. You'll get no better deal from Galba when the old man finally reaches Rome. Hell, if we are partners, I'll even give you the names of the men who betrayed you. I'm sure you're dying to know that.'

Nero pauses for a long while. 'There's no treasure,' he says at last. 'Or if there is one, I don't know where it is. Everyone knows I had people looking into it. But nothing came of it. People talk and will think what they want to think. But, I'm sorry to say, there is no ancient Carthiginian treasure I'm holding on to.'

The Fox shrugs. 'There's no rush. I'm now the only one who knows you're alive,' he says. 'This is your only option. You'll come to your senses soon enough.'

With that, the Fox and the other soldier leave.

When we are alone again, Dorpyhorus says to Nero, 'He's right, you know. His offer – it's our only option.'

Nero doesn't answer. Instead, he puts a piece of bread in his mouth and starts to chew.

# NERO

◆

*8 October, depth of night*
*City jail IV, Rome*

It will be a cold day in Elysium before I give the man who cut out my eyes half of Dido's treasure. I didn't obsess over the cipher for years, consumed by the mystery, night after night, only to see another man profit from it in the end. Anyway, I'm not even sure if I cracked the code. The epiphany came only weeks before the coup, so I didn't have time to confirm whether my conclusions were correct. And I'm not sure how word got around. I must have bragged in the middle of some drunken stupor, and now Terentius thinks it incontrovertible fact. Thankfully, weeks before my fall, gripped by paranoia, I committed the details to memory and then burned the cipher and all of the work I did to unlock it. So Terentius needs me. Doryphorus thinks he is our only chance to escape this prison and Rome. But I disagree. We do not need to give in. Not yet. Anyway, even a painful death would be more enjoyable than making that bastard a rich man.

Stories continue to swirl like sparrows. A new, particularly damning rumour is beginning to take root. Some are now claiming on the night I was taken, I ran from the city and took shelter in Phaon's villa with a gaggle of friends. (How convenient that the owner of said villa is now dead.) There – after I had decided all was lost but couldn't muster the courage to raise a blade – I had a friend cut my own throat. Epaphroditus.

My former freedman has now moved to the top of the list. No friend of mine would allow his name to be used in such a way. No friend of mine would let such lies circulate unanswered.

Doryphorus says the man is in hiding. He fears reprisals of the kind Phaon faced, for the wrongs he did while I ruled.

I was angry when Doryphorus told me. I know lies are part and parcel of Roman politics, and this type of rumour is to be expected. So why then did I erupt like Mount Etna when I heard this particular claim? Is it because the story somehow has a strand of truth? I too raised a sharp edge to my throat and contemplated death, but ultimately pulled back. Am I, like the Nero at Phaon's villa, a coward as well?

I have pondered this question all evening and come to the following conclusion: no, I am not a coward; I am simply not as Roman as I could be. My temperament has always been more Greek than Roman. To me, death is not all; I think it stupid to forgo life unnecessarily. My cock does not get hard when I hear the stories of Roman bravery every young boy is told. Stories such as the soldier travelling to Carthage to die by torture because he promised to. I have always thought: run, you idiot.

I'm not afraid to die. It's only that my priorities are different. First I seek revenge. That, at least, is very Roman of me.

Galba is a week away. Doryphorus and I have devised a plan, a way to escape, but it is too soon to carry out, and I am still too weak to travel. Can we wait until after Galba arrives in Rome? Terentius wants Dido's treasure, so he will keep me alive for the time being. Or am I wrong and Galba's executioners will soon be at my door?

Time will tell.

# MARCUS

*8 January, A.D. 69, sunset*
*The Quirinal Hill, Rome*

Galba arrived in Rome three months ago and the city already hates him. He's old and mean and decimated marines after they asked him for the coin Nymphidius had promised them. I didn't know what decimation was before Nero told me. Lots are drawn by an entire legion and one out of every ten men is killed. I didn't leave Master Creon's for two days afterwards because I was worried something might happen, like after Nero fell and people fought in the streets. But nothing's happened – not yet at least. Nero thinks it's only a matter of time before senators or the army move against Galba. 'They're missing me,' Nero said, 'and who can blame them.'

Nothing has changed since Galba came. I keep going to Nero every day, taking my lessons. I was worried Master would ask why Galba – who he thinks bought me – hasn't sent for me to come live at the palace. But Master doesn't care about anything other than wine and coin.

This morning Master said, 'You are coming with me to dinner.' But it's not until we are walking through the cold, dusty streets, as the sun is setting, with our cloaks wrapped twice around us that I learn we are going to Otho's.

'I'm in a tough spot here, Marcus,' he says as we're walking. 'You're Imperial property now. No one is to touch you. You heard it straight from the horse's mouth, like I did. But we're attending the home of one of Rome's most powerful men. And Otho has shown an interest in you, and he is a man used to getting what he wants.'

He says Otho's name and I think of the way he held my chin; my skin crawls.

Master keeps talking. 'We are to discuss business, he and I, but you never know. He may see you and remember what Galba stole away.

He may think, Who will know? And Marcus, you know, I am partial to that argument. If he does want to try what was taken away . . . why, the only way anyone will know is if you tell them. Otho will likely be emperor one day. This is a good opportunity for us both.'

Master stops walking. He bends down and looks me in the eye.

'Who knows what will happen tonight?' he says as he claws at my shoulder, digging in with his nails. 'But if you screw this up for me, I will grind your bones into a white slurry and sup on it for dinner. Understand?' He smiles, but he isn't happy.

He doesn't say anything the rest of the way.

At dinner, Master sits beside Otho. I stand close enough to hear them talk.

'Your funds have been most useful, Creon,' Otho says. 'Most useful indeed.'

'The soldiers were not reluctant, sir,' Master says. 'They required little encouragement to follow you.'

'Yes,' Otho says, 'I'm not surprised. The Hunchback has proven himself quite inept. Not only cruel – I don't need to list for you the needless deaths – but also his choice of heir. The Empire knows the younger Piso is a disastrous choice. If he had chosen me, if he had accepted my guidance these last few months in Rome . . .' He waves his hand. 'No matter. This is all in the past. Our path is set.'

'Yes, of course,' Master says. 'The city is behind you. But . . . May I ask? Are you . . .'

Otho sighs. 'Out with it, Creon. What are you concerned about?'

'What about the legions in the north?'

Otho makes a noise with his tongue: *tsk-tsk-tsk*. 'You mean the legions who refused to take the oath of allegiance to Galba, but have instead said they are at the disposal of the Roman people? Clearly they will fall into line once Galba is gone. Their refusal to swear the oath is further evidence we are in the right moving against Galba. The commander in upper Germany is a great friend of mine. And the commander in lower Germany – Vitellius's boy – he is more interested in banquets and orgies than raising a problem for Rome. Do you know it took him two months to travel north to his post after he was appointed in November? I suppose when you banquet four times a day and debauch a virgin at least once, you move at a snail's pace.'

Master waves his hand and I come over with a pitcher of wine. As I'm pouring, Otho notices me for the first time tonight.

'Ah,' he says. 'You've brought me young Marcus.' He looks at me even though he's talking to Master. My skin crawls. 'You are sly, Creon. Very sly. I can't recall what happened with my purchasing him before, but no matter. Leave him here tonight, will you? We can haggle the price another time. I will be generous.'

When Master nods, I want to retch.

Otho's voice gets quiet again. 'We will proceed in three days. There is a sacrifice to take place at the Temple of Apollo on the Palatine. I will need to attend; but I will make an excuse as to why I must leave. Then I will rush to the Praetorian camp where – if you have done your job and the money we have collected has done the trick – I am to be proclaimed emperor. The marines Galba decimated in October will escort me from door to door. Then we will find Galba – wherever he happens to be – and kill him.'

'What about the younger Piso?' Master Creon asks. 'Galba's heir.'

'Oh, he will have to die as well. The dullard.'

I feel sick near the end of dinner. Every time Otho laughs, my legs wobble and my head swims. I remember what Nero told me when Otho almost bought me from Master. 'Worn as the Appian Way,' he said.

Master Creon walks to the door. I follow behind with watery legs.

Otho says, 'Send me the bill for the boy tomorrow. Yes?'

'I would be remiss not to say the Imperial palace – Galba, I think – currently has the boy on loan.'

'What?' Otho asks.

'I'd explained this to your freedman in August.' Master's voice sounds like when he's telling tenants they have to pay more rent. 'You see Galba – or one of Galba's men – has paid for the boy to visit the palace every day. I am contractually bound not to lend him out or let another lay a hand on him.' He pauses, then says: 'Contracts, of course, can be broken for the right price.'

'You're born for business, aren't you, Creon,' Otho says. 'If he's Galba's boy right now, I don't want to rock the boat, as it were, not until he is gone and the purple mine.' He looks at me and says, 'I will claim my prize after I am emperor.'

Master grumbles all the way home. I make sure he doesn't see me smile.

The next day I tell Nero and Doryphorus everything I heard at Otho's. They talk about it all morning. 'This is our chance,' Doryphorus says to Nero, again and again. 'When the attempt is made on Galba's life, the city will be chaotic.' But Nero says he's not sure if the time is right – whatever that means.

Later, in the afternoon, after my lesson is over and I'm sweeping out the cells, the door opens and Icelus walks in.

I almost didn't recognise him. He looks better than when I saw him last. When he was a prisoner his tunic was torn and his beard mangy. But now he's wearing a fresh red tunic – silk, I think – with gold stitching, and matching pants like the northerners wear, and his face is shaved smooth. But he's still as wide as I remember, like an ox with his swishing steps.

He sees me and smiles. 'Afternoon, pup. What've you brought me today?'

I'm too surprised to say anything. I never thought I'd see him again.

Icelus walks towards me. He says, 'As talkative as ever, I see.' He slaps my shoulder. 'Well, good to see you all the same.'

'And who are you?' Doryphorus asks.

'Icelus.'

'Galba's freedman?' Doryphorus looks at Nero. 'So Galba knows . . .'

'Now, why would I tell him something like that?' Icelus picks up the stool and places it outside the cell. He sits. 'You can't go assaulting the principate with information. Otherwise, they'll drown in facts.' Icelus produces an apple and starts polishing it on his tunic. He takes a horse-size bite. He starts chewing and, with a full mouth, says, 'I think the prefect, Nymphidius, planned on bringing Nero here to Galba's attention. He thought he could profit from it. How is anyone's guess. Galba is not really one to negotiate. But I decided *not* to tell Galba and now the point is moot. Nymphidius is no more.'

Icelus swallows. *Gulp.*

'It took me ages to find this place again.' Icelus says. 'Blindfolded when I arrived, blindfolded when I left. But I have my ways.'

He takes another bite of his apple. He looks at me suddenly. He says, 'Feels like old times, doesn't it, pup? You and me. Here.'

He winks at me. The wet-swirly sound of his chewing fills the room. *Chomp chomp chomp.*

To Nero, he says, 'Galba is Emperor, but the city is not what I would call content. I'm feeling a bit restless myself. I haven't decided what I'm going to do with –' he waves his hand at Nero and his cell '– all this; whether I tell my prickly patron or not. Now, before you go offering suggestions, I've actually got one of my own. Something that would make my decision easy.'

Icelus takes another huge bite from his apple. After three bites, only the core is left.

'Dido's treasure,' he says. 'You've got it. I want it. A deal can be made there, I think.' He turns to look at me, and winks. 'Cunts and coin, eh, pup?'

Doryphorus starts to say something but Icelus cuts him off.

'This is where you protest like a virgin that wants it. "Not me! Not me!" And then I beg and plead, and I console, and I make you feel warm and cosy. "I'll take care of you," et cetera, et cetera. And then finally you relent, like you weren't going to in the first place, like you had a choice. Let's skip all that. I know you know where Dido's treasure is. I want it. Let's make a deal.'

Icelus stands up.

'I don't need an answer today. You're my contingency. My alternative plan if things with Galba go south. You've got time to think about it. But not a lifetime.'

With that, Icelus walks out.

The next morning, Doryphorus visits Master Creon's home before breakfast. He's waiting for me in the atrium. Elsie brings me to him. She stands and watches, with her arms crossed.

'We leave tomorrow,' Doryphorus says. His voice is low enough that Elsie can't hear. But she's frowning anyway. 'Nero asks that you accompany us.'

'Go? Where?' I ask.

'That's not for you to worry about, boy. If you choose to come, meet us by the river, at the docks of Scipio. We go by barge to the sea. If you aren't there, we go without you. We don't have enough coin at the moment to buy you out from Creon. So you'll need to slip out on your own.'

If I get caught running away, I'll be crucified. I've seen them do it to slaves. They stick you up on a post and leave you to rot, or stab you in the guts. Doryphorus guesses what I'm thinking.

'If you're a coward: fine. Stay here with your abusive master. It's all the same to me. Our barge leaves at sunset. Be there or don't. It's up to you.'

Doryphorus leaves and Elsie comes over to me. She says, 'What did he say?'

I tell her what Doryphorus said. Elsie pulls me close and squeezes me tight.

'I'm going to miss you, child.'

'I can't go, Elsie. I can't . . .'

'You must,' she says. 'There is nothing for you here. You must.'

I start to cry.

# XII

## Dinner at Ulpius's, Part I
### A.D. 79

# TITUS

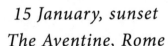

*15 January, sunset*
*The Aventine, Rome*

Ulpius has taken over Piso's old house on the Aventine, a behemoth of white stone from the days of the republic. After Piso was killed, another man – what was his name? Galarius? – occupied it for a few years before going bankrupt and killing himself. Now the property is considered bad luck, but I suppose that's not something a new man from Spain would know before putting his money down.

Ulpius. He's created quite the fuss since his arrival. Domitilla wasn't the only one who received an elaborate invitation to dinner. Expensive gifts were presented to many of the capital's great matrons. Tongues have been wagging ever since, opining on his origin, estimating the size of his coffers. We've had Spanish imports before, but none have captivated the city's attention like this.

'Shall I check ahead, sir?'

Ptolemy is beside me. Praetorians flank us, three a side, each with a torch lighting up the evening's twilight. Ptolemy wants to go ahead and ensure I'm not *too* early: Caesar's eldest son can't be the first to arrive. It's good having a slave who acts the snob. It allows you to pretend such things don't concern you.

'No, no. That's fine. Let's press on.'

The street outside is dotted with slaves conversing; empty litters sit side-by-side, like ships along a quay. I signal four Praetorians to wait out front. The remaining two follow Ptolemy and me up the walk.

The front door is elm, four men wide, with a bronze lion gripping a ring in its mouth. Before we've ascended the steps, the door opens revealing the plump little Parthian, Cyrus. When, I wonder, does he apply that black gunk around his eyes? Does he take it off at night? Or does he wear it permanently, like a tattoo?

Inside, the atrium is awash with silk and Canusian wool, sage green, pomegranate red, Aegean blue; golden bracelets *clink* as the upper crust of Rome gesture and point; conversations swing between friendly banter and teasing chuckles; oil lamps waver and hiss; and the smell of roasting boar, rosemary and lemon peel spawns a ravenous growl from my stomach.

'Titus Flavius Vespasianus,' Cyrus whirls his arm. 'Allow me to introduce your host, senator Lucius Ulpius Traianus.'

I follow the swing of Cyrus' arm to a man, bent over a walking stick, with a thick beard, equal parts grey and copper, and a rag tied across his eyes. For once, it seems, the rumours were true: Ulpius is blind. His age is difficult to place. He could be anywhere from forty to somewhere in his sixties. He looks old – old or he's lived a hard life.

'May I also introduce the senator's nephew, Marcus Ulpius.'

Cyrus points at a boy, seventeen or so, standing beside the elder Ulpius.

Neighbouring eyes watch intently as I meet our mysterious host.

'We are glad you could join us, Titus,' Ulpius says.

I nod, acknowledging the comment. 'Senator, is it? I thought I had met every senator.'

'Maybe now you have.'

'You've come from Spain?'

'Yes, from Spain.'

The boy surveys the crowd. Is he bored? He's meeting the Emperor's son and prefect of the Praetorian Guard, but by all appearances he is unimpressed, as though he has spent years in the presence of Caesar's house. Is this adolescence or something more sinister? Then again: is there anything more sinister than adolescence?

'Spain to Rome,' I say, 'a treacherous journey in winter.'

'Only when compared to the other seasons,' Ulpius replies.

Ptolemy clears his throat. He thinks the response impertinent. It was certainly odd, but I'm not sure if it offends me. Delicate questions begin to accumulate in my head. How did you lose your eyes? Where did your fortune come from? It is my business to know the answers, but now is not the time.

The Parthian springs to the door to open it for another guest. After Ptolemy helps me change into my dinner sandals, I take my leave so my host can continue his introductions.

I come upon Nerva and Secundus conversing at the other end of the atrium.

Nerva asks, 'And what does our great general make of Rome's newest senator?'

A lyre's silken notes drift in from the garden.

'I'm reserving judgement for now,' I say.

A slave hands me a cup of mulled wine.

'Eccentric though, isn't he?' Secundus asks.

I give a noncommittal shrug of my shoulders. In the garden beyond, I spot Domitilla's almond curls. Over the notes of a lyre, I hear Caecina's unruly laugh and I cannot help but frown.

'I don't understand the interest he's garnering.' Nerva says. 'A cripple.'

'Yet here we are,' I say. I nod my head at the tall, blue-eyed man, standing a few feet away. 'Is he new?'

'A Batavian.' Nerva smiles. 'You wouldn't believe the price I paid.'

'A Batavian?' Secundus is impressed. 'I hope you put him to work in the hunt or the gladiatorial matches. It'd be a shame to waste talent like that.'

'A dangerous breed,' I say, 'and stubborn. You'll have your work cut out for you.'

'I have my ways,' Nerva says. Then he asks, 'Is it true that your father intends to marry your sister to Marcellus?'

'Where did you hear that?' I ask, as unruffled as I can manage.

Nerva tips his head to the side, like a hawk watching from a bough. 'Oh, I hear many things. But this I found most disturbing. I worry whom Caesar aligns himself with. I worry he does not know who his true friends are.'

'Not to worry, Nerva,' I say. 'My father knows who is friend and who is foe.'

Secundus intervenes, astutely changing the subject. He relates an odd story, which happened moments before my arrival. Apparently, a merchant arrived with his wife and son, thinking they were invited guests. 'He was brimming with pride,' Secundus says, 'being invited to the same table as the Emperor's son. You could see it in the poor man's toothless grin. His name was Creon, if I heard properly. He and the Parthian Cyrus had a row the moment he arrived. The poor fellow raised his voice and held up a little roll of paper, claiming it was his invitation. The Parthian agreed the invitation bore his patron's seal, but said there must have been a mistake, because he (the merchant) surely was not invited to dinner. The younger Ulpius boy came over and inspected the invitation. He said, "I think you've been had, sir," and then peeled back the corner until he had two sheets of paper. "Someone has played a trick on you. We merely ordered linen from your fullery. That is what carried our family's seal." Someone pasted an invitation into the order for the fullery, a fake invitation. You should have seen the look on that man Creon's face as he realised he'd been made a fool. Very pathetic. He walked out without another word, unable to meet the eye of anyone, even the Parthian.'

'An odd episode,' Nerva says. 'I suspect we are in for more.'

# DOMITILLA

◆

*15 January, after sunset*
*The home of Lucius Ulpius Traianus, Rome*

'How *is* your sister?'

Calpurnia, Caecina's young wife, puts her hand on my arm. Her golden bracelets clatter against her wrist.

'She's well,' I say. 'It's far warmer in Capri than here.'

'Yes but –' Calpurnia lowers her voice to a whisper '– how is she *really*?'

She leans in, waiting for me to reveal our family's secrets.

The lyre player resumes after a short intermission. Two dancing girls spin on the portico.

'Calpurnia.' Antonia, Plautius' wife, materialises from the crowd. She gives me a look: *I'm here to rescue you.* We used to be close, Antonia and I, when we were younger. But we lost touch when she moved east with Plautius. It's good to have her back in the capital.

Antonia says, 'What's the story then?'

'Oh, Antonia,' Calpurnia says, straightening up. 'I didn't see you there.'

'Come, come,' Antonia says. She looks over her shoulder to ensure no one is listening. 'Tell us how he lost his eyes. What have you heard? You always have the inside track.'

Calpurnia aims her gaze at the floor for a moment, feigning modesty. 'Oh, I don't know what you mean.'

'No need for modesty,' Antonia says. 'We're all friends.'

'Well –' Calpurnia drops her voice to a whisper '– I've heard he brought it on himself, really.' She raises an eyebrow, showing her disapproval of what she's about to divulge. 'In the little Spanish town he's from – Hispalis or whatever it is – he didn't have an equal. He was the smartest, and the richest, and the handsomest – which isn't hard, I'm sure, near the ends of the earth, but still . . . Every girl in town naturally wanted to marry the man, and every father bent over backwards trying to make the match. But Ulpius was a cad. He wouldn't take a wife. Instead, using the promise of marriage, he secretly seduced one girl after the next, until he'd had every girl in town. Well, when their fathers found out . . .' Calpurnia pauses to sip her wine, hoping to build suspense. 'They took his eyes as punishment; a mob of them stormed his home. All those Spanish tribes may be in the Empire now, but they act the barbarian when given an excuse. The governor tried to instil order afterwards. He made each man pay Ulpius compensation, which is why he's so rich now. I've heard Ulpius says it was worth it, bedding those women in exchange for his eyes. Can you imagine? The depravity?'

Gods, what rumours does this woman say about me when I'm not around?

'Is your source sound?' Antonia asks. She's making fun, but Calpurnia doesn't notice.

'Very. I heard it from Cluvius's wife. Her husband knows Spanish traders.'

'Well, depravity aside,' Antonia says, 'Ulpius sounds quite experienced, doesn't he?'

Calpurnia raises both eyebrows this time. 'Antonia!'

I put my hand to my mouth to supress a giggle. Seeing my reaction – the reaction of Caesar's daughter – Calpurnia forces herself to laugh. She says, 'He's a cripple, Antonia. Don't be wicked.'

Caecina corners me before dinner is served. He's wearing the barbarian trousers he always wears and his cheeks have a ruddy glow from the wine. But even with his strange outfit, meant to cause controversy, and his decision to drink too much so early in the night, he remains charming and charismatic as ever. Little wonder the people think he and Titus are constant rivals. Both are in their early forties, handsome, and experienced soldiers. The main difference is that Caecina still has the hair he did as a boy of twenty, thick waves that curl at the back of his neck. That and his father is not master of all.

'How is your sister?' he asks, smiling as he always does, with his eyes rather than his lips. He touches my arm, just above the elbow. It's a warm, slightly flirtatious gesture. Is he doing it with the hope that Titus is watching? He has always had a knack for annoying Titus.

'Vespasia is fine,' I say. 'Why do you ask?'

'Why do I ask?' he says. 'She lost her husband. No doubt Titus had his reasons, but it doesn't make it any less hard.'

'I suppose not,' I say. 'But she is doing very well. I thank you for your concern.'

'She is enjoying Capri then?'

'Word does travel fast, doesn't it? I didn't know her current location was public knowledge. Yes, she is enjoying the Bay of Naples. The weather has been much kinder than here. I may join her.'

'I was thinking of heading south myself.' Caecina smiles mischievously. 'We could travel together. You know what they say: strength in numbers.'

Now I am certain he thinks Titus is watching.

'Would your wife be accompanying you?' I ask. 'I had the pleasure of speaking with Calpurnia earlier this evening.'

Caecina laughs. He is slightly drunk and our banter is endlessly amusing to him. He holds his cup in the air and rattles it. 'I am running low, Augusta. If you will excuse me.'

# CALENUS

*15 January, after sunset*
*Outside the home of Lucius Ulpius Traianus, Rome*

So far the night's been duller than a Greek play. But instead of watching some actor cry about his lot in life, I've spent most of the evening out in the cold, looking after Nerva's litter, while neighbouring slaves and freedmen praise their patron's various and wide-ranging virtues. Beside me are the slaves of some Imperial secretary by the name of Epaphroditus. (What a name! You need to take a breath halfway through.) They talk about the man as though he'd conquered the world, from Spain to India and back again. But he's only a freedman whose sole job is balancing ledgers. Not one of them has pride beyond what they have for their master. That's the difference between them and me. I was my own man once, before circumstance brought me low.

I'd worried about coming tonight, that maybe one of Caesar's friends would spot me and know who I am. But Nerva told me I was giving myself too much credit. 'The only soldiers who will be in attendance are Titus and Caecina, and neither has any idea who Julius Calenus is.' Easy for him to say. He's not a deserter.

During the civil war, once Cremona fell and there was nothing left of it but smouldering ruins and bloodied bodies lining the streets, Vespasian's forces rounded up all of the men who'd opposed them, those that were still standing. Men were picked to take messages to the armies in Spain and Gaul, to say Vespasian had won and to try to dissuade them from opposing him. Most of the officers were dead so they picked at random. A Flavian commander pointed at me and said, 'You're going to Spain. If anyone asks, you're a tribune.' But I didn't go to Spain or deliver their message. I ran.

I headed back to my piss-poor village in Gaul to reclaim my wife, who, after months of civil war, didn't know if I was alive or dead. She saw me stroll in to town and all she said was, 'Good, I was beginning to miss you.' A month or two later she started to cough, and six weeks after that I lost her for good.

Ever since, I've worried someone will spot me, especially one of Vespasian's men who sent me on a task I never finished, and they'd name me deserter and then nail me to a cross. Nerva doesn't know what happened, but he's smart enough to know I did something I'm not proud of. He says, 'Calenus, your anonymity is why you're valuable to me. I can assure you, your name will not make the history books. I can't stress enough how unimportant you are.'

I suppose he's right. It was nearly ten years ago, after all. But my stomach will always twist when I see a Flavian. Maybe that's not sufficient punishment for a deserter, but it's a punishment all the same.

Later in the evening, a dozen slaves exit Ulpius's house. I recognise one from across the street; I couldn't miss him. Ulpius's thick, one-eyed freedman. The Big Buck.

They spread out, going from one group of attendants to the next. I watch the Big Buck go to Epaphroditus's slaves first. He hands them a skin of wine, which they pass from one man to the next. The Big Buck takes the skin back and hands it to a little boy, who then runs it inside the house.

When he's done, the Big Buck walks over to me.

'Calenus,' he says. 'I thought I might find you here.'

The little boy runs back with a fresh skin of wine. He hands it to the Big Buck.

'Wine?' he asks.

'Never said no before,' I say. I take a long, deep drink and then hand him back the skin. 'Your master is a good man. Most patricians don't think of the help outside.'

'Ulpius is very generous,' he says. 'But it was my idea. Take another.'

He hands me the skin and I take another long drink. The blend is white, I think; nice and crisp, not too sweet. This Ulpius really does have means. Even the wine he gives the slaves is top notch. I hand back the skin and say, 'I never did catch your name.'

'Theseus,' he says.

Over his shoulder, I see the patrician boy, Marcus, walking towards us. Marcus sees me and smiles. 'Good evening, Calenus. Do you have everything you need? The wine is agreeable?'

'Yes,' I say. 'Top notch.'

The three of us are conversing very civilly. Anyone watching would never guess we killed two men on the road to Ostia four days ago.

'Dinner will be served soon,' the boy says. 'We could bring you inside and you could eat with Theseus.'

'I'm fine out here,' I say. 'Nerva wouldn't like it.'

He looks at Epaphroditus's slaves for a moment. Then to the Big Buck, he says, 'How goes it out here?'

'We're all done.'

'Good,' the boy says.

They head back inside, leaving me out in the cold, bored and hungry.

# TITUS

## 15 January, sunset
## The home of Lucius Ulpius Traianus, Rome

As the party slowly makes its way from the atrium and garden to the dinner table, Epaphroditus pulls me aside. Despite the occasion, he is dressed as he always is, sombrely, all in black. His dark goatee dangles like a dagger from his chin.

'I tracked your man.'

'Vettius?' I ask. 'The Pompeian knight? You found him.'

'Not exactly.' Epaphroditus snaps his fingers; a slave darts to his side and begins to whisper in his ear.

I look to my side and Ptolemy is there, stylus in his right hand, wax tablet in his left, ready to record. From where he conjured up these items, I don't know. But the boy has been with me long enough to know I may expectantly need a conversation recorded, even at a dinner party on the Aventine.

With his slave still whispering in his ear, Epaphroditus says, 'His name is Gaius Vettius. A knight from Pompeii. A gardener by trade, specialising in trees. Mainly, fig and pear.' The exchequer waves his hand. 'Yes, yes,' he snaps at his slave, 'I know the last bit.' The slave steps back and Epaphroditus says, 'Apparently this Vettius character has been missing since December. Three days before the Ides.'

'Missing?' I say, 'How do you know this?'

'One of my clerks knows a local aedile. He knew Vettius and pointed us in the direction of Vettius's former business partner,' the exchequer says. 'This is all my men could find. I trust this is helpful.'

What am I to do with this information? A local Pompeian gardener is missing. What does this have to do with Plautius? Each day I accumulate more questions than answers.

'Keep looking,' I say. 'If your men learn anything else, tell me immediately.'

# DOMITILLA

◆

*15 January, after sunset*
*The home of Lucius Ulpius Traianus, Rome*

The triclineum opens out onto the garden. It's a large, open room with three square tables surrounded by couches. On one wall there is a painting of a man in black armour standing on a chariot, which is dragging another man, naked and bloodied, with his arms splayed above his head. Achilles and Hector. Proud Achilles is staring straight ahead, his head held high. His horses – equally as proud – are as black as his armour. In the background, atop Troy's walls, a woman is wailing. Hector's widow, Andromache. The picture strikes me as very Roman: war and the men who fight it are pushed to the fore; the grief-stricken wife is acknowledged, but relegated to the background. I imagine the senator instructing the painter, holding up his hand, pinching the air with his thumb and index finger. 'Make the wife no bigger than this, please.'

I'm seated at Ulpius's table. He has given Titus the honour of the seat beside him, and I'm seated next to Titus. Secundus, Epaphroditus, the younger Ulpius (Marcus, I think, is his name), and old Graecina share our table. So too does the recently widowed Lepida. She continues to hide her blonde hair under a black shawl of mourning, which stands in contrast to her mischievous smile and constant banter. The remaining two tables are filled with senators, their wives, and Imperial staff. There is one empty seat, meant, I'm told, for Senator Marcellus. It seems my future husband decided to snub Ulpius's invitation.

Nerva's newest slave is a handsome, blue-eyed barbarian. He stands behind his patron at dinner. From the moment we sit down, I can feel his eyes on me. At first the attention is welcome – sometimes I worry I've grown too old to turn heads, that I've turned into the Widow, as some call me behind my back. But he persists to the point where it becomes inappropriate. When I meet his gaze, his eyes don't fall to the floor as they should. Instead, he smiles. Embarrassed, I immediately look away, hoping no one had witnessed the interaction or my smouldering cheeks.

The first course is Ferentum leeks, steeped in mint and hard-boiled eggs, topped with a relish of Danubian sea urchins. It's served with Falernian wine, a vintage, according to Ulpius, of thirty years.

The dinner, the decorations, the home itself – it is all tastefully done. I had expected this new, very rich man to throw a boorish party, but it's nothing of the kind.

'Tell us, Titus,' Lepida asks. 'What is the latest from Gaul?'

At the next table, Caecina is laughing boisterously.

Titus bites an egg in two. It feels an eternity since I last saw him out of his armour, relaxed and enjoying a meal. He says, 'Nothing beyond what was announced in the forum today. Sabinus, the Lingonian rebel the world thought dead, has been living in secret in Gaul.'

'What will happen to him?' Antonia asks.

'He will be executed,' Titus says.

Cyrus is standing behind Ulpius. He constantly leans down and whispers in his master's ear. I wonder whether he describing the conversation to Ulpius, telling him who spoke.

Antonia says, 'I have heard his wife hid him in an underground chamber, and she protected him, and now, after he was discovered and arrested, she sits outside the city jail where he is being held, night and day.'

I have heard this as well. I cannot escape the image: a miserable middle-aged woman, crouched in the snow, clothed in black, wailing for her husband. A barbarian Andromache.

While I find it affecting, Lepida laughs. She cannot fathom such devotion. How long did she wait to seduce Nero after her husband, Caius Cassius, was banished? A few days? A week?

Secundus chimes in. 'Rumour, my dear, pure rumour. We know little beyond what Titus has said. I'm sure this woman, Eponine, has already found another bed to keep her warm at night.'

'I think it romantic,' I say.

I can sense Titus tighten up, like a cat when a hound walks into the room. He doesn't want Caesar's daughter sympathising with a rebel. 'It was an act of treason,' he says.

Ulpius – for the first time – speaks. 'Can't it be both? Treasonous and romantic?'

Our mysterious host captivates the room; all other conversations fizzle.

Titus's response is short, both in content and tone. 'No,' he says, 'it cannot be both.'

The room watches Ulpius closely, but he is oblivious to the attention. He says, 'Caesar has spoken,' and leisurely sips his drink. Then he asks, 'Tell me, Titus, is there more news from Thrace, of the False Nero?'

'Nothing recent,' Titus says.

My left arm begins to tingle. I shift my weight from one elbow to the next and, with my newly freed but tingling arm, I reach for an olive.

Ulpius says, 'It's fascinating, isn't it, these men who claim to be Nero?'

Epaphroditus is keen to involve himself in the conversation. He says, 'The lower classes are mad, no better than animals. Little wonder they pine for the tyrant.'

Ulpius smiles. 'Come, there must be more to it than that. There were no imposters after Claudius or Caligula. There were none after Augustus. Yet there have been – how many? Three? Three men who claim they are Nero. And every time inspired followers have flocked to the name.' He takes another leisurely sip of wine, as though he is at the races. 'Surely, the explanation is not simply the lower classes are mad.'

Epaphroditus's cheeks, normally a sickly grey, flush with pink. He thinks Ulpius's response disrespectful. As one of Caesar's closest advisers, he is not used to being questioned by anyone but Caesar, let alone a fresh provincial. 'You say these men are inspired, do you?' he says. 'Treasonous talk, I'd say, especially for one newly come to Rome.'

I have no desire to see my host dragged away in chains after an idle comment. I draw a breath, about to intervene, when Titus puts his hand on my arm. I look to him, but his attention is on Ulpius, waiting to see how the man handles his sudden predicament. Our host, however, remains indifferent to the dangerous turn the night has taken.

'You are incorrect,' Ulpius says. 'Inspired merely means having a particular influence. The fact you've drawn more meaning from the word than the Latin allows is peculiar.' He nibbles at a watery leek. 'Very peculiar.'

Beside me, Titus snorts; he is amused. The tension in the room eases slightly. But Epaphroditus is not done. He says, 'The man was a villain.'

Ulpius shrugs. 'Aren't we all?'

It's now Titus's turn to get involved. 'You condone the tyrant's record?'

'No,' Ulpius says. 'I question the record itself. Its veracity.'

The room waits for Titus's response.

'I don't understand your point,' Titus says. 'Facts are facts.'

For a moment, through the marble wall, the sound of two slaves arguing – muffled, barely perceptible – is the only sound tempering the uncomfortable silence.

And then, perhaps tipped off by the smell, Ulpius says, 'Ah! The boar!' and every guest turns to watch three platters of wild boar paraded into the room. The platters are so heavy a slave is required at each end. 'Or should I say the boars,' Ulpius adds.

The room happily welcomes the distraction, and Ulpius is not asked to explain his odd comment.

Not long after the boar is served, the white-haired soldier my brother takes with him everywhere quietly enters the room. He walks up behind Titus and whispers in his ear. My brother frowns and then stands to go. He absently gives Ulpius his thanks, clearly forgetting the odd nature of their exchange, and leaves.

To my left, Lepida asks: 'And where is he off to at such an hour?'

The litter sways with the steps of palace slaves. Through silk curtains, the light of a dozen torches bleed together. Jacasta lies beside me. My head – light from the wine – rests on her arm. Her dry red hair tickles my cheek. She smells of rose petals and stale bread. The constant pitter-patter of slaves and Praetorians marching beside our litter sounds like rain.

'Where do you think your brother went?' Jacasta asks.

'He's been jealous of Ulpius since he arrived in Rome.' I say. 'Maybe he cooked the whole scene up to gain back the people's fascination.'

Jacasta asks, 'Do you think it concerned Plautius?' Her voice is earnest. It's possible she grew fond of Plautius during their time on Capri, when Plautius paid her to visit his room every night. I've always found Plautius unbearably ostentatious, but I think Jacasta thought him kind.

'I'm sure Plautius is alive and well.'

Our procession stops and the litter is gently lowered to the ground. A slave draws back the curtain and, taking my hand, helps me step out and onto the road. In the dark, the palace's white marble shines like the moon. Standing out front is my brother's white-haired soldier and two more Praetorians.

'Mistress,' he says, walking towards the litter. 'Titus has asked for your maid.' He points at Jacasta.

'Why?'

'Please, Mistress,' Virgilius says. 'He'd like her straight away.'

Jacasta follows the conversation, her head darting back and forth nervously.

I say, 'I will come as well.'

The soldier opens his mouth to say why this is not possible, but when he sees my resolve, he relents. 'Very well.'

Jacasta and I get back into the litter. This time the journey is far rougher, as the slaves rush to keep pace with Virgilius. Jacasta peeks out through the curtains to see where we are going. We pass the amphitheatre, still under construction, the forum, and then into the cattle market. The air is different this close to the Tiber, cooler, cleaner. We cross the square to a line of buildings. I can see Titus among dozens of Praetorians, his hands on his hips, watching our litter approach. He's changed into his armour again; his sword is strapped to his side.

Titus points at me once I'm out of the litter. 'You shouldn't have come.'

'What's this all about?' I ask.

Titus ignores the question. Virgilius whispers in his ear.

Across the square, the masts of moored ships sway in the river's current. Behind Titus, in front of a warehouse, two Praetorians stand on either side of a doorway. I notice for the first time a soldier a few paces from Titus, with a bucket of water. He's furiously scrubbing his hands together. His hands are stained a dark red.

'Is he all right?' Jacasta asks.

'Yes,' Titus says. 'He only slipped.'

'On what?'

He doesn't say.

'Titus, what is happening?' I ask. 'Why have you brought us here?'

'I need Jacasta,' he says. 'I need her to tell me if the man I've found is Plautius.'

'Can't you ask him?' Jacasta asks. 'The man you found.'

'No.' His voice is flat. He is the general, outlining the facts.

Jacasta's face is ashen.

'You know Plautius,' I say. 'Why do you need Jacasta?'

'I need someone who knows Plautius, intimately. I don't want to upset his wife. Not unnecessarily.'

Jacasta starts to shake. I put my arms around her.

'Where?' I ask.

Titus looks over his shoulder at the door flanked by soldiers. 'In there,' he says.

Titus takes Jacasta into the building, but insists I stay back. I watch as they disappear, descending into the darkness.

They are gone for what feels like an eternity. When they return, Titus is gently pulling Jacasta by the arm. Once on the street, Titus releases his grip and she falls to her knees. She retches out a watery, yellow mess. The bottoms of her bare feet are painted with a sticky crimson. I kneel beside her.

Panting, still trying to catch her breath, she says, 'It's not him.'

Titus is standing above us. To me, he says, 'The man down there has a birthmark; a purple splotch from his crotch to his navel. Jacasta says Plautius did not have such a mark.'

Jacasta tries to catch her breath.

'Thank you, Jacasta,' Titus says. 'You did well. You both did. Go home and rest.'

I want answers. I want to know what this strange, underground room is, and what has happened inside. But now is not the time. Titus is as disturbed as we are – more shaken than I have ever seen him. He will tell me when he is able. Now he needs to work, and I need to get Jacasta away from here.

We travel back to the palace in silence. Jacasta is rolled up into a ball beside me. I rub her back, offering what comfort I can.

For the second time tonight, our litter is placed at the foot of the palace steps. Jacasta and I step out and make our ascent. Once inside, walking down the wide, open halls, I can feel the night's events stalking my peace of mind. The hallways I've walked safely for years now feel menacing, as though danger lurks behind every corner.

In my room, we find braziers burning and lamps lit, awaiting my arrival. The room is empty – which is odd at this hour. Usually there are, at the very least, two slaves here to assist Jacasta.

Something is wrong.

'Mistress.'

Jacasta feels it too.

'Maybe we should ask for guards to wait at the door tonight?'

Then I see, sticking out from behind the bed, two legs, completely still; the balance of the body lost from view.

Jacasta grabs my arm; she screams.

She isn't looking at the legs behind the bed.

I turn to see a man, with a long beard and wild black hair. His menacing smile reveals yellow-black teeth and bloody gums.

He steps forward, a dagger in hand; blood drips from the blade.

# CALENUS

*15 January, first torch*
*Outside the home of Lucius Ulpius Traianus, Rome*

Theseus's wine was the best part of my night. After he and Marcus left, I stayed on the street, quietly waiting for the boredom to end. But there wasn't any relief when dinner was finally over. Nerva told me to stay.

'What do you want me to look for?' I asked.

'I don't know,' he said. 'Just watch. Tomorrow, tell me everything.'

And here I've stayed – sitting out in the cold for what feels like hours, with nothing yet to report – when Appius – Nerva's pudgy, snooty slave – comes running up the road. He's calling my name in those whispering-shouts people use when they're trying to be quiet and loud all at the same time. He can't see me until I step out of the alleyway.

'What do you want?'

'Nerva needs you.' He's sucking in big gulps of air, one after the next. I've never seen him run before. Whatever brought him here, it must be important.

'Where?'

'At the palace.'

I tell him to lead the way.

When I see Nerva waiting on the palace steps with a handful of Praetorians, I'm terrified I might be asked to go inside. I've never been inside the palace or even within a hundred yards of it. Nerva's home is the closest I've been to the murky patrician world. And the palace is a different pot of piss altogether. Not to mention it's filled with Flavians, men I fought against in Cremona before deserting and running north. An Auduan pleb and disgraced deserter should not enter the palace.

Nerva doesn't say hello or thank me for coming. He says, 'Come,' and turns and walks inside the palace. I pause on the threshold, with the eyes of half a dozen Praetorians on me.

Nerva turns back, annoyed. 'Hurry.' He starts walking again. I – the gods help me – follow.

Inside, the air is different. Flakes of gold dance in the air, swirling into my lungs with each breath. It's so thick I'll choke on it – cough and hack and suffocate until I'm dead. Then I notice the ceiling. In my apartment, I've got to duck when I move around. Here it's – I don't know how high. I've been to baths and temples with roofs like this before, but this is different. It makes me feel tiny, infinitely small, like I'm the lowliest person that ever snuck inside the palace walls, and the Emperor will have to crucify me in order to purify his home of marble. Only then, when I'm up on the cross, will he be able to scrape out the gold I hid away in my lungs.

'Stop it,' Nerva says. 'Whatever it is you're doing. It's impertinent. Keep your eyes and hands to yourself. And don't lag.'

We walk up a set of stairs. At the top, Nerva stops. He whispers so the guards can't hear, 'Translate in a way that favours me. Understand?'

He starts walking again, not waiting to hear that I haven't any idea what he means.

We enter a room with half a dozen Praetorians, two women huddled on a couch, and a dead, lifeless body near the door and another behind a bed ... A *bed*. Which means I'm in the bedroom of a member of the Imperial family. If Jupiter's lightning could fry me on the spot, I'd welcome it with open arms.

'Is this him?'

Titus – the Emperor's eldest son, prefect of the Praetorian Guard, the sacker of cities, the scourge of Jerusalem – is looking at me.

'Yes,' Nerva says. 'They've communicated before.'

'Good. Have him tell me what happened.' Titus points behind me. I turn to see the Batavian, sitting on the floor, with his back against the wall. Right in front of him is a dead body, face down, with blood pooling under its chest and belly. Somehow the Batavian looks relaxed, as though he's just sat down for dinner.

A Praetorian gives the Batavian a kick. The slave looks at the soldier, seizing him up, like he's about to cut his throat. But then he merely frowns and slowly gets to his feet.

Titus calls over the two women. When they get closer I see one of them is Domitilla, Caesar's daughter, who I've seen in the circus, from a distance. I recognise that almond hair, and the way she carries herself.

'Ask him,' Nerva says to me. 'Ask him what happened to this man.'

I ask the Batavian. He answers in stilted Cananefates. 'I kill.'

I translate, saying it loud enough for everyone to hear, 'He killed him.'

Caesar's daughter says, 'He saved my life.'

'Ask him why he's here,' Titus says. He looks tired and furious and ready to lay blame anywhere but at the feet of the dead man lying face down on the marble.

I ask the Batavian. He nods his head at Domitilla. 'Beautiful. Very.' He points at himself, 'I. Want.'

The crowd is hushed waiting for me to translate. Nerva looks like I'm holding his mother over a cliff. Meanwhile the Batavian is looking at Domitilla like a sad puppy. I notice for the first time her green stola is torn, at the shoulder and the hem, and her matching shawl is in pieces by the dead man.

'He says he heard a scream.'

Nerva exhales.

'And then what? He ran from Nerva's?' Titus doesn't believe a word. 'From the Quirinal to the Palatine?'

'He snuck out,' I say. 'To go for a walk. He'd never seen the palace before. A new slave to the city and all.'

Titus eyes me suspiciously. 'He told you that with all of four words, did he?'

Clearly, nothing gets past Caesar's son.

Three loud *whacks* echo along the walls and the room goes quiet. In walk ten lictors dressed in togas, white as German snow, carrying wooden rods over their shoulders. I know who's right behind them, so I drop to my knees, and bow my head to the mosaic-decorated floor. When I see the Emperor's boots, I close my eyes to wait for it to be over.

'Stop. Please rise. It's too late for such reverence.'

I can hear the rustle of people standing up, but I keep close to the marble: I'm not getting up without a personal invitation.

People start to talk.

'My dear, are you all right?'

'Yes, Father. I'm fine.'

'What happened?'

'Jacasta and I came back to the palace and a man was here, that man. We believe he killed two slaves and a soldier, and then waited for our return. When we arrived, he hit Jacasta, knocking her to the floor, and then he grabbed me by the hair, tore my dress, and was about to kill me . . . or worse. Then this man appeared. This slave. He saved my life.'

I keep my eyes squeezed shut.

'And you, my tall, blue-eyed friend. Who owns you?'

'I do, Caesar.'

'Well, Nerva, I owe you a debt of gratitude. You shall receive a generous gift.'

'Father, there is more to the story than this. This slave didn't just appear –'

'Titus, stop. Your scepticism is usually appreciated, but when the gods send a man to save the emperor's daughter, it is not for us to examine the details.'

'Yes, Father.'

'And what is this? Another dead body?'

After a moment of quiet, I feel Nerva's hot breath in my ear. 'Rise, Calenus. You're embarrassing me.'

I stand up. Caesar, Caesar's son and Caesar's daughter are all staring at me. Caesar's looking at me like I'd just sneezed on his breakfast. He says, 'You're a bit long in the tooth not to know what "rise" means, wouldn't you agree?'

I look around to see who he's talking to. When I realise it's me, I don't exactly piss myself, but I can feel white-hot fear creep to the edge of my cock.

Caesar says to Nerva, 'Is this one yours?'

'Yes, Caesar.'

'Well, I hope you don't need him to talk. Otherwise you didn't get your money's worth. Whatever you paid.'

On the walk back to Nerva's, the streets are empty except for a few carts making their deliveries. I'm beside Nerva. The Batavian is walking behind us with Appius.

'Well,' Nerva asks. 'What did he say?'

'You don't want to know.'

'I can hazard a guess. I saw the way he looked at her.'

I look back at the Batavian. I see a small patch of green fabric in his hand. Gods, the man is mad as a sack of eels. He's taken a piece of Domitilla's shawl as a prize.

Beside me, Nerva strokes the beard he doesn't have. 'If he's going to be this difficult, I may as well make money on him in hunts, maybe even the gladiatorial games.'

'You'll let a prize like him die in the arena?' I ask.

'Why not? The price I paid was good. I'm sure he'll give me a good return before he loses.'

'Caesar took a liking to him?'

'You couldn't even look at Caesar. And now you are an expert in what he favours?' Nerva says. 'You made quite the fool of yourself, didn't you?'

'I'd never met an emperor before. Or been in the palace.'

'He was a general once. You've met generals before. Or, at the very least, been more than a puddle in their presence.'

'Yes but now he's the Emperor, touched by the gods.'

Nerva stares at me for a bit. Then he laughs. 'The lower classes are fascinating, aren't they?'

Nerva suddenly sighs as though something has just occurred to him; he stops walking and turns to face me.

'I appreciate your assistance today, Calenus,' he says. 'I do. But I'm not sure how much work I'll have for you in the future.'

'What?' I say, bewildered. 'Why?'

'I've told you before, Calenus. Your value to me is in your anonymity. But you just entered the palace and met Caesar's family. That very ugly face of yours is known now.'

My heart drops down into my stomach: Nerva is my only way to make coin. If he drops me, I'm not sure how I'll live.

He sighs again. He's acting as though this is a hard decision, but I know he has ice for a heart.

'I appreciate all you've done, Calenus. Truly. But what would you have me do? I hired you to stalk the shadows and gather information. You can't exactly stalk the shadows if you're now a minor celebrity. But don't worry. I won't drop you outright. There will be a transition. I'll need help breaking him in.' He points at the Batavian.

I shake my head. I can't believe it. Bad fortune always seems to find me.

Nerva starts walking again. Like a slave – because I need his coin as long as he's offering – I hurry to catch up.

# TITUS

*15 January, depth of night*
*The Imperial palace, Rome*

Virgilius and I have three glasses of unmixed wine before we are ready
to talk about what we've seen. An oil lamp burns on my desk, another
on the side table. Ptolemy is in the corner, asleep on a stool.

'I've never seen anything like that before,' Virgilius says.

'Nor I,' I say.

We have seen our fair share of battles. But what we saw tonight . . .

'They say something similar happened to those captured in Teutoburg
Pass,' I say, referring to Rome's worst defeat, seventy years before, in the
forests of Germany. 'Their mouths sewn shut, their throats slit.'

'Why?' Virgilius asks. 'What purpose could it serve?'

I shrug. The question is simple, the answer elusive. 'The gods' favour;
to turn fortune; because life is precarious and we are all at the mercy
of the gods.'

We don't discuss the attempt on Domitilla's life. We've no information to know whether it is related to the body we found mutilated by
the Tiber. Father's words keep repeating in my head: *aspiring minds are
salivating.*

Later, Ptolemy ushers Secundus into my study, Halotus's bloodied
scroll in hand. He is out of breath and needs a moment to collect
himself.

'I received your note about what you discovered by the Tiber,' he
says. 'I didn't think I should wait to tell you what I've been able to
translate in the scroll we found on Halotus.'

'You think the two events are related?' Virgilius asks.

'I do,' Secundus says.

'Well,' I reply. 'What does it say?'

'It has been difficult because much of it was stained with blood when
Halotus died. But I am certain it contains instructions.'

'Instructions for what?' Virgilius asks.

'On sacrifice,' Secundus says, 'human sacrifice to a Germanic god. One I'd not heard of before.'

'And this god's name?'

'Torcus,' Secundus says. 'The god of the marsh.'

'And how does it relate to what we've found tonight?' I ask.

Secundus opens his mouth but he pauses, unsure of how to continue. I've never seen Secundus reluctant to speak of anything, least of all some foreign anomaly. Usually, he's fascinated by anything different. His reluctance is ominous.

'Out with it, Secundus,' I say. 'What do the instructions describe?'

He swallows and then describes a ghastly mutilation and murder.

'And is this what happened by the Tiber?' Virgilius asks.

'I believe so,' Secundus says, 'though I will need to inspect the scene.'

'What are you saying, Secundus?' I ask. 'You believe some cult is at work here in Rome?'

'It wouldn't be the first,' Secundus says. 'How was this chamber found?'

'A slave from the neighbouring warehouses found it by happenstance,' Virgilius says. 'As he was passing by, he saw what looked like light coming from under the door – a door to a warehouse he'd never seen used before. It was the middle of the night and the door was chained. He thought someone might have left an open flame. He went to the vigiles and told them, thinking there might be a reward for stopping a fire. The vigiles broke the lock and went inside to snuff out the flame. They found a torch, as they'd expected, and much more. They were in over their heads, so they notified the Praetorians.'

'How many murders have happened there which have gone unnoticed?' I ask rhetorically.

Quietly, we ponder the question.

Then Secundus asks, 'What about your father? This cult, the attempt of Domitilla's life – he may not be safe.'

'I will send him away,' I say. 'I believe that anywhere else is safer than Rome at the moment. He will go with only a select few, only those we know we can trust. No one will know his destination other than Caesar.'

Secundus nods in agreement. 'It is a good idea. A different schedule, a different location – it would make planning anything against him difficult.'

'And you,' I say to Virgilius. 'You will go south. You will find Plautius for me. We will learn more of whatever plot was being hatched in the south.'

Secundus and Virgilius leave.

I'm alone for a time at my desk, lost in thought, when, unannounced, she emerges from the dark, gliding out from the corridor like a ship. It's the middle of the night. She is alone.

'Antonia,' I say, 'is everything all right? How did you get in here?'

Her hair is no longer up, as it was at dinner; it hangs about her shoulders and conceals one of her oval, ox eyes. She sails toward me, silently. Her turquoise shawl shimmers in the lamplight. She comes to my side of the desk and leans against it.

'You left tonight . . . Was it Plautius?' she asks.

'No.'

Still looking away, she bends down and pinches the hem of her stola; she pulls it up just above her knees. She takes my hand and places it on her inner thigh, then pushes it higher.

Out of the corner of my eye, I see Ptolemy silently rise from his stool and, still half-asleep, float out of the room and into the dark of the palace.

I move with purpose now, confident we will not be disturbed.

# XIII

## Time to Go
### A.D. 69

# NERO

♦

*11 January, afternoon*
*City jail IV, Rome*

With my ear to the window and my chin resting on the stone sill, I hear Doryphorus below. He begins with expert, actor-ly precision.

'That's *not* sour wine.'

'It is too,' a soldier says, his voice heavy with drink.

'It's not.' Doryphorus sounds tipsy as well, but I suspect he's dead sober.

'It is!' says a different, equally drunk soldier.

'What do you mean?' says a third who may only be half drunk.

The second voice belongs to Juno. The third to Venus, I'm certain. I will never forget Venus's plebeian pitch.

'The swill you drink is soft,' Doryphorus says. 'It's for women and eunuchs. Now this –' I picture him holding up a jug of wine '– *this* is sour wine. *This* is the drink that will put hair on your back and make your balls drop.'

He is a wonder, isn't he? The way he can change not only his voice but also his character to suit the company he finds himself in. He always had a knack for this, but his years on stage have cultivated the talent. Now he is a chameleon. He can play an effeminate Persian one moment, a drunken soldier the next. It is particularly useful today because it has put my captors at ease. This will make our plan far easier to carry out.

Months ago, Doryphorus bought poison. Nothing too fancy, not the kind one uses to secretly kill a king, to make the regent's slow decline and eventual death seem natural. No, it was the cheap and obvious variety. Then Doryphorus began to cultivate a relationship with the soldiers keeping watch outside. He brought them wine, or shared theirs, and together they would drink, each session growing longer and more relaxed, until the men looked forward to it. At night, Doryphorus developed immunity to the poison by taking incrementally larger doses, so that if it came to it, if he had to drink the same poison as the soldiers, he wouldn't experience anything worse than an upset stomach.

'Well,' a soldier asks, 'are you going to offer us a drink or are you going to stand there all day holding that damned jug in the air?'

'All right, all right. If you women can handle it,' Doryphorus says.

I hear a fat whistle as a cork is removed from a jug.

The banter becomes incomprehensible, but I can tell from the swishing noise that each man is taking his turn with the jug.

'Aren't you going to have a drink?'

'Sure I will,' Doryphorus says.

A short swish of the jug.

'That wasn't much of a drink. I thought you were a . . .'

And then all I can hear is the sound of choking – glorious musical choking. One man at first, and then a chorus fills my ears.

Downstairs the door opens and I can hear a man leaping up the stairs. The door bursts open. 'It worked,' Doryphorus says. He rushes to the cell and starts to open it using the trick Marcus showed him, sticking two fingers into the lock.

But then he falls to his knees and starts to retch.

When he's finished and panting for air, I ask, 'Will you live?'

He spits. 'I'll live.'

'Then hurry. I want my face to be the last Venus's sees before breathing his last.'

For the first time in months, I'm on the move. Doryphorus has procured us a mule. I'm sitting behind him, clutching his soft middle, as we head south, to Rome. It's the sounds I find unnerving: the rustling of a tree, the bark of a dog, a growl somewhere behind us. In my cell, there was little stimulus beyond the voices of my various visitors; and the walls were tight and confining, which was – in a way – comforting. The unknown world, for ever dark, was scripted and controlled. Now, however, riding through the countryside, my true vulnerability is unearthed. Each sound could be a threat and I'd never know.

But I can stomach the uncertainty and fear and humility because I have finally brought one of the men who betrayed me to justice. Finally Venus is dead; poisoned and now lying in the dirt. A fittingly ignominious end for an oath breaker.

Once we pass through the city gate, I immediately feel the menacing proximity of the tenements and shops and flux of people around us. We force our way through the onslaught. It feels an eternity before Doryphorus says, 'We're here,' and helps me dismount.

For the tenth time today, I ask, 'You're certain he's here?'

And for the tenth time today, Doryphorus says, 'No, but it's the best intelligence we have.'

Of all the men who swore to protect my life above their own, those who had access to my chamber the night I was taken, Tigellinus and Epaphroditus are the only two who are not in hiding. Epaphroditus, though, has found favour with the Hunchback. He is in the palace and, for the time being, beyond my reach. This leaves Tigellinus. Apparently, he has fallen ill and may not be long for this world. His home on the Quirinal was plundered and burned after I disappeared. Now he is reduced to living in poverty, in a Suburrian hovel. I suspect the illness is fake, another one of his tricks, to avoid prosecution for his bloody acts as prefect. But we shall see.

Doryphorus helps me up the flight of stairs. A slave answers our knock at the door. His voice is ancient and weak. I imagine a very old man, with a monstrous hunch that drags him down toward the floor.

'We've come to pay our respects,' Doryphorus says. 'We hear the prefect is not long for this world.'

'No visitors,' the old slave says.

Doryphorus rummages in his pocket and then says, 'Let us have our time with him, old man.' I picture the silver coin he is holding up. 'This might see you through after he's gone.'

The door creaks open.

'This way.'

We step inside. Lurking beneath the trickery of cheap incense, the room stinks of mould and decay. It is the smell of death. Maybe Tigellinus is sick after all. We shuffle across the room and then I feel Doryphorus's hands take me by the shoulders and guide me down to a stool. Once seated – once the creak of the wood ceases – the rasping lungs of a dying man fill my ears.

'And who are you?'

It's a voice I heard nearly every day for seven years. I would know it anywhere.

'You don't recognise me?' I ask.

'I know no cripple,' he says. 'Bearded and filthy . . .' He takes a deep, sickly breath. 'You look like the beggar.'

'You know me,' I say. 'Look closer. Imagine the gods had not abandoned me. Imagine at this very moment, blue eyes met yours, not bandages and scars.'

I lean in.

Quietly, he says, 'No.' A long pause. 'No, no, no. You are . . . dead.'

'I assure you, Tigellinus: I am alive.'

'The furies come for me,' he mutters; his rasping breath quickens.

'I am alive, Tigellinus. I did not run from Rome. Three soldiers stole me away in the night and took my eyes. I have been imprisoned ever since. I am alive but you are correct: I am now a cripple, and I am a beggar. But I am not seeking coin or a free meal. Not from you. From you, I want answers – answers to questions I have been asking myself for many months.'

He mutters 'no' again and again.

'Who betrayed me?' I demand.

'Not I,' he says. 'Not I, not I.'

He coughs uncontrollably.

'Who then?'

'I don't know.'

Is this a performance? I knew him well. Usually I could see through his endless tricks. But it's difficult to evaluate a man's truthfulness without my eyes.

In the next room, I hear Doryphorus whispering with the slave.

'Who was guarding my room the night I went missing?'

'Spiculus,' he says. 'He and another gladiator. Hercules.'

'Where were you?'

'Asleep. In my chamber in the palace. I would never break my oath, Nero. Never.'

'Tell me what happened.'

His lungs rasp, greedily sucking in the stale air.

'I was woken in the night. By Spiculus. He said you were not in your bedchamber. He had been guarding your door but was called away on another matter. When he returned, you were gone. Or so he says. He took members of your bodyguard to search for you. I went to the Praetorian camp. By the time I was there – it was not yet sunrise – it was said that you'd fled the city. I thought you had abandoned me.'

He calls for wine. The old slave comes in and helps him take a drink.

He says, 'I'd gone to the camp to find Nymphidius, to speak with him about our next course of action. But with you gone, my life was in danger. I fled the camp with my slave Antonius.'

'What about my gladiators. What of Spiculus? Did you speak with him again?'

'No,' he says. 'I never spoke with anyone. I hid away. I heard Spiculus ran from the city.'

'Where?'

'I don't know.'

'Who had the key to my bedroom that night?' I demand.

He mutters to himself. Is he an old, sick man taxing his memory? Or a born liar playing another trick?

'Epaphroditus. Spiculus. Myself. And . . . I'm not sure who else.' He takes a deep breath. 'But my spies . . . they witnessed certain meetings, in the weeks before the coup.'

'What? Tell me.'

'The eunuch, Halotus, was observed meeting with Nymphidius several times in the months preceding your fall. I had started to investigate, but never learned more before the coup.'

Is this the truth? Tigellinus had spies throughout the palace, and Nymphidius was certainly involved in the coup. If he was meeting with Halotus . . . Halotus's involvement would not be surprising. I've always thought him a snivelling, worthless eunuch, my mother's lackey when she was alive. It seems my list is getting longer, not shorter.

'Did your spies find anything else?' I ask.

'I thought it nothing at the time.'

'What? Tell me.'

'In May, before the coup, while you were on the Bay . . .' He pauses, taking a deep breath. 'Another body was found . . .'

'What do you mean? What body?'

A hand – Tigellinus's hand – grips my cloak and pulls me down, close enough that my ear is inches from his lips. He whispers and his breath – the putrid smell of decay – envelops my face. He says a word I never thought I'd hear again.

'Torcus.'

His grip slackens and I pull away.

'Are you sure?' I ask.

He describes the body, with its mouth sewn shut and tongue removed.

'We didn't know for certain. And I didn't want to alarm you unnecessarily, especially with what was happening in the provinces. We were investigating . . . but then you disappeared.'

'Did you question anyone who was involved before?'

'No,' he says. 'Cassius was gone, banished to Sardinia. And you were infatuated with Lepida – you absolved her of past crimes and ordered she be unmolested in the future.'

He blames me for his failures. I choke back my anger.

'Why are you alive? You are the most hated man in Rome. The kin of those you'd killed should have seized the moment when I disappeared. You should be dead. Someone is protecting you. Who?'

He shakes his head. 'I never broke my oath.'

'Why are you alive, Tigellinus?'

In his voice, I can hear tears forming. 'After the legion in Gaul swore allegiance to Galba in May . . . I put the daughter of his right-hand man, Laco, under my protection. Also, his freedman, Icelus. I imprisoned him, rather than kill him, as you'd instructed. Somewhere safe, outside the city.'

'Why?'

'For this very reason. In case you fell from power and I was exposed. I hedged my bets. I have taken such measures before.'

'So you were protecting my enemies? We were at war, with legions revolting and swearing allegiance to Galba. You don't think Galba's freedman would have been valuable?'

He doesn't answer.

'You broke your oath, Tigellinus. You are as guilty as those who took my eyes.'

'No!' His voice is loud for the first time.

'Yes, you are just as guilty. You may not have openly plotted to bring me down. But you withheld information to save your own hide, knowing full well it put me more at risk. It's my fault. I lost sight of the man you were. I was content to let you apply your cruelty and indifference against others, to protect my interests. I'd forgotten that you were only loyal up to a point, so long as our interests were aligned.'

He mutters, 'No, no, no.'

I stand up to go. The stool topples over.

Tigellinus says, 'You will let me live?'

'Until the poison runs its course,' I say.

'What poison?'

Doryphorus chimes in. 'The poison you just drank. Your slave gave you up for a silver coin.'

'No,' Tigellinus says. His voice is defeated. 'No, no, no . . .'

We walk out without another word.

Outside on the street, before mounting our mule, Doryphorus revises the wax tablet and then hands it to me.

'Today has been productive,' he says.

I run my hands over the names, taking particular pleasure over the horizontal line through the names of those who broke their oath.

| Guilty | Guilt unknown |
|--------|---------------|
| Terentius (centurion) | Epaphroditus (chamberlain) |
| ~~Venus (soldier)~~ | ~~Phaon (chamberlain)~~ |
| ~~Juno (soldier)~~ | Spiculus (bodyguard) |
| ~~Nympidius (Praetorian prefect)~~ | |
| ~~Tigellinus (Praetorian prefect)~~ | Galba (False Emperor) |
| Halotus (the eunuch) | Otho (covets the throne) |
| | The Black Priest (?) |

'Yes,' I say. 'We've a long road ahead, and a plan that will take years to execute. But you're right: today was quite productive. Let us hope Marcus shares our success.'

# MARCUS

◆

*11 January, afternoon*
*The home of Proculus Creon, Rome*

I'm standing with Elsie in the kitchen when she drops three eggs, all at once; they splatter on the floor. 'Whoops,' she says, loud enough for anyone in the next room to hear. 'Marcus, you go to the market to get us more.'

She walks me through the side door and out into the alleyway. It's only when she's on one knee, looking me in the eyes that I can see she's crying. Just one or two tears – not like when I cry – but I've never seen her shed even one.

'I don't want to go,' I say. I start to cry as well.

'Why? You like carrying pots of piss every day?'

'I don't want to leave you?'

'Oh, Marcus . . .' Elsie pulls me close and squeezes me until I can't breathe. Then she takes my shoulders and pushes me back so she can look me in the eye. Another tear slides down her check. She says, 'You remember what Elsie told you? Yes? How the Chaldeans said you were destined for great things?'

I nod.

'Well, this is how it happens. Yes? Great things will come but you can't ignore the chance. If you stay here, one day Master will beat you too much, or he'll sell you to someone worse. The prisoner – this man who wants to take you with him – he's been good to you. He's teaching you things you'd never learn otherwise. You stay with him as long as you can, learn as much as you can, and great things will come. You understand?'

I nod.

'You go with him and you don't ever come back. Yes? Remember old Elsie, think about me every day if you'd like. But don't come back for me. Do you promise?'

I nod.

'Good.'

Elsie hugs me one last time before sending me off down the alleyway. I look back before turning the corner. She waves. I wipe my tears and go.

I make my way down the Caelian Hill towards the Tiber. The streets are empty – not a single person in sight; and it's so quiet I can hear water from the aqueduct filling each fountain as I walk past. I've never seen the city like this – deserted and quiet as a temple. I used to hate the noise and all the people, and I thought I would have liked being the only person in the street. But I don't. It's eerie, like someone is waiting for me around the next corner.

My plan is to cut between the Aventine and the Circus Maximus. But when I turn a corner – out of an alleyway to a wider road – I see a group of men blocking the way. There are twenty or thirty of them. They're talking casually, like they're waiting for something; but most of them are carrying swords or spears or axes. A few of them turn to look at me but, seeing as I'm just a slave boy on an errand, they turn back to whoever they were talking to.

To avoid them, I head north towards the Palatine. Maybe I can make my way between the palace and the forum. I start walking faster, almost running, because I will now have to take a longer route and I don't want to miss Nero. I turn a corner and slam into a man and my face crunches against hard silver and I fall backwards onto the bricks.

The world buzzes and pops.

I look up at the soldier standing over me. The sun is shining at his back, so his face is all shadow. I put a hand up to block the rays.

'And where are you off to, I wonder?'

The soldier takes a step towards me, into the shade of the building, and I finally see his face. It's the Fox.

I flip over onto my stomach and then get onto my knees and I'm about to take off and run as fast as I can when I feel a hand grab my hair and yank me up off the ground. Then my feet are dangling and my hair feels like it's on fire.

'You three thought you'd outsmarted me, didn't you?' He's yelling into my ear; little bits of spit are splattering all over that side of my face. 'I'm not letting all my hard work go to waste. You hear me, boy? You're going to take me to him. Understand?'

He drops me to the ground and I slam against the road. Then I feel his boot slam into my stomach and I bend at the waist like a broken twig. I start to wheeze, trying to catch my breath.

He grabs my tunic right below my chin, yanks me up again, and then he holds me against a brick wall. His little black eyes are furious. I feel something cold underneath my eye, then it burns . . .

He's sliced my cheek with a knife.

'Do you want to lose your eyes like he did?'

His blade reflects blinding white light.

'Where is he, boy? Tell me.'

I can feel myself clamming up like I always do – my chest tightening, my head wet and swimming. A voice – Nero's voice – tells me: *stay alive.*

'OK,' I say.

'OK what?'

'I'll . . . I can take you to him.'

'Where is he?'

Think, think, think.

'I don't know. . .'

*Think!*

'. . . but they've left a message for me. In the forum.'

'What kind of message?'

'I'll show you.'

'If you're lying, I'll cut your throat.'

We make our way to the forum and I try to think of something – anything – to get away. But I can't. The Fox is holding me by my tunic and he's got his knife out in case I try anything.

We emerge from an alleyway and walk into the forum, and it's as empty and quiet as the rest of the city except now, in the distance, people are yelling.

The Fox shakes me by the collar. 'Where?'

'There,' I say, pointing up at the Temple of Jupiter up on the top of the Capitoline Hill.

I'm not sure where I get the idea of a message. I want to stay alive and the best thing to do is to keep the Fox thinking we are going to Nero. I don't want to take him straight there because then he won't need me anymore. I said there was a message for me here in the forum, so now I need to find a message. There's always graffiti in Rome. Always. Everywhere. Red paint scrawled onto stone, saying whatever is on the person's mind. Even on temples like the Temple of Jupiter. The aediles will send slaves to come clean it off, but they can never keep up, and there's always more the next day. I figure graffiti could be the message.

We cross the forum to the Capitoline and start climbing the steep slope. The higher we go, the view of the city gets wider and wider. Somewhere over the Palatine, from behind the palace walls, there's a big swirl of black smoke spiralling up, up, up into the blue sky.

We reach the temple and the Fox says, 'Where is it boy? The message.'

I don't see any graffiti. 'Around the side.'

We walk around the side of the temple, following a stone path. We turn the corner to the far side of the building and I see red paint.

'There,' I say, pointing.

We walk closer. In big burgundy letters, it says:

## Nero is a Cunt

The Fox spins me around and slams me against the wall.

'Are you fucking with me, boy?' He holds the knife underneath my chin. 'Why shouldn't I just cut your throat right now?'

'It's code,' I say, surprising myself with the idea.

'Code for what?'

'Where I'm supposed to go next.'

'What does it mean?'

'Cunt means . . . the Appian Way.'

The Fox narrows his eyes.

'Cock means – or would've meant – the Flaminian Way.'

I don't want to mention the river, how we *actually* plan to leave.

'Will he be there? Will Nero be there?'

He wants to believe me.

'I think so. Yes.'

We go back to the forum the way we came. We can hear angry chatter from the surrounding alleyways. Then, on the left side of the square, a group of men emerge – soldiers mainly, but also men in tunics carrying swords and spears, and six slaves carrying a litter. I recognise one of the men near the litter. Icelus. At the other end of the forum, streaming out of the alleyways, there are soldiers (more than the other group) and men who're wearing leather breastplates and carrying wooden cudgels. There's one man behind the crowd sitting on a horse. I know him as well. Otho.

We're caught in the middle of the two sides. The Fox looks back and forth, from one side to the next. He doesn't know what to do.

At one end, the slaves put down the litter and pull open the drapes. Icelus pokes his head in and then helps a man get out. He might be the oldest man I've ever seen. When he's out, I can see his back is curved like a sickle, his face is grey and wrinkled, and his head is bald and covered in muddy spots.

The bigger crowd on the other side of the forum sees the old man step out of the litter and they get more excited. Some of them shout 'Galba' and 'murderer' and 'liar'. They start banging their weapons on the ground, as they start to walk towards Icelus's group.

The Fox sees the bigger group heading our way. He pushes me forward, away from both groups, but then a third group – more soldiers and other men carrying anything sharp, rakes and spears and axes – emerge from where we were headed.

'Dammit,' the Fox says. He turns to our left and we head for the smallest group, towards Icelus. As we walk, I can feel the group behind us getting closer, as the sound of their weapons – steel banging against steel – gets louder.

The old man walks towards us.

'Insolence!' he yells. I can barely hear his voice over the clatter and banging behind me. 'You shall all be punished for this. Severely punished!'

The Fox keeps pushing me along. He tries to take us wide of Icelus but the freedman finally sees us. His eyes go wide.

'You!' Icelus says. He starts running towards us. 'Stop.'

The crowd behind me is yelling louder now. They keep yelling 'murderer' or 'usurper' or 'imposter'. Others are yelling, 'Otho Caesar, Otho the Emperor' again and again.

Icelus runs straight at us. The Fox starts to take out his dagger but he doesn't do it before Icelus tackles him – *SMASH!* – and the three of us fall to the bricks. I sit up and see them fighting over the Fox's knife, rolling around on the ground. Behind them is chaos: men and soldiers, fighting and stabbing each other, screaming and groaning loader than the clanging of swords and shields and other weapons.

The Tiber is on the other side of the crowd. So is Nero and the boat that will take me from Rome. I know what I have to do. I'm shaking and my legs feel like mush . . . but I stand up and run as fast as I can into the crowd. I get bumped almost right away when a man's bum or hip knocks me down. On my way to the ground, I see an axe being raised. I fall to my knees and cower, waiting for my head to be smashed in . . . but the axe never comes. I open my eyes and see the flash of metal and the splattering of blood and men falling all around me.

I get up and start moving through the crowd again. People are too concerned with the fighting to care about a slave boy making his way through the battle.

In the middle of the fighting, a group of soldiers is standing in a circle with their backs to each other, facing the crowd. Behind them, a soldier is on his knees bent over something, hacking and sawing away with his sword. I keep moving. Over my shoulder, I look back and see the soldier on his knees stand up, his sword in one hand and the head of the old man in the other. The old man didn't have any hair, so the soldier is holding the severed head by the ear. He holds it above his head and howls like a wolf. Men keep chanting 'Otho Caesar!'

I keep my head down and push my way through the crowd. I don't look back.

I find the barge as the sun's last rays are disappearing. Nero and Doryphorus are on the ship. I run over the gangplank and then fall to the deck, exhausted.

'Close,' Doryphorus says. 'Very close.'

'Marcus,' Nero says. He bends down and reaches out with his hands, towards the sound of my heavy breathing. He kneels and puts one hand on my shoulder. 'I'm sure that wasn't easy, getting to this boat. You can tell me all about it later. First, let's get you some food and a spot of wine. Yes? We need you in good health. We've a long journey ahead.'

# XIV

## The Hunt Continues
### A.D. 79

# DOMITILLA

*4 April, afternoon*
*The Campus Martius, Rome*

The people chant his name before he enters the arena.

'Ba-*tavian*! Ba-*tavian*! Ba-*tavian*!'

The wooden arena rattles and sways.

'I do hope he doesn't disappoint,' Domitian says, pushing his black hair out of his eyes. He has recently returned from Campania, and hasn't yet seen the Batavian in action.

Three lions prowl the arena floor. One raises a leg and pees. A puddle of dark, wet sand doubles, then triples in size. Their fur looks metallic under the sun's glare.

Vespasia snorts sarcastically. 'He can't lose. His good luck charm is here.' She stares at me, waiting for me to acknowledge her wit. I won't give her the satisfaction.

Old Graecina sighs. 'Vespasia,' she says, 'do not indulge the rumours, even in jest. Caesar's family must be above reproach.'

'She's the one who wore green today,' Vespasia says. 'They're matching.'

Gods, am I never to wear green again?

'Why isn't Titus here?' Vespasia asks without taking her eyes off the arena.

'Titus thinks he's too good for the beast hunts,' Domitian says. 'He doesn't understand the sport's nuances.'

'Titus is meeting Cerialis today,' I say. 'Welcoming a victorious general is more important than the beast hunts.'

The steady beat of drums overtakes the crowds' chanting.

The doors at the far end of the arena open, slowly; a hush fills the stadium.

Domitian says quietly, 'I hope he at least survives the lions. We've arranged some stunning beasts.'

A man walks into the stadium; tall, graceful, moving with the controlled step of a soldier. He is holding a long spear and wearing barbarian trousers, a silver cuirass . . . and a green mask, which covers the top half of his head.

The crowd is silent.

He raises his spear above his head and the crowd erupts.

It has been three months since the Batavian saved my life. In the days that followed, Father sent Nerva a golden chest studded with emeralds to thank him. To the Batavian, he sent an Egyptian courtesan and a boy, gelded and drowning in perfume – Father is always one for contingencies. The Batavian was told he could have one, or both, and that Caesar thanked him for his bravery. The Batavian, however, refused both the courtesan and the boy. I was with Father when he heard. 'Should I have sent a sheep as well? I'll not spend more time learning what makes a slave's prick hard. Let him be content with the deed itself.'

Nerva entered the Batavian into the hunts the next month. I'd heard he did well his first two matches, and the crowd was beginning to grow fond of him. It wasn't until his third match, at the Quinquatria, when I saw him again. The hunt was held in the circus, on the third day of the festival. The Batavian came into the stadium and I gasped. He was wearing a silk mask – a particular shade of green I recognised: my shawl, part of it at least, the one that was torn the night he saved my life.

The Batavian made his name that day. There were half a dozen men fighting at once. After they had killed smaller game, into the arena trotted a rhinoceros. The beast ran into a group of hunters, flicking its horn, sending hunters into the air or trampling them under its massive hooves. Arrows and spears bounced off its hide. At the time, it looked as though every man in the arena would die. Then the Batavian threw his spear. The rhinoceros was standing still after a charge and the Batavian stood forty yards away. I am not one for violence or the hunts. But no one can deny the throw was magnificent. It hit the rhino directly in the eye. The remaining men, realising this was their only chance, rushed at the beast, hacking at it with their swords. The Batavian ran into the mêlée and grabbed the shaft of his spear. I closed my eyes . . .

When it was all over, the hunters – those still able to stand – came and bowed to the Emperor's box. Vespasia (who had finally returned from Capri) was with me, but she was off in the back rolling dice and laughing with some of our guests. So, to the crowd, it looked as though the hunters bowed only to me. I stood up and leaned over the railing. It was then that the Batavian took off his mask, kissed it and held it up, for me to see. The crowd understood: what else could it mean? He wore silk I had given him; I had given him my favour. Rumours spread. At first, it was merely said that we were lovers, that I visited him in his cell every night. Now the city claims we are in love, and married secretly, in a barbaric ritual overseen by a goat dressed as a druid priest. The patricians find the story distasteful. But the plebs adore us – the idea of us, at least. We are their favourite couple, despite the fact that we don't speak the same language and, only once, have I been within a hundred yards of him. The only benefit of the Batavian carrying on in this way is that it has halted the engagement to Marcellus – or at least, put it on hold. Marcellus told Titus he didn't want a wife of his 'cavorting' with a slave in public. Titus says Father will approach Marcellus again in the summer.

When the hunt is over, the scene is gruesome: the bodies of tigers, lions and one giraffe lie bleeding in the sand. Domitian's surprise – the giraffe – lacked the excitement he was hoping for. It was exotic, but felled easily.

The Batavian walks to the Emperor's box. He bows; his eyes are squarely on me. I squirm awkwardly in my chair.

'Should we leave you two alone,' Vespasia whispers.

Graecina says something about not encouraging him.

The Batavian removes his mask and kisses it.

The crowd erupts.

# CALENUS

*4 April, afternoon*
*The baths of Nero, Rome*

A man's bear paw slaps me on the back. I look up and, through the foggy mist of the baths, I see Fabius. I haven't seen him since we shared a cup a few months back and he begged me to join up with Montanus. He is naked and smiling, the twists of his beard weighed down with sweat.

'Calenus, you dog,' he says, taking a seat beside me, his bulk slapping against the stone.

Pipes spew hot air; the building gasps.

'Fabius,' I say. 'Where's your stick?'

He snorts. 'I don't need it for the likes of you.' He runs his hands over his head, slicking his long hair to his skull. 'You're not at the hunt?'

'I prefer the baths like this,' I say. 'Quiet.'

Usually, at this hour, the room would be full. Today, however, because of the hunt, there couldn't be more than a dozen people.

He says, 'You're missing your patron's new boy.'

I shrug. 'Watch a man kill a lion once, you don't need to see it again.'

'Maybe,' he says. 'But were you there for the rhino? I'd have paid to see that.'

'I was there. It was a fine throw.'

'The boy I hire talks about him incessantly,' Fabius says. 'He thinks the man is Achilles's ghost, back from the dead. He says that's why Caesar's daughter offers herself up to him every night. You can't say no to a demigod.'

'If my mother was a god,' I say, 'I'd not spend a single night in chains.'

Fabius laughs. 'Nor I, nor I.' He turns to look at me. His voice is suddenly grave. 'Must be hard, being the favourite of a man like Nerva. Then he drops you after he finds a prize like that.'

'Not my concern,' I say. 'I'm doing fine.'

'Well, if you need more coin, there's always more work.'

Fabius leans back, relaxing against the stone. He closes his eyes.

Something irritates, like a fly walking across the back of my neck.

'Why aren't you at the hunt, Fabius?'

'Oh, I prefer the bath's quiet as well.'

'You're false there, friend. The less swinging cock, the less reason for you to come.'

He opens one eye and aims it at me. He sighs, closes his eye again, and relaxes against the stone. He's reached a decision.

'You see,' he says. 'This is what I told Montanus: if you need more men, let me get Calenus. He's as quick with his wits as he is with a sword.'

'And what does Montanus need?' I ask. 'Wits or a sword?'

'There's some heavy work coming, Calenus. Work you and I are trained for.'

'What happened to your stick?'

'I'll need to sharpen it, I suppose.' Fabius sits up and once again runs his hands over his head, slicking his hair against his head. 'Let's be honest, shall we? You and I could make a wage as labourers, at the docks or in a warehouse. But we're veterans. We don't have it in us to lift and drag and pull after all those years working for the Empire. We've too much pride. It's not our fault we were on the losing side of a civil war. Is it? So we make a living other ways.'

'What's happening?' I ask.

'Do you think I know anything? This is the teat, though. Something is always festering, like a sore. And when it bursts, men like you and I go to work.'

A few months back – after Titus killed those boys in Baiae and all that business of the wolf in the forum, and then the body by the Tiber, mutilated by some strange cult – the city felt like it was going to boil over. But it's been quiet these last few weeks. I tell Fabius as much.

He puts his hands up to show his innocence. 'All I know is Montanus says we need a man who can use a blade if the need should arise.. Shit, Calenus! You think I want to know more than that? It doesn't matter, anyway. This is Rome: it's all extremes, good and bad. We get fresh water every day, surroundings like this –' he holds his arms up, capturing the enormity of the room '– but there's always brutality around the corner. What'd our old captain call it? "The machinery of Empire". The fuck if I can explain it.' He stands up. 'Men like you and me, all we can do is take the coin we're offered and hope we're on the right side when it's all said and done. If you want the work, you know where to find us.'

Fabius disappears into the steam, his sweaty feet slapping on the stone with each step.

Outside, after the dark of the baths, the sunlight is blinding. I shut my eyes and wait a moment. Then, as I'm walking down the steps, I see a litter in the street, with white silk swaying in the breeze. Four soldiers surround it. A redheaded girl, more freckles than not, walks toward me. Her face looks familiar, but I can't place it. It's not until she says her mistress would like a word and then points at the litter that I realise she's the Empress's girl.

I walk to the litter on watery legs. I feel as though a million eyes are on me, though no one is paying me a second glance.

The girl pulls back the curtain. I don't see Caesar's daughter because I'm already kneeling, with my head bent. I see only fat black stones.

'Do you know me, citizen?' she asks.

'Yes, Mistress.'

'We met once. Do you remember?'

'Yes, Mistress.'

'You seemed a loyal subject of Caesar's then. And are you still?'

'I am.'

I keep staring at the road.

'What is your name?'

'Calenus. Julius Calenus.'

'Calenus. A good name . . .'

Caesar's daughter said my name.

'Please stop looking at the road, Calenus. I'd like to see your face as we talk.' I look up at Caesar's daughter. She's lying on her side, propped up on an elbow. Her green shawl is draped over her head like a hood. Underneath: waves of almond hair, matching eyes, and white marble skin. Glinting gold hangs around her neck like a fancy noose. 'You are a veteran?' she asks.

'Yes, Mistress.'

'I thought so. You have the air about you. How is it that you work for Nerva?'

She means, *Why are you poor? Where's your plot of land every soldier works for?* What do I tell her? There was a civil war. I fought against your father. I am a deserter and a coward. Now here I am.

'Fortune abandoned me, Mistress.'

Caesar's daughter stares at me a moment. 'Well,' she says, 'let us hope she returns to you one day.'

I bow my head in thanks.

She says, 'I need you to deliver a message for me.'

'To Nerva? I might not be the right man. I've fallen out of favour as of late.'

'No, to the Batavian.'

'What would you have me say, Mistress?'

'Ask him to stop wearing his green mask, and to stop acknowledging me at the hunt.'

'He's a brute, Mistress. He doesn't speak my tongue and . . .'

'I only ask you to do your best, Calenus. Which I know you will.' She hands me a silver coin. 'Can I rely on you to keep this discreet?'

'Yes, of course, Mistress. I won't tell a soul.'

She gives me one last smile, then waves to the girl.

'Find me when it's done.'

She draws the silk curtain closed and a half a dozen slaves surround the litter and heave it up onto their shoulders. I watch the litter float across the forum and disappear around the corner.

I'm not sure what to make of this. Running errands for the Augusta. It could be a change in fortune, something I desperately need after Nerva dropped me. Then again, maybe it won't change anything. Time will tell, I suppose.

I make my way east, toward the Circus. By now the hunt will be over, and I should have time to visit the Batavian in his cell and deliver the Augusta's message before Nerva's men fetch him for the evening. It would be good to finish the job today, if I can.

I'm heading down a nameless street in the Subura, narrow and jammed with people, pushing my way through a crowd, when my shoulder collides with a woman. I'm twice as heavy as her, so the force sends her back a foot or two while I stay put. Then we stand there, staring at each other. Her hair is dark; half of it's braided and tied up in a twirl on the top of her head, like a sleeping cobra; while the other half is hanging around her shoulders, with a slight crinkle to each strand – planned the way women will plan that kind of thing. She's not young – she's seen four decades if she's seen one. But there's something about her. A confidence. An assuredness. It might be the way she stands, the way she pushes her chin up and away from her shoulders. She stands like a queen. I know her somehow, but I can't quite place it. I can tell she's thinking the same about me, so neither of us talks. And then suddenly it dawns on me: we met on the road to Ostia, when a legionary had her tied to the back of a horse.

She smiles knowingly. She remembers me as well. Hard to forget a man who's saved your life.

I hold up a coin, the last to my name. 'Buy you a drink?'

She looks me over, from toe to head.

'I cost more than a drink, soldier.' She smiles. 'What's your name?'

'Calenus,' I say. 'Yours?'

'You can call me Red.'

# TITUS

◆

*4 April, afternoon*
*Three miles north of Rome*

The camp is in an open valley two miles north of the city. The sun above is naked and bright in April's cloudless blue sky. Hooves whip and stab tall grass as we approach at a trot.

Soldiers hammering stakes into the ground drop their work and stand at attention as we draw near. The officer says, 'General,' as we slow to a stop. Virgilius and the rest of my escort wait with their comrades, while the officer takes me to Cerialis.

As we make our way through a maze of tents, I soak up the familiar sounds of camp: steel hammering steel, rock sharpening blades, anticipatory quiet followed by a flood of laughter. There is a weightlessness to it, with their latest battle behind them, and their next – at the very least – months away.

Beyond the flap of the general's tent, Cerialis is at his desk. He resembles the generals of old: square jaw, steady gaze, and manicured quaff. His patch of white hair – near his left temple, which he's had since birth – is his sole distinguishing feature, the one which sets him apart from the marble busts lining the palace niches.

He looks up from his rolls. 'Ah, Titus.' He stands and walks around his desk. He holds me by the shoulders. 'It's good to see you. It's been too long.' He points at a chair. 'Please. Sit.' Then, to unseen ears: 'Wine! Seawater!'

'You look much older than I remember,' I say.

He smiles. 'Well, I take heart in having my hair, a diminishing asset of yours, I see.'

Willpower stops me from reaching for my retreating hairline. I can't help but laugh. I have missed Cerialis.

We sit and receive our sour wine.

'Tell me everything,' I say. 'From the beginning.'

'Rome bores you,' he says. 'You miss the field. Don't shake your head. I know it's true. You're hoping to live vicariously through me. Well, I'm sorry to say, you will be disappointed. The story is not inspiring.'

'No?'

'No . . . Rome's glory was not advanced in our sack of Maronea and the capture of a few rebels.'

'Don't let the people hear you say that. Father has ordered an ovation. The games have already begun.'

'Has he? I was told it was something . . . less.'

'It will meet the definition of ovation, but it will be more . . . *mild* than most.'

In Rome, everything has its place, even parades, and there can be no stepping above one's station. Cerialis is not offended. He knows how this works.

'I don't dispute the decision,' he says. 'I will be mildly embarrassed given the circumstances.' He shrugs and sips his wine. He says, 'When did your father return to Rome?'

'Yesterday.'

'It was a fine decision to send him away.'

'Perhaps.'

'It was,' he says. 'With Caesar on the move, any attempt on his life would prove far more difficult than in Rome. And it gave the city a chance to breathe.'

'Yes, that's true. There cannot be plots against Caesar if there is no Caesar.'

'And there has been nothing since?' Cerialis asks. 'No murders? No plots discovered?'

I shake my head. 'No. Epaphroditus, the exchequer, went missing for a time, a month or so, after a dinner party held by a new senator named Ulpius. The exchequer returned with a ruined right arm and some story of long, drunken nights in the south.'

Cerialis frowns. He, like the rest of us, doesn't know what to make of the story.

'And Plautius remains missing?'

I nod. 'I sent Virgilius to the Bay but nothing came of it.'

'And what of the body by the Tiber?'

'We established a reward for anyone who could identify it. We said there was a birthmark, but not where or in what shape. Hundreds of people came to say it was their brother, or sister, or a colleague who owed them fifty sesterces. But no one could describe the birthmark with enough specificity.'

'What do you make of it?' Cerialis asks.

'Well, there was another murder, one only Father and a few others know of. The eunuch, Halotus.'

Cerialis raises an eyebrow. He takes a moment to consider this. If he's shocked at the murder of a procurator, he hides it well. 'Nero's former favourite?' he asks.

I explain to Cerialis the manner in which Halotus died, the scroll that he was carrying, and what Secundus translated from it. How these murders, or at the very least the one by the Tiber, was likely for some German god.

Cerialis is unperturbed. He was never much perturbed by anything. It's what makes him a good general.

'Come,' I say. 'I've answered your questions. Now answer mine. How did you take the False Nero?'

'There is not much to tell,' Cerialis says. 'I was in Illyricum with a legion, bringing to heel the hill tribes, when word came of the False Nero in Thrace. The reports weren't detailed, but men were flocking to him, that was obvious. I thought about writing to you to see whether I should move or not. But I decided I should move quickly rather than wait for instructions.'

'You made the right decision,' I say.

'As I said, I had one legion, just under six thousand men in total. I sent word to the legate of Asia, demanding three more. But I set off with mine straight away. We were undermanned, but able to move quickly. And we were in Thrace within the month. The False Nero and his army were last spotted near Abdera. "Spotted" is the wrong word. They sacked the city, raped the women, killed their husbands and made off with anything of value they could. I sent out scouts in three different directions, north, east and west. (The sea was south and we knew they didn't have ships.) The scouts returned with word that the False Nero had gone east, leaving a trail of wasted fields, burnt buildings, and corpses. You should have seen it. The destruction; it was as though Xerxes's army was heading west, not the twenty thousand thugs we eventually caught. We followed and eventually met them outside of Maronea.'

'Why not simply overtake them and raid their camp?' I ask. 'Why give him the opportunity for a fight?'

'Word is he's a former soldier, a former Praetorian. That is –' Cerialis smiles '– provided he's not Nero back from the dead. He had scouts. He knew we were coming. He picked the ground – at least I let him think he picked the ground – and he had his men lined up and ready for a fight.'

'Twenty thousand you said?'

'Thereabout.'

'Any horse?'

'Couldn't have been more than five hundred.'

'And you?'

'By then we'd met up with the Asian legions. We had just over twelve thousand.'

'Yet it was a rout.' I shake my head. 'You're a credit to the Empire.'

Cerialis acknowledges the compliment with a nod; he sips his wine.

'How did it unfold?'

Cerlialis's correspondence has already explained it all, but I want it again, detail by detail. Caesar's son wants the information; the former general misses the battle and this echo is all he has.

'Nothing dramatic. As I said, they only had five hundred horses. And our arms were far superior. We staged a line in front of his, but it wasn't anything more than a dummy line by the time his army advanced.' He uses a stylus and blocks of wood on his desk to show me. 'I had most of the men move to the flank. We tore into their side, pinched them like the claw of a crab at first, until the flank overwhelmed them.' He laughs. 'If the False Nero is a former Praetorian, he's not a credit to the unit. Maybe all you Praetorians are too fat on the spoils of the capital.'

'How many did you capture?'

'We took about two thousand alive. We didn't have enough men to take more. We'd hoped for ransoms, but these weren't rich men, thugs, farmers, idiots – not many with coin. We had some swear an oath of fealty to your father. The rest we sold in Pontus.'

I shake my head in disbelief. 'What possessed them to follow this man? Is there at least a resemblance with the tyrant?'

'I never saw him. But we interrogated his officers and a general consensus emerged. Based on what I'm told, I'd say this fake tyrant is shorter, and his hair is more red than the coppery-shade those Julio-Claudians all had.'

'How do his men describe him? Is he . . .' I search for the right word. 'Inspiring?'

Cerialis shakes his head. 'They were criminals, like I said. They wanted to rape and pillage. They didn't care who they were following.'

'And this False Nero may be an ex-Praetorian?'

'That's what his officers are saying. One in particular says he's been with him for close ten years. He has quite a lot to say, in fact.'

'Oh?'

'Yes, but it is better to hear it from the horse's mouth.'

We exit Cerialis's tent and make our way to the centre of the camp. Two guards stand in front of the prisoners' tent. Inside, it's dark and stinks of piss. There are four cages filled with a dozen or more men. While three of the cages are large enough that a man could stand without hindrance, the third does not quite reach my waist. Inside is a man, lying on his side, with his knees tucked into his chest. His chains rattle in time with his snore. His long brown hair is tangled filth. He is alive, but worn down, as a prisoner should be before an ovation.

Cerialis kicks the cage. Startled, the filthy prisoner wakes. Cerialis squats down to the ground, so his eyes are level with the prisoner's.

'You see this man here?' Cerialis points at me. 'He is Titus Flavius Vespasianus, prefect of the Praetorians and the Emperor's eldest son. If anyone were even considering showing you mercy, this would be the man. Tell him everything you told me and maybe he'll save that filthy neck of yours.'

'A sip of wine would help,' the prisoner says. His voice sounds hollow and empty.

Cerialis snaps his fingers and a soldier swoops in with a skin of wine. He hands it to Cerialis, who hands it to the prisoner. The prisoner takes a draught.

'All right,' Cerialis says, rattling the cage. 'Time to talk. Let's start with who the False Nero is.'

'His name is Terentius. He was a centurion in the Praetorian Guard, here in Rome.'

To Cerialis, I say, 'A name is useful. Very useful.'

Cerialis rattles the cage. 'And? What did this Terentius confide in you?'

'Nero is alive,' he says. 'He never committed suicide. Terentius stole him from the palace and imprisoned him.'

'And where is he now?' Cerailis prompts.

'Still there, I think, in some prison north of Rome.'

Cerialis looks at me and together we laugh.

As we're leaving, I say, 'It's amazing the tales men will tell to impress their own men.'

# XV

## From Oyster to Sardine
### A.D. 69

# MARCUS

◆

*2 February, dawn*
*Off the coast of Sardinia, the Tyrrhenian Sea*


Foamy white spray flies over the gunwales. I squeeze my eyes before a million drops of water hit me all at once. The bow goes up into the air and then the sea disappears and the ship falls and my stomach feels like when someone pulls a chair away as you're about to sit. Then: *crash!* Another wave slams into the boat and foamy white spray flies over the gunwales.

'Sheet in!' a sailor yells.

'Haa*aaaaaaaarrrrrrdddddd*,' another one yells.

Nero, Doryphorus and I are holding onto a rope tied to the mast. My knuckles are white. Doryphorus's face is pale and he's been retching for a while now. He's already lost his breakfast and last night's meal. Now all that comes out are yellow bubbles of sick.

We went straight from Rome to a city near the sea called Oyster. We stayed in a little apartment near the pier, and each day Doryphorus went to find a ship to take us away from Italy, while Nero and I stayed in the apartment, waiting.

Doryphorus and Nero argued a lot. They argued about money and about where to go next. Doryphorus said we need to go to Egypt for coin, but Nero wanted to find a friend of his who lived on an island called Sardine. And they argued about me. Doryphorus would whisper to Nero in Greek thinking I couldn't understand, but I'm learning faster than he thinks. I didn't understand everything, but I figured out enough to know Doryphorus thought they should leave me in Oyster, all by myself.

One day Doryphorus came back from the pier and said he'd found a ship that was leaving right away. We packed up our things, which wasn't very much, and rushed to the ship.

I couldn't believe the pier. There were so many ships, from little ones rowed by one man, to ones as big as the forum, rowed by an army. Each ship had amphorae being dragged on and off. I saw a giraffe's head from a distance (not the body, though), and I heard a trumpet that Nero said was an elephant.

Our ship wasn't very nice. It looked old with its yellow sail, and it stank of rotten vegetables. The captain was only wearing pants. His belly was huge and hairy; so were his arms and shoulders and back. His long, braided hair – brown with a bit of grey – was up in a bun. It reminded me of Elsie's. His crew looked like younger versions of him.

It was only when we were on the boat that I learned Nero had won the argument and we were sailing to Sardine. The wind was steady at first but got stronger and stronger as the day wore on. Soon the waves were big – 'rollers' the captain called them – and we were going right into them. The ship went up and down, up and down. It wasn't too long before I started to feel sick.

It's the afternoon when we finally see something, a green smudge in the distance, between the grey sky and scruffy blue sea.

'What's that?' I ask.

'Sardinia,' Doryphorus says.

'Why are we going there?'

'To ask a question,' Doryphorus says. 'Nero's brought us to a wild, lawless island to find one man and ask him a question – a question he'll likely answer with a lie.'

'I will know the truth of what happened,' Nero says to Doryphorus. 'Cassius was involved in Torcus once. He will have the answers I require. Anyway, I banished him when I was perfectly within my rights to have him killed. He is in my debt. At the very least, he owes me the truth.'

The boat suddenly pitches downwards and Doryphorus starts to retch again. I turn away so I don't have to see his grey tongue.

We keep sailing until the island doesn't look like an island anymore, until the smudge is so long and wide and green with trees it looks like there's no end in either direction. Then the captain shouts out orders and the ship comes to a halt and a little rowboat is lowered into the water; it hits the sea with a splash.

'All right,' the captain says, screaming over the wind. He bends down and unties the rope we've been holding on to. 'This is where you go it alone.'

Doryphorus is furious. 'What? You were to take us to shore. That was the agreement.'

'I'm changing the agreement. The sea's too rough and I am not being shipwrecked in Sardinia. Plus, the island's cursed and bandits rule. If I ordered my men to shore, I'd have a mutiny on my hands. I'm giving you a rowboat instead. A fair deal, I think.'

'And how are we to leave?' Doryphorus asks.

'The fuck if I care.'

The sailors help all three of us climb down a rope ladder. Doryphorus goes first. A wave pushes the tiny craft into the side of the ship just as he's putting his feet down. He slips and collapses in a heap in the bottom of the boat. Nero goes next. He takes a few steps on the rope ladder before Doryphorus takes him in his arms. I go last. Doryphorus doesn't help me at all, but gets the oars ready instead. I slip on the ladder and fall. My legs dip into the sea and my chest hits the gunwale.

'Hurry, boy,' Doryphorus says.

I wiggle and kick my legs again and again until I'm up and into the boat.

Doryphorus starts rowing us to shore. The waves help. We go fast for a bit, with a wave, but then it disappears and we slow down again. Then another wave comes and we speed up. Each time the boat rocks back and forth, and it feels like we might tip over.

Nero is lying on the floor of the rower. I'm beside him until Doryphorus yells, 'Get to the bow, boy, to even out the weight.' His eyes are wide with fear.

The waves keep sending us towards the shore.

'Sardinia has a certain smell this time of year, doesn't it?' Nero says.

A wave twice the size of any so far grabs our boat and sends us hurtling towards shore. The bow starts to aim away from shore, inch by inch, and the boat starts to tip . . .

And then the boat goes over and I'm in a rush of white foam, spinning and tumbling in every direction. I need to breathe badly and my chest is burning and just when I'm about to open my mouth underwater, the wave stops and I can fling my head up and out of the water and suck in a long, huge breath.

I flail my arms around hoping that's how you swim – but I know it will be no good and I'll sink like a stone and die right here. But my feet touch something. Sand. I can stand! With the water only up to my bellybutton. I smile and start to laugh – not believing my luck – but then I feel the sea sucking me back. That big wave that brought me in wants to suck me back out. Neptune isn't done with me. I know that if the wave sucks me out to sea I'll drown. So I start running towards shore. But my legs are underwater, so they're heavy and slow, and the sand slides away under my feet with each step and I don't go anywhere. I run as hard as I can, flailing my arms forward too, but I don't move. Neptune's wave keeps trying to suck me out, but I keep running away from it. But then Neptune's had enough and the sucking stops and I hear the roar of a wave. I look over my shoulder and I see another wall of water coming towards me, churning white foam as fast as a horse can run. With the sucking done, I can start to move forward again, towards shore, but the second wave hits me – *SMASH* – and white foam is everywhere; it slams me into the sandy sea floor and then sends me somersaulting.

When the second wave is done with me, I figure I've drowned and maybe drowning isn't so bad because it doesn't hurt, but I open my eyes and see the sun. I realise I'm not dead; I'm lying on the beach. Foamy surf laps my side. I look out to sea and see the ship heading south. It looks quiet and peaceful.

I want to cry out in celebration, but immediately I start to retch water I must have swallowed. When I'm done, I put my head down on the sand.

I doze for a while, not really sleeping, but I keep lying there collecting my energy, until I feel a poke, something hard stabbing my shoulder.

I look up. Beyond the glare of the sun, I see a handful of men surrounding me – ten, maybe eleven – with long beards, fur, carrying long axes and clubs and spears.

I retch one last time before they pull me up by the hair.

The walk through the forest is long and slow, all shadows and slivers of sunlight. Overhead the birds chirp, chirp, chirp. The bandits didn't bother tying me up; one of them threw me over his shoulder, without a word. His wet vest of wolf hide stinks of smoke and salty fish. With each step – up and down, up and down – my head and belly swirl and spin and I'd retch if I had anything left in my belly. I can stare at his backside; or, if I curl my head back, the line of bandits walking behind us. I think I can see another body over another bandit's shoulder. I hope it's Nero. He'll know what to do.

Soon there are voices ahead and then I can hear the hiss of a fire and the hammering of metal. We step out into a clearing splashed with sunlight.

'What's this?'

A hand pats my arse.

'Drift wood,' my captor says.

I'm taken into a hut. Inside, the bandit drops me behind a cage made from branches tied together. The floor isn't a floor at all, but sand. More bandits come in and two more bodies are dropped beside me. Nero and Doryphorus. I tell myself everything will be OK because Nero is here. My chest untwists a little.

The bandits walk out.

Nero says, 'Marcus?'

'Here,' I say. 'I'm here.'

Nero asks for Doryphorus and he says he's here too.

'Well,' Nero says, 'that was good fortune, wasn't it?'

Doryphorus says, 'Good fortune? Are you mad? They're going to roast us alive.' To me, he says, 'You think our blind leader is Jupiter himself, but believe me boy, he is mad. He'll be the death of both of us.'

Nero pushes himself up off the sand and sits cross-legged. He tightens the rag around his eyes. Doryphorus crawls over to the branches and starts shaking them, looking to see if any are loose.

'Nonsense,' Nero says. 'We were tired getting to shore. I could barely stand. It was useful to have men carry us.'

'And how do you know this is where we wanted to go? How many camps are there on this godsforsaken island? A dozen? Two dozen? There could be hundreds.'

'Keep faith, Doryphorus.'

'Faith? You're blind, we're being held captive, and we don't have a coin to our name. How can you keep faith?'

'Apollo favours me,' Nero says. 'Or maybe it is simply habit. I'm not sure frankly.'

Doryphorus flops onto the dirt and puts his head in his hands. 'You're mad.'

From the back corner of the hut, from the shadows, we hear a voice. 'Do you know the date?'

A man who'd been lying down in the sand sits up. His rusty beard is very long. I whisper to Nero, telling him there's another man in the cell. 'Yes,' Nero says, 'I gathered that.'

The man asks again, 'The date. Do you know it?'

Nero says, 'The second of February.'

'And the year?'

Nero says, 'It is the eight hundredth and twenty-second year since the foundation of Rome.'

The man gapes. 'By Hercules!'

Nero asks, 'How long have you been here?'

'A week tomorrow and it will be three years.'

'Who are you?' Nero asks.

'Ulpius,' the man says, 'Marcus Ulpius Traianus.'

Nero and the prisoner talk for a while. Nero asks all sorts of questions, mainly about his life here in the camp.

Nero asks, 'Who is in charge? What's his name?'

'Kortos used to be in charge. The large, black-bearded man who dragged the boy in here. But a few months ago another man arrived in the camp. He was bigger and stronger than Kortos, which I wouldn't have believed unless I saw it myself. He displaced Kortos. You know how bloodthirsty bandits do this: they fight with knives until one of them says uncle. Now he's in charge.'

'His name?'

'Spiculus.'

Nero laughs, slowly at first but then he laughs so hard he falls to his side and grabs his ribs.

'You see, Doryphorus,' he says. 'One must keep his faith.'

As the afternoon ends and the sun sets, the prisoner tells us his story. We sit quietly and listen.

'My home is Hispalis. It's a fine city, the finest in Spain; brick the colour of sand spread out beside a river of blue. It may not have the grandeur of Rome, or the clean lines of Alexandria. It doesn't have their history or their marble. But in Hispalis –' he sucks air into his nose, filling up his chest and then lets it out '– one can breathe.'

'My father made olive oil. He had three boys. I was the second eldest. He put my older brother and me to work in the family business, and sent the youngest off to serve in the army. My father was fine in business, good but not exceptional. He turned a reasonable profit and our family was comfortable. But when my brother and I took over, we expanded the enterprise. We bought more land and made more oil. Within two years we had tripled our annual earnings. So we bought more land and then tripled our earnings again. We began to travel across the Middle Sea, selling our product, securing more partners. For ten years we travelled across the Empire without incident, from Spain to Syria and back again. Then, three years ago, when crossing the Adriatic . . .'

He lets out a heavy sigh; he twirls his long dirty beard with a finger.

'. . . pirates. We saw them bearing down on us from the north. Four ships: smaller and faster than our lumbering merchant variety. My brother was the elder, so I differed to him in all things, including a crisis. When he saw the pirates, he screamed at our oarsmen, ordering them to row harder, demanding they save all our lives. For a time we stayed ahead of our pursuers. But our ship was too fat, too laden with the spoils of commerce. The ship's captain begged us to throw our amphorae overboard, to lighten the ship and ease its burden. My brother eventually agreed – but by then it was too late. The pirates overtook us. After grappling hooks dug into our gunwales, they shimmied up their ropes and stormed the ship. The fighting was swift and one-sided. Our oarsmen – slaves mainly – had little experience in combat. The pirates were professionals.

'We were chained and thrown in the hold of a ship. My brother and I – rich knights and citizens of Rome – found ourselves side-by-side with our own slaves. Their lot in life hadn't changed: they were slaves before and would remain so. Some, I am convinced, were hopeful, believing their lives might improve when they were sold again. (Rowing a merchant vessel is a hard life.) But for me the change in fortune was terrible; and for my brother, it was calamitous.

'He had a small nick on his thigh from the fighting, nothing more than a scratch, but we spent weeks below the deck and all I could do was watch as it festered. It stank of death long before the end. It was another three days until his body was removed from the hold and thrown into the sea. After I heard the splash from the hold, I whispered his dirge and wished him well on his journey.

'The pirates kept me below deck for months. Once a day, one of them would pour a few drops of water into my open mouth and press some bread or raw fish into my hand. The other captives were sold off, one by one, until I was the only man left. One day a fat oaf of a man walked in to the hold. His grizzled beard was so long, I didn't know where it ended and his vest of hide began. He crouched beside me and asked my name. I answered that question and each that followed with the truth. Applying my wits was beyond me. One of my captors said I'd fetch a fine ransom. The man in fur said that I'd been gone too long; my relations wouldn't believe I was still alive. Haggling followed, no different than any other sale, except they were haggling over a man's life, not a vat of oil. Back and forth they went, until I was eventually sold for ten denarii, the price of a decent ox.

'I was dragged to the deck at twilight. Yet for me the light was blinding. The dark blue sea and the red sky were the most beautiful I had ever seen. Tears streamed down my cheeks. I was put into a rowboat with more men in fur and jettisoned to shore. They had to carry me through the forest because my legs were weak from lack of use. I have lived here, in this cage of twigs, ever since, waiting in vain for my ransom to be paid. But with one brother dead and the other at war, the gods know when I will finally be set free. Yet I make due. If I'd gone from my former life to this jail, it would have been intolerable. But compared to the hold of a ship, this has been a paradise. The men bring me out at least once a day, sometimes for several hours. They even let me walk about the camp, because there is nowhere to escape to. You will not enjoy your time here. But you can endure it.'

Evening. Moonlight peeks between the cracks of the hut's branches; the room is silver, like a coin. We can hear the bandits laughing and singing. Their voices get louder. A fight breaks out, but then there is laughter again.

The door swings open and two of the bandits stumble in.

One of them says, 'What do you think the boy goes for?'

The other says, 'Hard to say, hard to say. Fair bit more than the cripple, I'd wager.'

They bind our wrists and drag us outside. There is a stage set up beside a massive fire. On it, one man is relaxing in a chair. His skin is the colour of wet sand and he's thick, especially at the neck, bald, and his left eye has a patch over it. He looks bored. Another bandit is standing behind him, whispering in his ear. He looks tiny compared to the one sitting. He's holding a wax tablet and a stylus. Dozens of bandits sit facing the stage. They're sitting on overturned logs or lying in the dirt, passing around skins of wine. Some are laughing; others are hollering at us. An apple core hits Doryphorus in the shoulder and bursts into tiny pieces. One bandit yells, 'Dead centre' and the rest explode with laughter.

We're dragged to a spot beside the fire.

Nero whispers, 'Is it him?'

Doryphorus looks at the stage. 'Yes, it's him.'

The little man with the wax tablet steps forward. He says, 'Senators! Senators! Order please. Order!'

The bandits hoot and howl; one of them hisses.

The little man yells, 'We are about to begin this evening's auction and we require *order*.'

The man with the eye patch lifts his hand and the crowd hushes.

It's so quiet I can hear a buzzing fly land on my shoulder.

'Spiculus!'

I look beside me. The voice is Nero's. He sounds brave, like Master lecturing a slave.

'Untie me at once.'

The man with the eye patch slides out to the edge of his chair. He stares at Nero, squinting his good eye. Then he stands up and walks to the edge of the stage.

The crowd stays quiet; I can hear the breeze tickling the branches overhead.

'And fetch me a cup of wine,' Nero bellows. 'I'm dreadfully thirsty.'

The one-eyed man hops off the stage and walks toward us. When he reaches Nero, he puts two fingers under Nero's chin, slowly forcing it up, and inspects Nero's face.

'Kill him!' a man in the crowd yells.

'Cut his throat,' yells another.

Doryphorus is shaking; so am I.

Nero whispers to the one-eyed man. 'Come now, Spiculus. Give your old Emperor a cup of wine. He's had a long journey to get here.'

And then the one-eyed man wraps his arms around Nero and I know this is it. Nero will be crushed to death and then they'll do the same to me. But then the one-eyed man laughs. He picks Nero up into the air and spins. I realize he's not crushing Nero; he's hugging him.

# XVI

## An Ovation
### A.D. 79

# DOMITILLA

◆

*5 April, morning*
*The cattle market, Rome*


The freedman waves his hand at the statue of Hercules behind him.

'You can see the problem, Augusta?'

Two slaves are on the podium, flanking the statute; neither stands taller than the demigod's stone nipples. They're holding up a purple toga, which would wrap three times around any man, but doesn't quite fit the statue.

'It doesn't fit?'

Pigs penned nearby squeal bloody murder; a cow, led by a boy, saunters past.

The freedman smiles and violently nods his head. 'Yes, exactly, Augusta.'

I catch Vespasia's smile out of the corner of my eye.

'Please do not call me Augusta.'

Vespasia whispers in my ear, 'Don't discourage him, sister. He thinks you're a goddess.'

I say, 'And why did you require my assistance?'

The freedman's smile evaporates; his bottom lip protrudes like a fresh wound. He says, 'You helped organise the triumph of Caesar and general Titus . . . I mean prefect Titus. It was an excellent occasion, I recall. Very well received.' The freedman sees my impatience and hurries up. 'And – and – and a new toga will need to be sewn for Hercules. I thought you could employ the same dressmakers who made the one used before.'

At Father's request, Vespasia and I, along with several other wives of notable senators, are inspecting tomorrow's parade route. Red strips of wool tied every fifty yards or so – to statues, fountains, shop stalls – mark the path. We've followed the route from the Campus

Martius, through the city walls and into the cattle market. It will swoop down from here into the forum and the circus, before twisting back up to the Capitoline. Tonight, as the sun sets, hundreds of slaves will sweep the path clean. Today, our main task is to check the decorations and remove any eye sores. This freedman's request, however, is too specific. Many of the important statues on the parade route, like Hercules, will be adorned in robes, bringing to life the gods; but the specifics are not my concern. I wonder if this freedman hasn't been too forward. Has the Batavian's bravado given the lower classes the wrong impression of me?

Thankfully, before I can answer, Jacasta steps between the freedman and me. She says, 'Mistress, I will find a solution. Please continue on.'

Vespasia takes me by the arm. 'Come, sister. Everyone is waiting for us.'

She spins me towards the group of women and Imperial secretaries waiting patiently.

Eight years ago, after Jerusalem finally fell, Father awarded a triumph to Titus and himself. With mother gone, and with Father and Titus preoccupied with matters of state, it fell to me to ensure the day was a success. The last triumph had been held nearly thirty years before, under Claudius, after his invasion of Britain. Given the lapse of time, we had some difficulty finding anyone who had been involved. Eventually we found a palace eunuch by the name of Posides. He was quite old, nearly deaf, and – for reasons I never learned – called me King Juba. But he knew the details of the procession, down to the last.

That day, as tomorrow will, the parade began in the Campus Martius. In the morning, before the sun rose, the troops lined up according to rank. Father and Titus, wearing garlands of laurel and purple robes with golden stars, emerged from the Temple of Isis where they had slept that night. After mounting a chariot, they led the troops through Rome to the Temple of Jupiter at the top of the Capitoline. Ahead of them were carts filled with the spoils of Judea: chests of gold, silver plates, jewels, men, women and children. At the head of the procession, there was a massive golden menorah taken from their great temple; its seven arms caught the sunlight and there was a gleam that rotated, back and forth like a twinkling star, as the cart carrying it bumped its way along the black brick road. Flower petals – pink and red and white – floated in the air. (It looked beautiful, but the magic was lost on me. I knew how much effort and Father's coin went into sourcing and distributing those petals. It would have been easier to simply throw coin.) Soldiers marched behind Titus and Father's chariot, thousands of them, laughing and answering calls from the crowd. Vespasia and I waited at the foot of the Temple of Jupiter. Father and Titus ascended the temple's steps, turned to the crowd and cries washed over them. It was the first time the city felt settled after the civil wars, the first time Father felt like Caesar. It was a good day.

On this occasion, however, Father has refused to grant Cerialis a triumph. 'It wouldn't be appropriate,' he said. 'The victory was against a band of criminals, not an army.' So rather than a triumph, Cerialis is to receive an ovation. The differences are few but significant. Cerialis will travel by foot, not chariot; he will wear myrtle, not laurels; his officers will follow him, while the rank and file will remain in camp; and Father has shortened the route considerably. He said, 'Let's not spend all day celebrating some other man's son.'

All of it I find amusing and slightly pathetic. Father and Titus often confuse politics with pride. They say, 'One cannot overstep their place,' as though the heavens would rain down on the capital if Cerialis went by chariot tomorrow rather than by foot. In truth, they see a hierarchy, with themselves at the top, and the world must make do with the space below. That's not politics. It's no different than a dog growling over its dinner.

We enter the forum in the afternoon. At the foot of the Capitoline Hill there is an unfinished stage. Saws work furiously; the sound resonates across the square, as though giants are snoring inside the surrounding temples.

Julia points at the pair of ivory thrones, which sit in the centre of the stage. 'Who will sit there? General Cerialis?'

Vespasia answers, 'Would your father allow another to take precedence? Never. Not in a hundred years.'

Julia and young Vip, cousin Sabinus's daughter, look at Vespasia for a moment before turning their attention back to the stage. I catch Vespasia's eye. *They're young. Don't poison their minds.*

I recognise contrition in Vespasia's face before she says, 'Those seats are for the Emperor and Titus. As the heads of state it is their responsibility to oversee the ovation.'

'Oh, I see,' Vip says, happy to contribute, whether she understands or not.

'Mistress,' Jacasta is behind me, whispering in my ear. 'Julius Calenus would like a word.'

'He's here? Where?'

Jacasta points in the direction of courthouse steps, on the other side of the square, where the grizzled ex-soldier is standing patiently.

'Another admirer?' Vespasia asks, smiling. This is a Batavian joke. She would have had a more biting comment, I think, if I hadn't chastised her moments before.

'Excuse me,' I say.

I cross the forum. Calenus starts to kneel as I draw close.

'We don't have to go through this again, Calenus? Do we?'

Calenus straightens up. 'Good afternoon, Mistress. Yes, sorry, Mistress.' He's an interesting character this one. An ex-soldier, living on Nerva's handouts. He must be disgraced in some way, having to earn a living like this. Or maybe he was just on the wrong side of the civil war. But there's something in those dark eyes of his, even with that grotesque scar running down his face . . . I trust him.

'How did you find me here?' I ask.

'By chance, Mistress. I recognised your girl.' He nods his head at Jacasta. 'I knew she wouldn't be too far from you. I thought I could speak to you away from the palace.'

'It makes you nervous, does it? The palace.'

'Yes.' His voice is sincere.

'And why is that? You've seen many battles in your day.'

He squints, considering the question. 'In battle you know who's with you and who's against you.'

'An astute observation. I assure you, Calenus, maintain your loyalty to me, and I guarantee you will have at least one friend in the palace.'

He nods. 'Yes, Mistress.'

'Well, don't keep me in suspense. You've sought me out. I take it you've spoken with –' I lower my voice '– him.'

'Yes, Mistress.'

'Well?'

'I did as you'd asked. I told him that he was embarrassing you, and that you wanted him to stop.'

'Did he understand?'

'Yes.'

There has never been a man of so few words. Stories come out one sentence at a time. 'Well?'

'He will stop.'

That should be enough to satisfy me, but I find myself wanting to know more. 'Did he say anything else?'

Calenus hesitates. He doesn't want to overstep his place.

'Speak freely, Calenus. Please. I will not be angry with what you tell me.'

Calenus clears his throat. 'He said he is sorry. He . . . he begs your forgiveness. He says . . . he says he loves you.'

My cheeks instantly smoulder with embarrassment. Behind me, Jacasta gasps with shock, as she should.

'Thank you, Calenus. I appreciate your diligence and . . . tact.' I wave my hand at Jacasta. She steps forward with a purse of coin. She presses three coins into Calenus's hands. How many draughts of wine will that buy him, I wonder?

I say, 'You are a good man, Calenus. I may come to call on you again, should the need arise.'

Calenus stutters his thanks before walking away, with his head down admiring the coins.

Jacasta and I watch him go. She says, 'You've made a friend for life, Mistress.'

'Yes,' I say. 'I think so.'

# TITUS

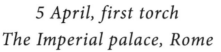

*5 April, first torch*
*The Imperial palace, Rome*

I find Father in his office, draped in a purple robe, sitting, with his feet propped up on a stool. A slave is on her knees, massaging his swollen, gout-ridden feet.

'How was your journey?'

'Bumpy,' he says, grimacing. 'It has left me tender.'

'I can see that.'

I sit beside Caesar.

He says, 'I see they're no further along with the amphitheatre since I left.'

Gone ten weeks and his first words to me are a complaint.

'They *are* further along. Much further.'

The slave on her knees looks up and smiles. She's pretty, save for her one thick eyebrow, rather than two. She seems familiar, but I cannot quite place where I've seen her before.

'How goes the preparation?' he asks.

'The ovation? Domitilla is handling it.'

'Good, good,' he says absently. 'And you met with Cerialis? What new information did he have to offer?'

I tell Father the story of the battle near Maronea, as Cerialis told it to me.

'An ovation for that?' Caesar shakes his head.

'The people won't care. Their only concern is the games.'

'I suppose,' Father says before changing the subject. 'I've allowed Ulpius to join the College of Augers.'

'That's ridiculous. How can he read the entrails of an animal? He's blind.'

'He paid me. That's how ... Careful!' Father yells at the girl, wincing. 'It's gout, not dough for tomorrow's bread. Where's the girl who normally does this? Where's Lesbia?'

The slave diverts her gaze. 'She's taken ill, master.'

Father sighs and shakes his head. 'Fine, fine. But be careful.' He wiggles in his chair, adjusting his robe.

The girl starts again and Father winces.

'Ulpius has also inquired about the consulships,' he continues. 'And to think, you said I put the price too high.'

Father recently had the idea to sell suffect consulships for past years, to raise money. He thought up and coming families would be interested in adding prestige to their lineage.

'If he'll pay that price,' I say, 'he's richer than I thought.'

'Don't be too hard on this man Ulpius. You don't understand the provincial's plight. It costs money, building a family's lineage, retrospectively.'

I raise an eyebrow. 'You talk as though you speak from experience.'

'You've had a much easier climb than I had. A provincial in Rome . . . it's not easy.'

'You forget,' I say, 'the old families of Rome consider me a provincial as well. My path has been easier than yours, I don't deny it; but it's been harder than you credit.'

'You had the finest tutors, any appointment you desired, unlimited coffers – your father is Emperor, for the love of Jove.'

'I said I don't deny my advantages were –'

'Yes, but you look down on Ulpius for buying titles and appointments. Careful you don't become the patrician snob you once despised. When your family is from a backwater like Spain, there are only two ways to change your place in the world: money and time. This man Ulpius is not content to wait, and I can't say I blame him.'

I put my hands up, showing defeat. 'Yes, Caesar, I will be more empathetic.'

Father's squint is sardonic. 'I didn't say that. Prefect of the Praetorians should not be empathic. I'm merely saying you shouldn't act the snob.'

Father suddenly grimaces, sucking in short, little breaths. To the slave with the one eyebrow, he barks, 'You are hopeless. Go find Lesbia. Don't come back.'

The slave with one eyebrow gives an embarrassed bow before shuffling out of the room.

Father turns his attention back to me. 'And what of Epaphroditus? Your letters explaining his disappearance were less than satisfactory.'

'I merely repeated what he told me,' I say.

'How long was he missing for?'

'Nearly a month,' I say. 'He attended Ulpius' dinner in January. Half a dozen guests watched him and his retinue leave at the end of the evening, but he never made it to the palace. His slaves went missing as well, so it was assumed they'd been behind it. And then one day Epaphroditus simply appeared, claiming he'd merely been drinking in the south. He'd needed a break, he said. But he was pale as moonlight, a cut and bruised cheek still healing, and his right arm hung lifeless in a sling. He looked as though he'd been to Hades and back, not enjoying the sun in the south. Ever since his return he has acted – I'm not sure of the right word – jittery, perhaps. His eyes dart around as though danger lurks in every shadow. There is more there than he has said, I'm sure of it.'

'Of course there is,' Caesar says. 'There is always more than what a man says. But does it matter? The hand in the forum happened months ago. Halotus is dead and Plautius remains missing, but – let us be honest – neither is a great loss for the Empire.'

'And what of the ambitious men you were concerned about? The men you said were salivating for your throne?'

Father shrugs. 'The danger will never pass, but clearly it's lessened. Unlike you, I was never much bothered by the body by the Tiber. This city has seen countless cults come and go. There's no evidence their machinations were aimed at me. The hand and Halotus's death were a concern, but it has been months now with no sign of sedition.'

My temper almost gets the better of me. He acts the benevolent prince now, but once there is any hint of sedition, he would say, 'Titus, you have failed me. Titus, find out who is responsible. Titus, cut their throats.'

Through clenched teeth, I say, 'If that is all?'

'For today, I suppose. I will see you tomorrow, at the ovation. Do your best to ensure there are no surprises, will you? I've had my fill for the year.'

# DOMITILLA

*6 April, morning*
*The forum, Rome*

The ovation starts in the third hour. We wait patiently at the end of it, on the stage at the foot of the Capitoline Hill. The road of black brick is empty; the city's populace, dressed in their best and brightest colours, cram either side. From our vantage, it looks as though a black snake is winding its way through a puddle of spilt paint, green and red and blue. The crowd roars in the distance. An impatient young girl at the edge of the road throws her petals into the air, and a handful of pink and white flecks float down to the bricks.

Vespasia and Julia are seated to my left; Father and Titus to my right. Julia starts to ask a question, but Vespasia shushes her. Beside the stage, there is a grandstand for respected senators and their wives.

The roar of the crowd grows louder. Excitement travels by proximity, from one person to the next. Collectively, we sense the parade approaching.

And then there is movement on the road; the crowd erupts; flower petals rain down.

Five mule-led wagons lead the procession. The first two carts carry the False Nero's officers, manacled and seated, with beards and menacing tattoos that stand in contrast to their forlorn expressions. The next two carry modest wooden chests and rusted arms – swords, spears and shields. Behind the wagons, by a distance of thirty paces or so, Cerialis is walking, waving to the crowd. His officers keep pace behind him.

After the four carts come to a stop in front of the stage, Cerialis walks to a spot directly in front of Father and kneels. Two Imperial freedman – one I don't recognise and Phoebus, the one Titus cannot stand – scamper to either side of Father's throne. Each takes an arm and help Caesar stand. Father pushes them away, flapping his arms like a gull, before gingerly making his way down the steps to Cerialis.

Phoebus trails behind carrying a pillow and, on top, a crown of myrtle. Cerialis – still on his knees – bows his head. Father takes the crown of shrubs off the pillow and places it on Cerialis's head.

Cerialis stands, turns to the crowd, and raises one arm above his head. The cheers from the crowd reach a crescendo and then Father and Cerialis walk back to the stage. Father takes his throne and Cerialis takes the open (more modest looking) seat beside Titus.

Two of Felix's officers jump into the back of the carts carrying the wooden chests and rusted arms. They look young, brimming with ego from the attention. I can see it in their wide grins and glowing eyes. One of them takes an old rusted axe and holds it above his head. The crowd cheers. Enthused, the soldier hacks at a chest's lock until it cracks open. Then he and his colleague swing open the top and begin throwing the coin held inside to the crowd. Next they turn to the neighbouring chest. Again, one of them uses the axe to crack open the lock. The lid swings open . . .

And out pops a man, stark naked, bearded, dishevelled, covered in mud and slime and the gods know what else.

Half the crowd immediately goes silent; while the other half – too far away to see what's happened, oblivious that a naked man just popped out of a crate – keeps cheering.

'By Hercules!' Father exclaims.

Vespasia chortles.

Julia use a curse word I didn't think she knew.

The two soldiers on the cart are stunned; they don't move an inch. The naked man steps – then falls – out of the crate and into the cart. He stands with wobbly legs and hops off the cart onto the road.

In the grandstand of patricians, a woman stands up. Antonia. Her face is ashen.

Titus is standing on the edge of the stage. His head swivels from Antonia to the man.

The naked man starts to run but trips on the bricks; he moves like a toddler, unused to his legs.

Jacasta is at my side. She leans in and whispers. 'Mistress, that's him. That's Lucius Plautius.'

# TITUS

◆

*6 April, sunset*
*The Imperial palace, Rome*

The marble hallway echoes with the sound of my approach. Virgilius –
leaning beside the doorway – salutes.

'He's cleaned up now. Just finished eating.'

'And Antonia?' I ask.

'She's in there as well,' Virgilius says. 'But other than her and a few
slaves, no one has talked with him, like you wanted.'

'An odd day,' I say.

Virgilius nods. 'Has your father cancelled the party?'

'No.' I say. Most of the city has no idea what had happened. The False
Nero's men were executed as planned. Father wants to act like nothing
happened – for now, at least. We were only just starting to put the mess
with the hand in January behind us. 'Tonight's celebrations are to go
ahead, as planned.'

Smiling, Virgilius says, 'Am I to miss another party?'

I ignore the question and push open the door.

Plautius – missing for months, now miraculously alive and well –
stands with his arms in the air, shoulder height. Slaves hover, wrapping
his toga around his formerly plump, now willowy, frame. Antonia is
sitting at the edge of the bed. Over the last three months, I've come to
know her mood. When her jaw is askew, she's annoyed; when her eyes
are wide, she's happy; when her bottom lip protrudes, she's sad. For the
first time, I see all three mix together on her face.

'Titus, old friend,' Plautius says happily. The dirt and grime and
smears of his own shit are gone; so is the smell. His face is freshly
shaved and his bald head shines like washed marble. He reeks of
flowery perfume.

'So,' I say, 'you've returned from the dead.'

'I'm like Orpheus, aren't I?'

Antonia's jaw slides further to the right. 'A poor comparison, I'd say.'

Eurydice wasn't as lucky as her lover, Orpheus. She remained in Hades.

'You seem in good spirits,' I say to Plautius.

'I'm finally back to Rome. I never thought I would see her again. Or my wife.'

The slaves finish dressing Plautius. I wave them away. Virgilius filters in quietly. He takes an inconspicuous place against the wall. Trailing behind him – sliding into the room before he notices – is Cleopatra. She's developed a knack for roaming the palace unmolested and finding me when it suits her. She saunters over to me and collapses in a heap. She begins to pant, tongue lolling out the side of her mouth.

I ask Plautius, 'What happened?'

'Can't this wait, Titus?' Antonia bristles. 'He's just been to hell and back.'

'Darling,' Plautius says. 'I'm fine. Really, I am.'

Antonia's head twitches in disagreement. She's angry. For the first time, I think: she didn't want her husband to return. It was just this week, one morning in bed, she was discussing the necessary paperwork. Did she think herself the next Empress of Rome?

I ask Antonia to leave me with Plautius and her anger doubles, but she reluctantly agrees.

Once Antonia has left, I say, 'Start at the beginning. Tell me everything.'

'The whole mess I put down to chance,' Plautius says. 'Unfortunate, unlucky chance.'

He begins with what I already knew, his arrival in Italy, how he was to stay in Baiae, while he searched for a summer home. He explains how he and his freedman Jecundus visited a brothel, the Stolen Glance, the very day they arrived in Miscenum. 'I was embarrassed at having attended,' he says, 'for I consider myself a moral man, Titus, a true Roman. But now, after what I have been through, I am beyond embarrassment.' He takes a deep, curative breath before continuing. 'I met Jecundus on the portico the next morning, hammers of alcohol banging away at my temples. After he politely inquired of my adventures, he told me about his night with this woman Red. Apparently, they sat and talked for hours. He said the woman had a charm about her, and Jecundus is not devoid of charm himself. After they had become good and drunk, she confided in him, telling him the story of the knight being abducted and the possible attempt to poison Caesar – the story I told to you in my letter. However, he didn't think much of it. He considered the whore your typical female, exaggerating some fright she'd had. But I couldn't leave it to chance. I care too much for you and your father.'

Plautius stares at me like a dutiful puppy.

He continues. 'I knew we had to find her again and learn everything we could. But our quest had to wait until after the baths: we needed to sober up. But by the time we returned to the Stolen Glance, she was gone. It would be more than two weeks before we stumbled upon her in the market. Understandably, she was scared. But she agreed to meet us the next day and take us to the knight's home.

'She lived in Miscenum, at the southern tip. Because I had business to attend to that morning, and I didn't want her changing her mind, I sent Jecundus early to ensure she kept her word. When I came to the apartment, Jecundus was dead and the whore was missing. Jecundus was known as being in my employ. I thought: if the murderer had no compunction killing a senator's freedman, what was to stop the murderer from murdering the senator himself? I took refuge in the nearest, least conspicuous place I could think of: the Stolen Glance. I stayed in the brothel for four days, living off stale bread and oily fish. Until one day the owner, a fat pimp the size of an ox-cart, suddenly demanded payment. He became the only vendor in all of Italy who is not content with a senator's word. I sent one of their boys to the house I was staying at, to fetch one of my slaves and coin. I was still waiting for him to return when two large thugs were given entry into my room.' Plautius shivers. 'After a swift beating, a sack was pulled over my head, my arms were bound behind my back, and I was dragged out into the street and thrown across the back of a horse. We travelled, but not very far.

'My sack was replaced with a blindfold and I was kept in a cage of wood. It stank of ammonia and my nose burned until the second day when it ceased to feel anything at all. I believe it was some attic above a fullery. It was not very Roman of me, but I was scared beyond my wits. I shivered and cried and called for help. I could hear my captors. I could hear them laugh and drink and dice. I could hear them plot. I was kept there for two days. On the third day, I was taken from the cage and my bonds undone. I was put on a chair, still with my blindfold on. I was told "the Boss" wished to speak to me. There I sat for I don't know how long. No one came. I eventually grew the nerve to steal a peek. I lifted my blindfold and saw there was no one around. I was sitting in a chair in an empty room. The door was ajar. I counted to ten. Then I ran.

'The door led to a balcony and stairs, which I followed down. I found myself on the pier, with ships tethered to the stone, one after the next. To my right, a group of men were approaching. Were they the one's that had taken me? I wasn't sure. To my left, another group of men were talking. I didn't know who was friend and who was foe, so I ran forward, across a gangplank and onto the nearest boat.

'I hid in the ship's hold, among amphorae of oil, sitting in an inch of water. I planned on waiting there until night, then make my way back to Baiae, but the boat raised its anchor that very afternoon. I wonder what you would have done, Titus? Would the great general have a plan? I certainly did not. I had no coin, no belongings. I kept below deck, thinking I might be able to sneak ashore at the ship's next stop, wherever that was. But I was found the next day. A sailor came below to check the amphorae for leaks. He jumped a foot in the air when he saw me. I was taken to the deck and brought to the captain. I explained who I was, how I would provide handsome reward for returning me to Rome – I had no interest in returning to Miscenum and my captors. Well, do you know what this villain of a captain said in response? "A senator, are you? Stowaways are always senators who've forgotten their purse." And then, Titus . . . and then they chained me to an oar and forced me to row.

'Those were the darkest days I've ever had in my life. It was only a few months, but it felt an eternity. I didn't think I'd ever escape. From sun up to sun down I rowed. My hands bled and blistered and then bled again. My skin burnt under the glare of the winter sun, until it was red and pink. My mouth was a desert; my tongue felt four times its size.

What little water they gave me did nothing. Wood splinters stabbed my bum and the back of my thighs.

'There were two men, one in front of me, the other behind, who sang all day long. They were all skin and bones, so I called the one Skin and the other Bones. I don't know what barbarian tongue they sang in, but it was awful. I didn't understand a word of it, except at the end of the chorus, they would yell "Again!" in Latin. I would go days without noticing it, but then I would explode with anger telling them to be quiet. They would laugh and the warden, a fat little man with a whip who paced the galleys all day long, would crack his whip above our heads and scream at us to be quiet. He thought I was having as much fun as Skin and Bones.

'We sailed west at first. Not that anyone told me where we were going. I know this merely from the fact we sailed away from the sunrise. We reached some barren barbarian port and emptied our hold of its amphorae, before filling it with more. Then we sailed east. I was certain we were sailing along the west coast of Italy. It was torture, knowing my salvation lay so close at hand. We passed through the Strait of Messina, Sicily on our right, Italy on our left. I cried thinking it would be the last time I lay eyes on the land of my birth. But we rounded up, and followed the coast north.

'I recognised Brindisium as we sailed into port. I had sailed into the very same port less than five months before. Once docked, we unloaded our last remaining amphorae. I saw the captain speaking with soldiers on the pier and then five of us were unchained. We were to help the warden carry amphorae to the legionary camp, which was pitched outside the city limits. I knew this was my only chance to escape from a life of slavery, so I waited for any opportunity to present itself. I don't understand why slaves don't always run when given the chance. Though, I suppose, slaves are slaves, and if they are caught they are crucified. Whereas I was a senator, illegally taken. It was a risk to run, but so long as I escaped, I did not face punishment.

'We arrived at the camp after dark. The warden, a former soldier, nostalgic for the "good old days", decided to get drunk. After we delivered the amphorae, we were sent to sleep in the slave tents. When everyone was asleep, I made my escape. I followed my nose to a tent with food.

(I had been starving for three months without reprieve.) I ate my fill of bread and roasted pig, and then brought the rest with me in a piece of linen for the journey to Rome. I also found a skin of water. I went from tent to tent trying to find something to wear for my walk to Rome, so I did not look the runaway slave. But then I heard the warden's voice, calling my name. (He called me Piglet, on account of my weight when I was taken. He persisted even as I lost the weight.) He must have checked in on the slaves and found me missing.

'I was in a tent filled with chests. I could hear the neighbouring tents being searched. I would have rather died than go back on the ship to row for the rest of my days. So I emptied one of the chests out, moving the golden and silver contents about the tent so it did not look conspicuous, stepped into the trunk, and brought the lid down. Unfortunately, the latch clicked shut and I was locked inside. But I had water and food, so I would not starve – at least not for a few days. You saw the crate – it was large enough, and light came in through the keyhole and the cracks between the wooden planks. And, I suppose, I had been so miserable in my brief life as a galley slave, I enjoyed the quiet.

'I listened to the warden come into the tent calling my name, cursing his "Little Piglet". But he soon moved on. The next morning, I felt the trunk lifted on to a cart and for two days felt it pitch and sway as we travelled. The crate was so small, the heat so stifling, I removed every stich of clothing, as though I were at the baths. After a day of rest, the cart was moving again. But this time I was surrounded by screaming men and women. It was so loud, I thought the trunk was being dragged into battle. I thought I had been wrong about docking in Brindisium, and we hadn't gone west to Rome, but instead north and mountain tribes in the Alps were attacking us. And then the crate opened and blinding brilliant light overwhelmed me. And . . . well, you saw what I did. I ran.'

Virgilius has an incredulous look on his face. He thinks the story impossible. As do I. But Plautius does have the burnt skin and calloused hands of a slave, not a senator.

Plautius says, 'I'm sorry, Titus. I've let you down. I wrote to you and said that you could count on me. But –' he holds his empty hands '– I've nothing to show for my efforts.'

'It's fine, Plautius. It's good that you're alive.'

Empty moments follow, as we quietly absorb his strange story. Then Virgilius asks, 'You said when you were held in Misenum, you heard your captors speak?'

'Plot,' I say. 'Plot is the word you used.'

'Yes,' Plautius says. 'I heard them speak about all sorts of things. I'm not sure much of it made sense. I don't recall any specific names.'

'Is there anything,' I ask, 'anything at all you heard which could identify a man?'

Plautius thinks. 'I heard them refer to two different men again and again. They never named them, but both descriptions stand out. And it was hard to miss they spoke so often of them. They called one the Turncoat. Does that mean anything to you?'

I exchange a look with Virgilius. His hand instinctively moves to rest on the hilt of his sword.

I say, 'Yes, Plautius. It does. It's the name everyone in the city uses for Caecina. How did you *not* know this?'

Plautius says uncomfortably, 'I'm sorry, Titus. But I've spent so many years in the provinces . . .'

Virgilius asks, 'You mentioned two men. Who was the other.'

'A name wasn't used for the other man.' Plautius relaxes slightly. 'They referred to a man who is no senator that I'm aware of . . .'

Virgilius and I bend our heads towards Plautius in anticipation, trying to meet what he is about to say halfway.

'They spoke of a blind man . . . filthy rich, according to them. So you can see my confusion there. In Rome there is no rich blind senator.'

'Oh, there is now, Plautius,' I say. 'There is now.'

# XVII

## Fetch Him for Me

### A.D. 69

# NERO

◆

*3 March, afternoon*
*Three miles inland, north-west coast of Sardinia*


This afternoon Marcus is learning to hunt. Spiculus and I sit on tree stumps outside his hut. He describes it all to me, patiently, providing context to the rowdy noise drifting across the camp. At the edge of the forest the men have painted a target on a tree. Each man has taken a turn throwing a spear. Marcus is then given a chance; but after each of his throws, another of the men needs to have another go. It sounds like children playing, not grown men giving a lesson.

The men erupt with cheers.

'The boy hit the target,' Spiculus says. 'Dead centre.'

'He learns quickly,' I say.

'He's been good for the men. He gives them a reason to behave, someone to impress.' Spiculus pours sour wine into wooden cups. He takes my hand and presses the cup into it. 'Who is he, then? You've never said. A slave?'

'He's not a slave,' I say.

'Like hell he's not.'

'He's not.'

Spiculus sighs. 'You've always had a thing for slaves, freeing them, raising them up. But what you're doing now . . . it's just not done.'

'And what am I doing?' I ask.

'I've no word for it because I've never seen it before. You're pretending he was never a slave. You're waving your arm like a witch, erasing his years of servitude. I can see it in the way you treat him. It's different from how you treated me or your other freedmen.'

'Are you jealous?'

Spiculus snorts. 'Like I said: it's dangerous. If anyone ever found out . . . at the very least, the boy would be crucified.'

I don't respond.

'I can't understand why you're bothering,' Spiculus says. 'A freedman can have many of the same advantages a full Roman citizen enjoys. How grand *are* your plans for the boy?'

'What does it matter whether he was a slave before or not?' I say. 'If I was emperor one day and a prisoner the next, why can't this boy be a slave one day and free the next?'

'You can't erase history,' Spiculus says. 'It doesn't work like that.'

'We shall see.'

'At least teach him to look men in the eye,' Spiculus says. 'That's what gives him away. He keeps his eyes aimed at the dirt, like a slave.'

We've been with Spiculus for nearly two months now, as we recover our strength and plan our next steps. I'm anxious to get to Carthage and press on, but it would be dangerous to rush ahead. Anyway, the time has been good for Marcus. Doryphorus continues to teach him to read and to write, and he has begun to teach him Greek. The bandits have shown him how to hunt – how to track, snare and spear game on this godsforsaken island. They've also taught him skills I wouldn't have thought to. He is already a better dice player than I ever was.

Our first night in the camp – after Spiculus learned who I was, and after he fed us and set us up in proper quarters – he took me to his tent. We drank sour wine and talked until dawn.

'Make your case,' I said.

'What case?'

'Prove you were not one of the men who betrayed me.'

'If I were,' he said, 'why wouldn't I kill you now and finish what I'd started?'

'Regret,' I said.

Spiculus laughed. 'Of all the emotions your murderer will feel, I don't think regret will be one of them.'

'You're avoiding the question,' I said. 'You sound guilty.'

'Caesar, please,' he said, growing serious. 'I owe everything to you. I would never have betrayed you. Before you, my master kept me chained in the street like a dog. He entered me in the fights without any training. He'd hand me a rusty helmet and a dull blade and wish me luck. To him, I was nothing more than fodder. But you saw me fight. You purchased me. You had me trained.'

'Your potential was undeniable,' I said, remembering the behemoth that darted like a fish.

'You made me a legend of the arena. You gave me my freedom. You gave me the honour of joining Caesar's personal bodyguard. I would never betray you.'

It's odd reading a man without your eyes, as difficult as reading a page. He was right, though: I did rescue him. I bought him, freeing him from his master's ignorance; and I had him trained – not only in combat, but in Greek, history, the poets, philosophy. If he was to represent Caesar in the arena, he must be more than a mere thug. I watched him grow from a timid beast into a man who inspired timidity. I'd always trusted him. The question was: should I continue to do so? Then again, what choice did I have?

We talked of the coup. He told me everything he could remember.

'Four years ago, you made me head of your personal bodyguard. Egos are what I dealt with, day in, day out. No doubt you knew of the rivalry between the Praetorians and your gladiators. But there was also a rivalry between the Praetorians themselves. Each Prefect had his own faction. Tigellinus's men would seek any advantage they could over Nymphidius's, and vice versa. And both groups would seek advantage over me and my gladiators.'

'You never raised any of this with me,' I said.

'Caesar shouldn't be concerned with petty squabbles. I make no excuses. I'm merely giving context for my failure. The coup occurred on the eighth of June. You attended the races and, by the end, you were drunk on sun and wine. I helped you from your litter and together we walked through the palace to your chamber. I had that evening off and should have left then. But Crixus was ill, so I took his place. Hercules was the other gladiator on duty.

'I remember what happened, the error I made . . . I would give anything to have those moments back. Two Praetorians arrived in the tenth hour to relieve their colleagues. They rounded the corner and, when they saw me, stopped dead in their tracks. They knew the rotations for the Praetorians and gladiators, so they were not expecting me. I didn't think anything of it at the time, but now I know they were scared; their plan was in jeopardy. Perhaps they planned on subduing Crixus and Hercules. But me? I fought in the arena for ten years. I never lost. What hope did two Praetorians have?

'But in the end, I was subdued – not by violence but through a trick; a simple trick only a child would fall for. It was the centurion who spoke to me, a redheaded man named Terentius. He told me your wife had a visitor, and wondered what we should do. You hadn't seen your wife in months. I knew she meant little to you. But the idea she would have a visitor at night was unacceptable: Caesar cannot be made a cuckold. This centurion clearly knew the love I bore you, and that I would rush to quash any possible embarrassment. So off I ran. When I returned, Hercules was dead and you were gone. I will never forgive myself.'

I didn't say anything. He shouldn't forgive himself. He was there to protect Caesar. He failed.

'I gathered my gladiators and we searched the remainder of the night, throughout the palace and then the city. But in the morning, the rumours began. It was said you had fled the city. Then the reprisals started. Your enemies began to gather up your supporters; we were ambushed in the street by a dozen soldiers. I was the only one who fought free. I hid until nightfall and then made my way to Ostia. I found a spot on a merchant ship from the east, who didn't know what the Emperor's favourite gladiator looked like. I'm sorry, Caesar,' he said. 'So very sorry.'

After Marcus's hunting lesson and dinner of fresh fish by the campfire, as we do now most nights, we retire to Spiculus's hut. We talk into the night. I can hear Marcus dreaming. (We've spent enough time together that I now know the slow, undulating measure of his breathing when he sleeps.) As he paces, Doryphorus's voice slides from one side of hut to the other. Spiculus is beside me. I can sense the space he eats up with his bulk. Perhaps it's the warmth he radiates, like the summer sun.

Word has come from Rome. (Somehow. Who knows how word travels from thief to thief, from Rome to Sardinia, across the sea.) January repeats itself. There are two emperors again. Joining Otho to the purple is Vitellius – gluttonous, debauched, frivolous Vitellius – whose troops in Gaul recently proclaimed him emperor.

'Vitellius marches south from Gaul,' Spiculus says. 'Otho has taken an army north to meet him. It is anyone's guess what such a war will look like.'

Spiculus knows both men from his days as my bodyguard. He watched them drink and carouse and whore, with not a care for the workings of empire. I remember one night when Vitellius passed out in a puddle of his own retch. Spiculus was the only one who could lift the elephant-sized senator and carry him home.

Now that I'm gone, the Empire is coming apart at the seams. It's satisfying, of course. Still, watching chaos consume what once was mine . . . it may not be heartbreaking, but I wouldn't say it's pleasurable either. It's like watching an ex-lover marry a brute. You think, See what you're missing, but in your heart there's the echo of regret, a mere sliver of grief, for the life she'll have.

'The war will take place in Italy, most likely,' I say, 'in the north. This is good for us. It is a distraction. The eyes of the Empire will be aimed north, as we dig for our fortune in the south.'

'Who will win?' Doryphorus asks.

'In the end,' I say, 'neither. Neither man has the constitution for leadership. They both lack what an emperor requires, the intelligence and dedication, the force of personality. Neither has that certain *je ne sais quoi.*'

The night wanes. Finally, we turn to Cassius, the man I banished to Sardinia.

'Can your men be trusted?' Doryphorus asks.

'Yes. If they are paid,' Spiculus says. 'If they are paid, they are predicable.'

'Maybe we shouldn't bother with Cassius,' Doryphorus says. 'You're not certain he was involved with Torcus, so there's no guarantee he knows anything.'

'There's no risk,' Spiculus says. 'My men will bring him here. They will return him. He will be blindfolded.'

'I came here for Cassius,' I add. 'We're not changing the plan now. Fetch him for me, Spiculus. Bring me the traitor whose life I spared.'

# MARCUS

*12 March, sunset*
*Three miles inland, north-west coast of Sardinia*


Spiculus and four of his friends are gone for nearly a week. When they return, Spiculus is carrying a man over his shoulder, tied up and blind-folded. They arrive at sunset. The campfire is already lit and crackling, and the air smells like smoky cedar. Some of the bandits – when they see Spiculus squirt out of the woods – start to whoop and bang their wooden weapons together.

When he's in the middle of camp, beside the campfire, Spiculus swings the man down off his shoulder and drops him onto the sand.

Doryphorus leads Nero by the hand, from his hut to the campfire.

Spiculus unties the man's gag.

Spiculus says, 'Say your name.'

The captive is shaking.

Spiculus gives him a kick. 'Your name.'

'Caiu . . . Caius Cassius,' the man says.

Nero yells over the racket: 'Not here. Somewhere more private.'

Two of the bandits grab Cassius by the arms and drag him into Spiculus's hut. Nero and Doryphorus follow.

I run after them but Doryphorus is waiting for me at the door. 'Run along, slave-with-a-consul's-name.'

'I want to see,' I say.

'This is the work of men, not boys.' He stands in the door until I walk away.

Once Doryphorus had ducked inside, I ran around the outside of the camp until I reach the back of Spiculus's hut. There, with their backs to me, are two bandits, peeking inside the hut through the cracks in the timber. They hear me approach and look back. It's the two who everyone calls Castor and Pollux because they are always together. One is older, with white hair and a bent back. The other has black hair and a scraggly beard.

Castor whispers, 'Quiet, boy.' He points at a free spot along the wall. 'There's space here.'

Pollux glares at me as I walk to the spot. '*Shhhhhh.*'

I close one eye and – with the other – stare between a crack in the timber. Inside the hut, the man named Cassius is sitting on a chair while two bandits tie him to it. Spiculus is pacing back and forth. Nero and Doryphorus are standing to the side.

Spiculus removes Cassius's blindfold.

Cassius spits at Spiculus. 'Scum! Why have you brought me here? I demand to know!'

Spiculus calmly wipes the spit from his cheek.

Doryphorus says, 'Since when do traitors get to make demands?'

Cassius starts fighting against the ropes. He screams, a rumbling '*aggghhhhhh*'.

Nero steps forward. 'Cassius. Stop.'

Cassius ignores Nero and keeps on grunting and flailing around like a madman.

Nero says, 'Cassius, I spared you your life once. Don't make me regret it.'

Cassius stops flailing. He squints trying to see Nero in the torchlight.

'Who are you?' he asks.

Nero steps forward and bends down. He removes the fabric covering his eyes.

'My beard is longer . . .'

Cassius keeps squinting, leaning forward.

'. . . and my eyes are gone . . .'

Cassius whispers, so softly I almost don't hear it: 'No.'

'Yes,' Nero says.

'But you're dead,' Cassius says.

'I most certainly am not,' Nero says. 'There is less of me, but I am otherwise alive and well.'

Beside me, Pollux says to Castor: 'Who is he, anyway?'

'Who do you mean? The blind fellow or the one they dragged in?'

'Oh, never mind.'

Nero steps closer to Cassius. He says, 'Come now, Cassius, you don't believe everything you heard, do you?'

'How?' Cassius shakes his head. 'How did this happen?'

'As a matter of fact, I was hoping *you* might be able to offer some insight into how events unfolded.'

'Me?' Cassius says 'Nero, I . . . I had nothing to do with whatever happened to you. I've been banished to this godsforsaken island for three years, long before your fall. I spend my days fighting off –' he looks at Spiculus '– rogues from other towns.'

Castor and Pollux start talking again. Their voices are all I can hear.

'Wait? The blind fellow is Nero? *The* Nero?'

'Who's that?'

'You dolt! The Emperor.'

'The cripple? You're joking. I thought the emperor was Claudius.'

'Claudius was the emperor nearly twenty years ago. Nero was after him. Don't you know anything?'

I turn and whisper, '*Shhhhh!*' And then put my eye back to the crack in the hut. I hear Cassius say, 'It was her. She worshiped the cult; she worshipped the Black Priest. Not me. She tried to kill you once and I'm sure she tried again.'

'Lepida?' Nero says. 'Nonsense. She wasn't a true believer. Not like you.'

'No, you had it backward. You had it backward then and you have it backward now. It was Lepida who was a true believer. When she got caught, she blamed it all on me.'

'Who else?' Nero asks. 'I want their names.'

Spiculus pulls out his dagger and steps toward Cassius.

'No, no,' Cassius says. 'I'll tell you everything. The eunuch. It's the eunuch who is to blame. Halotus. He and Lepida had something on every one of them, Torquatus, Tullinus. Please. *Please!* Tell him to put the dagger away.'

'And who was the Black Priest?' Nero asks.

'I'm not sure. A senator, I think. Lepida only mentioned the name once or twice. But she never said who. All I know is she was scared of him. The only thing that bitch was ever scared of.'

And then all I can hear is Castor and Pollux arguing behind me. They start to push each other until they go over in a heap and wrestle on the ground.

Spiculus (who must have heard and left the hut) is soon standing over them. He pulls Pollux off Castor and shoves him so hard that Pollux sprints for ten yards before falling to the ground. Spiculus points away from the hut and says to Castor, 'Go,' and Castor gets up and runs. Spiculus turns and sees me. 'Go, Marcus.' His voice is easier than the one he used for Castor and Pollux. 'This is not for your ears.'

I follow the other two into the woods away from the hut. Spiculus watches me go.

# NERO

*15 March, dawn*
*Three miles inland, north-west coast of Sardinia*

Spiculus leads me into the hovel that held me my first night on the island, the one the bandits call 'the Jail'. I hear the merchant Ulpius shuffle around on the sand.

'Well?' he asks.

'I have negotiated your release,' I say. 'You will keep up your end of the bargain?'

'I will owe you my life,' Ulpius the merchant says.

'Some men have poor memories.'

'True enough,' he says. 'But there's more in it for me than paying back my debt. I'm a merchant, you see, and my aim is profit. I'm very picky when choosing partners. For twenty years, I've pointed at particular men and said, "You have what it takes. You are going to thrive. I want to be in business with you." And this is what I have done with you. I've spent more than three years in this jail. You spent a matter of hours. Two days in the camp and you seemed to be running it. You're as smart as Minerva and just as resourceful. I'm tying myself to you for my own sake. One can only imagine what you'll do in Rome.'

'And your brother? The one still alive,' Spiculus asks. 'The soldier? Will he play the part?'

'He is my junior by seven years. He will do as he is told. And he will see the advantage.'

'And the likeness?' Spiculus asks. 'He resembles your brother? The one who died?'

I feel their eyes on me.

'It's close enough. His wounds will fill the gap.'

Good answers, all of them. Answers I can take solace in; answers we can move forward with.

It was good fortune meeting this merchant. Provincial origins, a missing brother – there is much to work with, useful holes for a cripple to fill. And it is good to have my story set before heading to Carthage. If I am right – if we really are about to discover a fortune – the world will want to know my name.

'Let him out.'

As Spiculus is unlocking the merchant's cell, a sullen voice croaks, 'And what about me?'

'Yes, Cassius?' I ask. 'What about you?'

'How long am I to remain a prisoner. I gave you the answers you required. I am an innocent man.'

'You answered my questions,' I say, 'and I am grateful for your assistance, Cassius. But if you were freed, how long would you wait before trying to profit from the knowledge that I am alive? You're desperate to get back to Rome and this would be your ticket.'

'So I'm to remain a prisoner?' Cassius is despondent. 'For the rest of my days?'

'You're alive, Cassius,' I say. 'It is a generous gift. You're just too stupid to know it.'

Cassius starts to weep.

Ulpius the merchant is beside me now; I can hear him dusting the sand from his tunic. 'Ready to go,' I ask.

'Lead the way, brother.'

# XVIII

## Two Prisoners, Two Stories
### A.D. 79

# TITUS

◆

*7 April, dawn*
*The carcer, Rome*

We follow the stairs down. The air is cold and wet. Virgilius leads the way with a torch. He'd taken Caecina here himself, sometime late last night. We decided to give him the night to fester. Regulus will have arrested Ulpius by now, and taken him to a different jail, outside the city walls. We thought it best to keep the two separated. Cracks in their story will show more easily, if they are not given a chance to confer.

The carcer is nearly as old as Rome itself, built by its fourth king, a subterranean prison dug into the side of the Capitoline, beside the Temple of Concord, where men are left to rot before their death. It has held some of Rome's greatest enemies, Jugurtha, Vercingetorix, Caratacus. Now it holds Rome's most recent.

We reach the upper level, which is a rectangular room, dark and empty, surrounded on all sides by cold stone. In the middle of the room is a circular hole, two men wide, with prison bars sealing our prisoner down below. Virgilius and I walk to the hole and look down. At first Caecina is out of sight. We call for him and he slides into view.

Caecina holds his hand to shield his eyes and squints. This is the first light he's seen in hours: it likely feels like the sun, rather than a lone torch. After his eyes adjust and he sees who stands above, he smiles disdainfully.

Somewhere, water drips.

'Confess,' I say, not wasting any time. 'Name all of the conspirators and we will permit you to open your veins in the privacy of your own home.'

'Confess?' Caecina asks, incredulous.

'Yes. Confess.'

Caecina laughs bitterly.

Virgilius says, 'The prefect is offering a window of mercy. But it is closing fast.'

'Confess to what?' Caecina asks. 'The charges have not been named. And I cannot guess what you have trumped up. If it's for what I've *actually* done, the laws of Rome are run roughshod.'

'Well, let's start with what you've *actually* done. Start with what you admit.'

Caecina harrumphs. 'Why play the part honest if the play is a comedy?'

He acts the victim well enough. It's how he survived the civil wars, how he tricked those who had a knife to his throat, again and again.

'What do you know of Torcus?' I demand. 'The god of the marsh.'

'I haven't the faintest idea what you're talking about,' Caecina says.

Virgilius looks at me. *Give him time to stew.*

Virgilius is right – all prisoners soften with time. But I need answers quickly. Whatever Plautius discovered – it was planned months ago. The gods know how much time we have left.

'You have until tomorrow,' I say to Caecina. 'Then we put your slaves to torture. Their blood will be on your hands.'

I follow Virgilius up the steps.

The building is two storeys of terracotta brick surrounded by a sea of green. Regulus – my patrician, entitled military tribune – and three soldiers are waiting out front.

Regulus grabs my horse's bridle as it slows to a stop. 'Prefect Titus,' he says. 'Ulpius is inside.'

'Good. Did he say anything when you arrested him?'

'No. He took it quite phlegmatically.'

A sign of guilt, perhaps?

'We treated him delicately, as you'd asked,' Regulus says. 'He already has a visitor.'

I step down from my horse. She's spent from the run and panting heavily; her black nostrils open and contract with a violent flourish.

'A visitor?'

'Yes,' Regulus says. 'Normally, I'd never allow such a thing, but Ulpius is, as you know, a cripple. It seemed indecent to stop a visitor.'

This is my fault. I told him to treat Ulpius differently. I only meant for him to arrest Ulpius in a civil manner, not to give the cripple free reign.

'Who?' I ask. 'Who is visiting him?'

'The man's nephew. The younger Ulpius.'

I can hear laughter as I near the top of the steps. I enter the room and find the boy, Marcus, sitting on a three-legged stool in front of the cell and Ulpius sitting – as Caecina did, as I suppose all prisoners sit – with his back against the wall, cross-legged.

Their laughter tails off when they see – or, in the elder man's case, hear – my arrival. Virgilius follows me inside.

Anger doesn't cloud my judgement as it did with Caecina. I can play this with more tact. I ask Virgilius, 'Do you know what I'm wondering?'

'What's that?' Virgilius asks.

'Who is more likely to laugh: the guilty or the insane?' I ask. 'I'm quite certain innocent men don't laugh after they've been arrested.'

The elder Ulpius pipes up. 'We are merely nostalgic.'

'Nostalgic?' I ask. 'I don't understand. You have been arrested before?'

'What do you care of past crimes?' Ulpius asks. 'This seems of the more recent variety.'

I shake my head. It will be tiring questioning this eccentric. He talks in circles.

'Where were you before your arrival in Rome?' Virgilius asks.

The boy answers, 'Spain, with stops in Marseilles and Civitavecchia.'

I point at Ulpius. 'Let him answer.'

Ulpius says, 'Oh, best to let Marcus give you the answers you're looking for. I could have been in Antioch for all I know.' He points at his rag-covered eyes. 'I've no way to corroborate. If someone says, "We are in Spain,"' who am I to argue?'

I exchange a look with Virgilius. *Are these two having fun?*

I say, 'You have been arrested on charges of treason.'

Ulpius tilts his head considering the charge. 'Yes, that seemed the likeliest explanation for bringing me here.'

The man's lack of fear is infuriating. 'If you do not answer my questions we will put your slaves to torture.'

Ulpius mutters something to the boy. I know four languages, but the tongue is not one I know. The boy gives a derisive snort.

A spasm of frustration travels the length of my arm and I automatically clench my fist: someone is plotting to poison Caesar and possibly his entire family, and yet these two are laughing at the thought of it.

'What do know you of a plot to poison Caesar?' I demand.

Ulpius says, 'You're right, Marcus.'

I look to the boy. 'Right? Right about what?'

The boy says, 'My uncle and I had been discussing history. The Empire's obsession with poison.'

Ulpius says, 'Great effort is made to sniff out plots against the Emperor – arrests, interrogations, torture. Marcus once posited: why not simply round up those who make poison? Ask them your questions.'

What nonsense. The man is casually chatting about the Empire's history, rather than pleading for his life.

Virgilius catches my eye. Leave him for now. *Let him think on this a bit longer.*

'Do you want my advice, Titus?' Ulpius asks. 'You are letting circumstance dictate character. Wise rulers make rather than react to circumstance.'

'What do you know of ruling?' My retort has an edge to it. This cripple is getting under my skin.

Ulpius shrugs. 'More than most. You know the Empire had such high hopes for you. A child of character, they said. There was a story I heard once, of a young Titus Vespasianus, who, as a mere boy, to protect his friend, stood in the path of Caesar. What happened to that boy, I wonder?'

The cold hand of the past touches me on the shoulders. I see Britannicus, my friend, Claudius' son, eight or so, lying on the marble, sobbing. I see his older, spoilt step-brother, Nero, standing, arm raised, with a cruel, twisted smile poisoning his lips. He is holding a wooden sword, the type gladiators train with. I stand between them. My eyes are closed, waiting for wood to collide with a yet-unknown part of my body.

I am quiet for too long. Virgilius raises a snowy eyebrow. *You're letting an old cripple get to you?*

I point my finger at Ulpius, as though he can see it. 'You have the night to think. In the morning, I want answers.'

Once we're outside, Virgilius looks around. 'The boy.'

We left Marcus with Ulpius. I was too distracted to notice.

To Regulus, I say, 'Go. Get the boy out. Drag him out if you have to.'

Regulus and two soldiers go inside. Soon we hear muffled shouts; then silence. Moments later, the boy calmly walks out of the jail. Alone. He stares at me contemptuously as he walks to his horse.

Regulus comes rushing out of the jail, minus his helmet. He is growling with rage. He rushes for the boy.

Out of the corner of my eye, I can see Virgilius stepping forward. His instinct is to stop Regulus, before he seriously harms the boy. But my intuition says differently. I've calmed down since Ulpius's comments; my mind is clear. I now see the boy differently, and I want to know him better. I grab Virgilius by the arm and give him a look: *let this play out.*

Regulus rushes at the boy, sword raised. The boy stands his ground before – at the very last second – casually stepping aside, as Regulus's sword swings down through the empty air. The boy crouches and grabs Regulus by the ankle. He stands, bringing Regulus's foot with him, and then Regulus – already off balance – falls face first to the grass. The boy pounces. He gives two heavy thumps to the back of the soldier's head, flips him over, and then hits the tribune three times in the face.

I let go of Virgilius's arm and he quickly moves to intervene. He rushes to the boy and picks him up in his arms, smothering his wild, flailing fists.

The boy is screaming. I'm not sure when he started; it goes and goes. I see him differently for the second time today. I'm not sure I've ever seen anyone, let alone a boy of seventeen, so filled with rage. He looks as though he wants the world to burn.

The other two soldiers finally come out of the jail, roughed up but alive. Thankfully.

Regulus is on his feet. His face is bloodied and his hair is tousled like a child after a nap. Bruises will follow. He pulls out a dagger hidden in his boot. 'Hold that little shit still,' he says as he wipes the blood from his mouth.

'Stop!' I say.

Regulus is incredulous. 'He will pay for what he has just done.'

'You should pay *him*,' I say. 'Give him silver and beg him to never speak of this again. You let a boy best you. Twice, by the looks of it.'

'You can't be serious. He must be punished for this . . . for this indignity.'

'You forget yourself, Regulus. You have let a child get the better of you. You've no one to blame but yourself. I will have to think about what punishment *you* should have. Of course, that's in addition to the ten lashings for speaking back to your superior officer.'

Regulus looks at the boy, then me. He growls in outrage, but keeps his mouth shut.

To the two soldiers, I say, 'Take Regulus back to camp. Have a centurion whip him. Ten lashes. Tell them why. If I don't see bloody welts on his back, I will find you and give you three times as many as he's due.'

Regulus's shoulders slump; his eyes slicken with a glossy sheen like he's about to sob. This will be a difficult embarrassment for him to live down. But he left me no choice. I won't have anyone question me publicly, especially one of my own soldiers.

Regulus walks in defeat to his horse. The two soldiers follow.

The boy is still in Virgilius's arms, but he is no longer struggling.

How do I handle this? I don't want to give him a beating; nor do I think it would have any effect.

After Regulus and the soldiers have untethered their horses and are riding east, towards the Praetorian camp, I signal for Virgilius to let the boy go. Once free, the boy takes two steps away from Virgilius. He straightens his tunic and belt.

A cow's bell clatters somewhere in the valley.

'Where did you learn to fight like that?' I ask.

The boy takes a deep breath. He looks about, weighing his options.

'The better question,' the boy says, 'is where did *your* man learn to fight? Isn't he a soldier?'

For all this boy knows, his life hangs in the balance. Yet, for me, all he has is disdain.

'I wouldn't call him a soldier.'

'No?' the boy asks.

'It takes more than the uniform,' I say. 'We are always looking for good young men in the legions.' I've arrested his uncle for treason and he has just finished assaulting three of my soldiers, yet I find myself trying to recruit him. Virgilius is smiling. He thinks it reckless, which, he will later say, is very unlike General Titus.

'You want me to be a soldier?' the boy snorts. 'Haven't you noticed? I eat soldiers alive. I can't very well do that if I'm one of them.'

'I could take you on my personal staff.'

I'm close to begging now. Virgilius is shaking his head. He can't believe it.

'I'd rather open my veins.' The boy is standing up straight now. Defiant.

I'm growing more aware – and more confident – in my intuition. This rage filled youth should be put to good use.

'Virgilius and I are going to take your advice. We're going to seek out the witches of Rome who make poison. Come with us. You can help clear your uncle's name.'

The boy asks, 'You're serious?'

'Yes,' I say.

Strange words echo from above. All three of us look up to the jail's lone window. It's small, with three iron bars, and darkened by the shadowy outline of a head. Ulpius' head. I recognise the language as Oscan – a language near extinction. It's an ancient saying, one little used. I vaguely recall it from childhood: if the snake is on your doorstep, invite him inside.

The boy shakes his head. He yells up at his uncle. He speaks in a language I don't know, not Oscan, or Greek, or Latin. Persian, maybe. Ulpius hollers back. He uses the same tongue.

Who are these two?

'The answer is no,' the boy says. Without another word, he walks to his horse, mounts it, and gallops across the plain.

# DOMITILLA

*7 April, afternoon*
*The Imperial palace, Rome*

Antonia and I are in the Atrium of Julia, admiring rare stones brought by my Illyrican jeweller Talthybius, when Vespasia bursts in from the hall. She is nearly spitting with rage.

'He has no right!' she says, ignoring our guests.

I put the emerald I'm holding down, meet Vespasia's eyes and say, calmly, 'A walk in the garden, sister?'

The tenor of my voice gives her pause. She looks at Antonia, then the jeweller. She smiles. 'Yes, thank you, sister.'

I excuse myself and together Vespasia and I exit, arm in arm.

When we are walking in the shade of the colonnade, I say, 'You know better than to act like that in front of people outside of the family.'

'I know,' she says. 'But Titus has no right.'

Her anger has lessened; but there is despair there, beneath the rancour.

'What is it?' I ask. 'What did he do?'

'He has arrested Caecina.'

I stop walking and stare into my younger sister's eyes. She's hinted at this for a while now, hasn't she? What did she say in January? *I have pursued love outside of my marriage.*

'How long?' I ask.

She diverts her eyes. She feigns embarrassment but I see her pride; she thinks Caecina a prize. 'Since October,' she says, 'of last year.'

I am unable to control my eyebrows, which rise an inch, maybe two. 'Vespasia! He is married. As were you.'

'I love him, sister.'

How many men has my sister claimed to have loved? I wonder if she has loved anyone but herself.

'Titus has falsely arrested him. He will kill him on a whim. You must speak with Titus. *Please.*'

'You know his history with Caecina. He will not listen.' I shake my head in disbelief: somehow she has persuaded me. 'We will have to speak to Caesar himself.'

# TITUS

*8 April, afternoon*
*The Imperial palace, Rome*


Phoebus, Father's loathsome secretary and freedman, finds me in my study.

'General Titus,' he says. As always, he has rolls of paper clutched in his little hands. 'Caesar sent me.'

I look up from my papers. 'Yes, that seemed likely. I couldn't imagine you thinking for yourself.'

Ptolemy – somewhere in the room, hidden from view – snickers.

Phoebus bares his sharp teeth.

'Caesar commands you to release your prisoners. Caecina and Ulpius.'

I put the roll of papyrus I'd been reading down.

'Does he?'

'He does,' Phoebus says, luxuriating over each word.

My response is firm but untroubled, as though I'm advising a misbehaving child. 'Tell Caesar, no.'

I reach for the roll of paper and resume reading. After a moment, after Phoebus runs through possible replies and determines none would do, I hear his sandals squeak along the palace floor, as he scutters back to Caesar.

Ptolemy appears at my side not long afterwards.

'Find my father,' I say, without looking up from my letter. 'I want to know when he is alone.'


Caesar's eyes are closed. Steam tickles his chin. His old body – once thick as a tree stump, but now thinning out with age – relaxes against the bath's marble wall.

'Father,' I say as I approach, 'I didn't know you were here.'

Father doesn't open his eyes, but a small, ironic smile curls the corner of his lips. 'No,' he says. 'Strange, I'd have thought you'd come running to apologise. It's not often Caesar is told "no".'

I sit down beside him and lean back against the marble. I suck the bright hot steam into my lungs; I let it out. Quietly, so that the slaves hovering nearby cannot hear, I say, 'I would have thought it would be *you* who would apologise. Sending your freedman to give me orders. Interfering with my investigation.'

'My freedman didn't give you an order. *I* did. He merely delivered it. Is it my fault that my son is so petty he bickers with my freedman? What did he do? Smile when he gave you the order. You are a soldier, Titus. If a man smiles when he delivers an order – what of it? Deal with it.'

'You could have asked me yourself,' I say, painfully aware of how childish I sound.

'By god!' Father sits up with a start. 'We are leading an empire. I have spoken to Plautius. I know the pretence on which you arrested both men. It is too tenuous – especially for men who are friends of the principate. Have you forgotten that there are men in this city who have much to gain from pointing the finger? We are not the Julio-Claudians who believed any bit of gossip concerning the principate.'

My frustration is only deepened by a memory of my sanctimonious words to Regulus, which seems a lifetime ago. What am I becoming, that I disregard my own counsel? Yet I am loath to relent; I press on.

'They are our friends now?' I ask.

'They have always been so. Caecina's defection secured us an important victory in the civil war. And Ulpius gave me a massive sum – funds we could not have taken the Empire without. And I worry your motives with Caecina are personal, not political.'

'That is an old story,' I say. Father means our fight during the Neptunalia, with wooden swords. The world thinks I'll never forgive Caecina for his victory and the way he laughed afterward. 'We were boys. It makes no difference to me now.'

'Not that,' Father says. 'Something else.' He watches me closely, reading my reaction. He knows something I don't. 'But it is nothing,' he says,

'Not to an old man who has lived a full life. If you don't know what I'm referring to, it's best you remain ignorant. In the end, it doesn't matter. Let them out. Now.'

I stand without a word. Whatever Father is referring to, he clearly doesn't intend to tell me now.

Before I leave, Father says, 'I don't know what you're concerned about. Plautius has returned, unharmed. The False Nero is defeated and fled east. I thought we'd agreed the crisis has passed.'

'There has always been more going on than Plautius' disappearance,' I say. 'The hand in the forum remains unexplained; your procurator was murdered, within the walls of Rome; and a man's body was mutilated by the Tiber.'

'The world is a violent place,' Father says. He relaxes against the marble wall again. 'Violent acts do not mean Caesar's life is in danger.'

'I have read things,' I say.

'What things?'

For the first time, I explain in detail Secundus' translation of the scrolls found on Halotus. 'Halotus' death was related in some way to the body by the Tiber. These are not random acts. There are forces at work in the city.'

Father waves his hand. 'What nonsense. There are always strange cults in Rome: Isis, Mithras, Christ. Romans are as promiscuous with their religions as they are with their wives. Religions come and go. And they're all dark in their own way. Don't let some scroll you found on a poisonous eunuch scare you. You're prefect of the Praetorians, for fuck's sake. Leave it.'

In the evening, well after the sun has set, as I sit lost in thought, aimlessly staring at the papers on my desk, Ptolemy leads senator Cluvius Rufus, the academic, into my office.

'Good evening, Titus,' Cluvius says. A wooden box is pinched under his arm. Rolls of papyrus stick out of the lid.

I stand – 'Cluvius' – and point at the seat across from my desk. 'Please.'

Cluvius sits. Ptolemy begins tidying papers.

'I hope I am not disturbing you,' Cluvius says. 'I know you are busy.'

'Not at all. In fact, I could use the distraction. How goes the writing?'

Cluvius bites his lip, considering the question. He is a particular case, Cluvius. Slight, with a patchy beard, and the delicate hands of a woman. He was one of Nero's favourites. He drank with Nero, caroused and gambled. I always thought he was as bad as his patron. Now, however, with Nero gone and the civil wars ten years behind us, he is the academic. He is writing a history, from Augustus to the present, and he has taken the task seriously. He sits at all hours in the libraries, scouring histories, family trees, edicts, dispatches, correspondence. A man can change – that is obvious – but to this degree? Was it a change in circumstance – with his patron gone and a new man to the purple – that led to this transformation? Or did it provide the opportunity to stop, exhale, and become the man he always was, the quiet intellectual sitting before me?

'The writing is coming along,' Cluvius says, 'slowly but surely. But I often feel as though I have bitten off more than I can chew. History is a difficult animal to master; it is a chimera, with too many heads.'

A chimera? I'm not sure the analogy is apt. In any event, I ask, 'Is that so?'

'Yes. Quite so. There is a plethora of information: documents, official and unofficial, first-hand accounts, second-hand accounts, commentary from this person or that. The information is endless. I could read day and night, until I was old and grey, and I still would not run out of material to review. On the other hand, the material is often contradictory and probably unreliable. And then there is the matter of direction, my literary bent, that is. What themes do I focus on? How do I balance one against the other?'

I am not sure I care, but to be polite, I ask: 'How so?'

'History is a narrative,' he says. 'You cannot write everything down or the story is lost.'

These are his concerns? The life of a writer: I would give my left arm. 'Otherwise,' I ask, 'it goes well?'

'Yes, yes. The support you and your father give is most welcome.'

Father has done much to cultivate Rome's men of letters. He is confident the policy will manifest itself in a way that favours the party. He says the trick to ensure favourable treatment is to not ask for it. 'Tell them to write something and they will bristle. But give them money and a safe city in which to write and the rest will follow.'

'In fact,' Cluvius continues, 'it is your family's support that has . . . *compelled* me to come here tonight. To draw something to your attention, something I discovered yesterday, which may be of assistance.'

'Oh?'

'You recall I was given access to Nero's letters?'

'Yes. But I thought there wasn't much there. You said it was mainly love letters, gambling chits, angry letters to architects. That sort of thing.'

'When you asked, I had not yet reviewed it in its entirety.' Cluvius chooses his words carefully. 'I have now reviewed all that I was given. For the most part, I was correct. The majority of the letters are as I described them. There are, however, a series of letters which he kept separate from his official letters – letters I do not believe anyone else has seen, other than perhaps the palace secretaries who made the copies before sending them out.'

'And these letters are of interest to me how?'

'Well . . .'

Cluvius continues to plod.

'. . . beyond being of interest to an historian, there is reference to certain . . .'

He is sitting at the edge of his chair, labouring over each word, his eyes aimed at the floor.

'. . . to certain religious practices conducted during Nero's day, which could be related . . .'

'Out with it, Cluvius. Related to what?'

Cluvius finally raises his eyes to mine. 'The body discovered by the Tiber.'

'Explain that. What do you mean?'

Cluvius seems relieved now that he's finished. 'Have you heard of Torcus before, the god of the marsh?

I sit up in my chair. He places a stack of paper on my desk. 'Nero exchanged letters with a barbarian, the famous Caratacus. I have marked the letters which are most pertinent to Torcus, but I suggest you read all of them in order to achieve context. Send word when you are done, if you wish to discuss it further.'

He reaches for the stack of letters. As he's walking out, I say, 'Cluvius . . .'

'Mm?'

'You know the chimera is fiction, yes?

'I do. Goodnight, Titus.'

# XIX

## The Personal Correspondence of Nero Claudius Caesar

### A.D. 65 to 68

*Rome, 3 January [A.D. 65]*
*Dear Caratacus:*

*Last night I dreamt of a coup. My own, actually, so I'm in a mood. I know the dreams of one man can put the next to sleep, but grant me this indulgence, old king: I have a point.*

*The dream began in the following manner. I was asleep, buried under soft silk, with naked, satisfied flesh spread out beside me. Then, without warning, soldiers burst through the door and dragged me out by the feet. They hurried me to my family's crypt and sealed me inside, alive. My screams for help went unanswered; the soldiers' taunts seeped through cracks in the stone. Hours stretched into days, days into weeks. A new man donned the purple and the Empire moved on. I did not. There I stayed, alone in the dark. Forgotten.*

*The dream was unsettling. However, it was not the violence of it that still haunts me, hours later. It was their common-ness. The soldiers, I mean. Each had a plain face and dark little eyes – men from some lowly Gallic town where there are few alternatives for breeding; where a plain face has no choice but to settle down with dark little eyes. And yet they wore the uniform that has conquered the world: steel cuirass, greaves, a sword at the hip, plumed helmet. The humdrum of humanity festooned in the greatness of Rome. The contrast was unnerving. It led to one thought in particular, one I'd never had before. You see: I may be a god, but unlike Jupiter, my power is divisible, divided up into every man who serves at my leisure. The true source of my godliness has a mind of its own, should he choose to use it.*

*My dream follows unfavourable portents. Never before (or so I am told) has there been such frequency of lightning. In Placentia, a calf was born with its head fused to its leg. Worst of all, a comet appeared three nights ago.*

*I consulted with the astrologer Balbilus. He has referred to his texts and conferred with the College of Augers. He is confident the portents are warnings, rather than the signs of anything inevitable. Remain vigilant, he says, and I shall rule for another twenty years.*

*My secretary Epaphroditus agrees with Balbilus. So too does the prefect Tigellinus. Trust in the gods, they say. Balbilus has never been wrong, they say.*

*I know they are right. Still, on a cold evening such as this, with only a lamp, papyrus and pen to keep me company, I find myself thinking of the advice you gave my uncle, Claudius Caesar, all those years ago. Do you remember? It was the first time we met. Claudius and the Imperial cortège paid a visit to your Italian estate. I was only a boy. It was the beginning of spring.*

*I remember a road of white stone that crunched under the wheels of our carriage. There was pollen in the air and my eyes itched. The sky was an empty blue. Your farm was two storeys of terracotta sitting atop a green hill. Truth be told, I was disappointed. You were the first king I had ever met, and the first barbarian. I expected a garrison manning parapets, trenches, screams in a guttural tongue, and foreign flags whipping in the wind. I knew that your defeat at Roman hands had come and gone, but I was young and life had not yet robbed me of my romanticism. I craved adventure. I was not prepared for a staff of ten, groves of olives and lemon, and an old man who waved as we came up the drive.*

*Claudius Caesar did not travel lightly. There were hundreds of us. Those who you could not accommodate in your home set up camp near the olive grove. In the evening, the musicians and dancers performed. There wasn't room in your garden, so ground was cleared on a nearby hill. Torches were lit. Wine was poured.*

*My uncle sat beside you. The two of you talked and talked. Mother insisted I sit close by, in order to hear how kings and emperors conversed. I remember Caesar sought your advice about Britannia, how to supress a tribe that was bristling under Roman rule. You told Caesar there was nothing to be done. 'One tribe or another will always be looking for a fight,' you said, 'whether against another tribe or Rome itself. That is the nature of the land you have conquered.'*

*My uncle responded with platitudes of the principate's unrivalled power. I will never forget your reply. You looked at Caesar – then, master of all – and said: 'Power is a ghost. One that will tire of haunting you soon enough.'*

*You spoke treason; yet Claudius did not have you arrested, or give you the back of his hand. He chewed on your words a while, then gave a slight nod of his head.*

*Your advice had great import for the Emperor then, and it has some for the Emperor now. You see: I find myself surrounded by men who marvel at my divinity, and commend my stewardship of the Empire – a stewardship that will last, according to them, sometime between now and eternity. But tonight, as I ready for bed, after a string of dark portents and evil dreams, I wonder: what would Caratacus say to me? What advice would Rome's most famous prisoner give?*

*It is an interesting topic: the nature of Caesar's power. Unfortunately, I cannot debate such things – at least not with my subjects. You have ruled; you understand. Men spy weakness like a hawk circling from above. Thoughtfulness is often twisted into vulnerability.*

*So I have imputed your past advice to my current circumstance. And I have considered your words for half the night. What is my response? Your advice contains some truth; I must concede the point. There have been four emperors before me. All met their end eventually. But your advice is premature. I grow more confident of this fact as I write. There will come a day when you are right, old friend, but today you are wrong.*

*Thank you for letting your Emperor write what he cannot say. The treasonous advice you gave to my uncle all those years ago, and which I imputed to you this evening – it is forgiven. You mean a great deal to me, as you did to my uncle. Plus, you were a king. You are given allowances others are not.*

*Send your prince some lemons so he knows you are well.*

*Yours,*

*Nero Claudius Caesar Imperàtor*

*Beneventum, 16 January [A.D. 65]*

*My Dear Emperor:*

*Of course I remember when we first met. It was a fine evening. The moon was full, which augured well, and the air was unseasonably crisp. It reminded me of home. I remember you were timid for a future emperor, soft-spoken and deferential, but bold in your own way. I watched you sit in rapt attention to the poets. I remember thinking, he is an artist – a good thing for a king to be, especially a Roman king. Romans lack artistry. Yours is an empire of engineers, heavy drinkers, and thieves. Roman art is merely Greek art, stolen and carted back on your well-built roads. An artist prince of Rome, I thought, now that would be a welcome change.*

*Never conflate hard truths with treason, my young king. That way tyranny lies. All things come to an end. To say as much does not amount to treason. It is merely honest observation. Which is something you, like your uncle before you, do not receive from your subjects and why letters are delivered to me with lunar regularity. And please do not misconstrue honest observation with desire. I hope your rule lasts as long as your astrologer predicts. Rome needs its artist prince.*

*You write asking for advice. But then, in the same letter, you anticipate and dismiss my advice. This is a trick of kings, I think; one I lost with my crown.*

*My advice – should you still covet it – is simple: drink, laugh, sing, read – read poetry and history and philosophy; travel and see the world. Love. You are still young – at least in this old man's eyes. Guzzle down all that life has to offer, while you can.*

*What news from the capital? My slave visited the market yesterday and returned with bad tidings. She reports that a woman was arrested in Miscenum on charges of treason. Word from the horse's mouth would be welcome, should you wish to give it, to fill my quiet days on the farm.*

*I hope you enjoy the lemons.*

*Yours,*

*Caratacus*

*Rome, 18 February [A.D. 65]*
*Dear Caratacus:*

*Much has happened since I wrote you last. The full details are yet unknown. This is what we do know.*

The slave woman you refer to was arrested in Miscenum after she asked a local captain to participate in a conspiracy to murder me, their Emperor. (I have great difficulty writing this even now, weeks later. Rage makes my arm shake.) She was arrested and questioned, but apparently knew little of the plot itself. It was not until recently that the simmering pot of intrigue finally boiled over.

Six nights ago, Flavius Scaevinus (a lazy, contemptible senator) emerged from a long, private conversation with Natlis, a knight with known republican sympathies. Scaevinus ordered his freedman, a man by the name of Milichus, to sharpen a blade. Scaeinus then revised his will, gave freedom to his favourite slaves and – boldest of all – had bandages prepared to staunch wounds he had not yet received.

This man Milichus put two and two together and, realising there was more to be gained by reporting what he had witnessed rather than being silent, ran to find me at the Servilian garden.

Scaevinus and Natalis were arrested and questioned under threat of torture until they named three conspirators, two senators and one knight. These three were brought to the Palace, separated, questioned, and each named two more accomplices.

There is a phenomenon I witnessed once when crossing the Alps. Snow – an army of it, miles wide – will slide down the face of a mountain, crushing everything in its path, building momentum as it falls. It is called an 'avalanche'. This is the only apt comparison to what transpired next. As we accumulated more names and brought those persons in for questioning, more names were given. This process was repeated again and again. And, like an avalanche, the momentum was devastating. We are still investigating with no end in sight.

Many have taken their own lives before they could be arrested; older, more distinguished patricians have been given the chance to do the same. The funeral pyres of the guilty, lit by their families, have been burning for two days. The devastation is so great that the very sky above the city is black with smoke and an acrid stench of burnt flesh fills my lungs this very moment. The white marble walls of the palace and forum and the city's temples are streaked black, and the populace wears black – nearly every citizen – so wide and pervasive was the conspiracy.

*I began questioning conspirators hoping to learn the reason for their treachery. I had to stop. There was no thread of reason, no common cause. Some sought revenge for affronts, however slight; some wanted the chance to rise with another; some thought me not worthy of the principate because I ride chariots in the circus and composed poetry and 'acted the Greek' – as though their lives weren't perfectly content otherwise.*

*Have you ever dealt with such a thing? You ruled for years, barbarians at that. Did you ever face such treachery?*

*Yours,*

*Nero Claudius Caesar Imperator*

*Beneventum, 1 March [A.D. 65]*

*My Dear Emperor:*

*I have your letter of 18 February and the advantage of further news from Rome. I have heard the man who orchestrated the plot was the elder Piso and, to escape the odium of his failed treachery, he has opened his veins.*

*I met Piso once, years ago. I recall he was quite tall, even by Celtic standards, with a little nose always aimed at the sky. He informed me of his noble birth the moment we met. Second only to your pedigree, he said, with ties to the royal family, stretching back to Rome's first kings. I am not surprised such a man was involved in the attempt on your life, only that he was their chosen leader. How could they not see his cruelty? His meanness? Such are coups, I suppose. One sees the chance to rise and little else.*

*I am also surprised – shocked, even – that your tutor, the great Seneca was involved. I am sorry, my friend. I know how much he meant to you. These are truly dark days.*

*To answer your question: no, I never dealt with such treachery. I believe that I benefited from factors beyond my control. In Britannia we had a common enemy: Rome. With our lives and freedom in the balance, we had no time to plot and conspire against one another. We focused our energies elsewhere, on Rome, on surviving. And my job was not desirable. Most didn't think themselves up to the task. Your circumstances are different. Rome has no enemies and your subjects see you enjoying life – the circus, your evenings spent gallivanting from one pub to the next (I have heard the stories), your beautiful wives and strapping young slaves. The crown did not appear heavy, but rather attractive.*

*There is a third factor, but I am not sure I have the words for it. It concerns your countrymen's endless desire to fight one another, the need for one citizen to sink his teeth into the next. The curse of the wolf is how it was explained to me, when I first came to Rome. A story for another day, perhaps.*

*Be well.*

*Caratacus*

*Rome, 7 April [A.D. 65]*
*Dear Caratacus:*

*The news, as you have heard it, is more or less correct, except for one point: Seneca was not in league with Piso – not directly. His involvement was more duplicitous. Seneca was asked to participate in the coup and, although he declined, he chose not to warn me. My former tutor – the man who guided me through my youth – knew I was to be killed. Yet he said nothing. It was an ingenious plan, I must admit. He stood to benefit whether the coup succeeded or not. If Piso was successful, he would have awarded Seneca for keeping quiet, and he would have required Seneca's experience as a statesman. It was Seneca's ticket back to Rome after I had sent him away. But if Piso was unsuccessful, Seneca remained uninvolved. Of course, Seneca failed to plan for the unlikely chance his meeting with Piso was observed and knowledge of the plot could be traced back to him.*

*One senator in particular was instrumental in bringing Seneca's involvement to light. His name is Cocceius Nerva. He produced two witnesses to the meeting between Piso and Seneca. They may have been spies planted by Nerva (I am not altogether naive), but their intelligence was corroborated and deemed correct.*

*I am trying to move on. At Nerva's suggestion, we have tried to recast the narrative. Piso and his colleagues intended to commit the deed in the Temple of the Sun. So there we have made sacrifices to the sun god, rams and cattle, thanking the god for delivering me from peril. As for the sword Scaevinus sharpened the night before he was discovered, I have inscribed on it 'To Jupiter the Avenger', and it will now be kept in the Temple of Jupiter on the Capitoline. The message: the gods are with Caesar; you should be as well.*

*What do you know of the curse of the wolf? I should like to hear a barbarian king's view on Rome's dark, bloody history, and your first days in Rome.*

*Sincerely,*
*Caesar*

*Beneventum, 8 April [A.D. 65]*
*My Dear Emperor:*

*If you want the story, then I must start at the beginning. I cannot recall what I told you of my first years in the capital. Forgive me if I trudge over ground already tilled.*

*After I lost the war, I was taken to Rome. It was my first time in Italy, my first time seeing the city the world never ceases to talk about. 'Welcome to civilisation,' they said when they dragged me to the city gates, chained like a criminal. I knew Latin even then. I'd learned it as a boy, when I travelled south to Gaul. My father had insisted, 'If you are to lead,' he said, 'you must learn the language of those men who rule to the south, those who will come for us one day, with their big noses and little legs and shining engines of war.' I learned a great deal – more than any Celt I knew – but I never understood this word, 'civilisation'. My tutor would often say, 'You come from the wilds, not civilisation.' But in Britannia – before the Romans came – we had cities and roads; we smelted iron and worked metal; we danced and sang and laughed and made love; we had kings – too many kings! 'Why,' I would ask my tutor, again and again, 'is my home "the Wilds"?' I never received an adequate reply.*

*It was not until I was standing outside the walls of Rome, defeated and chained, that the word was finally defined for me – not in words, but in the form of a city. And I thought: you can keep it.*

*Yes, in a way, their city – your city – was impressive: white marble and red brick everywhere, temples as tall as trees, arcades as long as valleys, and people – more people than I had ever seen, all milling around an expanse of brick and stone as though they owned it, with that peculiar Roman swagger; all manner of folk of every size, shape and shade. But gods was it loud, loud and dirty – dirtier than any village in Britannia. (Piss is meant for the forest, at the foot of a tree, seeping down into the roots. It is madness that you Romans collect it in jugs, walk around the city with it sloshing around, spilling out over the edge and on to the street or any passerby, and then use it to wash – wash! – your linen. Madness.) As I stood there in chains, I thought: this confluence of noise, dirt and piss was 'civilisation'? Who would choose this sea of filth and noise? Civilisation? No, I'd rather not.*

*I was kept locked away, somewhere beneath the city, a room with no windows, only walls of rough stone and the sound of water dripping, dripping, dripping. I had visitors, more than you would expect: rich men and their friends, their wives, sometimes even their children, who came to see a barbarian king under the yoke. They spoke assuming I couldn't understand them, discussing me like I was an animal. 'Oh, he is ghastly, isn't he dear?' 'Lucius, take a good look. If you are not good, he will come for you in the night.' 'Let's have a look at his cock!' I would sit there quietly, hoping to maintain my dignity, whatever of it remained.*

*One night, a woman visited me. Locusta. I had heard the name before, even far away in the 'wilds' of Britannia; a witch, famed for her spells and poisons. I had expected an ugly woman, old, with moles and wrinkles. (That's what witches are like in the north.) She was nothing of the kind. She had dark, lustrous hair, large purple eyes, and breasts that I will never forget bound up under a black stola and shawl; an ocean of flowing dark against perfect, milky white skin, like the moon against the night sky.*

*'I require the blood and semen of a king,' she said, holding a knife and a vial. 'How would you prefer to give it?'*

*Wanting to sound gallant for the beauty I saw before me, aching for any human contact, even a witch of Rome, I said, 'How ever you'd like.'*

*She was a vicious lover, pulling on my beard, biting my neck, scratching my back and my thighs, my scalp and my belly. She would take me inside her, reach around and grab my sack and then twist it, all while pulling my hair and screeching with evil pleasure, like an angry owl scaring away the day. She stayed with me the entire night. In between each tryst, she would lie quietly with her head on my chest, as a wife would, as mine had with me. Only once did she draw blood from my veins, dripping it into her vial for a purpose I did not care to know. It was during one of these interludes that she spoke to me of Rome and its dark history.*

*'There's no harm in you knowing the truth,' she said.*

*'Because I am to die.'*

*'No,' she said. 'You will not die – at least not for many years. But you will never leave Italy. No harm can come from your knowing Rome's secrets.'*

*And then she told me the story of the wolf.*

*'Rome is cursed,' she said. 'Some believe the blight originates in fratricide, when Romulus slew his brother Remus and drew the scorn of the gods. But this is incorrect. The curse predates the murder, to the wolf that suckled them as babes. You know of the twins, no?'*

*Her head was on my chest. When she asked this, she looked up at me, with her dark purple eyes, digging her chin into my chest and her hot breath blowing onto my clammy skin.*

*'Before Rome,' she said 'the great power in Italy was Alba Longa. Its king was Numitor. One day, Numitor's brother Amulius rose up, imprisoned Numitor, killed his sons and sold his daughter to the worshipers of Vestal, where she was to be a virgin dedicated to the gods. Though sworn to chastity, she nevertheless conceived after she was forced to lie with man or god. Some say it was Mars. Some say Hercules. Some say it was the pig farmer down the road. When Amulius learned his niece had produced not one but two contenders to his throne, he stole*

*the twin babes, carted them off to the Tiber, and left them to die in the reeds.'*

*By this point, the witch had folded her arms on top my chest and was staring straight into my eyes, and I could feel the beating of her heart against my belly.*

*'They were left to die,' she continued. 'But a she-wolf rescued them, offering them her milk. Many forget now, with the way Rome has mastered all, but wolves were once man's greatest enemy, hunting and eating our kin. The battle between man and wolf was waged for centuries. This is the source of Rome's taint. The she-wolf was not sent by the gods. She was evil, hate transformed into solidity, and her milk was a primordial blight that infected the twins who consumed it. It made the twins militant and strong, with more cunning and endurance than any man in the whole of Latium, skills that would be passed on to successive generations and lead to empire, but it turned them, twisting their souls; greed and ambition festered. When the twins grew into men, before claiming their right to the crown, Romulus slew his brother Remus. Because of the blight, this was simply a matter of time, and an act which would repeat itself again and again. Brother was to kill brother, citizen would kill citizen, for eternity, until time itself swallows up the empire and the world is at an end.'*

*We made love one more time when her story was finished. Afterwards, when she was dressing, wrapping her stola around her perfect white curves, I asked her how she knew I would live longer than my captors intended.*

*'I see much,' she said.*

*'But how is it I will live?'*

*'When you are brought to the senate, which you will be, appeal to their egos, theirs and yours. Do not show weakness, not to the descendants of Romulus. They would despise it.'*

*She was right. When the day finally came, I was brought before the senate, rows of white-haired men and matching white togas. Did your uncle ever tell you of my speech? Did one man's fate ever turn on so few lines?*

'You are great,' I began, and every man was wide-eyed with shock to find the barbarian before them speaking Latin. 'But I was great once too, a king and ruler of many nations. I should have entered this city as your friend, rather than your prisoner. My present lot is as glorious to you as it is degrading to myself . . . I had men and horses, arms and wealth. Is it any wonder I parted with them reluctantly? If you Romans choose to lord it over the world, does it follow that the world is to accept slavery? Were I to have been at once delivered up as a prisoner, neither my fall nor your triumph would have become famous. My punishment would be followed by oblivion, whereas, if you save my life, I shall be an everlasting memorial of your clemency.'

Your uncle was seated in the chair of a giant, adorned in white silk and Tyrian purple. As I spoke, he smiled at me, and, when I was finished, his colleagues in the senate nodded their heads in approval. The next day I was bathed, shaved, and brought before Caesar. 'You have appealed to Caesar's intellect and Caesar's mercy,' one of his freedman said. 'You are hereby pardoned. But you may never return to Britannia or leave Italy. You are, however, a king. You shall be treated accordingly. Caesar will provide for you.'

And here I have lived ever since, one hundred and fifty miles south of Rome, on an estate that grows grain in the spring, olives in the autumn, and lemons year round. Caratacus the king and slayer of Romans is now a farmer. My life as a barbarian general, waging war against an empire, seems like another life, that of a different man, one far stronger and braver than the one I find myself today. I have grown used to the Italian heat, also your strange manners and customs. But I miss the clear air of the north, the deep, dark greens of the forests; I miss brick-hard bread, and stews of roots and whatever meat is on hand. I miss my little niece, who was always caked in mud and singing to fairies grown men could not see; my niece who is now probably a mother herself . . . but I am content, in my way, as I grow old, tilling the earth by day, and, by night, writing to the master of all.

Enough. It is late. My lamp is nearly spent, as am I. To bed.

Yours,

Caratacus

*Rome, 12 April [A.D. 65]*
*Old King:*

*I had no idea you'd met Locusta. You should consider yourself lucky. Not only did you survive (which is more than most can say), but she clearly took a liking to you.*

*Do not take the story of the wolf to heart. People tell such stories to serve their own ends. It may be true; it may not. The truth is immaterial. Rome captured the world through ingenuity and engineering, not some curse passed down generation to generation. We built roads and armour and those shining engines of war your father feared. And we constructed a system of laws, which, most of the time, we try to follow. Yes, once in a while, Roman kills Roman, but these are outbursts – bloody and terrible, yes – but outbursts rather than the norm. The witch paints the world simply, as one must when making a point. In truth, the world is a mosaic, made of a million facts, considerations, motivations.*

*Yours,*
*Nero Claudius Caesar*


*Beneventum, 28 November [A.D. 65]*
*My Dear Emperor:*

*I have only just heard. I trust you are now safe. I cannot believe there was another attempt on your life. Rumours circulate; it is hard to believe what I am hearing. Send word when you are able.*

*Yours,*
*Caratacus*


*Rome, 19 December [A.D. 65]*
*Caratacus:*

*Yes, I am alive. Once again, I owe my life to Nerva and Tigellinus. The song was different, but the tune familiar. Men and women from distinguished families thought it their time to lead. So far, we have four* names: *Torquatus, Caius Cassius, his wife Lepida, and Tullinus (the kinsman of Marcellus, who I am sure you have met). At this point, the facts are muddled. Tullinus is the only one of the group to confess what he knows, and he is either possessed by the furies or he exaggerates to cast greater odium on the others and thereby save his own skin. What he says seems too incredible.*

*The story begins with Tullinus and Lepida. The two recently became lovers. One night, Lepida revealed to Tullinus that she was an adherent to a cult, one that he had never heard of. (Nor I, for that matter.) Torcus. He thought it another of the eastern cults that have made their way to Rome, of which the nobility will dabble, such as Dionysus or Mithras or Christ. Lepida asked Tullinus to take the rites with her. Tullinus says he did not think much of the invitation. Years ago, he had taken the rites of Dionysus. He imagined something similar: animal sacrifice in the dead of night, wine mixed with the blood of an animal, love-making in a wooded glen. He trusted Lepida. He would have followed her to Hades, he said. He agreed without hesitation.*

*One night, Tullinus was met at his home by two men dressed as priests, with blood-red tunics, with the folds over their heads like hoods, but each wore strange golden masks. The hour was late, well past midnight. Tullinus was blindfolded and put in a litter. He does not know where he was taken. The trek was long and winding. When the litter came to a stop, he was escorted down a zigzagging flight of stairs. Finally, he came to a stop and the blindfold was removed. The room was as dark and rugged as a cave, lit by spitting torches. (Or so Tullinus said. We have not been able to locate it.) There were more priestly figures, nearly a dozen, all wearing strange masks, except for one man in a cloak of black. At Tullinus's feet, there was a man on his knees, blindfolded, naked, shivering with fright, his cock shrivelled up to the size of a pea; and – according to Tullinus – this man's lips were sewn together.*

*The man in black began chanting in a foreign tongue. A knife was placed in Tullinus's hands . . . At this point, Tullinus' story stretches to extremes. Without corroborating evidence, it is difficult to believe. I cannot fathom Roman citizens acting as he describes. I suspect his*

*fear at the whole affair has poisoned his memory. Whatever tran-
spired, Tullinus tossed and turned seven restless nights before he was
arrested.*

*As it turns out, Nerva had kept a man watching Cassius, Lepida's
husband, for weeks. His spy (of which he now seems to have an endless
supply) had informed him Cassius and Lepida had plans to put their
nephew Torquatus on the throne. (Torquatus has loose ties to the royal
family going back to Augustus himself.) On the night in question, Nerva's man observed someone leaving in the dead of night. Luckily, his
man decided to follow and then watched a blindfolded Tullinus join this
person's litter. He followed them but soon lost the group somewhere in
the city's streets.*

*However slight, the information gathered was enough for Tigellinus to
arrest and question Tullinus. He cracked in a matter of hours, telling us
his fantastical tale. Tullinus swears there are more senators and Imperial
secretaries involved – dozens of the Empire's most powerful men. What
this new cult has to do with putting another man on the throne, I am not
entirely sure. I am not sure we will ever know.*

*In any event, Torquatus has taken his own life. Lepida is under house
arrest until I decide what to do with her. Cassius has been banished to
Sardinia. Although he was not directly implicated, I have my suspicions.
We continue to search for the other participants in this odd cult, but, so
far, we have had no luck.*

*Sincerely,*
*Caesar*

*Rome, 3 February [A.D. 66]*
*Caratacus:*

*Upon further reflection, this cult seems a dalliance to me, rather than
a true threat. I've come to learn much of it these last few weeks. You
see I have taken Lepida as a lover. She came to plead for her life after
the plot was discovered. I'd thought about banishing her along with
Cassius, her husband. But she is a great beauty, one of the finest in Rome.
It seemed a waste.*

*Truth be told, I cannot get enough of the woman, her blonde hair and green eyes, her pointy nose. We spend most nights together, gallivanting around the streets of Rome, drinking, carousing, making love. She's proven quite forthcoming about this so-called cult – so much so that I feel I could write a short history on it. She was forced into it by her husband, you see. She was never a true believer. Accordingly, she is able to provide an unbiased account of its origins and ideology. This is what she knows:*

*The story starts with the Teutoburg Pass in Germany. I understand that you are now a student of history since losing your crown. Are you familiar with Rome's worst defeat since Carrhae? It happened more than seventy years ago, while Augustus was still the emperor. At the time, before the humiliating defeat, it was taken as a given that Rome would conquer Germany. But treachery not only stopped Rome's advance, it sent us running the other way.*

*Varus was the local legate. One of his commanders was a man named Herman, a Latinised German who Varus trusted and relied on a great deal. One day Herman told Varus a tribe past the Rhine was planning to rebel against Rome. Varus moved at once, pulling three legions together and following Herman through the dark woods and slippery bogs beyond the Rhine. For days they marched in the rain, pushing their way through knee-deep mud, ducking as massive pines swatted at them like giants. Herman left under a pretence and, once out of sight, circled around and joined a massive host, a rare amalgamation of German's various (and usually warring) tribes. Herman had chosen the Teutoburg Pass to surprise Varus. It was the perfect location for an ambush. Ideal for a massacre.*

*According to Lepida, Varus had two boys on his staff, twins from a rich patrician family. They were too young to be soldiers, but their father was a hard man. To get his boys military experience early, he cashed in a favour with Varus. The boys were only ten or so. They were there when Varus's forces were massacred, and they watched afterwards as the Germans sacrificed thousands of Romans to their cruel gods. The twins were then taken as slaves by a group of Germanic priests, north, past the Elbe river, near the Baltic sea, to a marshy wasteland where this cult Torcus* resides. Lepida claims she doesn't know the twins' names. She calls them Romulus and Remus in jest. I don't believe her, but I'm not sure it matters what their names are.

Lepida says that different tribes across Germany deliver boys to this cult, to serve the god of the marsh. Each tribe is expected to deliver a boy each year. Many deliver disfigured sons – boys no one desires – so the bog is filled with men with strange disfigurements.

For months, the boys watched as men they'd served with, commanders who they had loved and admired were tortured. Their tongues removed and their mouths sewn shut, or their eyes plucked out. Most had their necks cut open and drained into golden cups.

Six years later, after the twins had practised the dark arts for years, after they had seen the power it gave the German warriors, these boys were travelling with a German host when they were overrun by the Roman general Germanicus (my grandfather) as he was exacting revenge for the Teutoburg Pass. After the battle, the boys were captured, identified and then brought back to Rome. No one knew of their dark dealings in the German bog. No one thought them responsible when their hard, belligerent father went missing within a month of their return.

Lepida says the twins bought a warehouse near the Tiber, hired men to dig deep in to the earth and create a pool perpetually filled by the Tiber, which was their German bog in Rome. The boys would go out at night, terrorizing the city, grabbing men or women and dragging them back to their layer, removing tongues, sowing mouths shut, drinking blood. They truly believed the force of the German gods brought them unlimited strength. These boys had sons to whom they taught the dark arts. And the cult slowly spread throughout Rome.

It was to this underground chamber that Cassius dragged Tullinus. Lepida swears she was only taken once. She was blindfolded and does not think she could find it again. She believes the cult is evil but had no choice given her husband's beliefs. She says Cassius, on the other hand, is a firm believer in Torcus. Fortunate for him, he was banished to Sardinia and escaped my wrath for now. If I had known the true extent of involvement before, I would not have given him the mild punishment of banishment.

*I asked Lepida why this cult wanted her cousin on the throne. She said the god of the marsh makes its adherents mad for power. Cassius would return to her after a ritual killing and he would think himself a god. They desired power like a man needs air in his lungs. 'This is why Rome will never take Germany,' she said. 'And why German tribes are for ever at war. Lust for blood is all they live for.'*

*When she told me this, I thought of Piso and all the other plots on my life I've uncovered. I wonder if there is a sliver of this German god in the heart of every man.*

*Yours,*

*Nero Claudius Caesar Imperator*

*Beneventum, 21 February [A.D. 66]*

*My Dear Emperor:*

*It would be a mistake to rely solely on what this woman Lepida says. I have heard of the god of the marsh and the cult that worships him. It is evil itself, truly. There were rumours in Britannia, of men and women, stolen by Germans, hauled to the bogs of Germany and forced to prac-tice their dark arts. The sect drives men mad. If captured, adherents are burned, so lost are their souls. What dark arts men are capable of.*

*Yours,*

*Caratacus*

*Rome, 2 April [A.D. 66]*

*Dear Caratacus:*

*You have always had a special place in my heart and I have often sought your advice, but do not overstep yourself, dear friend – especially in mat-ters of the heart. Remember I am your Emperor, your lord and master, and you exist because I allow it.*

*I am loath to admit it, but another plot on my life was discovered. I know not whether it is related to this cult Torcus. Lepida assures me it was not. I have left it to Nerva and Tigellinus to investigate and the Sen-ate to dole out punishment. Nerva seems to know what will happen in Rome before it does.*

*I have grown tired of the capital, the plots and the intrigue. So I have planned a trip to Greece. I will attend the great games of each city: the Olympian, the Delphic, the Isthmian. I will sing and race my horses against the best Greece has to offer.*

*Yours,*

*Caesar*

Beneventum, 2 January [A.D. 68]

My Dearest Emperor:

Last week, a delegation of senators passed through my estate. They said you had returned from Greece and are now in Neopolis. I hope this letter finds you there, refreshed and in good spirits.

How many months was my artist prince away? Fifteen? Have you adopted all Greek customs, I wonder? I can picture you now, long hair, beard to match, scrolls of papyrus unwound in your lap. Is this why you are visiting Neopolis, the Greekest city in all of Italy? How goes the saying? 'Captive Greece captured her uncivilised captor.'

What of this unrest in Gaul, of the legions refusing to take the oath? I am sure you have it all in hand. But this old, deposed king is bereft of facts and would appreciate anything more than rumour.

Yours,

Caratacus

Rome, 12 May [A.D. 68]

Dear Caratacus:

It is true, there has been unrest in Gaul and it has now spread to Spain. The latest news is that Vindex, the leader of the wayward legion in Gaul – proving himself not completely devoid of intelligence – declared, not for himself, but for Servius Galba, a senator with above average pedigree, in an attempt to legitimise his treachery. It is no matter. The gods are just. Galba and Vindex will learn the price of treachery soon enough.

Still, the ceaseless perfidy of my subjects is tiring. My nights are long and restless. Last night, I awoke after midnight, drenched in sweat, *screaming like a child. I dreamt I was at sea in a small boat. It was night. The sea was wild. Thunder crashed above me, with each ringing blue flash revealing waves as tall as the Pantheon. My ship's sail was intact and the shore was not too far away. I could have made it to safety, but the boat lacked a tiller. The ship, subservient to the currents and fate, drifted towards calamity. There was nothing I could do.*

*I find myself reminded of a dream that I had years ago, of being sealed inside my family's crypt, alive, at the hands of my own soldiers. Do you remember? A dark portent I mastered, as I will this most recent incubus.*

*Yours,*

*Nero*

# XX

## The Gardener
### A.D. 79

# TITUS

◆

*8 April, first torch*
*The Imperial palace, Rome*

By the time I've finished Nero's letters, I'm covered in a cold sweat. I'd been worried about the body by the river – I knew the threat was still out there. But this was only a dull suspicion. I didn't expect . . . this. And reading the slow, inevitable decline of Nero's principate only fuels my anxiety. He was vigilant and still did not see the end until it was on him. Have we been wrong all this time? Was it this German cult that finally brought him down? Did they try again for the throne but circumstance ruined their plan and the purple passed to Galba? Or was Galba an adherent?

I need to calm down. I need to think.

I yell for Ptolemy. 'Find Virgilius. Wake him if you have to.'

Virgilius arrives in my study, bleary-eyed and yawning; but he doesn't complain. His face is as expressionless as he reads Nero's letters. When he's finished he looks up and says, 'We've some work ahead.'

We talk for nearly an hour, debating what course to take.

'As I see it,' I say, 'we have three threads to pull. Cassius, Lepida and Tullinus.'

Virgilius leans back in his chair, nodding. 'Cassius was banished to Sardinia. We can send someone to find him, but that will take time. Lepida is here in Rome. Do we arrest her?'

Lepida, Nero's former mistress and ex-wife to Iulus, one of two men I put to death in Baiae last December. Lepida, who always seems on the periphery of tragedy, but never quite implicated herself.

'No. Not yet. She either isn't involved or, judging by how she played Nero, she is too smart to say anything she shouldn't. Better not to give away what we know. Not yet. For now, we wait.'

'Well, Tullinus is of no help.' Virgilius says. 'He's dead.'

'He is?' Now that Virgilius mentions him, I'm not sure I know much of Tullinus. He wasn't particularly important or influential. I'm not sure I ever met the man.

'He was Marcellus's nephew,' Virgilius says. 'He was with his uncle in Asia when he died, years ago.'

'How is it you know so much about Tullinus?'

Virgilius shrugs. 'His freedman lost money to me in a dice game. He ran off to Asia with his master before paying me back. I never saw the cheat again.'

Priests – thirty or so, blood-red cloaks, heads bowed and hooded – stream out of the temple and out into the forum. I work my way through the crowd and casually match stride with Marcellus.

'Good morning, Marcellus.'

'Eh?' Because of his hood, in order to set eyes on me, Marcellus has to turn not only his head, but his shoulders as well. 'Oh, Titus.' He stares at my priestly cloak. 'I didn't recognise you out of your armour. You hardly look the prince.'

I bite my tongue: I knew I'd have to put up with his snide comments in order to get the information I want.

'I wanted to ask you of your nephew, Tullinus.'

Marcellus stops walking. He bends forward, squinting his reptilian eyes, as though I'm a page he can't quite make out in the morning's pallid grey light.

'What?'

'Tullinus, your nephew.'

'What of him?'

'I wish to know how he died.'

Marcellus's bottom lip curdles. 'He drowned. Why do you ask?'

'Where did he drown? How?'

Marcellus sighs. 'He was on my staff when I was proconsul of Asia. When we were visiting Rhodes he got very drunk. He washed up on the shore the next morning. Now will you tell me why you wish to know how some lowly nephew of mine died six years ago?'

'What do you know of the trouble he was in under Nero? When Cassius was banished from Italy.'

Marcellus sneers; he waves his hand. 'That? He was manipulated by a pretty but very sick woman. Lepida. He didn't tell me more than that. I guessed the rest. As could you, if you took the time.'

'What do you know of Torcus?'

Marcellus' expression doesn't change. He shrugs. 'Is that a place or a person? Stop!' He holds up his hand. 'It doesn't matter. I've never heard of it. Or him. Are we done?'

I nod and Marcellus trudges off.

Virgilius meets me on my walk back to the palace. 'Any luck?' he asks.

'Tullinus drowned. That's all he would say.'

'Do you think he knows more?'

'Yes, but I am distrustful by nature.'

'And Lepida?' Virgilius asks.

'We wait.'

'So we are at an impasse.'

'Maybe,' I say. 'Maybe.'

Antonia visits in the afternoon. It is the first time we have shared a bed since Cerialis's ovation. I had been reluctant to continue after Plautius's miraculous return. I'd thought it was one thing when Plautius was missing and likely dead, but another when he was alive, within the city limits. I'd refused to see her for several days. But today I sent word, asking her to visit me discreetly. I'm not sure what changed. Maybe I truly care for her and I can't stay away. Maybe I just needed the distraction.

When we're finished, Antonia, still naked save for the pins in her hair and a gold bracelet on her wrist, pours herself a cup of wine and walks to my desk. She playfully traces her finger along the wood. Then she sits down and starts examining the papers I have left spread out.

Through the window, we can hear the call of a starling.

'Plautius is safe and sound,' she says, 'yet you're still hard at work I see?'

I roll on to my side and prop myself up with my elbow. 'There is more happening than the public knows. Men continue to plot to bring down Caesar.'

'Yes, but that is always the case.'

I snort sarcastically in reply. I think of Father's ten years in power beating back ambitious men. I think of Nero's letters and the plots he constantly faced. 'True. Very true.'

She holds up the bloodstained scroll found on Halotus. She tips her head to the side trying to make out the Germanic writing. 'Honestly, Titus . . . the things you collect.'

'All of it is important.'

'Oh,' she says, sceptically. 'What importance does this gibberish hold?'

'That is evidence of a cult,' I say, 'German in origin, which has infected Rome.'

She drops the scroll like it's on fire. 'I see. Well, that does sound important.' She picks up another piece of paper. 'But what's this? How can this be important?'

She is holding the note Ptolemy transcribed on Vettius, the knight who went missing in Pompeii; the note he put to paper after jotting down Epaphroditus's information that night at Ulpius' dinner party. Antonia reads it aloud. '*Name: Gaius Vettius; Class: Roman knight; Occupation: gardener; Specialty: fruit trees, particularly fig and pear; Missing: 12 December.*' She looks up from the paper. 'Honestly, Titus, what do you care of some knight in Pompeii?'

I explain this was the man her husband told me of, how he was interrogated and then went missing.

Antonia laughs. 'Proven wrong once again. I shall think twice before questioning prefect Titus's methods.' She considers Ptolemy's note again. 'You know they say that's how Livia poisoned Augustus.'

I reach for my tunic. Absently, I ask, 'What is?'

'Figs. Some said Livia wanted her husband, Augustus, out of the way to make way for her son, Tiberius. To avoid Augustus's tasters, she painted the palace figs with poison. He picked the poisoned fruit straight from the tree. It's nonsense, of course. Augustus died of natural causes. But,' she says with a sigh, 'that's what some say.'

All of a sudden the floor feels as though it has given way and I am falling. My stomach churns. How did I miss this?

I throw on my tunic and scream for Ptolemy. Antonia, still naked, runs to the bed and hides under the covers.

'What is it, Titus?' she asks. 'What's wrong?'

When Ptolemy arrives he diverts his eyes away from Antonia.

'Who is chief gardener of the palace?'

Ptolemy stares blankly back at me. 'I don't know.'

'Find out who and take me to him. And do this quietly, Ptolemy. No one is to know of my interest in the gardens. Do you understand?'

Ptolemy returns half an hour later and takes me and Virgilius to a man called One-Eyed Luke (though he has both eyes), a Jewish freedman who oversees the palace gardens.

'How many of the palace gardens have fig trees?'

'Four,' he says confidently. He explains there are different gardeners for each type of tree in each garden.

'Are you in charge of hiring these gardeners?'

'Sometimes,' he says. 'Sometimes I'm told who will do what.'

'When are the fig trees picked?'

'The harvest was thrown by the cold snap. We expect the next harvest this month.'

Luck. Luck is the only reason Caesar is still alive.

To Ptolemy, I say, 'No one is to pick, let alone eat, any of the fruit. Go. Find four slaves, each to guard one of the gardens.'

Virgilius says, 'If word gets out you know about the figs we lose any advantage we may have. And this palace has more leaks than a Thracian ship.'

I nod at this and to Ptolemy say, 'Have the slaves guard the trees during the day. Once the sun sets and the palace is asleep, we will have them picked clean and the fruit taken to a separate location, away from the palace. Pick four people you trust. Tell no one else.'

When it is just Virgilius and me, he asks. 'What do you think happened? Vettius was originally chosen to poison the trees and he wasn't up for it, so they killed him and found someone else?'

'We shall see.'

'What do you plan to do?' Virgilius asks.

'Find the tree that's been poisoned. If we find the tree we can find the man who poisoned it.'

'How?'

'Taste each one, I suppose.'

# XXI

## Dido's Gift
### A.D. 69

# MARCUS

## *2 April, afternoon*
## *The shores of Carthage, Africa*

Each step the mule takes I think will be its last. It's old and slow and so skinny that I can see every single one of its ribs beneath its hide. Every so often it will pause and the creaking wheels of our cart will stop and I think the mule won't take another step. But then Spiculus will whisper in its ear and pat its rear and it starts again.

Doryphorus, Nero and I are on the cart. Spiculus is walking beside the mule, holding its reins, encouraging it along. Beside us is a cliff. At the bottom, after a long, long drop, is the sea, crashing against the rocky shore. The back of my neck is sizzling under the African sun.

Doryphorus looks up from a roll of paper. To Spiculus, he says, 'Water.'

'No,' Spiculus says, looking back with his one good eye. 'We need to make sure we have enough for the trip back as well.'

Doryphorus swears under his breath.

I'm glad Spiculus is with us. I didn't know he was coming until we were leaving Sardinia. I was happy when Nero told me because Spiculus had started teaching me things Nero couldn't: how to throw a punch, track a boar, and bait a hook; which knot to use and why; how to sharpen a blade and start a fire. And he's nicer than Doryphorus. He doesn't get mad and scream at me. His voice is quiet (even though he's as big as a bull), and he doesn't mind telling me things twice or three times.

The day we left Sardinia the sky was grey and I thought a storm would come, but none did. All of the bandits saw us off. As we rowed out to sea, we could see a fight starting. Spiculus said it was to see who'd replace him as their leader. We didn't get to see who won.

We took a rowboat to a ship anchored in the deeper water, which was owned by merchants Spiculus knew. He said they owed him a favour, so they took us to Carthage for free. On the ride to Carthage, Doryphorus and Spiculus talked about money. We were running low and they wondered where we would get more. But Nero said there wasn't anything to worry about. He said we'd be rich soon enough.

Once we got to Carthage, we only had enough money to buy a mule, a cart, a skin of water and three loafs of stale bread. We didn't even have enough coin to buy a night at an inn, so we left right away, following Nero's instructions.

We've been on the road for hours. I'm sweaty and tired and hungry. And thirsty. I'm the thirstiest I've ever been. I want more water but Spiculus says we need to be careful.

'What if we run out of water?' I ask.

Nero is sitting beside me on the cart. He tries to ruffle my hair but misses and nearly pokes me in the eye. 'We won't, Marcus,' he says. 'We won't.'

I remember what Doryphorus said in Sardinia. How Nero was mad and would be the death of us.

'How do you know?' I ask.

'Maybe a story would help,' Spiculus says. 'To occupy the boy's mind.'

Nero nods. 'Yes, a wonderful idea. Why don't I tell you the story of where we are going.' He scratches his copper beard, which is now very long. 'Where to start? I've already told you about Queen Dido.'

'Yes,' I say, nodding.

'How she was buried with a massive treasure, with gold and silver and jewels, buried along the shores of Carthage?'

I keep nodding, then I remember he can't see me nod, so I say, 'Yes.'

'Well, what I haven't told you is that when I was emperor, a knight visited me. He said he knew the location of Dido's treasure. But he needed the resources of an emperor to dig it up. He had been a student in Alexandria, like you will be, when he stumbled upon his first clue. He was in the great library reading a play by Menander, *The Man from Ephesus*. The knight said it was his favourite play and he knew it by heart. He was midway through when he happened upon text that didn't belong. "The words were wrong," he told me, "nothing but gibberish." At first he was furious the book was ruined. But then, the oddity began to eat at him. He would return to the library every day after school and look at that damned page, hoping the answer would leap out and grab him by the shoulders. For months he read and reread the page. Then, one day, it occurred to him, the answer may be in the correct version of the text. So he found another copy of the play and compared the two. In the correct version, the chorus mused on Dido's lost treasure. This passage was missing in the altered version of the play. The knight pondered this – he thought about it for years until it occurred to him: the altered page is a cipher. He was sure of it. So he began decoding the cipher. He worked on it for years, first in his nights after school, and then, after he was finished his studies, in the office of the magistrate. After five years he decoded the first line. It read, "Follow these directions to the grave of Dido, Queen of Carthage." This, as you can imagine, spurred the man on. Decode the entire cipher and he'd find Dido's grave and the fortune she was buried with. The man continued to live a full life. He married, had five children, and became a prominent citizen. But he remained obsessed with decoding the cipher. Every night he plodded along, working letter by letter. And after twenty-five, he finally cracked it. Or so he thought.

'The cipher translated into directions from Carthage to the shore. He took his three sons and together they visited the site. He thought the fortune was buried under a mountain. He took one look at the mound of earth and thought, I'll never do it by myself. I'll need the help of a god. So he hired a ship and sailed to me, the nearest thing to a god on earth. He told me his story and I thought, why not? It was a whim, but of whims Caesar has an infinite supply. I gave him all the men and supplies he asked for. Month after month, the mountain was carted off, one pail of dirt at a time. But when it was all said and done, there was no treasure to speak of. There was nothing but a massive hole in the ground. It was all too much for the knight. He'd spent too many years stewing over his obsession to finally learn he'd been mistaken. Plus, he now owed me quite a bit of money – Caesar's help is never free. So, on the day I recalled my men from Carthage, he opened his veins.

'I learned of the knight's failure when I was in Greece. Several months later, when I'd finally returned to Rome, I found a chest of the knight's belongings waiting for me in my chamber – not his personal effects (I suppose those went to his wife), but the chest held the altered Menander play, and the knight's cipher. I had an aptitude for puzzles (as Caesar I'd had an aptitude for most things), so I sat down and gave the cipher a try. For months I kept coming back to it, feeling as though something was off . . . And something was off. Now, Marcus, it is true that Fortune is fickle, but this is especially true for idiots. The knight had made one small error that had ruined the entire translation; one little mistake – one letter missed – and the whole endeavour was ruined. The man had missed the "w" in west, and this small, stupid error sent him in the wrong direction from the start. He'd no hope of finding the treasure. But we do.'

'Before they took my eyes, I spent so many months learning the cipher and decoding that particular section of the altered play, that I memorised all the information we need. I knew where to go the moment we landed in Carthage. And this is where we are headed now.'

'So you'll be rich?' I ask.

'We,' Nero says. This time he finds my hair and ruffles it. '*We* will be rich.'

Spiculus pulls on the mule's reins and we come a stop. He looks at the paper he's holding and then the shore. 'This should be it.'

The shore looks as it has all day: a big drop down into the water. There's no city or anything for miles.

Doryphorus starts to curse. 'We're going to die poor and hungry,' he says, 'by the fucking seaside.'

'What is it?' Nero says. 'What's wrong?'

Spiculus starts pacing the shore, looking about intently.

'What's wrong?' Doryphorus is angry. He jumps off the wagon. 'We are going to die of poverty. Or thirst. That's what's wrong.'

Spiculus looks out over the edge of the cliff. He tosses a rock and a moment later we can hear a *plop* as it hits the sea.

'Calm down, Doryphorus,' Nero says. 'Calm down. Will someone explain to me where we are? Where is the treasure?'

Doryphorus starts swearing and kicking sand. He picks up a rock and throws it.

Spiculus starts to take off his clothes. Doryphorus stops swearing and watches Spiculus.

'What's happening?' Nero asks.

Once Spiculus is naked he walks to the cliff, stands with his toes over the edge, and then dives head first. He disappears from view.

'What's happening, for the love of Jove?' Nero says.

'Spiculus jumped,' I say.

'Good,' Nero says. 'I'm glad someone is trying something other than cursing.'

Doryphorus and I walk to edge and look over. We don't see Spiculus, just the sea.

After a while, too long for any man to hold his breath, I ask Nero if he's dead. Nero says, 'I hope not.'

And then we hear a huge splash below. We look over the edge and watch as Spiculus swims to the shore and carefully climbs the cliff face. When he's up and over the ledge and we see his hands are empty, Doryphorus starts cursing again.

'So he's returned with nothing?' Nero asks.

Doryphorus keeps cursing. His face is as red as a legionary's cape.

While still on his knees, Spiculus says, 'Not exactly,' and points at the necklace he's wearing – a necklace he wasn't wearing before. It's gold with fat green emeralds, three of them, dangling like juicy pears. Doryphorus gapes and then yells, 'Ho!' Nero keeps asking what happened.

After Doryphorus calms down, Spiculus explains how he found a cave underwater.

'And what's there?' Doryphorus asks. 'More than that necklace?'

'More gold and jewels than I've ever seen.'

Doryphorus starts swearing again, but this time he laughs in between the curse words.

We walk back to town laughing the whole way. We trade one of the three emeralds with a local jeweller for coin. We buy a rowboat, lots of long ropes, four horses and a week at an inn. We don't tell anyone else about what we've found. Spiculus says it's too dangerous, that someone would rob us if they knew.

That night, Nero says, 'Tomorrow, we go back for more. Much more. Spiculus, you can dive back to the cave with a rope?'

Spiculus nods.

'Good. Once you've secured each chest, we'll have the horses drag it up.'

'It will take days,' Spiculus says.

'Maybe,' Nero says. 'But we can leave some of the treasure where it is if necessary. It's lasted a thousand years, I'm sure it can last a few more. Either way, we will be the richest men in the Empire.'

# XXII

## An Experiment in Figs
### A.D. 79

# CALENUS

## *4 April, afternoon*
## *The Subura, Rome*

Red keeps me waiting for half of an hour. Maybe the client before stays too long. Or maybe she knows making a man wait only adds to the suspense and I'll want her even more. Either way, I don't care. As long as she walks through that door and invites me inside, I'm happy.

The waiting room is long and narrow; a bench that runs from one end to the other. To my left is a door that leads to the rooms. It's closed with a large fellow in front of it. Five other patrons are with me on the bench, waiting patiently. If I wasn't waiting for someone in particular, I'd be next. But I'm here for Red and only Red.

After I ran into Red in the street, I paid for the drink and everything else she was selling, and I've kept coming back to see her ever since.

I've asked her about the day we met and the men who'd kidnapped her. She didn't know why she'd been abducted. 'They weren't exactly the kind of men who would answer your questions.' She'd overheard something she shouldn't, she said, and stupidly told another customer when she was drunk and worrying about it, and that customer told someone else. 'Maybe one of them is to blame.' She said she'd learned her lesson and wasn't telling anyone anything, me included.

When the fight on the road started, she'd hid in the forest before making her way to Rome. 'There's no better place to hide than the biggest city in the Empire,' she said. 'And besides, no one would think to look for me here.' She got a job in this brothel and tried to get on with her life. 'I'm just keeping my head down,' she said. 'From here on out.'

After what feels like a week, the door finally opens and Red pokes her head out. 'Calenus,' she says. 'You weren't waiting long, were you?'

Red rolls off me, haphazardly pulls her stola on, and fetches a bottle of sour wine.

'One glass,' she says, 'then you'll have to go.'

I snatch my tunic off the floor and fish out what's left of the money Domitilla gave me.

'This,' I say, holding up a silver coin, 'should get me the rest of this hour and the next.'

She walks over and examines the coin. 'That, my dear friend, will get you the rest of the day.'

She hands me the drink and sits down beside me.

'You know I saw him today. The soldier who grabbed me.'

'What?' I sit up straight. My right hand clenches into a fist just thinking of that bastard. 'Where?'

'Oh, calm down, Calenus! Stop acting like a protective husband. I can take care of myself, thank you very much. Anyway, it happened in the forum. There were thousands of people around. And he's not looking for me in Rome. So unless I hit him over the head, he'll never find me.'

'It happened to us,' I say, recalling our collision in the Subura.

'True,' she says and reaches up and rubs the scar on my cheek. (She does this often. She says it's good luck.) 'But you and me have an affinity.'

'How do you know it was him?' I ask.

'Oh, I'm not likely to forget a beast like that. Plus he had that cut below his eye, the one you said you gave him. You'll be happy to know its healing badly.'

'Well, you come find me next time you see him.'

'Why?' She says, smiling. 'How's an old, washed up cripple like you going to protect me?'

'Its not for protection,' I say. 'Nerva told me he'd pay to know who he was. And it might help me get more work from him again.'

'You never told me what happened. Why did your patron drop you so quickly?'

I shrug. 'Because I went from a fly on the wall to Caesar's best friend.' I tell her the story of being brought to the palace to translate for the Batavian after he'd saved the Augusta's life. 'A man like me looses his value when people know my face – that's what Nerva said anyway.'

Red narrows her eyes. She thinks I'm boasting to impress her.

'The life you lead,' she says. 'So what will you do for money?'

'Not sure,' I say, depressed at my prospects. 'Nero still owes me coin. I can collect that.'

Red smiles. 'I thought you were a friend of the Royal family now. I'm sure Caesar could use the services of Julius Calenus?'

I laugh at the prospect. 'Imagine that?'

'Well,' she says, 'you'll think of something.'

'I always do.'

# DOMITILLA

♦

*10 April, afternoon*
*The gardens of Diana, Rome*

Vespasia and I find Titus on the second level of the colonnade, looking down into the garden of Diana. Cleopatra, his adopted mutt, is beside him, staring up at her master with affectionate eyes. Titus's hands are on the marble railing. He is bent over, watching everything like a bird of prey. Below there are four men sitting at a long, rectangular table. In front of each man there is a basket of figs; a wax tablet sits in front of each basket, numbered one to four. The men are all chewing; their mouths overflowing with freshly picked (and possibly poisoned) fruit. Behind the men, Titus's grizzled soldier Virgilius paces the length of the table.

We'd been searching for Titus all morning, from one end of the palace to the other, until Father let slip he could be found here, in the gardens of Diana, a little used, almost forgotten Imperial garden on the outskirts of the city.

Titus allows us to observe his experiment after swearing we would not tell a soul what we witnessed; and, for a time, we quietly watch the men aimlessly chew their possible demise. But then, not being able to bite my tongue any longer, I say, 'This seems ignoble, Titus. Even if they are criminals.'

From the corner of his mouth, without breaking his hawk-like observance, Titus says, 'They are all criminals, Domitilla, condemned to death. They are being put to better use here than in the arena.'

'It's cruel,' I say.

Titus straightens his back, then turns and looks me in the eye. 'These men are all convicts. Each one has volunteered. They know the stakes. I have promised to release anyone who lives. The man who dies will have a thousand sesterces sent to his family.'

Vespasia stops biting her nail, 'Domitilla is right. This is cruel.'

'You only think it cruel because it is novel,' Titus says. 'It's no crueller than the arena.'

'That's not true,' Vespasia says. 'This is different to the arena.'

Titus shakes his head. 'It may be different in form, but not substance. Every day you see cruelty and condone it. The Empire feeds off of it – it couldn't exist without it, no civilisation could. But you see it so often that you've grown used to it. It is only when the form is new that you notice it and raise an objection.' He finally looks at us. 'Cruelty is merely another word for novel. Once a practice becomes routine, it is no longer novel and therefore no longer cruel.'

'You're wrong,' I say with conviction. 'This is cruel.'

Vespasia says, 'I agree with Domitilla.'

Titus ignores us both; he is done explaining himself. We stand in silence, watching.

I miss my brother, the boy who would smile in the face of adversity. It was his constant calmness that I found supernatural. But this year has been too much for him – the unexplained events that he cannot attack head on. The hand in the forum, Plautius's disappearance, the body by the Tiber. I wonder if my brother, for the first time in his life, feels helpless.

It is quiet for a moment, almost serene, the only sound the slow monotony of chewing and, somewhere hidden, a bird coos.

And then the sound of choking is everywhere. A man stands up from the table, clutching his throat. White foam leaks from the corners of his mouth. He falls backwards and his fit of coughing is momentarily interrupted by the dull thud of his head hitting stone. He writhes for a time on the ground. Then there is only silence; his body is still.

Two Imperial slaves attend the cadaver and drag it away.

Titus calls down to his grey-haired soldier, Virgilius. 'What number?'

Virgilius is standing beside the now unmanned bushel of figs. 'Three,' he answers back.

The felons talk excitedly. They think they've earned a pardon.

'Why have you stopped?' Titus cries down to them. 'You're not done yet. I need each garden checked. You're not done until your bushel is done. Back to work.'

The three remaining men grow silent; their faces blanch. None, however, move.

Virgilius claps his hands. 'Move!'

Downcast, the convicts sit back at the table and reluctantly insert another barely-ripe fig into their mouths.

I roll the die and, when I see three ones making dog, I curse aloud. Antonia waits to see that I'm not too upset before laughing. She reaches for the die.

She says, 'I see your luck is no better than mine.'

I bite my lip, holding back more curses.

'No,' I say. 'But it does give us a good excuse to visit, doesn't it?'

'It does.' Antonia smiles. 'Do you know what your brother has been up to? I called on him yesterday but he was not at the palace.'

Since Titus swore me to secrecy, I am forced to say, 'I'm not sure. Off finding those working against Caesar, I suppose.'

Antonia tips her head to the side and rubs a spot on her neck just behind her ear; a cord tightens and her collarbone juts out. Unexpectedly, I picture my brother kissing this particular outcropping. I wince. One should not picture their brother doing such things. But there are rumours . . .

'Well,' Antonia says, 'whatever it is, Titus always chooses the best course.'

. . . and one can't help but believe the rumours when the alleged mistress is suddenly an expert on the alleged adulterer.

Antonia soon changes the subject. 'They are saying the False Nero has disappeared. The trail has gone cold.'

'Yes, but I am sure he will surface eventually. Strange, isn't it? How people would risk their life to follow such a man?'

'Oh, I'm not so sure,' Antonia says. 'I always thought the tyrant was handsome.'

I smile, appreciating Antonia's love of controversy. 'He was too short for my tastes,' I say.

'Ah, yes,' Antonia says; she grins. 'I'd forgotten you prefer your men tall – tall as a Batavian.'

I blush – though not as severely as I would have before. The Batavian has kept his promise, more or less. He has done nothing to embarrass me since Calenus spoke with him. It's what I wanted . . . and yet I find myself missing the attention. *His* attention. My worth has always been inextricably tied to Father. When a man showed interest, I was never sure of the reason: did he like me (my eyes, my wit, my love of poetry, the way I curl my hair) or did he like the wealth and connections that marrying Vespasian's daughter would bring? The Batavian was different. There was something simple in his blue gaze. It was unpolluted by politics or Rome's social hierarchy. But I know it's for the best: aside from the slight boost to one's morale, nothing good could have come from a Batavian's lingering blue eyes.

Later – after I am down three games to one – Plautius comes rushing into the atrium. He is gripping a piece of paper above his head. He is angry and visibly shaken.

'This is beyond the pale. Simply *ludicrous*.'

Antonia grimaces. She is embarrassed at her husband's lack of composure.

'What is it, Lucius?' she asks.

'Look at this.' Plautius thrusts a piece of paper into Antonia's face. 'They have brought a case against me. I can't even say why. It is too much, too much.'

'An action,' Antonia says. 'For what?'

Plautius sits and drops his head into his hands; he shakes his head back and forth; finally, he looks up. 'It is alleged that after my time at sea, I am no longer a free man.' His eyes tear up.

'I don't understand,' I say.

'The owner of the ship I was on. He says I was taken according to the law. He's brought an action, to prove I'm servile. To prove I'm his property.'

'Can he do such a thing?' Antonia is incredulous. 'To a senator?'

'It's a perversion of the law,' Plautius says. 'A court can restore a freeborn citizen his rights. It's done when freeborn children are put to work as slaves. This, though – this is mad. The ship's captain is manipulating ancient laws to steal a freeborn Roman citizen.'

'Why would a merchant do this?' Antonia asks. 'It's foolish to want a senator to row your ship.'

'It must be political,' I say. 'There must be an aim beyond putting Lucius back in chains.'

Plautius drops his head into his hands again. 'I won't go back to that boat. I can't.'

Antonia sits beside Plautius on the couch. Out of a sense of duty rather than true empathy, she pats Plautius's back. 'There, there.'

Plautius starts to sob.

# XXIII

## Alexandria
## A.D. 69

# NERO

◆

*23 May, morning*
*The home of Lucius Ulpius Traianus,*
*Alexandria, Egypt*

Doryphorus and I are on the balcony when Spiculus and Marcus trudge in. Their feet, still slick from their swim in the Great Harbour, slap the marble with each step.

'How was the lesson?' I ask.

'He's coming along,' Spiculus says. 'He will be better than me in no time.'

A slave takes my hand and then places a cup into the palm. He knows to wait until I've gripped it with both hands before letting go. He, like all of the other slaves we have purchased, speak only Aramaic, leaving us free to converse in Latin or Greek, without curious ears listening in.

'You've missed quite a lot while you've been swimming,' I say. 'A new emperor has been named.'

'Another one?' Spiculus asks.

'It's true,' Doryphorus says. 'The city prefect had the troops here in Alexandria declare a new man emperor. It's unfortunate Otho killed himself. We could have had three at one time.'

'Who?' Spiculus asks.

'Vespasian,' I say.

'The legate in Judea? The one you named?'

'The very one,' I say. 'Three years ago the man went into hiding after an ill-timed nap. Yet here he is, co-emperor of Rome.'

'Not of Rome,' Doryphorus says. 'He has only been declared emperor by the troops here in Alexandria and maybe in Judea. But if his pedigree is what you say it is, a provincial two generations removed from a Gaul, I cannot fathom the senate or the patricians bowing down to such a man.'

I shake my head. 'Armies are the ultimate counter-argument. The eastern legions were once famous for their lethargy. But they have lately been hardened by war. Vespasian is now backed by a formidable army. And look at the man he is up against. Vitellius is the lowliest of creatures. I enjoyed his company over a cup of wine or banquet – the man had appetites that took your breath away – but I would never have trusted him with the safe keeping of a mouse, let alone the Empire. It's only a matter of time before Vespasian wins. When he does, the senate will have no choice but to recognise him as Caesar.'

'Will the war come here?' Marcus asks tentatively. He loves Alexandria. To him, Rome is stiflingly hot, its people brutal. Alexandria is bright and mild, and here he is free, not a slave to a brute. He doesn't want Alexandria ruined by war.

Doryphorus, indifferent to the anxiety underlying the question, says, 'We can't be certain of anything. However, we can use this turn of events to our advantage.'

'How?' Spiculus asks.

'Assist Vespasian,' Doryphorus says. 'Place him in our debt.'

'And how does one get a general owing us a favour?' Spiculus asks.

'Empires cost money,' I say, 'and now money is something we have in ample supply. This will also provide an opportunity to advance the name of Ulpius.'

Doryphorus snorts. 'For the boy's sake?'

'For all of ours,' I snap.

'Come now, Doryphorus,' Spiculus pleads. 'We work to further the name of Ulpius now. We all agreed.'

'Yes,' I say. 'We best be getting on with it.'

'Welcome all.' The voice echoes across the portico. 'It is good to know support for our new emperor goes beyond the men in the barracks . . .'

A brine-spiced breeze gently licks the back of my neck.

'The city prefect is speaking.' Doryphorus's garlicky breath whispers in my ear. 'Vespasian is standing beside him.'

My self-reliance has improved since losing my eyes, but I still require help, especially when someone I have never heard before is speaking.

I need Doryphorus to explain the scene, point by point, who is speaking, where he is standing.

' '. . . may the gods favour Vespasian and the furies damn the traitors in Italy,' continues the voice I now know to be the city prefect. His name is Tiberius Alexander, appointed by me years ago. I remember a short man, balding, with a bulbous belly and thick black eyebrows, like two plump caterpillars asleep above each eye.

And Vespasian? I wonder whether he looks as he did when last I saw him. I was in Corinth when I sent for him, at the royal palace. We had sat down for dinner when Vespasian came bursting through the doors, his travel cloak dirty from the road, his balding grey hair in disarray. His fatty cheeks huffing and puffing. It was staged – 'You sent for me, Caesar, and I didn't stop until I laid eyes on you' – but I appreciated it all the same; the crowd was certainly impressed. Space was cleared at my table and he sat with me for the remainder of dinner. He had the good sense not to raise the issue of his untimely nap during one of my performances years before – a nap that sent him running from Rome. Water under the bridge if he was being given every general's dream: a war.

Doryphorus whispers in my ear. He says a secretary is going from guest to guest, gathering a sense of what donative each man will give.

When he comes to us, I ask, 'What is the highest donative so far?'

Flustered, the man cannot produce syntactical response: 'I . . . well . . .'

'Whatever it is, I will double it. I only ask for a word with the Emperor. A word and a favour.'

The secretary's silence tells me he is inexperienced in politics. He will have to learn quickly or he will be discarded.

There is no reply, only the dwindling sound of shuffling feet.

Doryphorus whispers in my ear: 'He has run off to his patron.'

'Yes,' I say. 'I gathered that.'

We are called over to Vespasian and Tiberius Alexander, the city prefect. I can hear the nasally sneer in the latter's voice.

'My freedman says you wish to make a generous donation to Vespasian Caesar's cause.'

'He is correct,' I say.

'Have we met before?' says a different voice. Vespasian's.

'No,' I say.

The city prefect asks, 'What is your name?'

'Lucius Ulpius Traianus.'

'Ulpius,' Vespasian says. 'The name is familiar.'

'My brother fought for you in Judea.'

'Ah, yes. I remember now,' Vespasian says. 'And where is your family from? I have forgotten.'

'Spain. My nephew and I now reside in Alexandria.'

The city prefect says, 'I have never seen you before, and I know everyone in Alexandria.'

'Do you? With a population of five hundred thousand, I cannot fathom such powers of recall.'

Vespasian interrupts. His concern is the donative, not the prefect's memory. 'For the donative, you asked for a word and a favour. We are giving you the word, what is the favour?'

'Entry to the senate and a posting for my brother.'

An incredulous guffaw from – I think – the city prefect. Vespasian, however, is more practical. He is a new man himself. He knows one does not need pedigree to be up to the task.

'Membership in the senate requires one million sesterces. You have holdings that meet this requirement.'

'I do. More than enough, actually.'

'And this is in addition to the donative you have already promised?' Vespasian asks.

'Yes.'

'And the posting?'

'Legate,' I say, 'or procurator, something along those lines.'

More incredulous laughter from the prefect. 'You cannot be ser—'

'There will be difficulty there,' Vespasian says, interrupting the prefect. 'After I take Rome, there will be many favours to pay back, and only so many provinces to go around. And Galba made appointments I'll be reluctant to overturn. Just this morning I met the man Galba named procurator of Asia. I swore I'd keep him where he is.'

He is negotiating. I've now promised to pay him a tidy sum. He will give in soon enough.

'There are smaller provinces, are there not? Cilicia perhaps?'

'Cilicia . . . yes, that is one I could agree to.' Vespasian circles the final point. 'And how long would it take for you to deliver the money?'

I smile. 'I could have it to you – I'm not sure. Tomorrow at the latest.'

Vespasian laughs, a hearty peasant's laugh, not the laugh of an emperor.

'Tomorrow will do just fine,' he says.

Never one to let information go unlearned, I say, 'May I ask, who is to be procurator of Asia?'

'Halotus,' he says.

Doryphorus' nails dig into my arm.

'Is he still in Alexandria?' I ask.

The prefect speaks up. His incredulity is gone, replaced with a blasé disinterest. 'He left this morning.'

Doryphorus — too quickly, with too much interest — asks: 'To Asia?'

The prefect answers the question with one of his own. 'Do you know Halotus?'

'Please excuse my slave,' I say. 'He bedded a man in Halotus' employ.' I pat Doryphorus on the head. 'He is a dog constantly looking for a leg to hump. He is a degenerate, through and through. But he has been with me so long – no one else knows how to dilute my wine the way I like it, or how to prepare my meals. I depend on him, degenerate or no.'

The peasant Emperor laughs again. He grabs me by the shoulder. We are becoming fast friends. 'If a man were judged by his freedmen,' he says, 'I'd have been sent to the mines years ago.'

'Thank you, Caesar,' I say, 'for your kindness. But you are certain it was Halotus?'

Vespasian says. 'Oh yes. Very sure. The eunuch is hard to miss. Eyes like a wolf, pale and hungry, but with the shoulders of a woman, and insolent as they come.'

I give him the derisive snort he was looking for. 'And who will he be working with? Who is to be proconsul?'

'I've named Marcellus proconsul of Asia.'

We talk for a while, hammering out the final details of the agreement. When we're done, he – I think it's Vespasian – grabs my hand and shakes it vigorously. He has all the grace of a man selling mules. 'We have a deal,' he says. 'I predict great things for the Ulpius clan.'

'Thank you –' I choke out the title I know I must use '– Caesar.'

Afterward, once we are home, Doryphorus, Spiculus and I meet on the balcony. Marcus is inside, asleep.

'So we've helped put another man on the throne,' Doryphorus says disapprovingly.

'There is no harm in it,' I say. 'Vespasian had no hand in my fall. He is merely seizing the opportunity presenting itself. There is no reason we can't make it so the man owes us a favour. We will owe him nothing and there is no reason we cannot turn on him later.'

'And what do we do about Halotus?' Spiculus asks. 'We know where he will be, but as procurator, he will be powerful and difficult to gain access to.'

'We wait,' I say.

'Where? In Ephesus?' Doryphorus asks.

'No,' I say. 'The capital of Asia will be his home turf, so to speak. We will find somewhere close that he will visit. Samos or Cyprus or Rhodes. Somewhere where we can continue Marcus's education. And we wait.'

'How do we know Halotus will come to wherever we are?'

'We don't,' I say. 'But we are not in a rush. We can afford to wait.'

# XXIV

## Trials and Tribulations
### A.D. 79

# DOMITILLA

◆

*18 April, afternoon*
*The Servilian gardens, Rome*

I find Father and Graecina, the grey-haired matron of the Plautii, under the crisscrossing boughs of an elm. The fruity aroma of whatever they are drinking perfumes the air.

'How goes the trial?' Father asks. 'You were there the entire day?'

'Yes,' I say, taking a seat. 'I saw it all.'

'Speak the truth, child,' Graecina says. 'How badly did Plautius embarrass our family?'

'He –' the pause gives me away, but I press on '– did well, considering the circumstance.'

'Circumstance?' Graecina's frown would freeze the Tiber. 'Do you mean the circumstance of him being an idiot? That cannot count as a credit in today's accounting.'

'No,' I counter, 'I refer to the prospect, however remote, of being made servile. Given what he has been through, with such a possibility looming, his anxiety has understandably run away from him.'

Graecina gives one of her dismissive *harrumphs*.

Father says, 'The action is only a prank. A stunt.'

'I don't disagree,' I say.

'My dear,' Graecina says, 'this is merely an attempt to embarrass the Plautii, by manipulating Rome's ancient laws and Plautius' unfortunate few months at sea. If Plautius were a better, more worthy man – if he was half the man my husband had been – he could turn these events to his advantage. But he is hopeless. He will not be named a slave, but he will, it seems, let our family be undermined in the process.'

Father shakes his head. 'This stunt is aimed at us as well. Ultimately. Your mother . . .' He sighs.

Mother's background has always been an embarrassment for our family. She was born free, a citizen of Rome, but her family was impoverished. She worked in another man's home for years, doing the work of a slave. Her life improved, and she achieved favoured status, but an action was required to prove she was freeborn. Father married her not long afterwards. When he ran for office, men spoke of mother's past; they made jokes. But since Father became Emperor no one has dared. It had been so long since the subject was raised Mother's past didn't occur to me when I first learned of the action against Plautius. I didn't realise the same laws that restored Mother's freedom were being used to chain Plautius to a paddle. And now Plautius's trial, and the Plautii's connection to our family, has given the city the excuse to once again discuss Mother's chequered past. Father thinks it a concerted effort to undermine him. We've no idea who is behind it. The ship's captain is a lowly merchant who would never have dared insult the Plautii like this. Someone is paying him for the right to bring the action and hired one of the city's best lawyers, Valerianus.

'Has Titus made any effort to find out who is behind this?' I ask.

'Not yet,' Father says.

'Must Titus do everything?' Graecina asks, in the tone only she could use with Caesar.

Father doesn't look up from his cup. He shifts in his seat and then his face contracts in a painful, gout-induced wince. He says, 'Titus is the only one I trust.'

Graecina rolls her eyes. 'Yes, that is obvious.'

Suddenly, I am struck with an idea. 'I have someone we could use,' I say. 'Someone inconspicuous.'

Father chuckles, derisively. 'Oh! Do you? An old colleague from the legions?'

Graecina stares at me, seizing me up. Without taking her milky eyes off me, she says, 'Caesar, one does not need a prick swinging between their legs in order to be useful. Tell me, my dear. Who are you suggesting?'

'His name is Calenus. An ex-soldier. He previously worked for Nerva.'

'Nerva?' Graecina says coldly. She has never taken to Nerva.

'Yes, but he is loyal to me now. I know it.'

Father asks, 'And what will your man do?'

'Whatever we need.'

# CALENUS

♦

*22 April, morning*
*Outside the home of Julius Valerianus, Rome*

I'm getting old; time to admit it. My back, my gimpy knee, my bony arse – everything hurts.

This is the fifth day I've been following the lawyer Valerianus. I've followed him from his home on the Quirinal, to the courts, and back again, hoping to learn something – anything that will help Domitilla. But he's a hard worker – no baths, no whores, no wine; just work and sleep. The days are dull but the nights are worse. I've got to make due in a narrow alleyway across from his home, camped out on an abandoned crate, which is about as comfortable as sleeping in a quarry, and there's nothing to do but drink sour wine and count the hours. It's been more than four days and I haven't learned anything except that my body's old and wine helps pass the time.

The job couldn't have come at a better time. Other than the fifty sesterces Nerva owes me, I was near broke when Domitilla's girl Jacasta found me and asked me to do this.

A strange mess, this action. To think one of the Plautii could end up a slave. Before I'd have been happy to see one of the teat's ancient, blue-blooded families fall. Plautii, Junii, Claudii – it's all the same to me. But now my loyalty is with Domitilla. She wants to know who's paying Valerianus, so that's what I'm going to find out.

The fifth day starts like the others. I watch the vendors come early, pushing their carts up the Quirinal: a baker, a butcher, a man delivering olives, another figs, a woman with spices, dried and fresh. But today, there's a new face: a woman, travelling on her own. There's something about her – hooded, alone, empty-handed. It makes my veteran hackles rise. So when she walks out – on a hunch – I follow.

She takes me on a tour of the city, through the cattle market, then north, by the theatre of Pompey and the baths of Nero, and then into narrow little streets near the Coline Gate. She finally stops at a canteen. The Spotted Pig, which sounds familiar but I can't quite place it.

Before heading inside, she turns to look behind her. I keep walking, without breaking stride. Out of the corner of my eye, I watch as she pulls back her hood and I get a good look at her face. She's young, with chestnut hair, and one eyebrow instead of two, thick and black. She goes into the canteen. I follow.

Despite the early hour, the canteen is busy. Men and women are drinking and laughing, with blood-red eyes and lazy heads dipping towards the table. For most of them, it's the end of a bender, not the start. I scan the room but the girl is gone. At the back, there are private rooms fashioned out of big swaths of canvas. The girl must be behind one of those, unless she's slipped out the back. I decide to wait at the bar. After I order a cup, a woman with wild black hair and a rash across the right side of her face sidles up to me. She's half my height and has to hop to get onto the stool. 'What do you like?' she asks.

'Away with you,' I say, 'I don't want any.'

'Come on, soldier,' she says, pawing at my crotch, 'the price goes up in the afternoon.'

I push the whore away and then give her a good kick to her backside. 'Go.'

Not long after I turn back to the bar, I feel the hand of a bear slap my shoulder.

'I knew you'd track us down.'

I turn to see Fabius and his wide, bearded face. With a jolt I remember where I'd heard the name of the canteen before. Fabius told me a few months back. He thinks I've come to join up.

'Come,' he says. A grin cuts his mud-brown beard in two. 'This way. Montanus awaits.' Fabius points at the private rooms in the back. I try to think of a plan, a way to politely decline, but it will ring false. Fabius told me where to find him if I wanted work, and here I am.

He walks me towards the back, towards one of the makeshift private rooms. When we are half a dozen paces away, the curtain is pulled back and, from behind it, out walks the girl with the one eyebrow. We pass each other and our eyes meet. Did she recognise me? But I've no chance to find out because Fabius keeps pulling me towards the makeshift room.

On the other side of the curtain, Montanus is lounging in a chair. It's been a few years, but he looks the same, for the most part. He's huge, my height plus another half, with scar rutted cheeks, dark eyes, and a chin like a slab of marble. His hair is different, though. It's longer now, touching his shoulders, and thinner with streaks of grey. Thick, protruding veins marble his neck and forearms. On either side, his ex-soldiers – boys I don't recognise – are standing, with their hands on the hilt of their swords.

Montanus recognises me, but he waits a moment before speaking. He always bristled at authority; orders were like poison he choked down. Now that he's finally the man in charge . . . I'm sure he relishes every minute of it; a leopard and his spots.

'Calenus,' Montanus says. 'I never thought you'd come.'

I look around the room, at the bare walls, the soldiers, at Montanus, stretching out time as best I can, hoping some plan will dawn on me. 'Oh?'

'You always chose the harder course over the easier.'

'Not sure I'd agree with that.'

'Come now,' he says, gloating. 'Admit it. You're a miserable bastard. How many towns did we take together? Ten? Twelve? You'd fight at the front of the line, risking your neck, and then when it was over and the men were given the night to do as we pleased, you'd return to camp.' He sneers. 'How does the saying go? Never trust a man who goes to the whorehouse for conversation.' He looks at his lackeys, soaking up their smiles. 'You always made life harder than it had to be. You'd rather hold the line than pillage.'

'All that screaming,' I say.

'There's screaming in battle,' Montanus says.

'Sure, but those are men. Screams from women and children, the octave is too high.'

He smiles; it's a satisfied grin. 'Tell me, why are you here?'

Before I can answer, behind me the curtain is pulled back and, on instinct – the soldier in me always wants to know who or what is behind him – I turn to see a man walk in.

I recognise him: the feeling is faint at first but quickly grows to certainty. It has been several months, and he is no longer wearing the

armour of a legionary, but rather only a simple tunic of light blue, but
his scar gives him away: the horizontal line an inch below his left eye;
the cut I gave him on the road from Ostia, the day I first saw Red.

Neither of us moves; we stare, each gradually recognising the other.
Time slows. I'm walking in mud.

The man works for Montanus. That much is plain. Which means I
helped kill two of Montanus's men.

Run. All I can think is *run*.

'You –' the man with the scar starts to say just before I grab his tunic
and run as hard as I can forward. We both burst through the curtain
and fall to the ground. I roll over the top of him, get to my feet, and run
towards the exit, leaving cries of surprise behind me. I'm just about to
reach the door when my feet are out from under me and I'm crashing to
the cold, brick floor. As I'm falling, out of the corner of my eye, I see it
was the little rash-covered whore who stuck out her leg and tripped me.

I hit the stone floor and the air flies from my lungs. Before I can
move, fists and feet rain down on me, pummelling me into submission.
Then I'm dragged back to Montanus.

Chaotic chatter soaks the canteen. Fabius and another man are
stamping on blackened curtains; grey smoke twists up from the dead-
ened flames. The private room is no longer a room.

Two men hold my arms. Then a hand grips my hair and my scalp
burns as my face is twisted upwards, towards Montanus's face. He
looms over me, like Jupiter. Now that he is standing, I remember how
huge the man is. He says, 'Are you mad?'

The man with the scar finally stands up, unwinding himself from the
curtains I left him in. He pulls Montanus aside and explains in whispers. Fabius leans towards the exchange, eavesdropping. He looks at
me and shakes his head. There won't be anything he can do.

# XXV

## Letters from a Stoic
### A.D. 73

# MARCUS

♦

## 1 September, morning
## The school of Musonius Rufus, the island of Rhodes

'Raising a child, shaping the boy into the man ...'

Musonius paces the portico. One hand is tucked into his armpit. The other is pressed into the depths of his white, curly beard, cupping his chin. The old man's mouth is gorged with his huge, yellowing teeth, like he's chewing chunks of piss-stained marble. When he speaks, it sounds like he's mid-meal, too rude to swallow before making his point.

'. . . it's every man's obligation, his duty.'

In the garden, under the canopy of an elm, a young girl walks by.

'What you teach a boy is far, far more important than leaving him a fortune ...'

I crane my neck to watch her; a few classmates do as well. Her little breasts poke out of her pale green chiton, her back curves like a snake, and her –

'Marcus!'

Musonius glares at me. Every boy – cross-legged on the floor – stares in my direction. Beside me, someone lets out a deep breath, thankful our tutor didn't just scream *his* name.

'Come here, Marcus.'

A beating from a stoic is the worst kind of beating – worse than those I'd receive from Master Creon. A stoic doesn't hit out of anger, but duty. It often lasts longer and is more exact. Worse yet, Musonius has a specific slave for the task: a muscled and very dumb Thracian. Aside from the Thracian, the other problem is my prick, which, thanks to the girl walking through the garden, is as hard as a gangplank. Sitting cross-legged, it is lost in shadowy folds of my tunic. Standing, however – standing is a different matter. Last month, Gaius stood up with his cock hard and the class pointed and laughed. Ever since, Peleus and his friends call him Happy Prick.

'Marcus,' Musonius says again. 'Come here. Now.'

The Thracian stands, sensing he will be needed soon.

Silence. Then, from the back of the classroom, a man's voice says: 'Musonius, I have a question.'

In unison, the class turns to see who spoke. I don't need to look. I know the voice. My cheeks, already smouldering, burn with embarrassment. Where did he come from? Why does he insist on interfering?

Musonius sighs. 'Ulpius, I must insist you stop sneaking into these lessons. It does the children a disservice to have my lesson constantly questioned.'

'Yes, of course,' Nero says. 'A dialogue has no place in philosophy.'

Musonius frowns. 'What is your question?'

'You said that it's more important to instruct a child, rather than to leave them wealth. You said that what a child learns is more important than the wealth he or she inherits.'

'Yes, I would have hoped this would be obvious to a man of your age. Knowledge is more important than wealth.'

Nero chuckles. I keep staring straight ahead, not wanting to look. If I don't look at him, then I'm not with him.

'Very well put, Musonius, very well put. I wonder, though, if given the choice, would you choose knowledge over the wealth? You have been kind enough to invite me to your home. I have experienced its splendour. I have been waited on by your army of slaves. I have dined at your dinner table. If put to the test, if only one were possible, would you really choose philosophy over that house of yours? And all those slaves?'

'Yes. Of course.'

'Splendid! A true philosopher.'

Musonius keeps frowning. He knows more is coming.

'I wonder, though . . . is such a response universal? If we were to go to a beggar in the street and offered him knowledge or, I don't know, a million sesterces, what do you think he would choose?'

I finally look over my shoulder. Across the colonnade, in the frame of the door, Nero is leaning on his cane. He looks like the beggar he described. How can someone who looks so old and broken – how can his voice sound like that? Like a drum.

'Yes,' Musonius says, 'if the man were acting in his best interests, he would choose wisdom.'

Nero smiles; he is enjoying himself. 'You are a true study of human nature. I wonder though, could we use your wealth to test the point? Could you donate one million sesterces to our beggar?'

Musonius hesitates. He says, 'We cannot hand wisdom to a beggar to make the exchange. It would be a pointless endeavour.'

'Much like the lesson itself, I'd say – though, admittedly, I am quite ignorant on this subject, as ignorant as the beggar we keep talking of. You see, I would have thought part of the problem would be your reluctance to part with one million sesterces. But tell me, I have one more question. Have you ever raised a child, Musonius? Are you a father?'

'I have dedicated my life to philosophy. To teaching and shaping the Empire's youth.'

'But you've never had a child yourself. Yet your views on education and rearing children are formed, and they are uncompromising?'

Musonius grimaces. 'Yes.'

'What luxury! You claim expertise on a subject you have no practical experience in. What amazing luxury you philosophers have. Truly! The tradesman is bristling with jealousy. Can you imagine the painter attending his patron's home? "I will paint you a grand mural," he says, and the patron asks, "What experience do you have?" to which the painter replies, "None, but I have thought a lot about painting. I feel quite strongly on how it should be done."'

We finally reach the point where Musonius screams at Nero, telling him to leave. The class is silent; we can hear Nero's cane tap-tap-tapping along the portico as he leaves. Musonius waits until the noise is finished before continuing his lesson. He is too flustered to remember he owes me a beating.

When school is over, Nero is waiting for me on the street. We walk back together. Nero takes my arm and I lead the way along the rocky path. Curls of turquoise, topped with white bubbles, lap against the rocky shore. I want to walk ahead and leave him behind, but I can't. He needs my help.

'You're quiet this afternoon,' Nero says.

I don't say anything.

'Well, point proven, I suppose.'

I spin around. Nero stumbles but doesn't fall.

'You embarrass me,' I say.

'Do I?'

'Everyone knew you interfered to save me from a beating, as though I couldn't take it.'

Nero still thinks I'm the quiet child who was afraid of everything.

'What of it?' he says. 'My tutors beat me regularly at your age. It did no good, only bad. Why not stop it if I can?'

'It embarrasses me. I look weak, like a child.'

'Are you no longer a child? You continue to speak like one, talking to your elder with such insolence. In fact, maybe you are getting *younger*? The boy I met had more respect.'

A pulse of fury shoots through my limbs like a shiver and I push Nero, not hard, but hard enough to knock him over. He lands arse first in the brown dirt, beside a green shrub.

He looks stunned. He doesn't try to get up.

'My point is proven,' he says, 'again.' He dusts his hands against each other. 'By aggregate, the argument is mine, I'd say.'

I storm off, leaving Nero sitting in the dirt.

Two hundred paces on, I see Spiculus walking out from the forest. Two rabbits are slung over his shoulder.

'Marcus!' he calls.

I keep walking and he calls my name again.

After an angry grunt, I halt.

Spiculus holds the rabbits up for me to admire. 'What do you think? I am tired of fish.'

'They're fine,' I say.

Spiculus frowns, disappointed with my reaction. He looks around. 'Where is your uncle?'

'He is *not* my uncle.'

Spiculus's back straightens; he scrutinises me with his good eye. I am breaking the rules. I am not supposed to break the fiction.

In a softer voice, Spiculus says, 'Where is he?'

I point back the way I came.

'You go back to the house.' He pats me on the shoulder and smiles. 'I'll see to him. Yes?'

'Fine.'

I stomp back to the house, alone.

# NERO

*1 September, afternoon*
*The shore, the island of Rhodes*


Spiculus helps me out of the dirt. I rub my tailbone.

'He would have left me to die,' I complain, bitterly. 'What happened to him? To my Marcus?'

Spiculus ignores the comment. He knows I could have made it home on my own, but hurt feelings made me sit in protest.

'He is a child who wants to be a man,' he says. 'It is a difficult period of one's life. Adolescence.'

'Is it? I wasn't much older than he is now when I was named Emperor. I managed.'

'Did you?'

Spiculus was not in Rome when I first rose to the purple, but he has heard stories, a boy fighting his mother for control – not just for himself, but for the machinery of Empire.

'All we ask of him is to attend class,' I say. 'To learn.'

'You are both too hard on the other. And you are both too stubborn.' He mulls this over. 'The problem is you are too alike.'

Spiculus's comment is meant to flatter, but I react like a barbarian. I poke him once, twice, somewhere in the midriff. 'Marcus is different.'

I will not admit this – not to the boy, not to Spiculus, not to anyone – but my fear is this: I will raise Marcus to be another Nero. Not the Nero of the tales currently in vogue, the stories told by those seeking Vespasian's favour, the tales of a bloodthirsty hedonist who murdered and screwed half the Empire. But after all these years divorced from my station, bereft of the unlimited power I once wielded, blind and physically helpless, I have come to a realisation: there is truth there, beneath the sanctimony, beneath the hypocrisy. I was spoilt, unfair, vengeful, lazy. I was profligate. I murdered and raped. (Can one consent if the man asking is a god?) I was selfish, mean, close-minded, cynical. I was a tyrant, a young sexed-up despot. Marcus will *not* be another Nero. I will not let that happen.

Spiculus, the gentleman warrior, immediately seeks reconciliation. 'Yes, Marcus is different.' He pats my shoulder. 'He is a good boy, struggling through a difficult time. Come. You can't see, but I have magnificent hares for dinner.'

I was in Greece before, while still the emperor, during my grand tour, and I remember the country's beauty. I can still feel it, though it is now only a dull sensation, a mere aftertaste of what I felt then. In truth, I've found this difficult, not being able to see it once more. I tell myself there are many things a man will never see once, let alone a second time. At least I saw Greece the one time ... But it is, without question, worse being here, living on the island, breathing its air, rather than thinking of it abstractly, as some distant memory. It's like having your lover in the next room after a long separation. She calls to you, whispers to you through the cracks in the stone, her soft flesh just out of reach. You think of her big, swishing lashes, and your body aches. I try to focus on the senses I still have: smell, touch, sound. All day I suck in the briny Aegean air and I sit on the portico, listening to the waves lap the shore, while the breeze runs along my arms and the back of my neck.

And I've found other ways to stave off bitterness, to fill the days as we wait for Halotus. Musonius is one. Marcus thinks I harass his tutor only to embarrass him or to save him from a beating. He doesn't realise I've despised the man for years. When I was emperor, he was a constant headache, using philosophy to undermine the principate. He persisted, year after year, until I banished him from Rome and he ran here, to Rhodes, and opened this school. My revenge (and daily entertainment) is banter, one question after the next. It's the screw I turn, day after day, as he tries to give his lessons.

Stoicism, like all philosophy, has value (that's why I send Marcus). But Musonius, like most philosophers, is worthless. His ideas have value, but the man is, without question, full of shit. This is one of the lessons I try to teach Marcus, the bird's eye view of the world, while his tutors teach him narrow, inflexible ideologies.

But Marcus no longer listens to me. The sweet boy who sat and listened with rapt attention to every word I said is gone, consumed by adolescence. In his place is a taller beast with only a vague resemblance to my sweet Marcus, but with a light dusting of hair above his lip (in my mind's eye anyway), an acidic smell that could fell a legion, and wandering eyes that rarely focus on anything other than a pair of tits (or so I'm told); a boy that disappears for hours at a time and gives inadequate explanations when he returns. And there is an anger now, beneath the surface; an anger that is often directed toward me, despite the fact he owes everything to me – his position, his education, the tunic on his back.

Is this normal? Is this how sons treat their father once they reach a certain age? I don't know. My father died when I was quite young. And the men my mother married afterwards did not meet the definition of 'father'.

Part of the problem is the slave woman, Elsie. Marcus's surrogate parent before he met me. He wanted us to purchase her, free her and bring her to Rhodes. But I wrote to Creon, his old master, and he'd sold the woman a year ago, and the man who bought her sold her a month later. I've sent letters across the Empire, tying to follow the chain of sale, but the trail has gone cold.

Spiculus thinks Marcus is having trouble because he is a slave masquerading as a senator's son. Doryphorus agrees. They think I've upset the natural order: one cannot eradicate the past, they say; and, if one tries, there are consequences. They don't understand. They haven't been through everything I have. They don't realise that it's all a trick – a play you've invited the world to attend. Being made a slave is arbitrary – as arbitrary as being named emperor. Once one is physically out of his chains, all that matters is what the world thinks. There's nothing more too it. So why not decide *what* Marcus is, rather than let the world decide for him.

We came here to wait for Halotus, but now I also wait for my sweet Marcus to return to me. But waiting is nothing. I was once the master of the known world; now I am the master of time. I will wait as long as I have to.

Doryphorus has returned from Ephesus a week early. He is waiting in the peristyle when Spiculus and I return.

'Any luck?' I ask as a slave helps me take a seat.

'Yes,' Doryphorus says. 'Some.' He sounds worn out from the road. I picture him dishevelled, streaked with dirt, possibly still in his eastern costume.

Spiculus is impatient. He says, 'Out with it, man.'

'We should wait for Marcus,' I say. 'Where is he?'

A slave answers. 'He has gone with Orestes, master.'

'He spites us openly now,' Doryphorus says. 'He should be punished.'

Orestes is the son of a farmer down the road, dirt poor, unconnected, and not someone with whom Marcus should be spending his time. After I told Marcus this, he began to spend even *more* time with the boy. A typical response of a thirteen-year-old, but frustrating all the same.

'Never mind,' I say. 'What happened in Ephesus?'

Doryphorus says. 'It took nearly two weeks, but I seduced a man on Marcellus's staff.'

Spiculus asks, 'Your disguise worked?'

'Yes, very well. Exceptionally well. I enjoyed playing the exotic.'

'Your Parthian accent was believable then?' I ask.

Doryphorus's voice is mock sadness. 'You wrong me, sir. I am an actor! There is no role I cannot achieve, no accent I cannot master.'

'In any event,' I say, 'it was a necessary precaution to ensure you were not recognised. Go on. Who did you seduce? What did you learn?'

'I found the canteen Marcellus's staff frequent. It was there that I struck up a conversation with the assistant secretary. We made love that very night.'

'He was not below the great Doryphorus?' Spiculus asks.

Doryphorus sighs. 'He was not the pick of the litter, if that is what you are asking. It was more to our advantage, though. He was grateful for the attention. He paid me back with information.'

Spiculus laughs.

'According to the assistant secretary, Halotus works very closely with Marcellus.'

'Does he?' I ask.

'There is more,' Doryphorus says. 'Marcellus intends to visit Rhodes next month.'

'That is good news,' Spiculus says. 'Halotus will likely accompany him.'

'Where the devil is Marcus?' I ask, annoyed.

'I will find him,' Spiculus says.

Spiculus leaves. Doryphorus continues his story.

# MARCUS

◆

*1 September, sunset*
*The shore, the island of Rhodes*

Orestes and I make our way to the water. We skip rocks to pass the time. Turquoise waves lap the shore.

'What did you learn today?' he asks.

'Nothing really.'

Orestes is short – shorter than me – with black eyes, black scruffy hair, and cheekbones that jut out like little hills. He doesn't go to school because his father can't afford it, and because he has to help with their flock. Orestes is poor (Nero calls him a pleb's pleb) but I still think he's lucky. His father doesn't tell him what to do or what to think or which famous general to measure himself against. Orestes can do what he wants once he's finished his chores. I met him when I was hiking through the hills behind our home. He and his father (who looks exactly like him but with more wrinkles and eyebrows twice as thick) were herding their flock up a hill. They were kind and they let me pet their sheep, so I started to go every day after school and help them.

I like spending time with Orestes because he's not like the rich, mean kids in Musonius's class – kids I'm nothing like because I'm not actually rich; I'm only pretend rich. I'm always afraid someone will find out I'm a slave and then I'll be laughed at or maybe even put on a cross and crucified. (Sometimes I dream Master Creon finds me and drags me back to his home and I have to carry urns of piss for the rest of my life.) But if Orestes found out I'm a slave, I wouldn't care and neither would he, because he's the son of a shepherd, and that isn't much better than being a slave.

I pick up a rock.

'Will you tell me about Alexander again?' he asks.

Orestes is my age, but I know more than him, a lot more. Sometimes I tell him about things I learned in school. He likes to hear about Alexander the Great most of all.

I throw the rock – spinning it with my wrist – and it bounces once, twice, three times, before sinking through the water. *Plop.* As I bend down for another rock, I start to tell Orestes about Alexander in Persia.

'Where's Persia?' he asks.

I look for the sun, which is close to setting, and then point in the opposite direction. 'That way, over the sea and across Asia.'

Orestes's mouth opens up. He has more questions, but he can't figure which to ask, or which ones not to, so he won't sound stupid.

'Well, well –' someone is behind us '– if it isn't the Marcus and his lover.'

We turn to see three boys on the crest of the hill, Peleus and two boys that follow him everywhere. Peleus is the largest boy in our class and everyone is afraid of him.

Peleus scrambles down to the rocky shore. His friends follow. To Orestes, he says, 'Hello there. Does Marcus give you what you like? Does he suck your cock?'

The other boys laugh. Peleus picks up a rock and throws it at me. I duck just in time. Then all four boys – Peleus and his friends – pick up rocks and start throwing them at me. Orestes stands in between and a rock hits him in the face. He bends down and I can see blood drip to the rocky shore.

Peleus and his friends run over and grab Orestes. They hold his arms behind his back. Peleus grabs his collar and, with his other hand, raises his fist.

'Come on, Marcus,' Peleus says. 'Come save your lover.'

I don't move. I feel frozen to the shore.

'What's happening here?'

Spiculus is on the crest of the hill. As he scrambles down, Peleus and his friends run away.

Before he leaves, Peleus smiles at me. A big, gloating, I-know-you're-a-coward smile.

Shame burns my skin like fire. I can't look Orestes in the eye.

# NERO

◆

*21 September, vesper*
*The home of Lucius Ulpius Traianus,*
*the island of Rhodes*

Finally, after years of waiting, the proconsul comes to Rhodes. Six days pass before we are invited to dinner. The richest and most important residents (by Rhodian standards, not Roman) are invited. Senators mainly, one or two knights, Commagenian royalty (embarrassingly deposed and transient), and a Parthian ambassador. The proconsul's presence has the island's inhabitants buzzing – they are excited, but there is an edge to it. Rhodes, when compared with Rome or Alexandria, is sleepy and provincial. So with the proconsul and his retinue – soldiers and attendants and staff numbering in the hundreds – the island feels overrun. The city is jammed with people and the markets have been laid to waste, as all supplies are diverted to the proconsular residence, a complex of white stone near the shore, which stands empty three hundred and sixty days of the year.

Marcellus has not left the residence since arriving, though his soldiers and freedmen walk through the city, day and night, leaving a swaggering path of entitled destruction as they go. I wonder if my retinue acted as badly when I travelled abroad. Actually, in truth, I know they did. I simply didn't care. How was I to know that one day *I* would be a mere citizen, fearful of falling victim to such behaviour?

With Halotus behind doors, we have waited and hoped for an invitation to dinner, for an excuse to get close enough and learn the answers we need. The arrival of the proconsul and his staff coincided with the disappearance of a man, a shepherd or farmer, something in that vein. He has been missing for two nights so far. Whether this is a sign of something sinister, we do not know.

The invitation to dinner came two days before the dinner itself. The late delivery means we were probably late additions, after more palatable guests dropped out.

We are all on edge as dinner approaches. Last night, I dreamt of men in golden masks drinking the blood of a shepherd. (In my dreams I still have my eyes.) When the deed was done and the men faded into the black of night, I went to the shepherd and turned the body over, rolling it face up in the freshly tilled dirt, and found the body belonged to Marcus – or he had the face I've given to Marcus in my dreams: soil black hair, green eyes, a hard chin and a gentle smile. But the corpse wasn't smiling; it was open-mouthed, with his tongue lolling between his teeth.

The dream is fresh in my mind the day we are to attend Marcellus's dinner. Marcus asks to help look for the missing shepherd. 'Most of the town is going,' he said. 'We are going to walk through the woods and along the shore from here to the next town. Please.'

'No,' I say, 'absolutely not. You know what's at stake tonight.'

'You won't even let me come to the dinner?'

'You're not invited. What am I to do about that? But we need you here in case anything happens.'

'Please!'

I tell him no and he runs off in a huff.

'Leave him,' Doryphorus says. 'He is still upset over the encounter by the beach. He will obey.'

We arrive at the residence in the eighth hour. The smell of roasting mint-drenched peacock greets us at the door. The air, as it has been all week, is cool, but when we enter the house the radiance of a hundred lamps envelops us, as though we are stepping into the sun.

Tonight, Doryphorus and Spiculus are my faceless attendants. Doryphorus takes my arm and leads me about the room. Spiculus – if he is sticking to the plan – slowly and inconspicuously loses himself in the building. He will find a place to hide and, when the party is over and all the guests have gone home and the residence is quiet, he will abduct the man I wish to speak to.

The dinner goes well enough, though I find I am not as important as I thought. I am relegated to the second table, along with two knights and the Parthian ambassador. The conversation is fine. I try to create controversy but the men are bland enough that they simply accept whatever strange notion I present as genuine fact. Doryphorus (once again in his Persian disguise) held up well when the Parthian ambassador questioned him. He gave a believable tale of leaving Parthia and finding himself in the employ of a Roman. It was entertaining, believable, brief – everything it needed to be.

Marcellus and Halotus sit at the main table. It's strange, Halotus' rise in fortune. I wonder what he has on Marcellus. In my court, he wouldn't have dreamt of sitting with senators. He was an Imperial freedman, yes, but a taster, nothing more. I try to listen to their conversation, to get a sense of their relationship. Is Marcellus anything more than Halotus' patron?

Dinner ends. No one notices Spiculus's absence as we leave. We go home and wait. Marcus is not up. Doryphorus thinks about waking him, saying he should be awake in case we need him, but I tell him to leave him be. 'Let him have his rest.'

We sit in the atrium. Doryphorus reads Homer aloud to pass the time. It is well after midnight when my ex-gladiator returns.

'Everything is ready,' he says.

'You didn't experience any trouble?' Doryphorus asks.

'None,' Spiculus says. 'I waited in his bedroom, hidden behind a curtain. When he returned, I subdued him, gagged him and dragged him out the window. The house was quiet, anyway, very quiet.' Spiculus grabs my arm. 'Come, I will take you to the man you have been dying to question.'

Spiculus leads us to the outskirts of town, to an old, abandoned hut we purchased months ago, sitting at the base of a hill, far beyond prying ears. The windows have been boarded up as a precaution.

Doryphorus leads me into the shack. I don't hear anything, which strikes me as odd. You would think a man recently abducted would struggle and yell for help. But the room is as quiet as a temple.

'Is he awake?' I ask.

Doryphorus whispers in my ear. 'He is awake. He seems at ease. Maybe he knows his time is up.'

'Remove his gag,' I say.

There is a brief rustling, then: 'Is it you?' The voice is cruel and easy. I picture Halotus' light blue, wolf-like eyes, his thin lips, his sneer. 'You won't believe me,' he says, 'but I had my suspicions at dinner.'

'What gave me away?'

'The frown you had when you were told you wouldn't be seated at the head table. It was the frown of a spoilt child. I can't count how many times I saw it in the past.'

'Well spotted,' I say, 'though you didn't do much with the conclusion, did you?'

'Perhaps.'

I can hear the smile in Halotus's voice. For the man who tasted my food every night, he has always possessed such inexplicable confidence.

'You are going to answer my questions, Halotus.'

'I had no role in your fall.'

'No? What of Torcus?'

There is a brief pause, then: 'You know the name, do you? Not altogether ignorant, I see. It is nothing. It is a dalliance.'

'It is a perversion.'

'Why? Because we murder man rather than beast. How is it different than the soldier? Or the Emperor?'

'Is that what you tell yourself? Is that how you justify your actions?'

He sighs like a mother exasperated with her child. 'Torcus had no hand in your fall; nor did I. It was a group of ambitious soldiers who wanted Galba's favour. They bribed your chamberlain, Epaphroditus. He let them into your bedroom.'

He speaks half-truths to convince me of a greater lie. The truth of it all is difficult to parse.

'Epaphroditus may be involved, but I know you were as well,' I say. 'You were working with Nymphidius and his centurion, Terentius. But they didn't stick to the plan. They didn't bring your man to the Praetorian camp and have him proclaimed emperor. I have your angry letter to Nymphidius complaining and vowing revenge.'

My bluff works. The eunuch doesn't deny authoring the letter we stole from Nymphidius. It feels good to have finally confirmed my suspicion.

He says, 'You are bursting with information, aren't you? Yes, we had a man chosen for the principate, but then Nymphidius – for whatever reason – double-crossed us. There's a lesson there: never trust the son of a concubine. But it's water under the bridge now. Nymphidius is gone. As are you, technically speaking . . . so tell me, Nero: how does it feel to know so many of the men you trusted jumped at the chance to bring you down?'

I shrug, trying to match his indifference. 'It has kept me busy,' I say. 'Was Marcellus the man you sought to put on my throne?'

'You should ask him yourself. He is but a short ride away.'

'Were Nymphidius and Terentius members of Torcus?'

'Those two? No, they had a different vice. They were soldiers.' He laughs. 'Do you know they are practising tonight?'

'Who is?'

'Why, the adherents, of course.'

I am silent. Is this another half-truth? Or a lie?

'They found two boys today . . .'

My heart, my lungs, my very flesh – every part of me ceases up.

'. . . you know one of them. You claim to be his uncle, which I seriously doubt, seeing as you are an only child.'

His self-assurance now makes sense. He knew since I walked in the door. He knew that Marcus was taken.

'Where is he?' I demand. 'Where have they taken him?'

'Release me,' Halotus says. I can hear the smile in his voice.

But then he is screaming. Spiculus (I presume) has applied pressure to compel him to speak. He has pulled his hair back and applied a blade to his neck; or he has broken a finger. I have to control myself, and Spiculus, or we will lose our only hope of knowing where Marcus is.

'Take his finger,' I say. 'The smallest.'

Halotus screams again, this time with blood-thinning vigour; and then he is moaning and sucking in deep breaths.

'Where is he?' My voice – which is all I have – is sharpened steel.

Silence.

'Another finger,' I say to Spiculus.

'No,' Halotus pants.

'Tell me now, at this very moment, where they've taken the boy, or Spiculus will take each finger, then your cock, then your eyes. There will be no second chance.'

Halotus names a valley we know, beyond the forest, a mile or two east. Before he is finished, Spiculus is through the door. I can hear it swing open and clatter against the wall. Doryphorus and I are right behind him, leaving nine-fingered Halotus, bleeding and panting for air.

# MARCUS

*21 September, first torch*
*The forest, the island of Rhodes*

All I can smell is horse. They've tied my ankles together and my wrists behind my back and thrown me over the side of a grey horse. My face is pressed against the animal's hot, hairy flesh. It smells of mouldy hay and sweat. I think Orestes is beside me, but I'm not certain. All I can see is the horse's furry shoulder and, out of the corner of my eye, torches lighting up the night.

People are walking beside me, in front and behind. I can hear their steps through the tall grass, but they aren't talking. I don't think I'd be as scared if they were talking.

I want to scream for help and hope that Spiculus or Nero can hear me. I want to scream because I'm scared and angry and I want to be away from here right now. But they've tied a gag around my mouth and the horse's back is digging into my stomach, sucking out my breath.

We walk and walk and walk, and my head gets woozy from the horse's rollicking steps.

I don't know why they've taken me or what they plan to do with me. All I know is that I don't want to die – not now that life is so much better than it used to be. Before I used to worry every day about Master beating me, or Giton thinking up some humiliation to put me through, or Mistress scolding me. But since I met Nero life has been so much better. I've learned how to read and how to write, how to speak Greek and I'm learning Persian. I've learned about the poets (the good ones and the bad). I've learned philosophy and mathematics. I've eaten oysters and drank Falernian wine. I've lived in Alexandria, the best city in the world. I've gone sailing and hunting. I've diced with bandits and found buried treasure.

I don't want to die. I want to live so badly that I start to cry. I cry so hard I start to whimper like a little girl. Nero would be disappointed.

'You must be courageous in death as well as in life. It matters how one dies.' But I can't help it.

When the horse finally stops walking, they pull me off it and drag me into a clearing in the trees and drop me on the grass. In the middle of the clearing is a large, flat-topped boulder. It looks like an altar. Beside it is a man dressed all in black. The other men or women, ten or so, are dressed in dark red, hooded cloaks. Beyond their hoods, each wears a mask, like an actor would wear, but made of gold.

Another person is dragged and dropped beside me. Orestes. I try to talk but there's a gag in my mouth and all that comes out is a harried mumble.

We're dragged to a spot beside the altar. The man in black looms over us. He starts to speak in a tongue I've never heard before. The red-cloaked priests move into a semi-circle around the altar. They begin to chant softly in the same language. It sounds like the hissing of snakes.

Two red priests grab Orestes and pull him up on to his knees: one grabs his shoulders, the other his head. Orestes's hands are still tied behind his back. His eyes are wide with terror.

The man in black moves forward. A knife is in his hand. One of the men in red, the one holding Orestes's head, grabs his jaw and forces his mouth open.

The hissing of the other men in red grows louder and faster.

Orestes starts to struggle, flailing his body like a fish out of water, but the red-cloaked men are holding him too tightly. Orestes stays put.

The man in black bends down, aims his blade at Orestes's mouth, inserts it and blood erupts from his lips.

I close my eyes because I can't watch. With my eyes closed, I notice I'm breathing fast and my heart is pounding. It's like I've been running all day.

Over the hissing chants of the men in red, it sounds like Orestes is drowning – drowning in his own blood. I bury my head into the grass. I keep sobbing. I don't stop.

Then a hand grabs my ankle. They start to drag me to the altar.

Two men in red are holding Orestes on the altar. The man in black has a golden bowl below Orestes's neck. It's filled with black water.

The man in black stands up and raises the golden bowl to his lips.

I close my eyes.

I can feel them drag me to the altar. I can feel two sets of hands position me onto my knees. I can hear the chanting speed up again, as the hissing snakes grow angrier. I can feel my mouth being pried open. My tongue starts to feel funny, tingly, as I wait for the steel knife.

I think of Elsie – I'm not sure why. I remember how she would feed me pistachios and tell me ghost stories. I want to smile but my mouth is pried open.

The hissing reaches a crescendo and then goes quiet. I wait for the blade.

But then I hear a man yelling. It's a screaming growl. A battle cry.

The grip on my jaw relaxes. I open my eyes.

The men in red are scattering. One or two are running away. The rest are running to the centre of the clearing, converging on someone or something I can't see. But then they start to fall like flies and I can see in their midst – his sword swinging in furious swipes – Spiculus, my friend.

One of the red priests grabs me by the collar. He stands behind me and then I can feel the point of his knife pinch my neck and warm blood trickle down to my collarbone.

I look back to Spiculus and see he's running straight at us, bodies of red priests strewn on the ground behind him. The man behind me yells at Spiculus in Greek, saying he'll cut my throat, but Spiculus keeps running – running as fast as I've ever seen him run – and when he gets closer, instead of cutting my throat, the man behind me raises his blade in self-defence, pointing it at Spiculus. Spiculus launches himself at the man and I duck just in time. Spiculus's momentum takes him and the other man down to the grass. Spiculus ends up on top, sitting on the man's chest, and then he's raining blows down like a hammer, one after the next. The red priest's blade slashes in self-defence, cutting Spiculus here and there, but then his blade is gone and his arms go slack. Spiculus grabs a rock twice the size of his fist and drums it into the man's scull, flattening it to a pulp.

I hear the crunch of a twig to my right and I turn and see three more red priests, blades in hand, slowly walking toward me, growling for blood. But then Doryphorus is standing between the red priests and me. He doesn't have a weapon. Spiculus gets to his feet and runs at the three red priests, rock still in hand. He crushs one skull, then the next. Behind him, another man lodges a blade into Spiculus's shoulder. Without stopping to remove it, Spiculus turns and hugs the man, pulling him in tight. Then I hear his ribs snap and Spiculus drops him to the ground. The man goes limp and falls to the grass like a rag. Howling with rage, Spiculus pulls the blade from his shoulder and slits the man's throat.

Spiculus looks up at me and, when he sees I'm alive, he sighs with relief. Suddenly he tenses; he stands. He is watching something behind me. I turn and see on the crest of the hill, the remaining adherents scatter and disappear. One of them stops. The man in the black cloak, his face hidden in shadow, turns back and watches for a moment, and then he is gone.

# NERO

*21 September, first torch*
*The forest, the island of Rhodes*

Doryphorus comes back for me when the fighting is done. He left me at the edge of the clearing, wrapping my arms around the trunk of a tree, and this is where he finds me moments later.

It is not until he says, 'He is alive,' that I can finally breathe. He takes my hand and walks me into the clearing.

Five men are dead, according to Doryphorus.

Pushing sentimentality aside, supressing my desire to hold Marcus myself, I say, 'Let us see if we can identify one of the bodies.'

Doryphorus leads me to the corpses. He lets go of my arm and I listen as he struggles to remove their masks.

When he's done, I ask, 'Well?'

'I recognise one.'

'Who?'

'Marcellus's nephew. Tullinus.'

'The boy I pardoned? You see, Doryphorus, it rarely pays to be magnanimous.'

We return to the shack to discover it empty: Halotus has escaped.

'How could this happen,' Doryphorus says. 'He was tied to the chair.'

I can hear Spiculus crouch down to the dirty floor. He says, 'There are footprints. Coming in . . . He had help.'

'We acted rashly,' Doryphorus says. 'One of us should have stayed with Halotus.'

'Marcus is alive,' I say. 'That is what matters tonight.'

'What will we do?' Spiculus asks.

'Halotus remains procurator of Asia,' I say. 'He remains powerful and we have lost the element of surprise. We are not safe here in Rhodes.'

'Are you saying we run?' Doryphorus asks.

'No,' I say. 'We grow powerful ourselves. We wait. We bide our time. We choose where and when we next meet.'

# XXVI

## Trust Your Hackles
### A.D. 79

# CALENUS

*22 April, first torch*
*The sewers, Rome*

I awake to the sound of rushing water and stone pressed against the left side of my face, cool and wet.

I open my eyes and the world is dark; my mind is groggy and grey. My wrists are bound behind my back.

Dark shapes argue, paces away.

'I know, I know.'

'Orders are orders.'

The air is damp and musty; it stinks of ancient piss.

'I know. Still . . .'

We are in the sewers, somewhere, in one of the sections where a man can stand without hindrance. Nearby a lamp flickers with a sickly glow.

How long have I been out? It must've been hours.

A dark shape lumbers over. Fabius. He kneels beside me. 'I'm sorry, old friend.'

My mind is covered with foggy cobwebs. I try to say something witty, but all I can muster is, 'Why?'

'Don't talk to that bastard.' A second dark shape waddles over. The miniature whore. She says, 'Wasted words, on a corpse.'

The third and final dark shape comes closer. My old friend with the scar. He's holding a rusty knife.

'I'm sorry, Calenus,' Fabius says as he grabs my scalp and pulls, twisting my chin up, exposing my neck; my Adam's apple feels naked and lonely, like having my cock for sale in the forum. 'Bad timing, that's all. Nothing to be done about it. Plans are set.'

The man with the scar kneels and then points at his cheek. 'Thought you got away with this, didn't you?'

The whore cackles.

My wits are slowly coming back; there's time yet to die with dignity. I meet the man's eyes and say, 'Never gave you a second thought.' Nearly content with my last words, I add, 'Cunt.'

With that I close my eyes and wait for the steel to slit my throat.

I have time for one thought: I can't believe I lived this long. Ten years in the legions, two on the run, eight living hand to mouth in Rome, running errands for senators and then the Imperial family. I should have met my end earlier. It was good fortune to live as long as I did.

The blade doesn't come.

I have time for a second thought: I'm glad I lived long enough to meet Red. That was good fortune, the very best. I think of the way she'd rub my scar for good luck, and I smile.

I keep waiting, but the blade never comes. Instead of feeling my neck peel open, I hear a yelp and a series of thuds, and then the iron grip holding my hair disappears and my head falls back to the bricks. I open my eyes.

Behind me, someone is untying my wrists.

'Are you all right?'

In front of me, the man with the scar is lying on the ground, holding a gory wound, gasping for air. There is another man wiping his blade onto the dying man's tunic. The light catches his eye patch and I realise it's the Big Buck, Ulpius's one-eyed freedman. Theseus.

The man behind me helps me sit up before walking over to Theseus. In the lamplight, I see it's Ulpius's patrician boy, Marcus.

A strange twist, I'd say. Very strange.

The boy says to Theseus, 'The girl ran off.'

Another body is splayed out on the ground. Fabius. He's rubbing his head and whimpering nonsense.

Theseus sits on Fabius, straddling his waist. He grabs Fabius by the tunic and pulls him up, bringing one eye level with two. He says, 'Who does Montanus work for?'

Fabius's face is white as a cloud. He looks around, trying to get his bearings. (He must have been hit on the head.) His eyes lock on his colleague – still gasping for air, one foot in Elysium now.

Theseus gives Fabius a furious shake. 'Who?'

'Look at him,' I say. I try to stand, but halfway up the grog returns tenfold, churning ear to ear, and I stumble back to the bricks. They wait until I'm ready to speak. After a moment, I nod my head at Fabius and say, 'His wits are gone. Give him a moment.'

They take my point: the boy helps me stand while Theseus drags Fabius to the wall and leans him against it. The boy hands me a skin of wine. I kneel beside Fabius and help him take a sip. When he's done he says, *ahhhhh,* and wipes his mouth.

'You were always decent, Calenus,' Fabius says. 'Always decent.'

'I'd have said the same about you,' I say. 'Until today.'

Fabius smiles. He looks up at Theseus and the boy who are looming over us. 'What now?'

Theseus says, 'For a start, you can tell us who Montanus works for.'

Fabius frowns. 'Or?'

Theseus shrugs.

Fabius frowns. 'Now how do I know that won't happen anyway?' He looks to me. 'Help me out old friend, Calenus. I'll share what I know, but I don't want today to be my last. I need assurances.'

I look at the other two and it's the boy (not Theseus) who nods. 'We will let you live, but you must leave Rome. Stay away until the summer.'

Fabius looks to me to corroborate. I say. 'You've my word, Fabius. Tell us what you know and you can go a free man. I'll even help you fight your way out if these boys change their mind.'

Fabius laughs and takes another draught of wine. 'Hell of a day.' He wipes his mouth. 'Where do I start? First off, you should know Montanus isn't a thief . . . well, I suppose he is, but he's more than that. He's a man of Minerva, an entrepreneur. There were a lot of soldiers out of work after the civil wars, after the man they backed lost, myself included. Montanus saw an opportunity there and he put us to good use. We do work for the trades mainly – getting rid of one man's competition, setting fires, breaking arms, that sort of thing. But we also work for senators and knights. I've a few names for you –' Fabius takes another sip of wine '– but the one I suspect you're after is senator Marcellus.'

'And why do you think Marcellus is who we are after?' the boy asks.

Fabius says, 'Because for months this whole city has been talking about some terrible, bloody murder by the Tiber. I figured that's what you were on about.'

'So you were involved in the murder?' the boy asks.

Fabius raises his hands up to show his innocence. 'Now don't go putting the knife in my hands. All we did was deliver the man up. Montanus said "get me so-and-so", so we went and got the man. We never drank his blood, or ate his insides, or whatever it is they did to him.'

Theseus adjusts his eye patch. 'Delivered up who? Who was killed?'

Fabius says, 'His name was Vettius, some knight from the Bay.'

'Are you certain?' the boy asks. 'Where you there when Marcellus hired Montanus?'

Fabius shakes his head. 'No, I suppose I wasn't. But I'm certain all the same. A few weeks before we grabbed the man, sometime in December, we went to see Marcellus, Montanus and I. Marcellus handed us a bag of coin the size of my arse and said, "Give this to Vettius. He'll knows what it's for." We did as he asked and we didn't hear anything for weeks. Then one day Montanus came back to the Spotted Pig and said we had to go south and nab Vettius. So we went and got the man, and we brought him north. We held him for nearly a week. Then we delivered him to a warehouse near the Tiber. It was the dead of night, cold as a Thracian's tit. Montanus knocked on a door and three of them came out, red cloaks and golden masks. It froze my blood. Montanus followed them inside, dragging Vettius behind him, leaving the rest of us on the stoop. And that was that. Next thing we hear is they'd found some bloodied body near the Tiber, right where we'd left him. Montanus never said anything more about it and we didn't ask.'

'And what of the hand?' Marcus asks. 'Was that Marcellus as well?'

Fabius shakes his head. 'Uh, uh. You see this is where things get – what's the word – convoluted.' He takes another sip of wine. 'A few months back Montanus took on a new customer. Some senator – at least, we think he's a senator; he pays well enough – but we've never met the man. He sends people instead of coming himself, with instructions and coin. A girl usually.'

'The girl from today?' I ask. 'The one with one eyebrow who met with Montanus?'

'The very one.' Fabius takes another draught of wine. He shifts his weight and grimaces. 'We did a few jobs for this senator. We stole an urn, beat up a slave – small stuff. Then one day the girl – she calls herself Livia – one day Livia shows up at the Spotted Pig with a mutt and a ring, solid gold. She says the dog's been trained. All we needed to do was get the hand of a grown man, put the ring on its finger, and then put the hand in the mutt's mouth on a certain day, at a certain time, and let it go.'

'Whose hand was it?' the boy asks.

'Can't remember who exactly,' Fabius says. 'Some poor bastard who didn't pay Montanus back money he'd borrowed. We killed him the day before, chopped his hand off and dumped the rest of him in the Tiber. Put enough rocks in a man's pockets and he'll be dragged half way to Ostia before he surfaces.'

Marcus asks, 'And what did this mysterious senator hire you to do next?'

'He's kept us busy all right. The very evening we set the mutt loose in the forum, Livia came back to see Montanus and asked us to kidnap two people on the Bay, a whore and a senator.'

'Plautius,' I say.

'Indeed,' Fabius says.

'Just kidnap?' Theseus asks.

Fabius puts his hands up again, showing his innocence. 'We didn't have anything to do with him rowing a boat for three months. Livia wanted us to grab him, hold him for a while, and feed him information. So that's what we did.'

'What do you mean, "feed him information"?' Theseus asks.

'We locked him in a room and talked outside the door. We were supposed to keep saying "Caecina" and "Ulpius", "the Turncoat" and "the Blind Man", shit like that, again and again. Like they were the one's giving us orders. Then we were supposed to let him escape – and we did. We made it easy for him. We left the door wide open. But instead of running to Rome and telling everyone what he'd heard, he went and found himself a job rowing a boat.' Fabius shakes his head. 'Not the sharpest of swords, that one.'

'So that colleague of yours –' I point at the man, now dead, who wears the scar I gave him '– I met him when he was bringing a woman north?'

Fabius nods. 'So I'm told. That's what he told Montanus, after you tried to run.'

'And why weren't you there?'

'I was with Plautius in Miscenum.'

'And you never asked why you were doing any of these tasks?' Marcus says.

Fabius is indignant. 'You inherited a pile, I can tell by the look of you. You've no idea what it's like to work. Beggars can't be choosers. And ask him –' he points at me '– you don't ask a man like Montanus, "And *why* are we doing such and such?"'

'And who tried to kill Caesar's daughter?' Theseus asks, arms crossed, rubbing his chin. 'Marcellus or this mysterious senator?'

Fabius shrugs. 'Can't say for certain. Montanus doesn't tell me everything. But I know the man who did it was one of Montanus's. Poor bastard. He'd fucked something up, lost Montanus twenty thousand when he got robbed on his way back from Ravenna. Montanus said, "Kill the Widow and the debt is forgiven." It was an impossible job, but he had no choice. You don't say no to Montanus.'

Fabius takes another sip of wine.

I say, 'A few weeks back, you said heavy work was coming. Do you remember? What did you mean?'

'Nothing in particular. You just hear things, second-hand. And Montanus was buying up more arms for the boys, cuirasses and swords. I just had a suspicion things were going that way. I've told you all I know.'

The questions stop and Fabius says, 'If that's all, I will be on my way.'

Theseus and Marcus nod. Fabius stands and says, 'Goodbye, Calenus. No hard feelings, I hope?'

I shake my head. 'Just buy me a cup next we meet.'

He smiles before disappearing around the bend.

When we're alone, Theseus asks me, 'And why did Montanus want you dead?'

I shrug. 'Hard to say.'

Nice as these boys were for saving my life, there's a chance their interests are different than Domitilla's. I need to report what I know to her and only her. So I'll buy them a cup, but as far as information, they can go jump in the Tiber.

Theseus frowns. His feelings are hurt; he thought we were friends.

Marcus takes over. 'You're working for Domitilla now. That's the way your loyalty lies. That's fine.' He puts his hand on my shoulder, like I'm his long-lost friend. 'Something is in the works, something aimed at Caesar and his family. When you know we are on the same side, come to us. We both have information the other does not.'

With that, they saunter off.

I emerge from the sewer in a daze, amazed that I'm still alive. It's not safe to go to mine, so I head to Red's. I pay the man at the front and he takes me to her room. I knock on the door and peek in. She's asleep, so I slink into the room and and lie beside her.

She starts to stir and I say, 'Not looking for anything other than a place to rest. Mine's not safe.' She doesn't say anything, but she throws her leg over my thigh. When she presses her face into my shoulder, I know she's happy I'm here. Her hot breath warms my cheek, which, like the rest of me, is still cold from the sewer.

There is a throbbing in my chest that will wake the room.

She kisses me, a little dab just shy of my lips. It feels different from the ones she's given me before, softer, sweeter. Another follows. I don't move, not wanting to spoil the moment. I hold my breath, to the point where I feel faint. She kisses me a third time, then a fourth. I am a statue, afraid to move. And I don't, not until – practical woman that she is – Red hitches up my tunic and grabs my member.

We make love, quietly. After I finish, she keeps me inside her, kissing me.

I fall asleep, thinking: this is the best day of my life, even if I had a knife to my throat for most of it.

The next day, it's near hour two when I make my way to the palace, a smile to end all smiles on my face. On the way, I see Chickpea, an old friend from the legions, named for the chickpea-sized mole on his nose.

'Ho! Calenus,' he says over the racket of the cattle market.

He goes to shake my hand and I pull him in for an embrace.

He looks at me sideways. 'You're mad! Have you time for a cup?'

'I do, indeed.'

Moments later we're under the awning of a market stall, bent over the bar.

Chickpea says, 'Lucky fellow, that Plautius. No?'

I'd forgotten: a decision was supposed to be reached yesterday, while I was indisposed.

'The ruling was in his favour then?'

'By a hair,' he says, 'two votes to one.'

I feel buoyed by this. It's good for Domitilla. 'A fair result,' I say.

'Fair?' Chickpea shakes his head. 'Justice for the rich, I'd say. A poor man would have stayed in his chains. It wouldn't matter how he got there.'

'Another reason why it's better to be rich.'

Chickpea nods.

Later, when we stand to leave, I see Nerva's slave Appius, the king of the portico, making his way down the road towards us.

'Ho!' I yell over the chatter of the crowd. 'Appius.'

He walks over, sceptical. 'Haven't seen you in a while. I thought you might be dead.'

'I've been working for the palace these days.'

'Have you now?' Appius is vaguely impressed. He looks Chickpea over, wondering if he's from the palace as well. To me, he says, 'You called me over to brag then?'

'No,' I say. 'Nerva owes me coin.'

Appius feigns shock; eyebrows raised. 'And you want me to pay you, do you?'

'Why not?' I ask. 'You carry your patron's purse around for him.' Realising I need him on my side, I add, 'And you've always been fair, Appius.' I turn to Chickpea. 'Wasn't I just telling you that? That Nerva's man Appius is one of the fairest in Rome?'

Chickpea doesn't miss a beat. 'This is the man? You said he was taller.'

It can't be more than the third compliment Appius has had his entire life. He nods, leans towards me, and says, 'Listen, you come by this afternoon and speak with Nerva. He's always in a good mood after the baths. If you're owed it, I've no doubt he'll pay.'

I slap Appius on the back. 'See! One of the fairest.'

Appius disappears into the crowd. I thank Chickpea for his quick thinking. He waves away the thanks. 'It was nothing.'

At the palace doors, I tell the guards, 'Phoenix,' the password Domitilla gave me, and one of them says, 'Wait here.' He comes back with Domitilla's redheaded girl Jacasta.

'Mistress Domitilla has gone to call on a friend this morning.'

'Well, I have news,' I say.

She says, 'And?'

'It concerns Valerianus and that rich Spaniard everyone talks about. Ulpius. It's a good story.'

'Well, tell me and I will tell Mistress.'

'I'd rather say it to her directly.'

She smiles. The girl is as plain as they come, but she has a good smile.

'Fine,' she says. 'Come back to the palace this afternoon. Mistress will have returned by then.'

I turn to go but she says, 'Wait,' and grabs my arm. She produces a thin gold necklace and a little velvet bag. 'Mistress was confident you would not let her down. She asked that you take this necklace as a token of her appreciation.'

I take the necklace and trace my thumb along the intricate threads of gold. It feels like embroidery, but with metal instead of string. I've seen necklaces like this before, but only at a distance; I've never felt one in my hands.

'And here –' she hands me the velvet pouch '– you should have enough there to rent your own lodging. Mistress will not want one of her bodyguards sharing an apartment with a dozen riffraff.'

I'm not sure I've heard her right. 'Bodyguard?'

'Oh, has she not told you yet? You are to be Domitilla's personal bodyguard. She would like a man she can trust. You may not be a Praetorian – Mistress doesn't care what happened in your past, but you clearly cannot be a soldier again. Still: the personal bodyguard of Caesar's eldest daughter is a worthy achievement.'

I can't believe it, the turn in fortune. I can't believe it. My arms are shaking and my mouth is open like a fish. I think: collect yourself, Calenus.

I stand at attention. 'I will be back this afternoon.'

I head straight for Nerva's after the palace. I'm suddenly flush with coin, but every little bit helps. Also, fortune is on my side today. Why waste it?

Appius greets me at the door. The compliment I'd paid him this morning has worn off. He looks confused at my presence. 'Oh, Calenus,' he says. 'Of course. Come along.'

We find Nerva alone in his study, behind a long desk. He's so short his shoulders are barely higher than the wood.

'Come to beg for more coin, have you?' he asks.

I take a seat across from him. 'Only what you owe me.'

Nerva frowns. 'I see. And how much is that?'

'Ten sesterces.'

Another frown. He unwinds a roll of papyrus and begins to read it. He may pay me, but he will make me wait first.

There are noises behind me – feet slapping on marble, the clearing of a throat – and Nerva looks up. His face changes – only slightly, but even the smallest change to Nerva's stony bust is news. I turn back to see who's behind me.

Appius is standing in the atrium, on the threshold to the office, with his head down, reading a wax tablet. Beside him is a girl – *the* girl with the one eyebrow, the one I followed to the Spotted Pig and who met with Montanus. Our eyes meet. If she recognises me, she doesn't show it. I collect myself as best I can before turning back to face Nerva.

When I turn back, the change in Nerva's face is gone. He is back to plain, unreadable Nerva again. Calmly, he says, 'Not now, Appius.'

I fight the urge to turn back and watch the girl go.

Nerva says, 'All right, Calenus. Let's get you what you're owed.'

He stands, walks to a cabinet behind the desk and pulls open a drawer. His back is to me and he fumbles in the drawer for a moment. He returns with a change purse, and then, on his desk, counts out ten sesterces.

Nerva is as rich as Midas, but he's always reluctant to hand over coin. The girl, that look on his face – my hackles are raised. I should leave. Right now. But the coin – my coin – is right there on the desk.

'Here you are. As promised.'

He picks up the stack of coins and takes a step toward me, but then two coins fall from his hands. He puts the remaining coin back down on the desk and then nods towards the fallen coin. 'Quickly, Calenus. Before I take them back.'

I bend down to pick up the coins. Out of the corner of my eye I see Nerva take a step closer. As I'm raising my head, Nerva is there, only a few inches away.

And then I feel a sting in my neck . . .

The pain grows, from a bee sting to an inferno. I put my hand to my neck and, when I pull it away, it's painted red.

The room trembles . . .

I fall to the ground.

Nerva stands over me. He meets my terrified gaze. 'A waste,' he says as he wipes the blade on his tunic; a dark blot pools on the vermillion cloth, just below his ribs.

Liquid trickles from my mouth. Blood. My blood.

'I'm sorry, Calenus,' he says. 'But I can't have you interfering and undermining years of careful planning. I'm well placed now. I won't let some soldier with a schoolboy crush get in the way.'

Nerva squats down. He pats my pocket and pulls out my change purse. I'm too weak to stop him. Inside the pouch he finds the gold necklace. He holds it up to the light. 'Hm.' He pockets the necklace and stands up.

'And I'm sorry you won't be around to see how I pull it all off. Marcellus and his cult will come and go . . .'

My neck throbs; I try to breathe – all I want is to take a fucking breath – but I can't; it's like sucking air from a stone.

'. . . but I will be Rome's constant, like the Capitoline, like the Aventine.'

He steps over me and calmly calls, 'Appius!'

The burning churn in my neck eases. The room dilutes. My eyes shut. I sink down into a wave of warmth.

Red. I think of Red.

I hear Nerva say, 'Clean this up.'

The world slips through my fingers . . .

# XXVII

## Dinner at Ulpius's, Part II
### A.D. 79

# SPICULUS

◆

*11 January, cockcrow*
*Outside the home of Eprius Marcellus, Rome*

Marcus and I use a wagon and a mule for cover. In the morning, before the sun rises, we park it out front of Marcellus's home and remove the wheel, crack a spoke, and lean it against the wagon, giving it the impression it cracked all on its own. We're dressed in simple tunics, unwashed and rumpled, with hooded cloaks. When we're finished, I say, 'What do you think? Just two delivery men trying to fix their cart.'

'It will work for now,' Marcus says. 'But we'll need something different if we don't get him tonight.'

The sun rises and the street starts to fill. The day is uneventful for the most part. In the afternoon a vigiles gives us a hard time. But after Marcus hands him a gold coin he smiles and tells us to take our time.

Around hour six we see him. It is the first time in six years.

Halotus emerges from the alleyway beside Marcellus's home. Even after all this time, he still has the same round belly that juts out, skinny arms, long legs, small head and wolf-like eyes. Marcus and I busy ourselves with the cart. We pretend to talk about the broken wheel, but our eyes are fixed on Halotus.

Marcus sighs. 'He was right. Damn it. He's always right. Not only did the letter work, he came straight to Marcellus. I suppose we'll have to listen to Nero say "I told you so", but at least we know where Halotus is staying.'

I say, 'Just because Halotus is staying with Marcellus, it doesn't mean he is the Black Priest or involved in Nero's fall.'

'Nero will disagree.'

'Halotus's guilt is obvious. With Marcellus, we still don't know.'

Six months ago, Nero paid the Spanish governor for a letter he had in Titus's hand, and then paid a forger to match it, and the seal, and commissioned a letter to Halotus, recalling the eunuch to Rome. Marcus and I were sceptical it would work. We were wrong.

'If he was here before us,' I say, 'we need to be careful. If he's spoken to Titus, he could know he was tricked to come to Rome. His guard could be up.'

Halotus returns after dark. The streets are empty. We call him over on the pretence of helping us with the wheel. As Marcus distracts him, I wrap my arms around him and Marcus quickly stuffs a rag in his mouth and then a sack over his head, and we drag him into the covered portion of the wagon and tie him up. Then, as if all is well, we attach the wheel and drive the cart back to our new home on the Aventine. 'I fear Nero will want to do something dramatic,' I say. 'He has waited a long time for this.'

'Yes,' Marcus says, 'that is a fair bet.'

Nero chooses the Tarpean Rock. He says it's fitting because this was how traitors were killed during the republic. We go under the cover of dark. We take Halotus in the wagon to the foot of the Capitoline and then we drag him up the hill's steep slope and walk him to the Tarpean's ledge.

There is a cold wind here, one that we didn't feel in the forum below.

Nero says, 'Can he see me?'

Marcus removes the sack over Halotus's head. The rag remains in the eunuch's mouth.

'He can now.'

'Hello, Halotus,' Nero says. 'It has been too long. The last time we did this, you successfully talked your way free. Today, I think we'll keep you quiet. Yes?'

Halotus' pale eyes are oceans of terror. He tries to scream but it's lost in the wet rag.

'Stand him up,' Nero says.

Doryphorus and I pull Halotus to his feet. Behind us is an immense drop to the forum.

Halotus starts to talk but it's muffled by the rag in his throat. His voice gradually rises in intensity.

The cold wind continues to blow.

Marcus positions Nero in front of Halotus. Nero reaches out and touches Halotus's face, confirming the eunuch's position.

Halotus is now screaming into his rag and struggling against my grip.

Then Nero issues one swift kick to Halotus's stomach and the eunuch steps back, only there is nothing but air behind him, and he falls quickly and quietly before splattering against the forum floor like a melon.

'Cross him off the list,' Nero says.

Doryphorus takes out the worn wax tablet that has followed us across the Empire, with the names we have been pursuing for many years.

| *Guilty* | *Guilt unknown* |
|---|---|
| *Terentius (centurion)* | *Epaphroditus (chamberlain, telling lies)* |
| ~~*Venus (soldier)*~~ | ~~*Phaon (chamberlain)*~~ |
| ~~*Juno (soldier)*~~ | |
| ~~*Nympidius (Praetorian prefect)*~~ | |
| ~~*Halotus (chamberlain)*~~ | ~~*Galba (False Emperor)*~~ |
| ~~*Tigellinus (Praetorian prefect)*~~ | ~~*Otho (covets the throne)*~~ |
| *The Black Priest* | *Lepida (mistress)* |

'And now?' Doryphorus asks.

'Next is Epaphroditus,' Nero says. 'Our dinner guest.'

# NERO

◆

As Titus is giving his answer, some sprawling response littered with un-inventive Stoicisms (or, to be more specific, Seneca-isms, that's how uninventive the man's ideas are), Doryphorus leans into my ear and whispers, 'Epaphroditus has drunk the poison.'

He calls it poison, but I'm not sure it meets the definition. Poison kills. What Epaphroditus drank will put him to sleep for a short time; nothing more. At the moment, Spiculus is outside giving the same concoction to Epaphroditus's slaves.

Lepida is here, my first time in the same room with my former mistress in a decade. It is anticlimactic. I've wondered for years whether she played me for a fool; whether she was somehow involved in my fall; whether she seduced Caesar and convinced him she was nothing more than a victim of Torcus, not an adherent. I'd planned on learning the truth, and I will. But not tonight. Maybe the wind has gone out of my sails after waiting for so long to bring Halotus to justice. Or maybe my feelings for the woman linger just enough that I am reluctant to move swiftly. Either way, tonight she will escape my machinations. Marcellus will also avoid my reach for the moment, given his decision to decline my invitation to dinner. Spiculus, our collective conscience, refuses to move against him without certainty. It doesn't matter. Tonight I have Epaphroditus. Apollo willing, he will tell me everything I need to know.

Marcus is quiet and sullen throughout dinner. We received word just before sailing for Rome: the slave woman, Elsie, may be in Sicily. It's impossible to know for certain; and I think Marcus will eventually have to be the one to go and see for himself. But I've told him he cannot go until we are finished here, until Torcus is routed out and destroyed. Marcus was furious. He swore and carried on. 'We've waited six years, what's another month?' I insisted but I think it was Spiculus who swayed him in the end. Marcus often suspects I'm manipulating him, rather than being honest. Spiculus, on the other hand, clearly has never said anything he didn't mean. Marcus trusts him.

Marcus agreed to wait, but he has been particularly combative since arriving in Italy. The incident on the road from Ostia to Rome is one example – though, after our shared experiences together, we all hate soldiers and their arbitrary cruelty and tendency to prey on the weak. We likely would have intervened on behalf of that poor woman, being dragged behind that centurion's horse, whether or not Marcus was itching for a fight.

Spiculus continues to blame me. 'He tries to meet your expectations. He thinks you want him to be the wild boy who fights legionaries in the streets, so that is what he does, even if it's not in his nature. You waved your hand and said he was no longer a slave, but a patrician, brave and noble. He is confused and angry and constantly trying to impress you.' I disagree, of course. (None of this is my fault. I saved the boy from a life of servitude for Jove's sake.) I go to Doryphorus for support, but he is not helpful. 'He needs something to fuck,' he says. 'When you're that age, it's a panacea; it has a way of letting the bee out of the jar, and the incessant, furious buzzing can finally cease.'

After dinner is done and the guests are filtering out, I take my leave. I go to my bedroom to rest as Spiculus and Marcus follow Epaphroditus through the dark streets of the city. If all goes according to plan, they will watch as Epaphroditus and his retinue collapse to the bricks.

I sleep an hour or so before Doryphorus gently rocks my shoulder and whispers, 'They're back.'

I take my stick in one hand and Doryphorus's arm in the other. Together we walk to the stables.

I'm greeted by muffled screams. Our guest, I gather, is gagged and the sleeping tonic has already worn off.

Doryphorus directs me so that I am standing in front of Epaphroditus. We have done this enough that Doryphorus knows how to proceed.

I ask, 'If we remove the rag in your mouth, will you agree not to scream?'

'He nodded,' Doryphorus whispers.

'Remove the gag,' I say.

The sound of a mouth – of a tongue testing its dry surroundings – tells me the gag has been removed.

As I have done before, I lean in and remove my blindfold. 'Do you recognise me?' I ask.

Silence.

'It has been many years. My beard is longer, with traces of grey. My eyes are gone.'

Silence.

'Come, you must know who I am.'

'It isn't possible,' our prisoner whispers.

'No? Why? Because you cut my throat?'

Silence.

I say, 'You conspired to bring me down, to take my eyes. Why? I was good to you.'

'Nero?' There is a long pause; an eternity of silence. Then: 'I . . .'

Again, he is at a loss.

'Out with it. I have waited more than a decade for an answer from you. Halotus says you were in it together. Do you deny it?'

'What? No! Halotus is mad. He and the others . . .'

'What others?'

'Nero, I, I, I –'

To Spiculus, I say, 'His arm first.'

I hear a dull snap, like a twig being broken under a blanket and Epaphroditus screams in pain.

When he's done screaming, through his heavy panting, he says, 'No! I will tell you everything. I never betrayed you. I never broke my oath. I am loyal. I was always loyal. It was Halotus. I had no choice.'

'Speak,' I say. 'I am listening.'

'It was because I caught him . . .'

He takes several deep breaths, trying to settle himself before telling me the story I have waited years to hear.

'It was March, before the legions started to revolt. I entered the wrong room of the palace. I happened upon Halotus and your wife. They were making love.'

I snort. 'He was a eunuch.'

'He was, yes, but there are different types. His shaft was intact.'

I signal for him to continue.

'Halotus and your wife were embraced, her stola hiked up ... Halotus saw me. They both did. I ran away and didn't say a word. I didn't want Halotus's ire. Or your wife's. I outranked Halotus, but you know his reputation. It's said he helped poison your uncle, Claudius Caesar. What would he do to me? I thought if I kept quiet, he would leave me alone. A child's plan, but I couldn't think of any other. He waited two weeks before he approached me. It was after the races, before dinner, during those quiet hours when half the palace is napping. He said he appreciated my tact. He wanted to bring me into his sect as a show of thanks. It would change my life, he said. I was happy we were not at odds and, to me, one sect is as good as any other. So I agreed. Halotus told me to be ready the night of the Ides. When the day came, four men came for me in the depth of night. They were wearing red cloaks and golden masks. They blindfolded me and took me to the Tiber. I knew it was the Tiber because I could hear the ships moving in the swell. Then we descended some steps, until we were in the heart of the earth. My blindfold was removed and I was surrounded by ghostly priests with golden masks. A man was dragged before me. He was naked and his mouth sewn shut. I heard Halotus's voice in my ear. "Cut his throat or you do not leave here tonight." I had nowhere to turn, no way out.'

Epaphroditus begins to sob.

'We did terrible things. It was not just murder. It was human sacrifice to some devil of a god. We drank the man's blood and ate his tongue. The gods help me, but I did it. When the ceremony was over, Halotus told me I was now tied to him and his cult. If I told anyone what I saw him doing with your wife, he would produce witnesses to the human sacrifice I had performed. For three months, I didn't sleep. I was beside myself. And then, one night, Halotus came to see me again. He said in two weeks' time, I was to leave the key to your chamber in the library, inside a scroll.'

'Ah, I see. So you left the key, on the night he asked, dooming your patron, your Emperor, your god, a man who never did you any harm?'

'Never did me harm? You had me beaten three times that year for little cause. You took my wife for sport. You did me harm, Caesar. Often.' He is angry but still in tears. His voice sounds exhausted. 'But I never broke my oath. I didn't betray you.'

Doryphorus asks, 'What happened next?'

'I left the key because I had no choice. But – I swear – I never meant you harm. Halotus said I was only helping him embezzle money. Everyone stole from you and you didn't care. Your coffers were infinite. Gods do not run low on money. He said he needed to access certain ledgers. I had no idea leaving the key would lead to what it did. So I left it, as Halotus told me to, and that night I awoke to the sounds of chaos. I stalked the halls and saw men fighting. I even saw an Imperial secretary cut down. So I ran and I hid. It was only after I'd emerged from hiding that I learned the world – or half of it at least – thought I'd assisted in your suicide. But the story saved my life. Galba, not only kept me alive, he made me exchequer because of it. I could not dispute it. I had no choice.'

'You poor man,' I say, sarcastically. 'So many choices beyond your control.'

'But Caesar, I have never had any involvement with Torcus since your fall. I am not a believer. They know this. They have let me be. Please, please spare my life.'

I can feel eyes on me, not only our prisoner, but Spiculus, Doryphorus, and Marcus. The room wishes to know if this man will live or die. I know Spiculus will be against killing the man. And I'm not sure what Marcus would make of mercy. His anger is for Halotus and the Black Priest, the men responsible for killing his friend Orestes before his eyes.

I shake my head, not at our captive, but at myself. There was a time, not long ago, when this traitor would have breathed his last the moment his story was done. But now? Bloodthirsty revenge has grown stale; plans change; revenge – its constituent parts – ebb and flow.

'We will hold you for now, old friend, to test the validity of your story. And I will ponder the appropriate punishment.'

# XXVIII

## A Trap is Set
### A.D. 79

# DOMITILLA

*23 April, noon*
*The Imperial palace, Rome*

We wait for Calenus all afternoon. We see neither hide nor hair.

'I thought your man was reliable,' Titus says. He considers this a victory, even if it sets us back. He thinks my involvement in the matters of state impertinent. He is worse than Father.

'Calenus is reliable,' I say. 'Something must be wrong.'

'He was a drunkard, sister. I smelled the wine on him myself. He means well, but let's leave him to the canteens, yes? Matters of state take precedence over your little project.'

'He will come,' I say. 'Or something has gone wrong.'

'Wrong?' Titus raises an eyebrow; his voice is condescendingly smug. I hate it when he is smug. 'You continue your vigilance while he rots in a canteen. He mentioned Ulpius when he spoke to Jacasta. I will go to Ulpius myself. He will finally tell me of his involvement. I will get the answers we need.'

Cleopatra is curled up by my feet. She raises her head, realizing Titus is leaving. Titus tells her to stay and – the quick learner that she is – she puts her head back down and falls asleep.

Titus walks out and I begin to pace.

After an hour, I walk to the front gate to enquire with the guards whether, for some reason, Calenus was refused entry. Cleopatra – who has grown fond of me these last few months – follows. On my way, I happen upon Nerva and his slave Appius.

'Senator Nerva,' I say.

Nerva gives a slight, respectful bow. 'Domitilla.'

Cleopatra wags her tail with vigour and pushes her head between Nerva's knees.

'I am glad to see you,' I say. 'You know Julius Calenus, do you not?'

Doing his best to ignore Cleopatra, Nerva nods. 'Of course.'

'I was expecting him here at the palace this morning. But he has not come.'

'You were expecting him?' Nerva looks confused for a moment and then nods. 'Ah, yes. I had heard he was running errands for you. That is most unlike Calenus. He was a reliable man. Except, of course, when the drink takes hold of him.' He tilts his head slightly; the movement is cold, predatory. 'He has had a difficult life. Occasionally, he seeks solace in a cup. Many men from the civil war are like this, as I'm sure you know.'

I notice for the first time a dark stain on his vermillion tunic, barely visible under his cloak, inches above his right hip. It looks like a wound.

'Are you all right?' I ask.

'Oh that?' he says, inspecting his hip. 'This morning's sacrifice. I had only my tunic with which to wipe the blade.'

Cleopatra – her tail still wagging – sits on her bum and makes a noise. It is not so much a bark as a hello.

I say, 'She acts as though you're long lost friends?'

'I'm not sure how,' Nerva says. 'I've never seen her before.'

I nod absently, my mind already drifting back to Calenus. 'If you will excuse me,' I say.

'Good day,' Nerva says before gliding away down the marbled hallway.

Titus returns in the afternoon. He is furious.

'I should have him killed.'

He is pacing while I remain seated.

'Who?' I ask.

'Ulpius. The man's impertinence is shocking.'

'Tell me what happened.'

'That damned slave of his, the Persian, did most of the talking. Ulpius would whisper in the slave's ear and then the slave would tell me what Ulpius said, as though Ulpius didn't speak Latin or Greek. I should have him arrested. The arrogance of that man.'

'Let me try,' I say.

Titus shakes his head. 'What could you possibly do?'

'He's taken a liking to me. There is no harm in trying.'

Titus shrugs. 'Fine. But if you can get any information from that eccentric, you're a better man than I.'

The Persian escorts me to the garden where Ulpius is drinking sweetened wine. Neither man seems surprised at my visit. There is even a cup of wine waiting for me.

After pleasantries, Ulpius says, 'Your brother is unbearable. The capital has soured the great general.'

'He is my brother,' I say, gently. 'And we need your help.'

'My help? Why? Help with what?'

'Let us not pretend, Ulpius. I have a man Calenus who works for me. He mentioned your name in relation to Valerianus and the suit brought against Plautius.'

He is apathetic. 'And?'

'The action brought against Plautius is aimed at undermining my father and the Imperial family. Quite possibly, it is aimed at overthrowing the Emperor.'

'And how do you know I'm not involved?' he asks. He is smiling his strange, eccentric smile. 'How do you know *I* don't have designs on the throne?'

I consider the question. I hadn't thought of this before.

'Father says you helped us during the civil wars.'

'Yes, but a man can change his mind.'

His tone – for the most part – remains flat, but there are undercurrents of mischief; he enjoys leading me astray.

'Yes,' I say, 'but you do not desire the throne. It would bore you, I think. Maybe not the power itself, but all that comes along with it, the politics and the squabbling. You might have ambition, and you have some personal aim moving here to the capital, but the throne is not one of them.'

He snorts with pleasure. 'You've twice the charm of your brother.' He thinks a moment and then says, 'And I suppose we've reached a dead end ourselves . . . all right, I will help.'

'You will?'

'Yes. Come tonight,' he says. 'I must confer with my colleagues. And what I have to tell you – it is easier to understand at night, away from the light of day.'

'May I bring Titus?'

He sighs. 'If you must.'

# TITUS

♦

## 23 April, sunset
## The home of Lucius Ulpius Traianus, Rome

Ulpius is in the peristyle of his home, sitting under a cypress with a blanket over his lap. It is dusk and the air is cooling quickly. Marcus is with him, as is the one-eyed man Theseus and the Parthian. Virgilius is with me; so too is Domitilla. She insisted on coming, and – I must admit – she has a way with this eccentric.

Conciliatory as always, Domitilla speaks first: 'Thank you for agreeing to meet. We are grateful to learn what you know.'

'I will tell you what we know of the plot against your father,' Ulpius says, 'but there are conditions.'

The man's arrogance is startling. I am Caesar's son and he is going to dictate conditions to me? My pulse pounds and I am about to tell him what I think, when Domitilla puts her hand on my arm.

'What are they?' she asks.

'I will tell you everything that you need to know, I give you my word, but you may have questions about *how* we know what we know. We would like to keep our privacy. If I chose not to answer a particular question, that is too bad for you. Is that clear?'

Domitilla knows I cannot answer such impertinence, so she answers for me. 'Yes. We understand.'

'Good,' Ulpius says. 'Well, where to begin?' He leans back in his chair. 'The knight Vettius was hired to paint poison on the figs in the palace. I think, Titus, you already knew this. The aim was to kill the Imperial family.'

Taken aback, I ask, 'And how do you know this?'

'Ah, now here I will refer back to our terms.' Ulpius says. 'I do not wish to say.'

I bite my tongue.

Ulpius says, 'Coin was offered to Vettius, but then those who hired him did not think this sufficient. They desired something more, a pact sealed in the ways of the ancients.'

'Torcus,' I say.

Ulpius looks surprised; he claps his hands three times very slowly. 'Bravo, Titus. Bravo. Maybe you are not all fire and sword after all. Yes, the cult of Torcus, from the bogs of Germany. Adherents have infiltrated Roman society since Rome's defeat at the Teutoburg Pass.

'Evil itself,' I say, echoing the words I read in Caratacus' letter.

Ulpius pauses; his mouth purses slightly. 'Yes, very well-informed, aren't you.'

I shake my head. 'I know very little.'

'Well,' Ulpius says, 'I wish I could say the same. We have seen much of Torcus these past few years.' Ulpius hesitates, censoring himself. 'An ex-freedman from Nero's court, Halotus, your father's procurator in Asia, was an adherent. Five years ago, he and senator Marcellus, another adherent, tried to kill Marcus.'

Domitilla gasps at the name Marcellus. We exchange a look: you would have had me marry such a man.

The one-eyed man clears his throat.

Ulpius says, 'Well, truth be told, we are still not certain about Marcellus.'

'And are you the one responsible for Halotus's murder?' I ask.

Ulpius scratches his white-copper beard. He is being cute and I do not like it. 'I think anyone would be reluctant to admit killing a procurator, vested as they are with Caesar's power. But I can assure you his death is not related to any attempt on your father or the principate. Quite the opposite, in fact.'

'We understand,' Domitilla says. 'Please go on.'

Ulpius clears his throat. 'Where was I? Ah, yes, the body you discovered by the Tiber. That was the knight Vettius. Those plotting to take the purple did not trust that he would follow through on their instructions. So Vettius was brought to Rome. Torcus adherents use human sacrifice – murder – to forge oaths and therefore tie each other to a common cause. I take it Vettius was a better man than most and refused. So he became another victim.'

Domitilla asks, 'I don't understand. Vettius was killed before he painted the figs? Yet when Titus had them tested, one grove was entirely poisoned.'

'I think your brother could answer that,' Ulpius says.

I had been holding on to this bit of information as well, but apparently Ulpius knows everything I do and more.

'One month ago,' I say, 'when it was decided Father would return from his absence from the city, Phoebus, the Imperial secretary, sacked one of the palace gardeners and hired a new one, the one responsible for the garden of Venus. I suspect this is the man who poisoned the figs.'

Ulpius is nodding. 'Their original plot was not discovered, so they tried again. This time with a more compliant gardener.'

'What of the hand then?' Virgilius asks. 'And Plautius?'

'This is – so to speak – where the plot thickens.' Ulpius is smiling. The eccentric is enjoying himself. 'The hand and Plautius's disappearance were part of the second plot.'

'The second plot?' Virgilius furrows his brow.

'There is always more than one plot,' Ulpius says. 'There are more than a thousand senators, only a fraction of which have your father's favour. And there are even more knights. And you have Praetorians looking to rise by tying themselves to a senator on the make. By my calculation, Nero averaged three plots a year.'

'So what of the second plot? Who is behind that?' I ask, with growing impatience.

'That I do not know,' Ulpius says. 'We are fairly certain the hand in the forum and Plautius's disappearance were more subtle attempts to undermine Caesar, not necessarily a plot to kill him. But whoever is behind it, he is far more discreet than the followers of Torcus. His technique – I must admit – is quite clever. He hires the same thugs as Torcus, which helps insulate him from discovery. For anyone asking questions – if they lacked the necessary deliberateness – it would be easy to conclude Torcus is responsible for all of it.'

'Is it Caecina?' I ask, already convinced of his involvement.

'No, I don't believe so.'

Ulpius explains how Marcus and Theseus saved Calenus this morning, in the sewers, before Calenus drank himself into a stupor. Apparently, they interrogated someone. Ulpius explains everything they learned about this gang and its leader, Montanus. How they were apparently hired by Marcellus and another mysterious figure.

'I do not think Caecina is involved,' Ulpius says. 'He is a playboy. He is content bedding the beauties of Rome. And this shadowy figure had Montanus fed false information to Plautius while he was imprisoned, which aimed to frame myself and Caecina. For Caecina to set himself up like that . . . I think it unlikely.'

Domitilla asks: 'Fed him information? How?'

Ulpius says, 'Plautius told your brother he overheard his captors speaking of a "blind man" and "the Turncoat". He says reference was made to both men repeatedly, and then he escaped. Plautius is slow-witted enough that this transparent attempt to mislead was lost on him. He genuinely thought he overheard sound information before escaping. The plan had been to let him escape and come to Rome, so that he could – I suppose – run and tell you what he'd heard. But he panicked and found himself paddling a ship for several months. If you want to know who this mysterious senator is, I would look first at those who knew Plautius was in the south; someone who had the head start to have him abducted.'

I try to recall who I told. Father, certainly. Antonia, Regulus, Virgilius, and Ptolemy. Were there more? 'That is a hopeless exercise. What if a person I told inadvertently told someone else?'

Ulpius nods. 'Yes, there is difficulty there.'

'And who made the attempt on my life?' Domitilla asks.

'It was one of Montanus's men, certainly,' Ulpius says. 'But we do not think it was Marcellus who arranged it. He was engaged to you at the time. It was a great rise in fortune. And it would have legitimised his claim to the throne. If Caesar and his sons were dead, Domitilla's husband would be a natural choice for emperor. We suspect it was the same shadowy figure who orchestrated the hand, someone who sought to ensure Marcellus's claim to the throne no stronger than anyone else's, by ending the engagement to Caesar's daughter – ending it the simplest way possible.'

Domitilla blanches at the callousness of Roman politics.

Finally, I ask: 'Who are the members of Torcus?'

Ulpius counts names on his fingers. 'Marcellus, we are almost certain. Lepida, I think. Likely Phoebus, given what we know of the fig trees. Praetorians will be involved as well, but we do not know which.'

'Why do you suspect Praetorians are involved?' Domitilla asks.

'It is not a suspicion, but an inevitability,' Ulpius says. 'The days of the senate naming the emperor are gone. Now the Praetorian Guard rules Rome. The senate cowers and does what they say. Your father was smart enough to understand this. That's why he named Titus prefect. But those below him could be swayed by the promise of money or a promotion.'

Theseus says, 'It is likely that at least one of your officers is involved. The conspirators will need an officer to take control of the situation. You will be dead, so an officer will be able to fill the void and rush their chosen man off to the Praetorian camp to have him proclaimed emperor. Do you know of any unhappy, prideful officers?'

'Of course. Most officers are prideful and unhappy.' I think of Regulus, though this is the first time I think him capable of such a thing. Our collective ignorance is frustrating. It eats at me. 'So you have more questions than answers, Ulpius.'

'That is true,' Ulpius says. 'But I also have a plan.'

Virgilius finally speaks up. 'A plan?' We have moved from theory to actionable tasks, his bread and oil.

'Yes,' Ulpius says, 'we set a trap.'

'A trap?' Domitilla asks, sceptically.

'My sources inside the palace have told me the story of the figs,' Ulpius says. 'It's good you have kept the experiment quiet.'

'You are not short of information, are you, Ulpius?'

Ulpius smiles. 'We are on the same side, Titus. Do not worry about what I know. I think we can use the figs to our advantage. Throw a feast. Serve figs. Let the guests think they are from the palace. Anyone who declines to eat them – well, we will have our traitors.'

Virgilius snorts with approval; he appreciates boldness.

'And what of the second plot,' Domitilla asks. 'What of this shadowy figure?'

'A battle for another day,' Ulpius says.

'What's your interest in this?' I say to Ulpius. 'This is all because the cult tried to kill Marcus?'

'In part, yes. I am loath to forgive a transgression. And I have a favour to ask . . .'

Here it is. I should get a stylus and tablet to record the appointments he seeks, and the elephant size chest of coin.

'I would like a word,' Ulpius says, 'in private.'

# DOMITILLA

◆

*30 April, sunset*
*The Campus Martius, Rome*

The guests begin to arrive as the sun is setting; thirty senators and their wives, Imperial secretaries, knights, and a handful of Praetorians. Titus and I wrote the guest list ourselves. Marcellus, Lepida, Caecina, Phoebus and their hangers-on were the first names added. Others followed. Influential senators, such as Nerva, and people in our inner circle, like cousin Sabinus, Epaphroditus, Secundus and Graecina. And those we are almost certain are not involved, such as Vespasia and Domitian, because their absence would be conspicuous. Titus also invited several Praetorian officers. I think he suspects one in particular, though he hasn't said who. And of course Ulpius and Marcus. Word spread quickly once the invitations started to go out. It is now considered the event of the year. Father is not one for lavish parties, so a massive banquet thrown by Caesar instantly captured the city's attention.

We've cleared space in the Campus Martius as Nero used to do, draining the lake and filling it with tables and couches. Ulpius suggested it. 'Being away from the palace may make the conspirators bolder,' he said. 'Plus it makes for a better party.' Dozens of couches are set up along four long tables, all facing each other creating a perfect square. Massive torches are lit. Slaves – hundreds of them – weave to and fro. The April air – cool but not cold – fuses with the torches, giving the air a pitch-perfect warmth. 'A good evening to catch a traitor,' Titus says as we make our way from the palace, arm in arm.

Father knows the plan and he is happy with it. 'Fine, fine,' he said. 'Make me the bait. Titus is the better hook in any event.' We haven't told anyone else, as Ulpius advised. 'You don't know who you can trust,' he said. We haven't even told Vespasia or Domitian. Father likely told Graecina but he tells her everything.

Vespasia and I greet the guests as they arrive. Vespasia's hair is crimped and twirled into a heap on her head. Her shoulders and neck jut out of pink silk. As is often the case, my style is more conservative: less curls, less skin, less blush.

Ulpius and Marcus, accompanied by the Persian and Theseus, are among the first to arrive.

'My dear,' Ulpius says. 'There will be a fine turnout by all reports.'

'Let us hope so,' I say.

'Excuse my sister,' Vespasia says, oblivious to the conversation's subtext. 'She has never been described as an optimist.'

'There is nothing wrong with a little caution, my dear.' Ulpius says. 'I will see you inside.'

Nerva arrives with the Batavian. Ever since the Batavian became famous in the wild beast hunts, Nerva brings him to every public event. Thankfully, the Batavian keeps his blue eyes aimed at the ground and Vespasia has no fodder for a joke.

Epaphroditus arrives alone. He moves gingerly, as he always does after his unexplained disappearance, with his useless arm in a sling. He speaks politely, eyes aimed at the ground, and shuffles inside.

Caecina and his wife are the next to arrive. While I am speaking to his wife, Caecina and Vespasia's eyes lock – only for a moment, but it is unmistakeable. How did I not know they were lovers before she confessed? They are as conspicuous as a gladiator in a toga.

After the last guest arrives, Vespasia and I make our way to the tables. We pass under an arch made entirely of rose and myrtle, golden in the torchlight. Vespasia was put in charge of the decorations and I think she may have out done herself. She thinks this a true banquet, not a ruse to flush out traitors.

I have arranged to sit with Ulpius. I have grown to like the man's company, and I want his insights as the evening progresses.

We had determined the figs should be served with the second course, to let the guests get comfortable, but not too late that conspirators may be too drunk and unable to react properly.

The first course is oysters and fresh fish from the Bay, which the palace slaves carry out on polished silver trays with matching domes and reveal the dish all at once, with a flourish. A slave announces the dish and its origin.

'Your brother should sit,' Ulpius says. 'His pacing makes him look like he is waiting for calamity.'

For a moment, the fact he knows my brother is pacing catches me off guard, until I recall that his Persian whispers everything in his ear.

'Titus is always pacing.' I say. 'It would seem strange if he were not. If he was laughing the entire party would run home and barricade themselves inside.'

Ulpius puts his hands up. 'I relent,' he says, smiling.

At the table across from us, Father is sitting beside Secundus and Graecina. Two seats over is Marcellus. Beside him is Lepida, Nero's former mistress. The Praetorian officers are sitting to my right, twenty or so. Tonight they have set aside their armour in favour of brightly coloured tunics and dinner jackets. A feast is one of their few opportunities to show their sense of style. Half of them appear quite drunk, laughing and yelling and carrying on. The other half are quiet. One in particular – what is his name? Regulus, I think – is watching Titus with a scowl.

Vespasia is seated at the table on my left. She stands up and excuses herself. As she walks away from her table, she looks over her shoulder and smiles at Caecina. The exchange is subtle; I doubt I would have noticed if I didn't know what I do.

The Persian is pulled away by Theseus. Ulpius says to me, 'My dear, I am without my eyes so to speak. The second course will be out soon. I would ask you describe what you see. In particular, the exchequer Epaphroditus. I am curious what he does.'

I agree to do as Ulpius asks and then, almost on cue, a parade of slaves march out with the second course. Domed silver platters are placed onto the tables and all at once – in a flourish – the tops are removed. A slave announces, 'Figs, fresh from the palace gardens.'

I try to watch everyone, to see what they do in this exact moment. Titus is to my right, behind his officer's table, observing. His grey-haired soldier Virgilus is beside him. Marcellus is motionless, like a statue. He does not reach for the figs, but instead whispers to Lepida. At the same time, Caecina stands up and walks from the table. But is he running from the figs or to my sister? Epaphroditus takes a fig and, throwing his head back, drops it with aplomb into his mouth.

'Epaphroditus ate a fig, so too did senator Nerva,' I say to Ulpius. 'Marcellus has not. Nor did Caecina or Lepida.'

'Epaphroditus ate a fig, did he? Good. *Good*. A man of his word, it seems.'

I'm about to ask Ulpius what he means when Marcellus stands. So too does the officer Regulus. Marcellus – in an instant – disappears in a ring of his slaves. Regulus tries to step away from the table but Virgilius is there. He grabs Regulus by the collar, spins him around . . .

And then they are wrestling, fighting over a dagger each grips above their heads. A fight in the midst of a banquet seems surreal. Most guests watch in quiet shock.

Titus meanwhile is walking at full pace towards Caecina. Titus calls his name. Caecina turns. Titus draws his blade (hidden under his tunic) and slashes at Caecina. The blade cuts at his neck and shoulder. A splash of dark blood flies through the air. Caecina collapses.

Chaos ensues. Two dozen armed Praetorians surround the banquet. Titus is shouting out orders. The guests are crying out in shock. Several of the Praetorian officers are trying to fight their way out.

Vespasia runs back into the square. She falls to Caecina's bloodied body, sobbing and screaming. She is hysterical. Titus stands confused for a moment, but the general takes over. He speaks to his soldiers pointing at Lepida and then in the direction Marcellus went.

I sense movement behind me. I turn and see the Batavian, standing a few paces behind me, watching the chaos intently. I wonder what he is doing – his duty is to Nerva and Nerva is not in the vicinity. And then I realise he is standing guard over me, amid the bedlam. I stand up and step back from the table. The Batavian steps in front of me. He turns back and says, 'Safe.'

Ulpius is standing now; he grabs my arm. 'What is happening, my dear?'

I turn back to the tables. I say, 'Lepida has been taken into custody. So too has the Praetorian Regulus. Marcellus has escaped with several Praetorian officers. Caecina has been . . . I think he is dead.'

'I see,' Ulpius says. 'And Caesar lives?'

In the chaos, I had forgotten about Father. I look to him. He is standing behind his couch. Secundus holds him by the shoulder. A slave girl hands Father a cup of wine. Father downs the cup and hands it back to the girl. When the slave girl turns, I see her face. Her one, thick eyebrow reminds me of my grandmother.

# TITUS

*1 May, cockcrow*
*The forum, at the foot of the Capitoline Hill, Rome*

We wait for the sun to rise. The Temple of Jupiter sits in shadow at the top of the Capitoline. Massive columns of white marble surround the building; the black beyond hides an army of traitors.

'How many are inside?' I ask.

We are kneeling. In front of us, spread out on the ground is a model of the forum and the hill we are about to take, made from blocks of wood, little branches, and a stale, hard-as-hooves loaf of bread. Behind us, a mass of Praetorians stand at the ready.

'Two hundred, I'd say,' Virgilius says. 'But that is only a guess.'

'How many do we have?'

'After the defections, about the same number, I'd say.'

'How many armoured Praetorians do they have?'

'Sixty, maybe seventy, I think. But many of the others are former soldiers – Montanus and his men,' Virgilius says. 'And they have the high ground. Taking the temple will be difficult.'

After Marcellus and his fellow conspirators were exposed, the banquet descended into chaos. Somehow Marcellus and a handful of traitors and their slaves fought their way free. I took half of our men and whisked Father off to the palace. Meanwhile Virgilius and others followed the traitors into the city. A few skirmishes occurred in the streets until Marcellus rendez-voused with Montanus and his band of criminals. Clearly they had planned for such an event. Outnumbered, Virgilius had to back down. The conspirators rallied together and took refuge in the Temple of Jupiter, easily the most difficult building in all of Rome to take by force. Difficult, but not impossible.

Behind me, over my shoulder, Marcus says, 'What of Cerialis's men?'

He and Theseus have joined us, as though we'd invited them to our counsel. I should tell him to leave (this is no place for a boy), but I've no time. Anyway, I'd made a promise to his uncle.

'They started marching north three days ago,' Virgilius says.

'We cannot wait for them,' I say. 'This ends today.'

'Do you have a plan?' Virgilius asks.

Virgilius and I have fought many battles together. Every so often I would devise an ingenious plan that saved lives and brought victory, quickly and efficiently. This is not one of those times.

'There is no plan. When the sun rises we take the hill. The longer we give them, the deeper they'll dig in. We concentrate our forces here.' I point at the loaf of bread, which is the Temple of Jupiter in our model.

Virgilius looks at Marcus. 'If he is going to come with us, he'd better have a cuirass. And a sword.'

The sun peeks over the Aventine and the world is awash in May's brilliant morning light. I take my sword from its scabbard, raise it into the air, and tip it forward. More than one hundred soldiers start to advance. The sound of us jogging up the hill – armour rattling, heavy breathing – overtakes the eerie quiet.

Halfway up the hill, the twenty men holding the battering ram take the lead. One man starts a bloodcurdling cry; then the rest of the men chime in and a wall of furious screaming advances against Rome's greatest monument.

The battling ram slides between two massive columns of marble and slams against the temple doors and a hollow *thud* momentarily drowns out the screaming. Three times the ram is swung before the doors open with a thunderous crash.

The battling ram is dragged back and soldiers stream into the temple. The two brave men who went first get no more than a step or two inside before they are falling back onto the colonnade, bloodied and dying. Two more soldiers try and meet the same fate. I'm behind the next two, with Virgilius beside me, and we grab them by the belt and push them through the door. We are working with them, but they are also fodder, because wars cannot be won without fodder. We burst into the dark temple and a small army of traitors stab and swipe at us with sword and spear, as we push our way inside. The two men in front of Virgilius and I fall to the floor and we press forward, ramming our shields into the men in our path, stabbing our short blades when they are off balance. Muscle and sinew make way for steel but bone – the shoulder blade, I think – stops my sword dead. I pull out my blade and the man falls to the floor. Out of the corner of my eye, I see a blade flashing down toward my head; I turn, knowing I'm too late and I will be soon be dead, knowing I was careless pushing my way into this crowd of traitors without enough men to guard my flank, careless to the point I deserve to die by some disgraced soldier's hand; but Virgilius is there, shield held high, sending the blow harmlessly to the side, and then I stab my assailant with three short controlled thrusts to the neck and the man's blade falls from his grip and harmlessly clatters on the temple floor.

The screams of terror and anger and physical exhaustion are overtaken by my voice, calling my soldiers to me. And then my men are around us and we form a circle, backs aimed at the other, protecting each other's flank. The traitors' attention is on us, the circle of ten or so soldiers in the middle of the temple, letting more men stream through the doors. The battle is incrementally easier now, knowing my back is safe – and an increment in battle is everything.

I stab and slash while trying to get a sense of the room. Over the top of the battle, I can see a giant guarding a corner of the room. Montanus. It has to be, if the descriptions of the man are accurate. He is guarding something, likely his meal ticket, Marcellus. They can wait, for now. I see the boy Marcus and the freedman Theseus, working together, back to back, holding their own. By the door, there are dozens of my men, dead and gone. We took heavy losses getting in here, but the battle is beginning to turn. There is a cadence to battle, a musical beat, and it shifts as the fight wanes. It took years to learn how to hear it, to feel its ebb and flow; but I am an expert now, my ear pitch-perfect. Even with my eyes closed, I would know the battle is ours.

As the fight continues, the staccato of steel against steel is occasionally broken by the long, lugubrious moans of men dying. I find myself outside again, on the colonnade, fighting between marble columns. The sun is up now, unhindered in the blue.

Through the din I see Marcus, at the edge of the hill, with his hand shielding his eyes from the sun, observing. Something clicks, a conclusion is reached, and he is running down the Capitoline's slope.

Marcellus. He is chasing Marcellus.

The battle has turned and the day is ours; but Marcellus cannot be allowed to escape. I chase after Marcus, down the hill, the ground falling away from me, and then through the forum. I sprint through the square into an alleyway. Then I follow a rabbit warren of curves, bending and turning, this way and that, with Marcus just out of sight.

I'm not sure whether I've lost him or not (I have made countless turns since I saw him last), so I slow my pace and, over my heavy dog-like panting, I listen.

Something is ahead of me. I move quietly towards the sound, with short efficient steps. I turn the corner and the alleyway opens up slightly, from one spear length wide to three. Marcus is there, with his back to me. Over his shoulder, I can see the giant Montanus, a sword in each hand. He is facing Marcus, like a cornered bear. Behind him, someone is cowering against the brick wall. Marcellus.

We are all breathing heavily. No one says a word.

Marcus twirls his blade the way gladiators do, to get the crowd behind them. I make a note: if we survive this encounter, I shall have to teach him how a soldier fights. There is never a twirl.

Marcus has surprised me before. But I think this man Montanus will prove too much. He is three times the boy's size and a trained soldier.

The giant takes three deep breaths and I know he will strike at any moment.

I grab Marcus's shoulder and yank him back as hard as I can. Marcus back pedals and falls to the ground behind me. At the same time, Montanus screams and flies toward us.

My sword is up just in time – just before the first blade would have cut my neck in two. The force of the collision sends me back and I stumble until I'm down on one knee, and then I raise my sword to meet Montanus's just in time. We continue like this, a barrage of swords, cutting down towards me, and my sword only just saving my skin. Then the force of his blows are too much and I fall back. I see Montanus' other sword go high into the air, higher than any before, to maximise the momentum and cleave me in two, but then a shadow leaps over me, before I've even hit the ground, and Marcus's flashing blade plunges into Montanus's exposed armpit. Montanus screams in agony and his foot slams into Marcus's stomach. I jump to my feet and put one hand on Montanus'shoulder and begin to stab his flesh with a frenzied animal pace. Then Marcus is beside me, ploughing his blade deep into Montanus's flesh.

Montanus falls to the ground. His last words are a whispering gasp; his eyes go wide, listless and empty.

I walk to Marcellus who is sitting on the ground, with his back against the bricks. He looks dejected. He will not put up a fight now. He made his play and he lost.

I stand over him.

'No trial then?' Marcellus says. He is looking at my sword, not me.

I shake my head. No.

Marcellus fiddles with his earlobe, like a child.

I raise my sword to his chin and gently angle it up, so he's forced to look me in the eyes. He meets my stare, but only for a moment. Then his eyes lose focus and he looks away.

I am about to push my blade into the traitor's neck, when I feel a hand gently take my arm.

I turn to Marcus.

'Put him on trial,' he says.

I shake off his hand. 'You'd give him a trial? Didn't he murder your friend and try to murder you?'

'He did.'

'He would have killed me and my family.' My voice is rising despite my best efforts. 'There would have been no trial.'

'Yes,' the boy says. 'But he is a villain. You are Caesar's son.'

For a moment, the only sound is heavy breathing, mine, the boys, Marcellus's.

It pains me to admit it, to take advice from a boy, but he is right.

I sheath my sword and haul Marcellus up by the ear.

'Trial it is.' I say.

# NERO

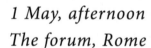

*1 May, afternoon*
*The forum, Rome*

I look for Marcus after the battle. Doryphorus guides me through the smoking, bloody chaos that is the forum. At first, he'd refused to take me anywhere. He had taken me home after the banquet to keep me safe. But I insisted, in the way only an ex-Caesar can, and he eventually complied.

It is sometime near the end of the second hour. Doryphorus walks me to the foot of the Capitoline, but even that is not close enough.

'Put him in my arms,' I say.

Doryphorus drags me through a crowd of tired soldiers laughing over their victory – laughing in the euphoric way only men who have cheated death can laugh. A body is pushed into my arms and, by the way it attempts to squirm free, I know it is Marcus.

'My boy,' I say. 'My boy.'

'I'm fine,' Marcus says. He lets his body relax and, eventually, returns my embrace. 'Marcellus has been arrested. He will be put on trial.'

'My boy,' I say again, only now realising how concerned I was for his safety. 'You did it.'

'There is still so much more to do. Terentius is in the east and the man who staged the hand in the forum. . .'

'Ssshhh,' I say. 'Battles for another day. I'm proud of you.'

Marcus pushes his way out of my arms. 'Proud? You won't be proud when you find out what I've done. I could have killed Marcellus. I had the opportunity. But I convinced Titus to put him on trial.'

'And why would that disappoint me?'

'You've killed every man responsible for your fall from power. But I let Marcellus live.'

I reach out for Marcus's hand. I snap it in my claws and squeeze. I wish – not for the first time – I could look him in the eyes.

'Yes, I admit, once all I wanted was to bring death to those who earned it and then retake the throne. But . . .'

I've hinted at this before, but never told him outright – I've never told any of them outright. Not Marcus or Doryphorus; not even Spiculus. They assumed the end goal was the purple, to be Caesar once more.

'But I have come to realise that is not what I want. That night we almost lost you, on Rhodes – it was that night I realised you are more important to me than revenge. In fact, you *are* my revenge.'

'What?'

I cannot see his eyes. I wish I could see his eyes.

'I cannot take the purple back, Marcus. It is lost to me. And I am no longer the man who was emperor. He is dead and gone, and all that remains is a cripple – a brilliant, humorous cripple, but a cripple all the same. However, I have a better plan. You are my revenge because *you* will retake the purple. You will be emperor one day, the greatest Rome has ever known. That is why I have asked Titus to take you on his personal staff. He will give you the training you require.'

Marcus is angry. 'That is idiotic. I cannot lead. I have servitude in my blood. I am a coward.'

'What?' I say, almost laughing at the absurdity. I reach out for his shoulders, to find them and give the boy a shake. 'You're no coward.'

'I have been a coward my whole life. I have always been afraid. You called me coward yourself.'

'No I didn't.'

'You did. Here in Rome, when you were still prisoner.'

'Why, that's false.'

'You did. You said I was no Germanicus, that I'm not even a Corbulo.'

'What?'

'You once told me a man is either a Germanicus or a Corbulo. He either possesses magnificence of mind or he does not.'

What is the boy talking about? I've no recollection of this conversation.

'Are you sure?' I ask. 'It sounds a stupid distinction. Explain it to me? I'm not sure I even understand it.'

According to the boy, I told him a story years ago, while I was still imprisoned, my eyes recently gone. I've no recollection but he remembers it word for word. Gods, I must have told him this to light a fire under him, but I've created a dichotomy to the world, one he's tried to force himself into. I wasn't a father then. I didn't know the power of my words.

'My boy, you've forgotten one of the first lessons I ever gave you. Know your man. You can listen to what a man tells you, but you have to understand the man himself, look at him critically. I was broken then, still shallow and self-absorbed, speaking to hear my own voice. Gods, I'm like that now. What I told you was rubbish. I never met my grandfather. I've no idea the man he was. I knew Corbulo, and I would describe him as neither coward nor brave.'

'I let Orestes die,' Marcus says suddenly. His voice cracks; he is on the verge of tears. 'I could have stopped it.'

Spiculus once said Marcus and I are too similar. I thought it true at the time; but now, listening to the boy's anger at himself, and his melancholy, I realise we couldn't be more different. At his age, I thought myself infallible ('king shit', as my tutors used to say). Any good in the world was thanks to me, and any bad another man's fault. Marcus, however, blames himself for everything. He puts so much on his shoulders, it is a wonder he doesn't collapse.

'No, you could not have stopped it,' I say. 'You were a child then. All the gods asked of you was to stop those men from doing so again, from polluting the Empire with their dark arts. And you've done that. You're the bravest man I know.'

Marcus is crying.

His shoulders are in my grip. I pull him in close.

'I'm proud of you,' I say, squeezing him tightly. 'So very proud.'

Yes, Marcus and I are different. And he is the better man.

# XXIX

## Epilogue
### A.D. 79

# DOMITILLA

◆

*4 May, sunset*
*The Imperial palace, Rome*

The night of Titus's victory, while there was still the hum of excitement coursing through the palace, as we drank wine and planned future festivities, Father took ill. Although the illness was not particularly serious, it detracted from our collective mood. Father's doctors advised that he should go north, where a cooler climate will be less oppressive over the summer months ahead. Titus thought it a good idea. We were victorious against Marcellus and his ilk, but we are not invincible. If Father is going to be bedridden, recovering from whatever illness he has, he should be away from the city's more jaundiced eyes.

I visit Father the night before he is to depart. I cross paths with a man as I walk in. He is tall, in a black robe, with matching beard, and deep-set eyes. He stops to bow as I pass him by.

Father is in bed, sitting, with blankets of purple silk strewn over his legs, and his face is lit up by a constellation of braziers stationed around his bed. The room smells of burnt oil, sweat, and incense, heavy with cinnamon and clove.

'Father,' I say, 'How are you?'

I take a seat on a stool beside him. Four blobs of perspiration dot his forehead. One pops and slides to the tip of his nose.

'Fine, fine,' he says.

'Who was that man?'

'The man who was just here? He is my physician.'

'Oh, I remember you having a different man, a little Greek fellow.'

'Yes, well, that man was clueless with my gout. So I've replaced him with a man who comes highly recommended by Nerva. He has done wonders already. I'm confident he can handle a cold.'

I fuss with Father's pillow, fluffing it while he leans forward.

'Oh, is it only a cold now?'

He smiles before letting a puppy-sized cough escape. 'Yes, this a cold. Nothing more.' He winces with discomfort, shifts his weight, winces again. He says, 'How is your sister?'

'She is . . . upset. She hasn't left Caecina's side.'

Father's eyebrow curls in surprise. 'Still alive, eh? I predicted today would be his last. I saw the blow Titus landed. It cleaved the Turncoat's collarbone in two. Most men would have expired on the spot. It appears the playboy is made of sterner stuff than I thought. Do we have your sister to thank?'

'She has hired excellent doctors.'

'Will he live?'

'Titus thinks not.'

Caesar nods. 'It is easier that way. Marcellus's trial will have fewer . . . distractions with Caecina gone.' Something occurs to Caesar. He says, 'Does the city know my daughter sits at the bedside of a conspirator?'

'I don't believe he was a conspirator, Father. I think Titus was mistaken.'

'What does that matter? Once an accusation is made it's as good as true. Oh don't look at me like that, my dear. I didn't make the people the way they are; I didn't make them devoid of intelligence and happy to accept the worst. Titus named Caecina a traitor when he drew his blade. Whether he is or not, there is no going back now, not in the people's eyes.'

What does one say to that?

He says, 'Talk to her. She should not be with him.'

'You know Vespasia. She is stubborn.'

'Well, make her understand. I've no doubt you will be able to.' He fiddles with his sheets. 'Would you get your father another blanket?'

I walk only a pace or two before a slave hands me a blanket. I flick it open above the bed and let it drift down, slow as a snowflake, over Caesar's person. I resume my vigilance on the stool.

He says, 'You have been a help, my dear, these last few weeks. I have made a note of it; I have learned my lesson. I intend to involve you more in matters of state – behind the scenes of course – you are a woman and this is Rome after all – but you are an asset the principate intends to use.' Father is staring at the mound his belly makes under his purple sheets. Finally, he turns his eyes to mine; he smiles. 'I'd forgotten you've your grandmother's blood in you, a streak of strength that overcomes your sex. The Sabine stubbornness, she called it. Do you know I was scared shitless of the woman? So was my father. Hell, so was all of Reate. She was a pipsqueak, the size of a child, but her voice was a hammer; she could bludgeon you with it. My father was twice the size of her and a veteran, but it didn't matter. She said jump and he said how high.' Father stares dreamily at the wall, remembering ghosts. 'Voice and pedigree . . . in any marriage, those are the best weapons, good breeding and a voice that will carry.'

Father coughs; he shifts his weight three times until he gives up.

'I will need you to use your voice in the coming months.'

'What do you mean?'

'Your brother loves you. You help humanise the general, when he allows it. When I am gone, you must make sure he relies on you.'

'When you are gone? You mean while you are recovering in Reate?'

Father doesn't answer.

He takes my hands in his; he looks me in the eye. On the surface, to anyone watching, the act is nothing of note, only a father holding his daughter's hands. But the sudden act of intimacy reminds me how little there has been between us. He smiles and, in the corner of his left eye, there may be a glimmer of a tear. But this is all he is able to muster.

I promise to do all that Caesar asks before standing to leave. As I'm walking away, I hear him bellow for wine.

The litter pitches and sways. The silk drapes, normally green, filter the setting sun's last gasps and are now as orange as a clementine. Jacasta is beside me, reading names off a list. (I have forgotten why.) I have gradually stopped paying attention, and now the names blend together, into one long, monotonous, rollicking poem of Roman elite, of Luciuses, Guises, and Antoniuses, of Marcuses, Faustuses and Numeriuses. My mind is preoccupied; it circles back, again and again, to Father and the glimmer in his eye. When one's father, the consummate general – the man who took maybe an hour to mourn the wife he loved before returning to the stack of correspondence on his desk – when such a man is sentimental, life feels infinitely short, painfully precarious.

Over the footsteps of the slaves, I can hear the *chip-chip-chip* of the labourers building Father's amphitheatre. I pull back the drape and Jacasta stops reading her list.

'Mistress,' Jacasta says. 'You do not want to invite leering.'

'Stop,' I say and the litter immediately halts. 'Down,' I say and the litter softly floats to the bricks.

I put out my hand and another – hard with callouses, hairy knuckles – takes it and helps me out of the litter. Jacasta follows. We stand, side by side, looking at the amphitheatre. Beside it is the Colossus, the massive statue of bronze built to honour Sol, the sun god. In the dwindling light, it looks dark and menacing.

I point at the statue. 'Do you know Nero had the face of Sol fashioned to mirror his own?'

'Did he?'

'But when Father was named emperor, he had the masons bend and fashion it until it looked like anyone but Nero.'

'Why?' Jacasta asks.

'Father said it wouldn't do having Nero's face – his royal lineage – staring down on the people, day in, day out. He said, "One's legacy is only as good as those who follow will allow."'

Jacasta smiles, 'And will your legacy be a good one?'

'I'm a woman. I fear I'll be forgotten altogether. Or I will be a line or two in the record. "A loyal sister. She liked the colour green."'

'Better than a slave's.'

'Yes, I suppose that's true. But it's all rubble in the end.' I point at the amphitheatre. 'That is Father's legacy, or so he thinks, but it will be gone one day. Dusty rubble.'

'Well, I'm glad they changed the statue,' Jacasta says. 'Nero was quite ugly, wasn't he?'

'No, I don't think that's true. I only met him a handful of times, but I remember him as quite handsome. You know I heard Father complain when the masons were done altering it; he said they'd kept Nero's chin.' I hold my hand up in front of me, as far away as the arm will allow and block my view of the top half of the statue's head, leaving the mouth and chin. I close one eye and focus the other. Jacasta does the same.

'The chin is fine,' Jacasta says. 'Not handsome, but not ugly.'

'Hmm . . .'

'What is it, Mistress?'

'If one squints, the chin has a likeness to Ulpius.'

'Does it?'

'I think it does. I wonder if Ulpius shares any blood with the tyrant? Some distant relative who ran off to Spain perhaps. Wouldn't that make for a good story?'

'I don't see it, Mistress. I think the chin is like Titus's,' Jacasta says. 'He's very handsome, your brother.'

I drop my hand. Hearing another woman talk of my brother's good looks has ruined my fun.

'Come along, Jacasta,' I say, heading back toward the litter. 'Let us go home.'

We climb back into the litter; the drapes fall back, obscuring the view; the litter lifts up, off the bricks, and we head for my family's home atop the Palatine.

# MARCUS

◆

*5 May, afternoon*
*The farm of Gaius Priscus, Sicily*

We race along the winding dirt road. The house at the top of the hill is the colour of a stalk of wheat. I can feel my heart pumping furiously over the thud of my horse's hoofs raining down on the earth. Spiculus trails me by twenty yards. He calls out, asking me to slow down.

'If you keep up that pace, you'll ruin the horse and we we'll have to walk back to Rome.'

Realising he's right, I pull on my reins and bring the horse to a halt. As Spiculus gets closer, I can see he's smiling. 'I know you're eager, Marcus, but she can wait another hour.' He takes a sip from his skin of wine, then looks off at the sun-baked house with half-closed eyes. 'Anyway, she has no idea you're coming. This will be a pleasant surprise.'

In unison, we resume at an easy trot.

'You don't think she'll be angry with me?' I ask. 'She's been living as a slave all these years. Meanwhile I've been living like a senator's son.'

'Not *like* a senator's son,' Spiculus says. 'You *are* a senator's son. And no slave ever begrudged a man for being free. I was a slave for nearly twenty years. I never once held it against anyone for taking their freedom once it was granted.'

Spiculus watches me for a moment, scrutinising my face. He's known me a long time now. He knows my mood better than I do, and can often guess what I'm thinking. Today is a good example.

'She doesn't think you abandoned her, Marcus. You were a child. And she was like your mother. She was happy you escaped and she'll be happy to see the man you've become.'

My heart clenches like a fist. I'm not sure what would be harder, if Elsie was mad at me or if she was proud of me. Either way, I will always feel like I abandoned her.

I spur my horse forward so Spiculus can't see my face and read my thoughts.

At the top of the hill a man is waiting for us. He's so slight at first I thought he was a child. But once we're closer, I can see his white beard and dry, cracked skin.

'And you are?' he asks, one eye on his wax tablet.

'Marcus Ulpius,' I say.

'Ah,' he says, 'the mysterious benefactor. I've never seen a man purchase a slave by letter, without laying eyes on her first, and then demand she be given no task until your arrival. Master Priscus couldn't believe it.'

'I'm glad to be of interest,' I say, trying to seem at ease.

'Yes, well, I hope you are not disappointed. From your instructions, it seemed you thought she were some great beauty that you didn't want spoilt by hard work.'

'And is she not beautiful?' I ask.

'Why she's older than me,' the old slave exclaims.

Spiculus interjects: 'If you don't mind, sir, it has been a long ride. We would like to see her and be on our way.'

The old slave nods his head and takes us into the garden, which is bordered on all four sides by a colonnade. In the middle of the garden there is a woman. She's sitting at a table, a basket of pomegranates at her side. One pomegranate is cut in two and she's beating the back of one half, the rounded end, and letting the red seeds fall into a bowl. She isn't facing us, but I can tell she's old, with her bent back and limp, grey hair, which she's wearing up in a bun. I signal for the old slave and Spiculus to wait under the colonnade. I make my way to the woman, right up to her side, and say, 'I told them to let you rest until we arrive.'

She slowly turns to face me. She's older than I remember, more fragile. She looks up and squints in the sunlight. I kneel, so we are eye to eye – as she used to do with me.

She studies my face for a long while. Then she's shocked – but only for a moment; she smiles. 'Look at you,' she says as she takes me in. 'Just look at you. The stars are never wrong. Yes? I'll have to find my

Chaldean priest and tell him he was right.' Her smile finally cracks and turns into a sob. She reaches out, grabs my shoulders, and drags me in close. She's crying heavily now, as am I.

'My Marcus,' she says. 'My little Marcus, the boy from the Tiber.'

# Historical Note

In June A.D. 68, after thirteen years as the emperor of Rome, Nero fell from power. According to the surviving accounts, when faced with mutinying legions in the provinces and disloyal Praetorians in Rome, believing all was lost, Nero fled to his freedman's villa and committed suicide. Nero was a tyrant, so said the ancient historians, and his suicide a welcome day for the Empire. This remains the predominant view to this day.

And yet, when scrutinised, this story doesn't quite add up. In the years that followed Nero's fall, at least three men claimed to be the deposed emperor alive and well. These imposters were remarkable and frequent enough that they were given their very own label: the False Neros. Rather than draw disdain (as one would expect when someone claims to be a deposed tyrant), they drew support. Nero was a name worth fighting for – at least for some.

The idea of a False Nero is itself an outlier. Nero was the fifth emperor of Rome. There were no false Augustuses or Tiberiuses. Caligula wasn't spotted after his death; nor was Claudius. What was different about Nero? Did the people love him more than the emperors who came before and after? Was his death more mysterious? We don't know. But it's clear that Nero, his reputation and suicide, is not quite the open and shut case the ancient historians would have you believe.

Nero is one example of a larger issue. Engaging with the past, particularly the first century A.D., is treacherous. For the events of the empire, the acts of the Caesars and their subjects, we mainly rely on three men: Tacitus, Suetonius and Cassius Dio. None was contemporaneous, but rather wrote decades or, in the case of Dio, more than a century later; all three wrote from one perspective – male and aristocratic; and all three were not only historians, but politicians as well – men who looked to advance under an entirely different regime. And the Flavian Dynasty, which began with Vespasian in A.D. 69, had every reason to cast, or encourage, aspersions on the dynasty that preceded it, the Julio-Claudians. No doubt this was par-ticularly important for the last Julio-Claudian, Nero. Of the three historians, Tacitus is considered the most reliable. Unfortunately, his accounts of Nero's fall, all but one of the False Neros, and most of Vespasian's reign have been lost.

Of course the predominant view is not the only view. Classicists have begun to reconsider Nero's reputation. Some scrutinise the extant record (Edward Champlin's *Nero*, for example). Or there is the refresh-ingly frank Mary Beard, who, in *SPQR* (among other places), admits we will never know what did or did not happen under Nero, Vespasian or any other emperor. I am partial to this view. My background is in the law and the rules of evidence. The lawyer in me found it strange, even unfair, on what little evidence Nero and the other 'monsters' of the early Empire were condemned. The ancient historians merely relate what others claim to have observed. It would be inadmissible in court because it is hearsay evidence, which, by its very nature, is unreliable.

It is in the context of this contradictory and unreliable record that this story resides, from Nero's fall to Trajan's rise to the principate. This is a work of fiction, and I have taken certain liberties authors allow themselves. But I have also strived to offer a story that is accurate in its own way, one that can fill the gap scholarship cannot, and seize on the unexplained contradictions, unanswered questions, or biased accounts, for a period of history of which little has survived.

# Cast of Characters

## A.D. 68

**Nero and his courtiers**
Nero, Emperor of Rome
Phaon, Imperial secretary
Epaphroditus, Imperial chamberlain
Halotus, eunuch and Imperial chamberlain
Spiculus, one-eyed ex-gladiator and personal bodyguard to Nero

**The Praetorian Guard**
Nymphidius Sabinus, co-prefect of the Praetorian guard
Tigellinus, co-prefect of the Praetorian guard
Terentius, centurion, aka the Fox
'Venus', soldier in the Praetorian guard
'Juno', soldier in the Praetorian guard

**The house of Proculus Creon**
Proculus Creon, freedman and entrepreneur
Mistress Creon, wife to Creon
Giton, Creon's son
Elsie, slave and cook to Creon
Socrates, slave to Creon
Marcus, slave to Creon

**Senators**
Galba (aka the Hunchback), senator and successor to Nero as Emperor of Rome
Otho, senator, former friend of Nero and presumptive heir to Galba
Vitellius, commander in lower Germany, famous for his appetites

**Freedman**
Icelus, freedman to Galba, imprisoned in Rome at the time of Nero's fall
Doryphorus, freedman turned actor

# A.D. 79

**The Flavians**
Vespasian, former general and Emperor of Rome
Titus, prefect of the Praetorian guard, victorious general in the Jewish war and the Emperor's eldest son
Domitian, second born (and often forgotten) son of Vespasian
Domitilla, eldest daughter of Vespasian and widower
Vespasia, second born daughter of Vespasian and recent widow of Asinius
Julia, daughter to Titus
Sabinus, nephew to Vespasian, recently named rex sacrorum
Vip, daughter to Sabinus

**Imperial staff and courtiers**
Phoebus, Imperial secretary
Epaphroditus, exchequer and Imperial freedman

**The Plautii**
Graecina, wife to deceased general and ex-consul, Aulus Plautius, close friend to Vespasian
Lucius Plautius, hapless senator and friend of the Flavians
Antonia, wife to Plautius

**Senators**
Secundus (aka Pliny the Elder), soldier, senator, scientist and close adviser to the Emperor
Cocceius Nerva, senator and former member of Nero's consilium
Eprius Marcellus, influential senator under Nero and Vespasian
Caecina Alienus (aka the Turncoat), former commander during the civil wars
Cerialis, general charged with defeating the False Nero
Caius Cassius, banished to Sardinia by Nero
Cluvius Rufus, former courtier of Nero turned historian under the Flavians
Julius Valerianus, high-priced lawyer

**Women of Rome**
Lepida, widower of Iulus and former mistress of Nero
Calpurnia, wife of Caecina

**The house of Ulpius**
Lucius Ulpius Traianus, blind wealthy senator from Spain
Marcus, nephew to Lucius Ulpius
Theseus (aka the Big Buck), one-eyed freedman
Cyrus, Parthian freedman

**The Praetorian Guard**
Regulus, military tribune and patrician
Virgilius, Titus's right-hand man

**Ex-soldiers in Rome**
Julius Calenus, disgraced ex-soldier stalking the shadows for Nerva
Montanus, hired thug and head of criminal gang
Fabius, former colleague of Calenus, works for Montanus

**Slaves**
Ptolemy, slave to Titus
Jacasta, slave to Domitilla
Appius, slave to Nerva

**On the Bay of Naples**
Vettius, missing Pompeian knight
Red, prostitute who witnessed Vettius' abduction

**Barbarians**
The Batavian, a slave purchased by Nerva; likely former Batavian soldier, one of the most feared of all Germanic tribes
Caratacus, deposed barbarian king from Britannia, pardoned by Claudius Caesar

# Acknowledgements

The author's note at the beginning of this work was distilled from *Life and Leisure in Ancient Rome* by J.P.V.D. Balsdon. The other works that I could not have written this book without and would highly recommend include: *The Roman Way*, by Edith Hamilton; *Daily Life in Ancient Rome* by Jerome Carcopino; *69 A.D.: the Year of the Four Emperors* by Gwyn Morgan; *Nero* by Edward Champlin; *Religions of Rome*, Volumes I and II, by Mary Beard, John North and Simon Price; *The Forum Reconstruction, a Reconstruction and Architectural Guide*, by Gilbert J. Gorski & James E. Packer; *The Twelve Caesars* by Suetonius (Penguin Classics edition translated by Robert Graves); *The Annals* and *The Histories* by Tacitus (The Modern Library edition, translated by Alfred John Church and William Jackson Brodribb); *The Oxford Classical Dictionary*, edited by Simon Hornblower, Antony Spawforth & Esther Eidinow; *Vespasian* by Barbara Levick; *Dynasty* by Tom Holland; *The Roman Forum* by David Watkin; and Mary Beard's oeuvre, including *the Roman Triumph, the Fires of Vesuvius: Pompeii Lost and Found, SPQR*, and *Confronting the Classics*.

I am indebted to my agent, Sam Copeland, for his enthusiasm, conviction, and tireless efforts; and everyone at Bonnier/Twenty7, particularly my editor, Joel Richardson, for his insight and steady editorial-hand. Without Sam and Joel, I doubt this book would have seen the light of day.

My thanks to my creative writing instructor, Chis Wakling, and classmates (Beth Alliband, Nicolas Hodges, Nick Ledlie, Stuart Blake, Marjorie Orr, Marialena Carr, Downith Monaghan, Penny Glidewell, Tawnee Hill, Lacey Fisher, Luke Hupton, Jordan Followwill, Clarissa Goenawan, and Kate MacWhannell) for their insight and commentary on the novel's earlier drafts.

I am grateful to Robert Rueter, managing partner at my firm, for approving and encouraging a leave absence to finish the book.

Thank you to my parents, Howard Barbaree and Lynn Lightfoot, for their unwavering love and support, and the example of hard work and dedication they have provided throughout my life.

Finally, I am forever grateful to my wife, Anna, and her discerning intelligence, without which I would be lost.

Want to read
# NEW BOOKS
before anyone else?

Like getting
# FREE BOOKS?

Enjoy sharing your
# OPINIONS?

Discover

# READERS
# FIRST
Read. Love. Share.

Get your first free book just by signing up at
## readersfirst.co.uk